P9-DMY-025

Rvrkw copy
950

DISCARD

BETHARD
COLLEGE
LIBRARY

813.54 SA39L
Salzman, Mark.
The Laughing Sutra

GAYLORD S

ALSO BY MARK SALZMAN

Iron & Silk

THE
LAUGHING
SUTRA

THE
LAUGHING
SUTRA

A Novel

Mark Salzman

Random House
New York

Copyright © 1991 by Mark Salzman

All rights reserved under International and Pan-American Copyright Conventions.
Published in the United States by Random House, Inc., New York, and
simultaneously in Canada by Random House of Canada Limited, Toronto.

Library of Congress Cataloging-in-Publication Data

Salzman, Mark.
The laughing sutra : a novel / Mark Salzman.
p.   cm.
ISBN 0-394-57009-X
I. Title.
PS3569.A4627L3 1990
813'.54—dc20   90-53136

Manufactured in the United States of America
24689753
First Edition

Book design by JoAnne Metsch

THE
LAUGHING
SUTRA

1

IN THE SEVENTH YEAR OF THE PEOPLE'S REPUBLIC OF China (1956), in a remote village in Yunnan Province, Kuo Hsiao-mei gave birth to a son with extraordinarily well developed earlobes. In many parts of Asia, long earlobes are considered a sign of great wisdom; Buddhist and Taoist deities are usually depicted as having earlobes that hang down practically to their shoulders. So Kuo named her son Sheng-hui, meaning "Flourishing Knowledge," and believed that the boy would grow up to be a famous scholar. Kuo took her son to the village fortune-teller, expecting him to confirm her belief, but after determining the exact hour of the boy's birth, throwing yarrow sticks, and consulting the *I Ching,* the fortune-teller came to a different conclusion.

"The boy," he said, shaking his head gravely, "will leave home when he is very young. He will encounter sorrow and loss as he grows up. Then he will wander all over the world."

This was hardly what Kuo wished to hear, so she cursed the old man and reminded him that he had once predicted she would marry a northerner and move to Peking, but in fact she was an unwed mother and still stuck in Yunnan.

Kuo decided that if Sheng-hui was going to become a scholar, he would have to learn early how to read and write. One day, while picking tea leaves, she had an idea; she took some of the leaves home and wrote a single Chinese character on the back of each. She showed the characters to Sheng-hui one at a time, at the same time loudly pronouncing them, in the hope that he would imitate her and eventually connect the characters to the sounds. Sheng-hui was only a few weeks old, however, and did not appear to be aware of the leaves dangling in front of him, nor did he seem capable of producing the appropriate sounds. But Kuo did not give up. Each night, after returning from the fields, she lit a candle in the reed hut and flashed the leaves in front of Sheng-hui as he suckled at her breast.

After a year of this, he showed little progress toward recognizing the characters written on the leaves, but one day he reached out and grabbed the leaf in his mother's hand and swallowed it. That leaf happened to have the character *yu*, meaning travel, written on it. This alarmed Kuo, because it reminded her of the old man's prediction. After trying unsuccessfully to get Sheng-hui to cough up "travel," she wrote *liu tsai chia*—"stay at home"—three times on another leaf and forced him to swallow it. So ended Sheng-hui's early education.

IN 1960 A FAMINE struck most of China, partially due to a series of natural disasters but mainly thanks to the economic policy known as "the Great Leap Forward." Part of the Great Leap Forward involved destroying vegetable and fruit crops and replacing them with rice fields, because Chairman Mao thought that fruits and vegetables hinted of bourgeois decadence. Kuo's village had cultivated mango, banana, and citrus fruits for centuries, but visiting political cadres forced the villagers to chop down all the trees and plant rice. That spring there was a drought, so the rice crop was spoiled as well. At the end of that summer, with nothing to harvest, Kuo and many of her fellow villagers had to forage for dry brushwood, which they gathered into huge bundles, carried on their backs to the village, and sold in the outdoor market. In no time at all, brushwood became scarce around the village, forcing Kuo to wander farther and farther out into the hills to gather it.

On one of these exhausting journeys, with Sheng-hui marching beside her, dutifully holding some twigs, Kuo came upon an unfamiliar valley thick with black bamboo, a rare variety whose graceful stalks and branches look as if they are carved of ebony. They found a path that led them through the bamboo grove down to a river, where they heard a steady roar coming from somewhere downstream. Deciding to put their work aside for a while, they dropped their loads and walked along the riverbank in the direction of the roaring sound. It got louder and louder, and the bamboo forest got thicker and thicker, until all of a sudden the river and forest simply ended at a sheer cliff and opened up into blue sky. Surprised, Kuo and Sheng-hui nearly tumbled over the edge of the waterfall.

Catching their breath, they made their way as close to the edge as they could safely get, but even then they could not see the bottom of the waterfall for all the mist kicked up by the crashing water. As they stared down in wonder, they heard a sound behind them, and turned around in time to see a deer crashing through the bamboo forest, leaping away frantically. Kuo could hardly conceal her delight.

"This is a special place!" she exclaimed. "A deer is a sign that an immortal lives somewhere nearby!"

Sheng-hui looked back at the falls and asked, "What's an immortal?"

"It's a magical being," his mother answered, "a person who never dies."

"Why don't they die?" Sheng-hui wanted to know.

"Because they are living Buddhas," said Kuo, clasping her hands together in prayer.

"What do they look like?" Sheng-hui asked.

"They have long white beards and bald heads because they're so old. And they have long earlobes like you, that's why you'll be so smart. And they collect rare herbs in valleys that are hidden by mist, so no one will see them. There's plenty of mist at the bottom of the falls, so maybe an immortal lives down there! We should say a prayer now." Kuo bowed her head and began chanting, but Sheng-hui tugged at her ragged skirt.

"Why does a deer mean an immortal lives here?"

Kuo frowned for a moment, then answered patiently, "Because deer are afraid of ordinary men, but they aren't afraid of immortals. Immortals are so gentle they can ride deer like horses!"

"So why did the deer run away?" Sheng-hui asked.

"Because it saw us!" Kuo snapped. "Now keep quiet while I pray to Buddha for good luck."

When she had finished her prayers, Kuo suggested that they take a refreshing bath in one of the shallow pools along the riverbank. Just as they got up to their knees in the clear, chilly water, Kuo sensed someone behind them. She turned and saw a man, ragged and desperate-looking, stumbling out from the bamboo grove. He walked toward them uncertainly, and Kuo pulled Sheng-hui toward her. As the man closed on them, she picked her son up and thought of trying to run across the river, but she quickly realized that the current would pull them over the waterfall. She screamed for help as loudly as she could, but no one answered.

The man grabbed them and dragged them both ashore. He shoved the boy aside and wrestled Kuo to the ground, but she clawed at his eyes and throat. He bellowed in pain, yet he managed to grab both her wrists with one hand. But when he drew his other hand back to strike her, Sheng-hui seized it with both hands and bit down with all his might, holding on like a wild animal. Cursing, the man dragged Sheng-hui toward the water, pried the boy loose, and threw him into the deep part of the river.

Kuo struggled to her feet and charged desperately toward the river, but the man grabbed her and held on while the boy thrashed and coughed in the rushing current, heading straight for the falls. Just as he went over the edge, he let out a piercing shriek. When Kuo saw that, the world became dark for her, and she felt no more pain.

The man shook her as hard as he could. He wanted her to be alert so that she would be afraid of him. She did not wake up, though, so he dragged her to the river as well, threw her in, and let the current pull her toward her son.

11

"IT MAY SEEM CONFUSING," THE OLD MONK POINTED out, "that Buddhist literature often reminds us that true knowledge cannot be found in books. If that is so, why is there any Buddhist literature at all?"

After a pause, he continued:

"When asked this question, an enlightened master once said, 'If I see the moon, but you do not, I will point at it. First you will watch my finger to see where it goes. Eventually, however, you must take your eyes off my finger and find the moon yourself.' So it is with the sutras. They point you toward the truth, but must not be confused with truth itself.

"You might ask yourself then, 'Why should I read the sutras at all, if they do not contain the truth, if they cannot tell me the true nature of reality? Why waste time on them?' But then you would be making a grievous mistake. How would you know where to look for truth if the sutras did not point you in the right direction? Would you look under your bed? In the woods, per-haps?"

After another pause, the monk shook his head wistfully, then said, "No, one wouldn't know where to look, of course. That is why one must keep reading."

His lecture ended, the monk Wei-ching took off his glasses, wiped them clean with a piece of cloth, then dabbed at his forehead. A white cat, his only audience, yawned, licked a paw, then slipped out of the tiny hut to chase rats on the grounds of the ruined temple. It had been a dreadful summer, and even at night it was still sweltering. Wei-ching sighed, then opened one of the drawers of a large wooden cabinet behind him and removed a scroll from it. He carefully unrolled the sutra, placed a few smooth river stones on the corners as paperweights, put his glasses back on, and began reading.

Wei-ching had been living alone here for nearly twenty years. The temple had once sheltered more than a dozen monks, but during the war with Japan it had been almost completely demolished by an unfortunate accident. A group of Chinese soldiers marching toward Kun-ming to bring supplies to a besieged airstrip camped near the temple one night. Just before daybreak, a soldier on guard duty, trying desperately to stay awake, smoked a cigarette as he paced back and forth in the woods. When he heard the signal announcing that his company was breaking camp, he flicked the cigarette aside and joined his comrades. By the time the brushfire began, the soldiers were already on their way.

When the fire reached the temple, the other monks fled to safety, but Wei-ching stayed behind. Fearless for his own life, he carried bundle after bundle of the scrolls from the temple library to the river, and tossed them in where the fire could not reach them. Only when he was sure he had removed all of the scrolls did he jump into the river himself and swim to safety.

When the fire died down, Wei-ching returned and dragged the scrolls out of the river. Then he carefully unrolled them and hung them to dry on charred tree branches. Realizing that soon the water-damaged scrolls would crumble and fall apart, he built himself a little hut in the ruins of the temple and spent the rest of the war years transcribing the sutras onto fresh rolls of cloth.

Before that time, he had felt indifferent toward the scriptures, believing that meditation alone led to enlightenment. But the pious act of copying them out, character by character, page by page, chapter by chapter, gradually changed his mind. He came to believe that the fire was not an accident at all but a sign indicating that he must devote himself to the study and preservation of sacred literature. He gave himself the religious name Wei-ching, which means "Guardian of Scriptures," and after the war made a pilgrimage each year to a different part of China to visit other temple libraries. Whenever he found a sutra not in his own collection, he copied it out and brought it back with him. His goal was to assemble a complete library of the major Buddhist scriptures in his lifetime, and by the age of sixty-four he had located and painstakingly copied out all of them except one—a sutra so rare Wei-ching could not even be sure that it still existed.

Just after the Communist revolution, Wei-ching traveled northwest to visit the Tun-huang Buddhist caves in Kansu Province. Tun-huang used to be an important oasis along the old Silk Road, the last truly Chinese city before one ventured west into the murderous Takla Makan Desert on the way to India and beyond. Traders who stopped there paid handsomely to maintain and improve the religious paintings, statues, and libraries in the caves, hoping that such pious donations would build up enough good karma to get them through the deserts and back to China alive. When ocean routes made the treacherous overland journey unnecessary, the caves were abandoned to the desert and forgotten for nearly a thousand years.

In 1906 a lone monk was living there when an explorer under commission from the British Museum, Sir Aurel Stein, stumbled on the caves and brought many of their treasures back with him to England. After that, a large number of foreign archeologists and collectors flocked to the caves, taking most of the best artwork and scrolls out of China. Around 1920 the Chinese government somewhat belatedly forbade any further looting from the caves and made Tun-huang a museum.

When Wei-ching got there in 1952, the old monk who had been living at Tun-huang was still alive. He confided that in 1948 another rich foreigner, an American named Fo-lan, had visited the caves. He was another museum collector, and made it clear he wanted to buy some religious artifacts in spite of the government ban. At that time, China was devastated from the war with Japan and then the fighting between the Nationalists and Communists, so a corrupt local official made a deal with the American and sold him a few statues and a trunkful of scrolls. According to the old monk, that trunk contained the last extant copy of the Laughing Sutra, a scroll so precious that whoever understood its message would instantly perceive his Buddha-nature, and—this was the remarkable part—achieve physical immortality as well.

At first Wei-ching was skeptical; if this sutra was genuine, how could it be that he had never heard of it? The Buddhist canon had been copied and spread over libraries in China for nearly two thousand years. It seemed hard to believe that a sutra that offered both enlightenment and immortality could have disappeared so completely. But the monk from the caves insisted it was genuine. The reason the Laughing Sutra had been ignored, he said, was that few could recognize its true value.

The sutra was based on a private sermon Gautama Buddha gave to one of his most talented disciples. In that sermon, Buddha described the formless, chaotic nature of existence. He insisted that the human situation is utterly hopeless, the universe unknowable, and our individual souls mere illusions. When the disciple heard this, he tumbled into fathomless despair. In that moment of total surrender, he directly perceived that he had been enlightened and immortal from the very beginning, and dissolved into laughter so profound and free from delusion that even the stones around him shook in sympathy.

Unfortunately, the monk said, most people who read the Laughing Sutra misinterpret the disciple's response as derisive laughter and assume that he took Buddha for a fool. That is why the sutra never became popular, and why that particular disciple had long since fallen into obscurity. After hearing this testimony, Wei-ching vowed to travel to America to recover the Laughing Sutra, both to attain immortality for himself and to make the sutra available to others.

111

IT WAS GETTING DARK OUT, SO WEI-CHING PUT AWAY
the book he was reading and called the cat in
for the evening. He lit a gas lamp, washed his
hands and face in a bucket of cold river
water, ate some warm rice gruel, then sat
down on the little rug in front of his cot and
chanted his evening prayers. Lately, he had
been praying to Kuan-yin, the Goddess of
Mercy, asking her to look out for him now
that he was about to embark on his pilgrimage to America.

Toward the end of his prayer, he felt an
odd tingling sensation in his chest. He paid
little attention to it, since he noticed as he got
older that he had new aches and pains all the
time, and kept on chanting. Then he heard a
knock at the flimsy door to his room. Unused
to visitors in the remote temple, he hesitated
before answering. The knocking ceased, and
Wei-ching peered out of a crack in the wall
to see if he could catch a glimpse of his visitor. He looked around but saw nothing except for the fleeting image of a fingertip just
before it poked him gingerly in the eye. Wei-
ching fell back onto his mat, rubbing his eye,
and heard a voice say in a strangely archaic
dialect, "Open the door or I will remove it."

Wei-ching, now trembling with fear, opened the door expecting to see a soldier or bandit, but instead he saw a man unlike any he had ever seen before.

The visitor wore a ragged suit of leather armor of a sort that Wei-ching had only seen in ancient woodblock prints. He was of average height but powerfully built, and fearsome to look at. His arms and chest were covered with dark hair, and his facial hair grew out under his cheekbones almost all the way to his nose. He had thick eyebrows that swept up toward his temples, and a pair of burning yellow eyes that did not blink or even seem to move. He carried a rusted iron pole that glistened dark and wet on one end. Lichen and moss covered his armor, as if he had lain outdoors for years without moving. Wei-ching thought he looked like a bronze statue come to life.

"You live alone here, isn't that true?" the visitor asked. Wei-ching managed to nod, but for some reason he could not bring himself to speak. He noticed that the tingling sensation in his chest had become more pronounced.

"You have a guest," the visitor said, and pointed to a shivering, naked boy with long earlobes standing nearby.

"Someone tried to kill this boy today," the strange man continued. "I happened to be nearby, so I was able to save him. Unfortunately, I was not able to save his mother." The visitor frowned and looked at the boy. "He needs dry clothes and some food. After that, you can find out where he lives and return him to his village."

Wei-ching made a great effort to regain the use of his tongue, and finally blurted out, "But you should take him to the police! I am just a monk; I wouldn't know how to take care of him! And I am about to begin a long journey, so I won't have time to—"

The visitor's eyes narrowed and seemed to burn even more fiercely. Wei-ching felt the tingling in his chest even more strongly, as if an electric current were passing through his body, making his arms and legs feel heavy. The strange man raised his right hand and pointed at Wei-ching. "You are a monk, and you have vowed to alleviate suffering. This boy is suffering, so it is your duty to assist him. You will postpone your journey and care for the boy!"

"B-but what about the murderer?" Wei-ching asked. "What if he comes here? Shouldn't you—"

The stranger's upper lip twitched with anger. Wei-ching noticed that he had long eyeteeth, like a wild animal's. "The murderer will not come here," the stranger said. "He has been punished in a manner suiting his crime." Then he came so close to Wei-ching that their noses almost touched. Wei-ching was terrified, but found he could not budge.

"If anyone asks," the stranger hissed, looking hard at Wei-ching with his unblinking eyes, "the boy wandered here on his own. You never saw me. If you say otherwise, you will regret it." With that, the stranger left, carrying his rusted pole, and Wei-ching led the shaking boy into the temple.

IV

AT AROUND MIDNIGHT, SHENG-HUI BEGAN SHIVERING so hard that his chattering woke the old monk. Wei-ching laid his own blanket and his extra clothing over the boy and gave him some herb tea, but the chills turned to fever and Sheng-hui fell into a delirium. Wei-ching sat up all night with him. The next morning he hurried to the nearest village to find a doctor. Unfortunately, the only doctor in the vicinity was a poorly trained "barefoot doctor" who could only recommend that Wei-ching keep the boy warm and quiet.

The boy dropped in and out of consciousness for four days, during which Wei-ching hardly slept or ate for worry. During the worst spells of fever, Sheng-hui cried out for his mother and mumbled in a dialect Wei-ching couldn't understand. When at last the fever broke, Sheng-hui seemed shrunk to half his original size, and his eyes looked like those of an old man. Most worrisome, though, was that he seemed to have lost the ability to speak. His mouth would open purposefully, but no sound would come out, and he would sit there frozen, like a picture of someone caught in midsentence. Eventually, the boy would panic, and tears would fill his eyes, but even his crying was soundless.

When the boy was strong enough to walk, Wei-ching led him around to all the nearest villages to find out what he could about the foundling's background. No one recognized the child or had any clues as to where he might have come from. If Sheng-hui could have spoken, someone might have recognized his village dialect, but whenever anyone asked him a question, the poor child only stared back anxiously. Finally, Wei-ching and Sheng-hui made the long day's journey to Ling-feng, the closest town large enough to have a police station, but the police had no information about a missing woman or child. Since Kuo had no living relatives in the village, her starving neighbors there assumed she had decided to take her son to a place less stricken by the famine.

Days, and then weeks, passed, but the boy's identity remained a mystery. Wei-ching hoped that some kind village couple with no children or only daughters would offer to adopt him, but perhaps because of the famine or the little boy's muteness, no one did. Wei-ching had lived alone most of his life, away from the cares of the material world, and feared that raising a boy would distract him from his pursuit of enlightenment, not to mention his search for the Laughing Sutra. Still, he couldn't bear to think of leaving the child at an orphanage. "Perhaps," Wei-ching began to say to himself, "it is Buddha's will that I care for the child."

When a month went by and Sheng-hui still could not speak, Wei-ching began to fear that perhaps the boy had been permanently damaged by the fever. The old monk despaired to think that he, who had such a passion for learning, might spend the rest of his life caring for a moron. To try to prevent this, Wei-ching began reading sutras aloud to the boy at night, hoping that it might nudge his brain awake.

Actually, Sheng-hui's brain worked fine, but whenever he tried to speak, it felt as if a pair of invisible hands clutched his throat and squeezed it shut. The harder he struggled to force the words through, the tighter the hands squeezed, until he could hardly breathe. As the weeks passed, though, he came to understand the old monk's dialect, and gained strength from the chores Wei-ching gave him around the temple.

Wei-ching, in the meantime, both pleased and disappointed himself by growing fond of the boy. He knew that to attain the spiritual goal of enlightenment one had to cast off all attachments to the world, especially emotional ones. On the other hand, by showing the boy mercy, he was almost certainly acquiring good karma for himself, so even if he failed to attain enlightenment in this life, he would definitely have a better chance in the next one. Also, small things like watching how much the boy enjoyed eating or playing with the cat brought Wei-ching unexpected pleasure. His only regret was that, considering how arthritic he was already and how many years it would be before the child could take care of himself, Wei-ching would probably never be able to make the long pilgrimage that he had planned for so many years.

IN TIME, THOUGH, Wei-ching began to entertain the dim hope that one day the orphan would make the journey for him. With that in mind, he named the boy Hsun-ching, which means "Seeker of Sutras." But even with such a fortuitous name, Wei-ching thought, how would the child become interested enough in sutras to want to travel to the other side of the earth in search of one? Most people didn't appreciate that sort of religious literature until well into middle age. Wei-ching realized that his only hope was to appeal to something in the boy more universal than a desire for spiritual advancement: a love of adventure. Toward this end, Wei-ching stopped reading sutras to the boy at night and instead began reading him *Journey to the West*, a famous novel about a T'ang dynasty monk and his magical companion, who walked all the way from China to India to find Buddhist texts.

One rainy evening Wei-ching was reading a particularly excit-ing chapter in which the priest's magical companion, known as the Monkey King, had to use his prowess in the martial arts to subdue a formidable pig-demon. Just at the climax of their battle, a strong gust of wind flung the temple door open and extin-guished the lamp.

"I guess the fight will have to wait until tomorrow," said Wei-ching, getting up to close the door. Suddenly, out of the blackness, a small voice pleaded, "But does Monkey win?"

Wei-ching turned around and stared in the direction of the boy. "You spoke!" he nearly shouted. Hsun-ching was even more shocked than the old man; the words had just fallen out of him. He opened his mouth to say more, but the words became like a crowd of men trying to crawl out of a single window in a burning building, crushing against each other in a panic. He felt the invisible hands bear down on his throat once again, and he was unable to say anything more that night.

Over the next few weeks, though, the invisible hands loosened their hold, and perhaps because he had been mute for so long, Hsun-ching became obsessed with language. He talked incessantly, mostly in the form of questions about the Monkey King, and when Wei-ching begged for some peace and quiet, the boy simply talked to himself. It was a remarkable recovery, but not a complete one. Whenever Hsun-ching got overexcited, he began to stutter and had to wait until he calmed down before he could speak fluently again.

Now that young Hsun-ching could talk, Wei-ching tried once again to find out where he was from, how he had become separated from his family, and the identity of the strange-looking man who had brought him to the temple. As much as he wanted to, though, Hsun-ching couldn't answer any of those questions; he could see his mother clearly in his mind, their house and their village, but he remembered nothing about the day they wandered out to the waterfall.

Wei-ching, in the meantime, took it as a good omen that the boy had taken such an interest in *Journey to the West.* He began to read from the novel in the morning as well as the evening. Even that wasn't enough for Hsun-ching, though; he wanted to hear about Monkey all day long. Finally, he begged Wei-ching to teach him to read so he could devour the novel on his own. This request delighted the pious scholar, and he turned back to the beginning right away, so that Hsun-ching could learn the characters as they went.

Hsun-ching's obsession with speaking quickly shifted toward

reading about Monkey and his adventures. It turned out that he was gifted with a nearly photographic memory, so that within only a few months he knew enough characters to read more than a page a day. By the end of the year, he was able to read all by himself, using a dictionary to look up the unfamiliar words and only occasionally having to ask Wei-ching for help.

One autumn day Wei-ching returned from his herb garden to find Hsun-ching lying facedown on his cot, crying. He asked the boy what was wrong, but Hsun-ching was so upset he could only stutter. Wei-ching made him some chrysanthemum tea, which soothes the nerves. When Hsun-ching had settled down enough to explain the cause of his unhappiness, he pointed to the foot of his bed, where the tattered, yellowed novel lay, and blurted out, "I f-f-finished it!"

Wei-ching thought this should be cause for celebration, but Hsun-ching felt as if the world had ended. No more adventures for Monkey, no more demons to vanquish, no more corrupt bureaucrats to tweak, no more savage deserts to cross. What was left?

Wei-ching realized that what the boy needed was a sense of accomplishment to make up for his sense of loss. He patted him on the shoulder. "You have finished your first book. It is a very important moment. But to show that you are ready now to move on to other books, you must do what all great scholars do when they finish their first books."

"Wh-what do they d-d-do?" Hsun-ching asked.

Wei-ching straightened himself up to look more formal and said gravely, "You must show your understanding of what you read. You must tell me the story in your own words. Are you prepared to do that?"

"B-b-but . . . you already know the story," Hsun-ching protested.

"That doesn't matter! I want to know if *you* know the story!" Wei-ching countered. "Your report should be complete, and you may take as long as you like. Are you ready?"

Hsun-ching sat up and dried his face on his sleeve. The old white cat jumped on his lap and purred loudly, which helped cheer him up, and he began to think back to the first chapter of the novel, which he had started reading almost two years before. He felt a thrill of pleasure as he recalled the story of Monkey's birth.

"Th-the name of the book is *Journey to the West*," he began. "It's about Sun Wu-k'ung, the Monkey King, who—"

"No, no—it's about the Buddhist monk Hsüan-tsang!" Wei-ching interrupted. "He is really the main character!"

"It's m-m-my rep-p-port," Hsun-ching said, lowering his head and beginning to stutter. Wei-ching apologized, told the boy to relax, and let him continue.

"Th-th-the Monkey King hatched out of a stone egg more than two thousand years ago. He was a stone monkey, but he was as smart as a man, and he could talk. Also, h-he was very strong and brave. He became king of a band of regular monkeys, and led them to a magical place known as Flowers and Fruit Mountain, where they lived and played for years and years.

"After a while, though, Monkey got bored with swinging around and eating fruit day after day, so he left the mountain to find a famous Taoist master who could teach him magic secrets. Monkey found this man and became his best student. H-he learned how to somersault over clouds, change himself into any animal or object he wanted, and make an army of spirit-monkeys by pulling some of his chairs out, chewing them up, then blowing the pieces into the air! Each piece became a tiny soldier.

"When Monkey finished his training, he traveled under the oceans to the palace of a D-D-Dragon King, who had a great collection of magic weapons. Monkey went there and found a giant staff called the Compliant Golden Rod, which weighed thirteen thousand, five hundred pounds. He picked it up easily. Then he found out why it was named the 'compliant' rod—when he mentioned that it was too long to be carried around, it changed just like that to the size of a sewing needle! Monkey slipped it behind his ear and announced to the Dragon King that he wanted to keep it. When the Dragon King said no, Monkey h-h-hit him over the head with the staff and told him not to be so stingy toward his guests!

"Then he made his way up to heaven, where he just walked into the palace of the Jade Emperor, ate all the Peaches of Immortality, and ruined an important party for high-ranking immortals! H-he wasn't afraid of any of them! After that, he called himself "Great Sage Equal to Heaven." This made the Jade Emperor very mad—he called Monkey a conceited ape! So he sent a whole army of heavenly warriors down to earth to punish Monkey. B-b-but Monkey was such a good fighter he sent them all back to heaven beat up and crying!

"At last Buddha invited Monkey up to heaven, where he challenged Monkey to a test. He said to Monkey, 'I hear that you can somersault over the clouds for great distances. But I don't think you can even jump out of the palm of my hand! If you can, we will give you the Jade Emperor's palace. But if you fail, you will be a p-p-prisoner!' Monkey said, 'I can do that easily!' Buddha stretched out his hand and told Monkey to prove it. Monkey hopped onto his hand, then did one of his somersaults, and he jumped more than thirty-six thousand miles. When he landed, he was at the base of a great mountain range that had five pink mountains. To prove he had been there, he p-p-pissed on one of the mountains, then somersaulted back thirty-six thousand miles and landed right on the B-B-Buddha's palm!

"But then the Buddha got mad and yelled, 'Foolish ape! You jumped nowhere! You never got out of my hand.' He pointed to the base of one of his fingers, where Monkey saw a tiny puddle of piss! Before Monkey could say anything else, Buddha's hand grew huge and closed on Monkey, then he threw Monkey into a m-m-mountain p-p-prison!

"Monkey stayed there for over five hundred years, and all he had to eat was iron pellets! At last, Buddha said he would let Monkey go, but only if Monkey would do a good deed."

"And what was that deed?" Wei-ching asked, thankful that at last they had reached the relevant part of the story.

"M-M-Monkey had to protect Hsüan-tsang on his trip to India."

"And who was Hsüan-tsang? Where did he come from?" Wei-ching asked.

"He was a famous monk. Before he was born, a bad man killed his father and married his mother. When Hsüan-tsang was born, the bad man wanted to kill him, because he said it wasn't his baby. So the mother put the baby on a little boat and put him on a river, hoping that somebody would find him and take care of him. He floated down the river, and a monk found him, so he grew up in a temple. Kind of like me now."

"Yes." Wei-ching smiled. "Kind of like you. Then what happened?"

"Th-then he grew up and became a famous monk and decided to go to India with Monkey," Hsun-ching answered, rushing through what he felt was the most boring part of the story. "The problem was, Hsüan-tsang was a c-c-crybaby! They had to go through all sorts of dangerous places, in deserts and mountains, where there were lots of demons. Whenever the monsters attacked, though, he just started crying and gave up, so Monkey had to save him all the time. The first monster he fought was—"

"That's all right," Wei-ching interrupted again, "you don't have to tell me about all of the monsters. What about their pilgrimage to India—what did they do when they got there?"

Hsun-ching pouted. "The m-m-monsters are the best part."

"Yes, of course," Wei-ching sighed, "but you can tell me about them another time. Today I would like to know how the story ended."

"W-w-well," the boy continued, "they finally got to India, where Buddha gave all the sutras to Hsüan-tsang. Then they went back to China, and Monkey went back up to heaven. B-B-Buddha forgave him, and now Monkey lives there with the other immortals, and he can do wh-wh-whatever he wants for the rest of eternity!"

Wei-ching was disappointed that Hsun-ching seemed so much more interested in the fairy-tale character of the Monkey King than in the historical character Hsüan-tsang and his holy mission. Still, he nodded his approval, then asked expectantly, "And what do you feel after reading this book? Would you want to be like Hsüan-tsang someday and make a great journey like that?"

Flushed with excitement, Hsun-ching answered breathlessly, "N-n-no! Hsüan-tsang was a w-w-weakling! I want to be like M-Monkey and kill m-m-monsters!"

·   ·   ·

AFTER THAT DAY, Wei-ching began teaching Hsun-ching classical Chinese. That way, he reasoned, the boy's desire to kill monsters would be gradually replaced by a desire to read old books. Hsun-ching did not show much enthusiasm for this austere language, but nevertheless learned it at an astonishing rate.

By the time Hsun-ching was nine, he had read samples of poetry, history, and even some of *The Analects of Confucius.* Wei-ching also tried to lead him through the some of the more important sutras, but Hsun-ching found these hopelessly boring. Wei-ching eventually had to admit that the Buddhist canon was hardly designed to appeal to little boys, so he postponed that part of Hsun-ching's education until later. Instead, he dug out of his book collection an old English-language primer he had bought for himself years ago in Nanking, and told the boy to teach himself English. He felt convinced now that karma had pointed to Hsun-ching as the one to make the pilgrimage: He had been miraculously saved from certain death and then raised by a Buddhist monk, just like Hsüan-tsang more than a thousand years before, and he had been moved to speak again by the novel about Hsüan-tsang's journey to India. Also, according to his official biography, Hsüan-tsang had long earlobes, and Hsun-ching shared this physical trait. It would be an unpardonable sin if Wei-ching did not do everything he could to prepare Hsun-ching to follow the T'ang monk's example. And since Hsun-ching's modern pilgrimage would take him to America, it made sense to encourage him to learn English.

When Hsun-ching reached the end of the primer, Wei-ching decided to take him to Kun-ming, the capital city of Yunnan Province, where they could find more advanced English books. Also, it would be a good chance for Hsun-ching to get out of the forest and see the world. In their five years together they had taken plenty of trips to nearby villages to buy supplies, but Hsun-ching had never seen more than a few dozen people at once.

Wearing their best saffron-dyed robes, they packed some food and started walking toward the closest town with a bus station, about twenty miles west from their temple following the river upstream.

After several hours they rounded a bend and saw a waterfall. Wei-ching smiled. "This is called the Dragon's Breath Waterfall, because the mist kicked up by the falls looks like steam puffing out of a dragon's mouth." Wei-ching imagined how spectacular the sight must look to someone who had never seen it, but the boy looked pale and sullen.

"What's the matter?" Wei-ching asked. Hsun-ching only shrugged his shoulders, so they got back on the path and resumed their walk.

To get to the top of the falls, they had to climb a precarious stairway carved right into the side of the cliff. When they at last reached the top, Wei-ching suggested they have a little rest near the edge to enjoy the view. Hsun-ching seemed willing, but as soon as he got near the edge, he felt ill, so they ended up having their rest in the bamboo grove nearby.

That night they camped out under the stars in a grass clearing. After a good meal of rice gruel steamed in plantain leaves, they lay on their backs and talked about what they would do and see in Kun-ming. Long after Wei-ching had fallen asleep, Hsun-ching was still awake. He was thinking about that waterfall; something about it was familiar, but he couldn't quite remember what it was.

v

THEY GOT AN EARLY START THE NEXT MORNING AND
reached Shao-yang just after dawn. More
than three thousand people lived there, and
almost all of them were out on the streets,
riding their bicycles to work, pulling huge
carts, or walking back from the outdoor market laden with vegetables and fish. At one
intersection, two bicycles had collided, and a
large crowd gathered to watch the fallen rid-
ers argue.

The bus station was really just a muddy
parking lot. Wei-ching bought their tickets
from an old woman sitting on a bamboo
stool. She told them that the Kun-ming bus
didn't leave for another hour, so they wandered through town in search of breakfast.
At the outdoor market, they found a stall
that served soybean milk and *yut'iao*, which is
something like a doughnut.

"Watch me," Wei-ching said, holding his
yut'iao with a piece of newspaper so the hot oil
would not burn his fingers. He dipped the end
of it into the cold soy milk, then took a large
bite out of it. "This way," he said once he had
swallowed it, "you get hot and cold, solid and
liquid, at the same time. It is a balance of
opposites, which helps the digestion."

Hsun-ching had never had such a fancy breakfast before. He followed Wei-ching's instructions and dipped the *yut'iao* in the milk, but once he put one end into his mouth, he just kept stuffing and chewing until the whole thing disappeared in one huge bite. Wei-ching had to laugh; with his cheeks full of dough and his eyes wide open with excitement, Hsun-ching looked more like a famished squirrel than a young monk.

WHEN THE NUMBER-FOUR bus arrived in Kun-ming after a bumpy seven-hour ride, Wei-ching and Hsun-ching got up stiffly and hobbled out of the vehicle. There had not been nearly enough seats on the bus for everyone, so Hsun-ching and Wei-ching had been forced to sit on the floor with baskets of fruit piled up on their laps. That was uncomfortable, but some people had to stand the whole way.

Once he had shaken the stiffness out of his limbs, Hsun-ching took his first look at the city. Curved tile roofs, handsome teak-wood balconies jutting out from the old houses along the streets, and the solemn, ancient wall that surrounded the city—all of it glowed with the pale color of sunset and left him speechless with admiration. "Let's have some foreign food," Wei-ching said, interrupting the boy's reverie, and he pointed to a mud-walled building with three tables set up inside it that advertised itself as a French restaurant.

The French had built a railroad from their colony in Indochina up to Kun-ming in 1921, and had a community of missionaries and mining engineers in that city for many years. After 1949 the French, like most of the Westerners in China, were forced to leave, but they left behind a good hotel, some great recipes, and the best pastry shops in China. The maître d', waiter, chef, and manager of this humble establishment was a man named Kuei who claimed to have worked at the French hotel back in the twenties and thirties.

Chef Kuei did not say what his job had been in the French hotel, but it evidently had little to do with preparing food. He served the two monks a watery Chinese soup, a few slices of canned Yunnan ham, then a main course of a very bony steamed fish. It was served without the head or tail, which the chef enthusiastically called "French style." After dinner he gave them each a taste of a locally produced brandy, which Hsun-ching could not finish, but Wei-ching declared miraculous.

After dinner Wei-ching mentioned to the chef, who was by now quite red-faced after helping himself to several glasses of the brandy, that they had come to Kun-ming to get English manuals for Hsun-ching. The old man said, "That's easy enough! The Foreign-Language Bookstore is right down the street, where Liberation Road crosses Broad Masses Avenue."

Wei-ching winced. "Those aren't really street names, are they?" he asked. The chef put his finger to his lips, signaling Wei-ching not to speak so loudly, then rolled his bloodshot eyes and nodded his head with resignation. Then, as if he were suddenly in a hurry to make their table available for more customers, he gave the two monks the address of a dormitory where they could get beds for a reasonable price.

When they had settled down for the night, Hsun-ching spoke up. "Master—I thought Buddhist monks never eat meat or drink, but tonight we had fish, ham, and liquor. What will happen to us now?"

Wei-ching picked at his teeth for a moment, then said, "It is true that one should not eat meat or drink liquor. But it is even more true that a Buddhist must be compassionate. That man needed to prepare us a good meal, to redeem himself for ignoring religion during his life. If we had refused, we would have prevented him from carrying out a pious act and gaining merit. So you see, we soiled ourselves temporarily, that he might be cleansed."

THE NEXT DAY they went to the Foreign-Language Bookstore and bought several English textbooks, a few English novels, a large English-Chinese dictionary, and a pocket world atlas with dozens of maps in it. Their main business done, they spent the rest of the day sightseeing, then took a local bus to a Buddhist temple outside the city. They announced themselves to the abbot's assistant and joined the other monks as they filed silently into the temple dining hall.

After standing and chanting prayers for some time, the abbot

struck a large wooden fish with a hammer, signaling everyone to
sit down and eat. Hsun-ching turned to Wei-ching and started to
ask, "Why isn't anyone talking?," but Wei-ching kicked his shin
and indicated for him to keep silent. The monks ate quickly,
believing that a monk should waste as little time as possible
tending to earthly necessities, and all seemed to finish in unison.
The abbot stood up, struck the wooden fish again, then led the
monks in a quiet march back to the meditation hall.

Candlelight and incense smoke filled the hall as the monks
took their places on little square mats on the floor. Hsun-ching
looked around in wonder at all the sculptures of deities, bod-
hisattvas, demons, and the Buddha himself. He had never seen
such lifelike statues before, and when the chanting started and a
trance seemed to come over everyone in the hall, Hsun-ching
almost expected the wooden figures to spring to life. During the
first chant another group of monks floated in without a sound and
took their places toward the back of the hall. Hsun-ching thought
that something about these monks looked odd; when they
opened their mouths to join in the chant, he realized that they
were not monks at all but nuns. With their shaved heads and
heavy robes, he hadn't been able to tell from looking.

Then the abbot struck a huge bell, and Hsun-ching clapped his
hands over his ears, thinking they would surely burst. He had
never heard such a rich, penetrating sound before, and it frightened him. But when the nuns began chanting, this time by themselves, he took his hands away and let their clear, high voices
soothe him. The next time the abbot struck the bell, Hsun-ching
was better prepared for it, and the sound seemed to fill him with
strength. Hsun-ching looked over and saw Wei-ching listening
with his eyes closed and his mouth fixed in a half-smile. After
a while, Hsun-ching closed his eyes too and let his mind wander
as the nuns sang. He remembered very little about his mother,
but the nuns' voices reminded him of how she sang in the fields
as she worked.

THE TRIP TO Kun-ming was a great success, but bad news awaited
them on their return. The white cat, whom Hsun-ching had come
to love dearly, was missing. At first they thought she might have

just wandered farther than usual on one of her hunting trips, but after a week they resigned themselves to the probability that she had herself fallen prey to an owl or wild dog. Hsun-ching was crushed, and even Wei-ching felt the loss sorely—for nearly ten years the cat had done a fine job of protecting his scrolls from gnawing rodents. To make the boy feel better, Wei-ching performed a dignified funeral ceremony for her by the river. When he finished, he said, "There is a poem that I think would be appropriate for this occasion. It was written by the Sung-dynasty poet Mei Yao-ch'en, and the title is "An Offering for the Cat." Would you like me to recite it for you?"

Hsun-ching nodded. Wei-ching looked out over the river, closed his eyes, and recited from memory:

> Since I got my cat Five White
> the rats left my books alone.
> This morning Five White died.
> I make offerings of rice and fish,
> bury you in the river
> and chant from the sutras—I
> wouldn't slight you.
>
> Once you caught a rat,
> and ran around the garden with it
> squeaking in your mouth.
> You thought it might scare the other rats
> and keep the house clear of them.
>
> When we'd come aboard the boat
> you shared our cabin, and though
> we had nothing but meager rations,
> we ate them without fear of rat droppings
> and gnawing—all because you were diligent.
> A good deal more than the pigs and
> chickens.
>
> People love to boast about their stallions;
> they tell me nothing can compare
> to a horse or donkey—
> enough!—I don't want to argue the point,
> only cry for you a little.

Not long after, Hsun-ching began speeding through the English textbooks. Within a year, he was able to read, with occasional peeks at the dictionary, *The Adventures of Tom Sawyer*. He especially liked the dramatic chase in the cave, because it reminded him of the sorts of situations Monkey would get into.

Meanwhile Wei-ching's arthritis worsened, but as Hsun-ching got older, he was able to do most of the cooking, cleaning, and farming for the two of them. He was ten years old now, and in most respects acted like an adult. Wei-ching began to think that in just a few years, the boy would be old enough to make his pilgrimage to America, if he was willing. In December of 1966, though, the Red Guards visited their temple, and Hsun-ching's life changed abruptly for a second time.

That day Hsun-ching had gone to the village downstream to buy salt and soybeans. When he returned, it was already dark out, so he was able to see the huge fire long before he reached the temple. He dropped his packages and started running. He heard people shouting, and assumed that they were helping to put out the fire. But when he reached the temple, he found Wei-ching, his hands tied behind his back, surrounded by a group of teenagers wearing army clothing and bright red kerchiefs. They forced Wei-ching to kneel with his head down as they shouted and spat at him, while a smaller group made sure that the pile they had made of Wei-ching's scrolls burned steadily. Hsun-ching pushed his way through the group and ran over to Wei-ching.

A young man with a bright red face and a rifle, apparently the leader of the revolutionaries, shouted, "You want to protect the old man from revolutionary justice? Don't you know that is a counterrevolutionary act, and a crime?" Hsun-ching didn't say anything, but gripped Wei-ching even harder. This made the young man with the gun furious, and he struck Hsun-ching over the head with the butt of his rifle.

When he woke up, his hands were tied behind his back, and a welt throbbed on the back of his head. He felt nauseous too, but then he threw up and felt better. He sat up painfully, and saw that he was a prisoner of the group of teenagers who had burned Wei-ching's books the night before. The young man with the rifle came over when he saw that Hsun-ching was conscious. "So you're alive—you're lucky! If you confess, maybe you'll be allowed to become a Red Guard and join us in the Great Proletarian Cultural Revolution!"

"What's that?" Hsun-ching asked.

"Reactionary pig! You don't even know about it? We are Chairman Mao's True Soldiers, and we follow his orders to make revolution throughout the land to overthrow bourgeois capitalist reactionary thought, and smash feudal counterrevolutionary forces everywhere!"

In the daylight, Hsun-ching could see that this young man couldn't be more than sixteen years old. "Wh-why did you b-burn Master's b-b-b—?" he started to ask. The young man shoved him roughly to the ground. "There are no masters in the New Society! Only comrades! Let me hear you say it, dog! Say comrade!"

Hsun-ching tried desperately to say the word "comrade," but he was so upset he couldn't force the word out.

"All traces of feudalism must be destroyed!" screamed the Red Guard. "Down with counterrevolutionaries, and long live Chairman Mao! Old books, old religions, old paintings, old buildings, old statues, old thinking—all must be destroyed in the revolution!"

A bunch of children burned Master's books and spat on him! Hsun-ching thought, and this made him black with anger. He wished he were bigger, so he could beat the lot of them to death, but his thoughts of vengeance were interrupted when he realized that Wei-ching was nowhere to be seen. "Hey," he yelled to the revolutionaries, "wh-where is my c-c-c-comrade?"

The leader of the True Soldiers walked back over, forcing the smile off his face and replacing it with an expression of determined zeal. "Good. You are learning. From now on, you will address all the citizens of New China as 'Comrade'! Don't forget it!"

"Is he here?" Hsun-ching asked again. The young man laughed derisively. "What are you, a crybaby? You miss an old man so much? No, he isn't here! He is a product of the Old Society, and is beyond help! He can't be a Little Red Guard! Forget him! You have left him behind! You have started a new life as a revolutionary!"

"Is h-h-he all right?" Hsun-ching asked.

"Yes, he's alive. He made a full confession of his crimes. But I know that type—he just said the words, and didn't mean a bit of it! He's a bourgeois intellectual, a parasite feeding off the blood of the masses! And he perpetuates superstition to fool the people into being passive! Has he filled you up with old-fashioned ideas? Don't even think of lying, or you'll pay for it!"

Hsun-ching stared at the ground. "He t-taught me to read and write."

"Well, the masses don't need all that intellectual crap!" the boy screamed. "Do you understand?" Hsun-ching didn't respond, so the boy kicked him in the face. Hsun-ching thought his head would burst, but he managed to say, "Yes . . . yes!" which kept the boy from kicking him any more.

"Good," the Little Red Guard said. "Now, if you want the old man to stay alive, you will come with us and help us make revolution. There are reactionaries and counterrevolutionary factions all around us, so we need more comrades to help us defend the Great Chairman Mao's true directives. If you come with us and cooperate, we will let the old man live. But if you give us any trouble, or try to escape and go running home to your old master, we'll follow you there and kill him in front of your eyes—do you understand?"

Hsun-ching nodded. Tears ran down his cheeks, but he refused to make a sound, and he vowed to himself that even if he had to wait until he grew up, he would get revenge.

VI

IN LATE 1966, AT THE BEGINNING OF THE CULTURAL
Revolution, Red Guards were encouraged to
roam across China to "make revolution" and
otherwise maintain the atmosphere of tur-
moil Mao needed to bring down his political
foes. The Red Guard rode all the trains for
free, and could demand food and lodging
pretty much anywhere, anytime. Hsun-ching
and Chairman Mao's True Soldiers rode
mostly on the backs of trucks while they
searched for counterrevolutionaries in rural
Yunnan. About a month after Hsun-ching
joined them, their leader, whose name was Li
Shu-men, announced that they were to leave
immediately on a "revolutionary pilgrimage." First they would go to Ch'ang-sha to
visit Chairman Mao's home, then on to Peking, where there was to be a huge rally of
Red Guards, at which Chairman Mao himself
was to appear.

The True Soldiers' first stop was Kun-
ming. Their train for Ch'ang-sha didn't leave
until the next day, so Li Shu-men suggested
that they make revolution for a few hours.
They visited a school campus, but other Red
Guards had already been there and had broken all the windows, so there wasn't much to

do. Then a truck rode by with at least fifty Red Guards on it, armed with hoes, sticks, hammers, and a few rifles. "Go to the Pure Land Temple," they called down to the True Soldiers, "we're going to clean it up at last!"

When Hsun-ching heard this, he felt sick to his stomach, for this was the temple he and Wei-ching visited less than a year before. But he said nothing. In the weeks he had spent with Li and his followers, he had seen them drag teachers out of schools and beat them mercilessly for no reason at all, so he shuddered to think what they might do to Wei-ching if he gave them something to be angry about.

By the time they reached the temple, most of the important work—defacing the paintings and calligraphy, ripping the heads off statues, harrassing the poor monks—had already been carried out. But the True Soldiers quickly gave themselves the task of carving the sayings of Chairman Mao into the giant bell. By nightfall the bell glistened with the Great Helmsman's utterances, and Li pronounced their work done. As they marched out of the temple grounds, Hsun-ching heard the nuns chanting, and a chill came over him. He guessed that they had seen the destruction going on, and decided to carry out their evening chant in the woods. Worried that the True Soldiers might hear them and go beat them up, Hsun-ching cried out, "Let us yell slogans in praise of Ch-Ch-Chairman Mao!" A chorus of shouts followed instantly, drowning out the nuns' singing, and Hsun-ching was allowed to carry the red flag for a while.

At Ch'ang-sha the True Soldiers ran into problems. It was rainy and cold in Hunan, and the younger members of the group began to get homesick. Most of them had never ventured outside their own villages before, so even a city the size of Ch'ang-sha intimidated them. Some of the True Soldiers asked if they could go back to Yunnan and make sure that the revolution was doing all right, so that when Li and his companions returned from Peking, they could be assured of a strong home base from which to carry out further missions.

Li spat with disgust. He said he didn't want to make revolution with a bunch of mama's boys. Anyone unwilling to go to Peking was a phony revolutionary and should be tried by the people for crimes against Chairman Mao, he said, whereupon about half of his group burst into tears. Li stood up and announced he was taking the next train to Peking, and anyone who was a true revolutionary could follow him; the rest could go home for all he cared. Five boys stalked out with him, leaving twenty-nine wimpering True Soldiers and Hsun-ching huddled together in an empty classroom of Number Two Middle School, shivering from the cold and wondering how they were going to get food without Li and his rifle. They did not know that the worst part of the Cultural Revolution was coming to an end, or that at that very moment the People's Liberation Army was combing Ch'ang-sha for Red Guards to disarm and bring under control.

With Li gone, Hsun-ching saw no reason to stay with the True Soldiers, and prepared to begin his journey home. But the True Soldiers begged him to stick with them, and when the youngest of them all, known only as Hsiao Hamma (Little Toad) because of the rash of warts all over his head, buried his face in Hsun-ching's lap and wept, he relented and agreed to lead them as far as Kun-ming.

On the way to the railroad station they heard gunshots. As they rounded the last corner onto May First Road, they saw several truckloads of soldiers engaged in fierce battle with some Red Guards holed up in an abandoned factory. They watched in terror as a group of the Red Guards stormed out of the factory in a desperate attempt to overwhelm the soldiers, only to be cut down easily by the soldiers' superior weapons. The surviving Red Guards dropped their rifles, came out of the building, and surrendered.

A soldier with a bullhorn announced that, by order of Chairman Mao and the Communist party of China, all Red Guards were to surrender immediately. If they did so peacefully, the state would treat them fairly and return them to their homes. Hsun-ching and the True Soldiers immediately put their hands over their heads and came forward. As they walked toward the soldiers, they had to pass the bodies of the fallen Red Guards, whereupon little Hamma screamed and fainted in a heap. Hsun-ching ran over to help him and saw that the poor boy had stumbled over the body of Li Shu-men, lying on his back with his mouth open and a bullet through his eye. "Bad actions produce bad karma," Hsun-ching muttered as he picked up Hamma and carried him over to the army men.

The soldiers brought all of the surrendered Red Guards to a large detention center set up in a field on the outskirts of the city. Hsun-ching and his companions were sitting in a small circle waiting for their turn to be interrogated when a large officer with no nose strode over to them and asked who their leader was. The True Soldiers pointed to Hsun-ching. "You come with me," the officer said, then he turned smartly and marched into a drab cement building nearby. Hsun-ching tried to get up, but Hamma, who had been sleeping with his head on Hsun-ching's shoulder, would not let him go. "I have to go with that man," Hsun-ching said. Hamma didn't say anything, but stood up and followed him into the dark building.

The man with no nose led them into a room with only a single chair and a bare light bulb hanging from the ceiling. "Sit down," he said roughly to Hsun-ching. Then he noticed Hamma. "Who are you?" he barked. "I said I only wanted the leader of your group to come."

Hamma was too frightened to say anything, but he would not let go of Hsun-ching's arm.

The big man spat. "Fine with me."

Partly true to their word, the army sent home the Red Guards who surrendered peacefully—most of them, that is. The leaders of each faction, who had encouraged their peers to misinterpret the Great Chairman's words and translate them into violent crimes against the people, were to be reeducated through labor in the countryside. Only by living and working with the peasants could they understand the Chairman's "true" intentions, and make revolution in a way that benefited the broad masses. Hsun-ching, Hamma, and a group of older boys were to leave the next morning for an impoverished commune in the deep countryside of Hunan.

"The peasants in that commune are starving largely because of the madness created by the Red Guards," the man with no nose said, "so it is fitting that you should go there to help them."

"How long will we have to stay there?" Hsun-ching asked.

"As long as necessary," the man answered, and then he nodded to a soldier standing in the back of the room, who took Hsun-ching and Hamma by the collars and led them out of the building.

THE COMMUNE LAY in a remote area of western Hunan that could only be reached by truck from Ch'ang-sha. After two days of tortuous driving, they reached their destination: a small village in Funghsien County, surrounded by grotesquely shaped mountains carved over the centuries by wind and water. Many of the mountains looked like huge animal or human figures, and since billows of mist almost always drifted at their feet, one had the unsettling impression that these were giants moving slowly across the valley.

Hsun-ching and Hamma had to live, along with the other former revolutionaries, on the floor of a primitive barn. They were each given a wide straw hat, two pairs of green pants, two green shirts, a pair of sturdy shoes, and a heavy, quilted army coat. The coats were so long that they dragged on the ground when Hsun-ching and Hamma wore them. No other possessions were allowed, and a party cadre made weekly inspections of the barn to make sure that the new "workers" were not hiding any counterrevolutionary materials, such as books or toys. They learned to drag plows without the help of animals—since the peasants had no animals except for their pigs and a few thin chickens—how to plant and harvest rice, how to patch clothing with woven rice husks, and how to rebuild thatched roofs after storms blew them off. They also had to endure nightly "struggle" meetings where their ideology was rectified by zealous party members, and learned what it meant to live on the verge of starvation.

Hamma told Hsun-ching that he had been taken into custody by the True Soldiers after the Red Guards had beaten his parents to death. The two boys became close friends, and Hsun-ching promised to take Hamma, who was only nine, with him to live in the temple after they were released. Months, and then years, passed, though, and they were not released.

In 1970 Hamma contracted encephalitis from an infected mosquito, and after suffering terribly for fifteen days, died in the middle of the night. He was twelve years old. Funeral services had been banned in China as useless remnants of a feudal past, so the peasants took Hamma's emaciated body and buried it on a little hill not far from their commune. Hsun-ching sat near the grave long after everyone else had returned home and thought about Hamma's short life. He remembered the prayers he and Wei-ching used to recite together to Kuan-yin, the Goddess of Mercy. He went over them again and again in his mind, this time thinking carefully about the meaning of each word, and at last he said aloud to the mound of earth next to him, "If there were really a Buddha, or a Goddess of Mercy, this couldn't have happened."

BY 1973, MOST of the people "sent down" to the countryside had returned to their homes, but Hunan was a stronghold for radical Maoists, so it was not until 1976, after the fall of the Gang of Four, that word came to the commune that Hsun-ching was free to go. Nearly ten years had passed since Chairman Mao's True Soldiers dragged him away from Wei-ching, and Hsun-ching was now twenty years old. He hitched a ride on a truck to Ch'ang-sha, then took a train to Kun-ming, which had changed greatly from when he last saw it. From there he rode the bus to Shao-yang, which now followed paved roads, then walked until he came to the ruins of the old temple where he used to live.

Hsun-ching stopped a few yards from the door and looked around at the place. The building was in complete disrepair, and the garden was unkempt and overgrown with weeds. Hsun-ching's heart pounded in his chest, and his knees felt weak as he imagined what he might find when he walked inside. He pushed the brushwood door open, but before he looked inside, he heard a faint voice say, "You're early today, Old Chou."

Wei-ching lay on a cot with a blanket over his legs. He squinted up at Hsun-ching.

"I knew you would come," the old monk said quietly, then he closed his eyes and smiled. "Buddha be praised."

That night Hsun-ching told Wei-ching what had happened to him after the Red Guards took him away. "But what have you been eating?" he asked after finishing his own story, "You aren't growing anything in the garden."

Wei-ching said, "After you left, I did not know if I would ever see you again. After five years, I gave up hope, and decided to leave this place and go to the Pure Land Temple in Kun-ming, where at least there would be other monks to care for me when I couldn't feed myself anymore. But then something wonderful happened. I was walking past that waterfall—the one on the way to Shao-yang—and I saw something. . . ." He paused and shook his head slowly.

"Let's say, for now, that I saw something that convinced me you were alive, and that you would return. So I turned right around and decided to wait here for you, no matter how long it took. Around three years ago my legs became so bad I could no longer tend the garden. Fortunately, Buddha be praised, some pious lay people in the village have helped me by bringing me food and water every evening. I thought you were one of them when you came in!"

Later that evening one of the villagers, a ruddy-faced old woman with her hair pulled back into two short pigtails, walked into the temple with a covered pot full of rice porridge and minced vegetables. She was startled when she saw Hsun-ching, but Wei-ching said, "Old Chou—this is the boy I told you about!"

The woman's eyes widened with surprise. She rushed out of the temple and went all the way back to the village to fetch more food.

THE VERY NEXT morning, Hsun-ching started fixing up the temple and clearing out space for a new garden. He had learned a lot about building and planting out in the countryside, so that within a few months Wei-ching's home looked better than ever. One day, Hsun-ching wrapped Wei-ching in some blankets, carried him outdoors, and propped him up in a chair so he could watch as Hsun-ching worked.

"Can you grow kumquats here?" Wei-chung asked. "I've always liked kumquats."

"I can grow just about anything you like!" Hsun-ching boasted. "You tell me what you want, and I'll plant it."

Wei-chung laughed and said, "Too bad you can't plant books."

Hsun-ching put down his trowel and looked up at the old man. For the first time in many years, he recalled that Wei-chung had once had an ambition of going abroad in search of a single scroll.

"What was the name of that sutra? The one that was in another country?" Hsun-ching suddenly inquired. Wei-ching shifted in his chair but tried not to show much interest.

"You mean the Laughing Sutra?"

"Yes—why did you want it so badly, when you had so many others?"

Wei-ching rearranged the blanket around his shoulders so that his right hand could stretch out in front of him. He spread his arthritic fingers as wide as he could and said, "If a man were born without a pinky, do you think it would affect him much?"

Hsun-ching thought about it for a moment, then said he didn't think it would make much difference.

"But what if he were born without a thumb?" Wei-ching asked. Hsun-ching had to admit that without a thumb, a man's hand would be rendered almost useless. Wei-ching nodded slowly and said, "The sutras are like fingers. They allow you to grasp the dharma, the true nature of existence, which of course brings enlightenment. I have read and meditated upon every sutra except one, but so far they have been useless to me, as I remain unenlightened. They are like the four fingers without a thumb. I am certain that once I read the Laughing Sutra, I will at last be able to grasp the dharma of Gautama Buddha."

"And where is this sutra now?" Hsun-ching asked. "You never told me much about it when I was a boy."

"That is because you never asked," Wei-ching responded, sitting up straighter in his chair. "You never showed much interest in sacred literature, as you might recall. Your only interests seemed to be reading about the Monkey King and playing with my old white cat! But since you have asked, now I will tell you. The Laughing Sutra was one of the texts brought from India to China by Hsüan-tsang in the T'ang dynasty. Most of those texts became very popular and spread all over China, but the Laughing Sutra, which is supposedly very difficult to understand, fell into obscurity. Perhaps as few as two people have read it in the last thousand years!"

"So how do you know about it, then?" Hsun-ching asked.

"I heard about this sutra when I visited the Buddhist caves at Tun-huang. The monk who tended the grounds told me that an American bought it illegally in 1948."

"But how did you think you could find it?" Hsun-ching asked. "America is a huge country!"

Wei-ching wrung his shiny hands and said, "That is true, but the world is small for merchants. This Fo-lan was a merchant of sorts, and like most people of his kind, he had a wallet full of cards with his name and address on them. He had given one to the monk at Tun-huang, who was happy to give it to me."

Hsun-ching stood up and shook the dirt off the knees of his trousers. He walked over and squatted on the ground next to Wei-ching's chair, poking at the ground with his trowel and frowning.

"But how were you going to get to America in the first place?" he asked. "Chinese people can't go there. It's a capitalist country."

"Anything is possible when your intentions are pure. I planned to walk west, toward Tibet. I have heard that the mountain passes leading to Nepal are poorly guarded. From there, one would simply continue west toward Europe. I'm sure it would be easy to get from Europe to America, because those countries are all friendly with each other."

"So why didn't you go?" Hsun-ching asked.

Wei-ching stopped wringing his hands, but his face remained expressionless. "My karma did not allow it. It was Buddha's will that I raise you instead."

Hsun-ching had dug a little hole in the ground in front of him and couldn't decide whether to keep digging or to fill it back up. "Do you believe it is Buddha's will that I get the sutra?" he finally asked.

"Only you would know that," Wei-ching answered carefully. "If it is Buddha's will that you make such a pilgrimage, he will make it clear to you."

THAT NIGHT HSUN-CHING couldn't sleep. He got up quietly, put on the tattered army coat he had worn for ten years, and built a small fire near the temple. He was watching the flames consume a fresh log when a dozen ants scrambled out of a knot in the wood and searched for a way out of the inferno. They ran back and forth along the log, but fire surrounded them. Hsun-ching got a morbid thrill from their predicament; he wondered how he would feel if he were trapped in the same way. How would the ants die? Would they just stop moving all of a sudden? Or would they struggle to the last instant and then make a final, desperate leap just in case they might get beyond the fire? At that moment, a question popped into his head: "Would I be letting these ants die if Wei-ching were sitting next to me?," and he kicked the log out of the fire, sending the ants flying to safety.

He thought about how, during his ten years in Hunan, not a single day went by where he did not dream of having his life with Wei-ching restored. Now that he had at last been reunited with his beloved master, though, something was wrong. He was beginning to feel empty again, the way he had on those endless nights in the barn with nothing to do and nothing to look forward to except another miserable day. But he couldn't understand why he was feeling that way now.

Since his return, he had begun comparing himself to the old monk. Wei-ching was educated, disciplined, and deeply religious, and he was the gentlest man Hsun-ching had ever known. He had real character, the result of living with a sense of purpose, and of making decisions according to what he believed was right and wrong. Hsun-ching, on the other hand, had no idea what it was like to have a sense of purpose. Most of the decisions in his life had been made for him, and as a result his own sense of right and wrong was rudimentary: Don't hurt people, don't eat spoiled food, don't argue with party members. He feared he had no character at all, and little hope of developing one. If those ten years of his life hadn't been taken away from him, he wondered, what would he have been like? If he hadn't seen Hamma die in the countryside, would he still have some sort of faith? If he hadn't been forbidden to read, would he have continued his classical education and eventually been qualified to get a job in a city like Kun-ming, where he could have taken care of Wei-ching and made his last years more comfortable?

That night he decided to try to find the Laughing Sutra for Wei-ching, not because he thought the sutra had any real value, and certainly not out of a sense of adventure; he would probably be caught at the border and sent to a labor camp for another ten years. He decided to go because he knew it would make Wei-ching happy, and because he couldn't think of any other way to make his own life seem less of a waste.

WHEN HSUN-CHING broke the news to Wei-ching that he planned to make the journey to the West, the old monk at first tried not to seem excited about it. He knew that happy events were just as illusory and transient as sad events, and that one must be detached from them all to attain a true understanding of reality. On the other hand, this news meant that Buddha was certainly on his side in this endeavor and would undoubtedly lead Hsun-ching safely through his mission, and that Wei-ching would be able to read the last sutra and become enlightened at last. In the end, he gave in to a few moments of euphoria, and told Hsun-ching that this was the happiest day of his life.

He advised Hsun-ching not to leave until late spring so that by the time he reached Tibet, the mountain passes would be clear of the heaviest snows. He had one other bit of advice: "It will be a long and arduous journey, and you are still just a boy. I would feel much better if you had a companion on the trip."

"I'm twenty," Hsun-ching laughed, "and besides, who would go on a trip like this?"

Wei-ching held onto the frame of his cot and struggled to sit up. He leaned toward Hsun-ching.

"I think there is someone who would go with you. Buddha has pointed him out to us." The old man reached out and took hold of Hsun-ching's arm. "Do you remember how I told you that when I had given up hope for your return, I saw something that reminded me of you? Something that made me know you would come back?"

Hsun-ching nodded. He had never seen Wei-ching so dramatic, and he wasn't sure what to make of it.

"Well, I was traveling by that waterfall on the way to Shao-yang. It was early morning, before dawn, and the base of the falls was so thick with fog I could barely see my hands in front of my face. I decided to sit down and wait for daylight, because I was afraid I might stumble and fall down. As I sat there, I thought I heard something moving not far from me. I wasn't sure what it was, but it sounded big. I thought maybe it was a deer, but then I heard a strange whooshing sound and then a terrible crack! I was very frightened, so I didn't move or make a sound. I started to feel an awful pressure in my chest, and thought my heart was failing, when all of a sudden the fog lifted, and in the moonlight I could see who was making the noise!"

Wei-ching stopped talking and tightened his grip on Hsun-ching's arm.

"Well—who was it?" Hsun-ching asked.

"It was the man who saved you!" Wei-ching gasped. "He was wearing the same strange clothing, and had the same iron rod that I saw the night he brought you to me. He was swinging it like it was a piece of grass—that was what made the sounds. I tell you—no ordinary man could do what he did with that rod. I stood up and tried to run to him, but he looked at me and I felt like all the strength ran out of my body. I couldn't even speak. He just pointed at me and stood there for the longest time."

Hsun-ching stared at Wei-ching with wide eyes, waiting for the old man to continue. Wei-ching, exhausted from sitting up for so long, let go of Hsun-ching's arm and lowered himself onto the cot. He closed his eyes. "This will sound foolish, I know, but you must believe me. The man who saved you is no man! The armor he is wearing must be over two thousand years old, and I believe he has been wearing it since it was made—do you understand? His iron staff—I'm sure you or I couldn't even lift it, and he swings it as if it were nothing!

"At last he lowered his finger and spoke. He reminded me that I had vowed never to tell anyone I had seen him. Well, may Buddha forgive me, I am breaking that vow today! He and you were brought together for a purpose—it's so obvious! How can I stand in the way of karma? May Buddha forgive me for breaking my vow . . . may Buddha forgive me."

VII

HSUN-CHING DID NOT SHARE WEI-CHING'S BELIEF
that he had been saved by a supernatural
being who had been put on earth to help him
find a sutra. Still, if this was in fact the same
man who delivered him to Wei-ching's temple, Hsun-ching wanted to find him. Perhaps
he knew something about Hsun-ching's
mother, and how he had become separated
from her. Hsun-ching hurried to the nearby
village and found Old Chou washing clothes
by pounding them against smooth stones on
the bank of the river. He told her he had to
leave for a day, and asked if she could bring
Wei-ching something for dinner. Then he
bought some rice balls for himself, packed
them in a canvas bag, and followed the path
upstream toward the waterfall.

He reached it just at twilight and rested at
the base, where the roaring water kicked up
spectacular clouds of mist. He called out a
few times, but when no one answered began
to sense how futile this search probably was.
After all, it had been five years since Wei-
ching saw the man—he could be anywhere
by now. He walked up and down the riverbank, looking for any signs that an odd her-
mit who swung an iron pole lived nearby, but

saw nothing but water, mud, mist, and bamboo. At least, he thought, I'm going to cool my feet. Taking off his sandals and rolling his trousers up above his knees, he waded into the river and got as close as he could to the falls. Part of the wall of water was transparent, and he noticed that there seemed to be a cave on the other side of the water. He was tempted to run through the wall to explore the cave, but it was already nearly dark out and getting chilly in the forest, and wet clothes would make for a long, uncomfortable night.

He waded back out of the river and had his dinner of rice balls, then prepared for the long walk back. He took one more look at the waterfall, and again felt an urge to explore the cave behind it. It seemed like a childish thing to do, since he knew perfectly well there would be nothing to see but a dark hole in the rocks, but Hsun-ching couldn't resist the impulse. He looked around furtively to make sure no one was around, then stripped off his clothes and waded toward the falls. When he got up close to the crashing water, though, he got nervous. He wondered how hard the water would feel, falling from that height. What if it crushed him or knocked him unconscious? He would drown, and Wei-ching would wait for him, thinking he must have gone ahead and left for America. He also began to feel silly, standing there stark naked and preparing to dash himself face first into, most likely, a big rock. But he couldn't go without having tried, so he clenched his teeth, braced himself for the shock of the cold water, and threw himself forward.

The water was so cold and hit him so hard he saw stars and his whole body went numb, but he managed to stay conscious. When he opened his eyes, he found himself on his hands and knees in the mouth of a large cave, much larger than he had imagined. His heart was pounding in his chest, and his whole body tingled.

The cave looked about twenty feet high and twenty-five feet across, but Hsun-ching couldn't see how deeply it went into the side of the cliff. He followed it about a hundred feet back, where it ended abruptly. In the near-darkness, Hsun-ching could see that the walls of the cave had depressions in them large enough for a man to sit in, but he could find no signs that anyone had been there before him. Disappointed, he walked back toward the mouth of the cave. About halfway there, he hit something hard with his big toe, then heard a loud clank as the object fell to the ground. He clutched his throbbing toe and howled with pain.

When he had determined that nothing was broken, he groped around with his hands until he felt something smooth and hard near the wall of the cave. He pushed his fingers under it and lifted. As he brought it up, the dim light from the mouth of the cave fell on it, and he saw that he was holding one end of a long iron rod. It weighed about thirty pounds and stood five feet high. He looked at the wall of the cave where the rod had stood. His eyes followed the wall up about ten feet to one of those man-sized depressions, which held a boulder. Suddenly, the tingling sensation all over his body intensified. The hair on the back of his neck slowly raised, and he heard a terrific buzzing in his ears. Two yellow points appeared in the boulder and glittered brilliantly in the dimness.

Slowly, the boulder moved, and Hsun-ching realized that it was not a boulder at all but a living creature huddled into a tight ball and covered with dried mud. The creature shuddered violently, then jumped to the ground like a cat. When it straightened up, Hsun-ching saw the armor and the yellow eyes and felt as if he were looking at a character from a long-forgotten dream. When he saw the long teeth behind the curled lip, though, Hsun-ching knew it was no dream, and remembered everything.

He remembered seeing his mother beaten, the sensation of being thrown into the water, being pulled downstream, and then—falling, falling, and everything going black. He remembered waking up in those strange arms, being carried through the night woods, arriving at the temple, listening to the strange, rasping voice and Wei-ching's frightened answers in an unfamiliar language, and then watching as his savior disappeared.

Hsun-ching could not speak. "M-m- . . . m-m-m—"

The creature glared down at him, but said nothing. Hsun-ching struggled for speech, concentrating on the first word.

"M-m-my . . . m-m-mother . . ."

The creature continued to glare at him, then looked out toward the mouth of the cave.

"Is your mother out there?" he asked, in a dialect Hsun-ching could barely understand. Hsun-ching shook his head. The creature picked up the iron rod and pointed one end of it at Hsun-ching.

"What are you saying?" it demanded.

Hsun-ching looked at his own hands and counted the fingers, hoping that would calm him down enough to be able to speak. "You . . . s-s-saved m-my . . . life. . . ."

The creature growled, "I came in here a few hours ago to get out of the rain, and fell asleep. I didn't save anybody."

Hsun-ching shook his head. "Sixteen years ago . . . a man threw me . . . off the . . . w-w-waterfall! You caught me! Wh-wh-what h-h-happened to m-m-my m-m-m—?"

The man frowned and said, "What makes you think it was me who saved you?"

Hsun-ching hid his face in his hands. "It w-w-was you."

The man's eyes narrowed even further, and he fell silent.

"Where is my m-mother?" Hsun-ching pleaded.

The creature leaned his iron pole against the side of the cave and looked out again toward the waterfall. At last he said, "She came over the falls when I was carrying you out of the water. There was nothing I could do." He brushed some dirt off his arms, then turned to look at Hsun-ching.

"But I assure you that the man who killed your mother did not go unpunished. I caught him at the top of the waterfall and said that if he told the truth, I would spare his life. So he told the truth, and I killed him. It was very satisfying."

Hsun-ching did not move or speak, and the creature seemed to become angry again. "How did you know I would still be here?" He grabbed Hsun-ching roughly by the shoulder and dragged him to his feet.

"The old man told you, didn't he?" the man growled. Hsun-ching opened his mouth to deny it, but the man shook him so hard he could hardly breathe.

"How many other people know about this?" the man demanded, pulling Hsun-ching's face close to his own.

Hsun-ching shook his head. "No one! He would n-n- . . . n-never tell anyone else! He had a reason for telling me!"

"What was that?" the man asked, looking as if he might rip Hsun-ching to pieces at any moment. Hsun-ching told him about Wei-ching and the Laughing Sutra. "He thinks that it is Buddha's will that you help me find it! He doesn't think you're a regular man! He thinks you're a—a ghost or something! That's the only reason he told me! P-p-please don't be angry with him!"

The man loosened his grip on Hsun-ching's shoulder.

"B-b-but that's not why I came here," Hsun-ching continued. "I . . . I just wanted to find out about my mother."

The man nodded slowly and asked, "And now that you have found out, what do you plan to do?"

Hsun-ching looked straight into the man's golden eyes. "Wh-who are you?"

The man scowled and said, "I'm a man who wants to be left alone." He tossed Hsun-ching away from him, then picked up his iron pole.

"Th-then I'll leave you alone," Hsun-ching said.

"And what will you tell the old monk when you go back?" the man asked.

"I—I'll tell him that I saw you, and—"

"And what? That he should forget that he saw me, and leave me alone like you will?"

Hsun-ching nodded weakly.

"Fine. Then he will say, 'But he is a ghost! What sort of man lives in a cave, can catch children when they drop more than one hundred feet, and can swing an iron staff around as if it were made of paper? And why hasn't he aged in sixteen years?' What will you say then? You will have to come back here to ask me those questions—isn't that right?"

Hsun-ching hadn't thought of those things; he began to get frightened again, and instinctively backed away from the man.

"Why don't I save you a trip, then, and get this over with now," said the man in a quiet voice. "Think about what you have seen and what you have heard from your master. Who do you think I am?"

Hsun-ching could only shake his head. He tried desperately to find the reasonable explanation for these things, but without success.

"I guess it doesn't matter, does it?" the man said. "That monk knows who I am. He'll send you back here, or he will find a way to come here himself. And soon others will find out, and before long there will be a line reaching to Ch'ang An of people who will want to have a look at me. So the important question is—what do I do about you and your old master?"

Hsun-ching said, "Wh-wh-what do you mean, Master knows who you are? Who are you?"

The man glared at Hsun-ching, then shook his head. He lifted the iron rod and said, "Come here," then disappeared through the wall of water.

Hsun-ching flung himself after. The creature was already walking up the riverbank toward a small clearing. Outside the cave in the evening light, Hsun-ching could see him more clearly. The lichen growing on his armor really made him look like a statue. He walked with a springy step that looked more animal than human, and Hsun-ching noticed that his eyes did not move in their sockets; when he wanted to look at things, he turned his entire head.

"This is what the old man saw that day," the man said. He gestured to a dead tree. "Try to move this."

Hsun-ching dragged himself out of the water, walked over to the tree, and tugged at it. Of course, it did not budge.

"Now stand over there," the man said. He looked straight into Hsun-ching's eyes, and his body seemed to tense. Hsun-ching once again felt a terrific pressure in his chest, as if the man's gaze were forcing his rib cage to collapse. The man lifted the rod, then swung it, ripping the tree out of the ground with a single terrify-ing stroke. His eyes never left Hsun-ching as the tree crashed into the river. When at last he turned his eyes away, Hsun-ching felt the pressure in his chest diminish.

"Now you have seen what your master saw," he said. "So I ask you again—who do you think I am?"

No human being Hsun-ching knew of could have felled that tree. A strange calm came over him and he said, "You're not a man, are you?"

The man spat angrily and said, "You see? This is why I have

to live in caves, running whenever anyone finds me. I *am* a man, do you understand? Isn't it strange enough that you are born out of a gob of sperm and grow into a man with two arms and two legs, and live for seventy or eighty years? No one hounds *you* to the ends of the earth to ask you why you were made that way, or expects you to explain the world and save people from death and sadness! I was born the same way you were, but you are a handsome boy and I am a very ugly man! I'm stronger than ten of you, but I'm still a man! I bleed, I get tired, I'm getting old, and I have to shit and piss like everyone else!"

The man shook his head in disgust and jammed the pole into the ground with a powerful thrust. "I had parents just like you did! I even remember mine. You know why? Because I still remember when they threw me into a well to drown me. A fortune-teller told my parents I was a demon—why else would I be so ugly?"

"B-but," Hsun-ching said in a trembling voice, "with your strength, you could do whatever you wanted—you have what all men want!"

The man's eyes grew wide with fury. "Do they?" he snarled. "All men want my strength, but I am the only man to have it, so all men fear and envy me! I have no friends, no wife. Who would sleep with someone who looks like this?" he asked, pointing at his own face. "I can defeat anyone in combat, but I am no wiser than other men because of this, and my days are far more boring than yours, I assure you! Who would want that?"

He pulled the heavy rod out of the ground, and it seemed to come alive in his hands as he moved it. Then he pointed one end of it at Hsun-ching.

"But let's talk about you now. You're going to go to some strange country to find the sutra that you think will make you immortal. Haven't you figured out by now that those scrolls are worthless? Do monks live any longer than merchants or whores? No! But I suppose you think it will be different when you read them."

"I'm not interested in the sutra," Hsun-ching said. "I know it is worthless."

The man sniffed the air and looked at him suspiciously. "But you're a monk—you live out at that temple, and you plan to go around the world for a roll of paper, isn't that right?"

"I'm doing that to please Master. I promised him I would. He won't live much longer." Hsun-ching walked over to his clothes and put them on. "I am sorry I disturbed you," he said to the man. "I promise you I won't come back."

The man thrust out his staff and blocked Hsun-ching's way. "What makes you think I'm going to let you go?"

Hsun-ching was beyond fear now; he looked straight into the man's eyes and asked without stuttering, "You saved me before. Are you going to kill me now?"

The man's yellow eyes burned into him without moving or blinking. "What will you tell your master?" he asked in an even voice.

"I'm going to tell him the truth. I'll tell him you want to be left alone, and he'll never speak to anyone else about you. Don't hurt him; it's not his fault that he saw you. He won't live much longer anyway."

The man slowly lowered his staff, still glaring. Hsun-ching began to walk away but then stopped, bowed to the man, and said, "Thank you for killing the man who murdered my mother."

The strange man watched as Hsun-ching disappeared down the path along the river, then slashed at the air with a furious swing of his staff, and stalked back toward the roaring falls.

"IT IS A very sad thing," Wei-ching said, "that a man like that is so alone in the world. Buddha be merciful—human beings are so stupid! In my lifetime, there have been two world wars, two civil wars, and the Cultural Revolution. All of them were caused by stupidity. And now I've seen an immortal—a true miracle—and I learn that he is lonely and bitter. All this merely proves the wisdom of Buddha, for he said that all life is suffering. Even so, it's very, very sad."

Hsun-ching nodded and poured some tea for the old monk. Wei-ching sipped it, then said, "I believe we have not seen the last of that man, however. There must be some reason Buddha brought you together, some purpose for it! In any case, only Buddha himself knows what it is, and he will reveal it to us when the proper time comes."

"Master," Hsun-ching said, "the man said that you knew who he was."

Wei-ching said nothing for a while. Then, "He did?"

"Yes. Do you know him?"

All of a sudden Wei-ching seemed to freeze, and Hsun-ching was afraid he had stopped breathing. Then a smile crept onto Wei-ching's face, and he seemed lost in a reverie for a few moments. He blinked, looked back at Hsun-ching, and said, "Yes. Perhaps I do. Did you say he mentioned a line of people who wanted to look at him reaching to Ch'ang An?"

"Yes," said Hsun-ching. "Why do you ask that?"

"Well, Ch'ang An was once the capital of China. It's been called Sian since the Ming Dynasty."

"But who is he?"

"It is so obvious!" Wei-chung declared. "It's been obvious from the beginning! But we, who have so little faith, just couldn't see it."

"Who is he?" Hsun-ching repeated, feeling frightened all over again.

"It would be useless for me to tell you," Wei-ching said. "It would only sound foolish to you now. No, you must discover his identity for yourself. How and when I do not know, but I am sure it will happen. For now, we must not speak of him anymore, but only concentrate on your journey. I suggest that you go to Kun-ming right away and get some new maps, an English dictionary, and sturdy clothing."

Hsun-ching pleaded with Wei-ching not to keep any secrets from him, but the old man would say nothing more about the man behind the waterfall.

After a couple of months, Hsun-ching went to Kun-ming to buy the supplies he needed. On his way to Shao-yang, he had to pass the waterfall. He was sorely tempted to go back into the cave and ask the man who he really was, but he had given the man his word not to return, and he was beginning to think that perhaps he and Wei-ching had blown the whole thing out of proportion. Just because the man was very strong did not have to mean that he was divine, or wise, or even honest.

It only took Hsun-ching a day to buy the things he needed in Kun-ming, but he stayed on a second day to visit the Pure Land Temple. When he got there, his heart sank, for the temple was in ruins, but stepping inside, he found a few monks still living there. They said they were just now beginning to fix the place up, now that the Gang of Four had been smashed. It had been used as a garage for army trucks and motorcycles for seven years. Hsun-ching asked about the nuns, but the monks said that only two of them survived the Cultural Revolution. "And now," one of the monks added, "the government forbids young people from becoming monks or nuns, so our community can't rebuild itself. In twenty years, there won't be any of us left, and Buddhism will disappear in China."

THE WINTER PASSED quickly for Hsun-ching, perhaps because for the first time since he'd decided to learn to read, he had a sense of purpose. Before he knew it, spring had nearly passed, and it was time for his departure. That morning, Hsun-ching and Wei-ching got up early and chanted a long sutra together. Then, after breakfast, they parted.

"Be careful, and may Buddha be with you. You are like a son to me," Wei-ching said.

"I'll come back soon," Hsun-ching said, and he left the temple with tears in his eyes.

About two hundred yards into the forest, Hsun-ching heard a voice say, *"Hai."*

He turned and saw, lying across a thick branch of a tree about fifteen feet in the air, the strange man in his suit of ancient armor, casually fingering his iron staff. Hsun-ching dropped his bedroll.

"Please don't hurt us," Hsun-ching begged.

The man hopped down from the tree. "I'm not going to hurt anybody. I'm going with you," he said.

Hsun-ching didn't know what to say; at last he asked, "Wh-wh-why?"

The man looked around for a minute, tapped the ground with

his staff, then frowned. "Because I was getting bored in that damn cave, and I've never seen that part of the world, and because it amuses me that you would travel halfway across the earth to make an old man happy." He grinned, showing his long, evil-looking teeth, and said, "Show me your maps."

VIII

AS HSUN-CHING SPREAD OUT HIS MAPS IN THE SHADE of a mango tree that had survived the Cultural Revolution, the man narrowed his eyes and looked closely at him. "I don't believe I know your name."

Hsun-ching looked up from his maps. "Master gave me the religious name Hsunching. He hoped it would inspire me to go on this trip."

"But what is your real name? The name your parents gave you?"

"I don't know."

"Mm," the man said, nodding thoughtfully.

"And—how shall I address you?" Hsunching asked.

"My family name is Sun. I don't remember my given name. I've been a military man all my life, so why don't you call me 'Colonel.' That's what I'm used to."

"Colonel Sun—I still don't understand why you want to go with me. We'll probably get caught, and—"

"You want to know the real reason I'm coming along?" the colonel interrupted. Hsun-ching nodded gently; he didn't want to anger the man again.

"I'm coming because after you kicked over my pole and woke me up, I couldn't get back to sleep again. And I have nothing else to do right now. It's that simple. Now show me the route you had in mind."

Hsun-ching decided it best not to pursue the matter for the time being, and looked down at his maps. "There are a few ways we could go," he said, "but I'm not sure any of them will work. Our biggest problem will be crossing borders. Master thinks we should go this way, across Tibet, then through a mountain pass to Nepal. He thinks there wouldn't be many guards there, because the mountains are so high."

"He's right about that," Colonel Sun said, "but forget about it. It's cold up there. We have to find a better route."

Hsun-ching showed the colonel the heavy coat and boots he had bought in Kun-ming, and said that they could buy similar equipment for him if he worried about the cold, but the colonel shook his head.

"There isn't a man or animal in the world that I fear, but the one thing I cannot bear is sneezing. I caught a cold once in Mongolia, and I had a sneezing fit that lasted nearly two weeks. I couldn't eat or sleep for that whole time, and nearly died. I would rather fight the whole Imperial Army than wander around where there will be snow." He scratched his chin for a while, then pointed at the map with a hairy finger. Hsun-ching noticed that the colonel's nails were like talons, and he felt himself getting nervous. He hadn't the faintest idea what sort of man the colonel really was, and what if he turned out to be mad? He could crush Hsun-ching's skull with one easy swing of his pole.

"Look here," the colonel said, "what's this big city on the water, south of Canton?"

"That's Hong Kong."

The colonel nodded. "Do a lot of boats stop there?"

"Yes, of course. It's a port city."

"Well, what do you want to crawl across Asia for? Let's go to Hong Kong and find a boat headed for this country you call America! Sailors don't ask questions if you can lift things and scrub floors."

Hsun-ching shook his head doubtfully. "I don't think we can get into Hong Kong," he said.

"What do you mean?" the colonel asked. "It's in China—we don't have to cross any borders to get there."

"Yes, we do; Hong Kong is a British colony. I've heard there is a huge barbed wire fence between Hong Kong and the mainland," Hsun-ching said. "There are armed guards set up to make sure no one crosses it."

The colonel's eyes narrowed with disbelief. "How is it that foreigners can build such a fence in China?"

"The British didn't build the fence," Hsun-ching answered. "We did. This is New China, and the leaders of New China say they want to keep capitalists out. But actually, I've heard that the real reason for the fence is to keep us communists in. Hong Kong is supposed to be some kind of paradise."

"Then we're going there for sure," the colonel said. He looked at the map again. "Who are capit- . . . those two words you just said?"

"Communists and capitalists? How can you not know those words?"

"I don't know as many fancy words as you do," the colonel said, with a trace of resentment. "I didn't have an old man to take care of me and teach me to read and write when I was little."

Hsun-ching reddened with shame. "Well . . . the world is basically divided into two kinds of countries—communist countries, and capitalist countries. A capitalist country is a place where people own things privately and can become more wealthy than other people. They use money to get whatever they want, and can oppress poor people. A communist country is a place where the government owns everything. That way, everyone is equal, and no one can be oppressed. Without money, people share willingly with each other and help each other rather than just helping themselves. Everyone works for the good of the people, not just for personal gain."

Colonel Sun thought about this for a moment, then burst into derisive laughter. "The capitalists sound pretty normal," he observed, "but that communist arrangement sounds like a lot of crap to me."

"Well, yes, I've thought that sometimes," Hsun-ching said nervously, "but you must be careful who you say that to! In China you can be thrown in jail, or worse, for speaking against communism."

"So what else is new?" the colonel said. "Every time someone starts a new dynasty here, he kills anyone who speaks against him. Who's the new emperor?"

Out of habit, Hsun-ching carefully looked around out before answering. "There are no emperors in New China! There was someone like that—Chairman Mao. But he's dead now, and the Gang of Four have been smashed."

"If the tyrant is dead, then things will probably get better in a few decades," the colonel observed. "What's the name of the new dynasty?"

Hsun-ching's eyes opened wide with fear. "How can you say that? This is the People's Republic of China! There's no ruling class, only the Communist party—how can you possibly not know that? It's been that way for almost thirty years!"

"Arrogant child! Is it really so impossible for you to believe that I have better things to do than keeping track of government officials and their endless petty intrigues?" the colonel asked dryly. "Just tell me this: Is America communist or capitalist?"

"Capitalist—America is the most capitalist country of all."

"That's good news," the colonel said, "for if we find this scroll, we can just buy it from the owner instead of having to steal it from some nut who doesn't believe in money. That will be much easier."

"Yes, but we still have to get there. How are we going to get by that fence?"

The colonel leaned against the mango tree and scratched his back against it. "Let's have a look at it first, then we'll choose a plan. Right now we should decide how to get from here to the border. Do we walk, or do we try to get on one of those things with wheels that are driven by fire?"

"You mean a train?" Hsun-ching asked, unable to conceal his incredulity. "You don't know the word for that either?"

The colonel seemed to take offense at this, and answered sharply, "No I don't, but I am quite sure that I could ride one as

well as any man, and probably better. You just tell me how, and
I'll be fine."

Hsun-ching, not knowing what to make of the colonel's behavior, apologized for sounding rude. He said that it would be
very easy to reach Canton, which was near the Hong Kong border, by train from Kun-ming. Hsun-ching folded his maps, and
they began walking toward Shao-yang. But after a few hundred
yards, Hsun-ching said quietly, "Colonel Sun—I have thought of
one other small problem. Those clothes you are wearing . . . aren't
they going to attract a lot of attention?"

The colonel looked down at his ancient suit. "Why?"

"Because . . . because no one wears clothes like that anymore."

"Oh. Then I suppose I will have to wear something on top of
them. When we reach Shao-yang, you go on ahead and buy me
some clothes."

"Why don't you just leave the old clothes here in China?
Won't it be uncomfortable, always wearing two layers of clothing?"

"What?" the colonel barked. "Leave this armor behind? This
belonged to Shih Huang Ti himself!"

Shih Huang Ti was the founder of the Ch'in dynasty, which
began in 221 B.C. He was the man who commissioned the building
of the Great Wall, who standardized the Chinese script, and who
burned the country's books and buried 460 scholars alive to
discourage anyone from "studying from the past to criticize the
present." Hsun-ching didn't want to anger the colonel, but he
doubted that the suit of armor could possibly be authentic. "But,
Colonel Sun—how do you know it was Shih Huang Ti's armor?"

The colonel frowned. "Because I took it from him myself."

Hsun-ching realized he must be joking. "Are you a grave rob-
ber?" he asked, smiling.

The colonel looked disgusted. "Do you think I am the sort of
man who would do such a cowardly thing? I'll tell you how I
know it was his armor. Shih Huang Ti was a very superstitious
man. Some time after he had taken power, a meteor fell to earth,
and on it was written, 'After the death of the Primal Dragon, the
empire will be divided.' Shih Huang became obsessed with immortality after that. He began to call himself the 'Perfected

Being,' equal to the Jade Emperor, and claimed that no one, man or demon, could stand against him. Then a fortune-teller convinced him that the true elixir of immortality was to be found on P'eng-lai, the legendary island protected by sea monsters. So Shih Huang went all the way to the Eastern Sea and shot a whale with a crossbow, thinking that would pacify the gods and force them to welcome him into their community. That was bad news, for once emperors think they are equal to the gods, they quickly go mad, and the whole country suffers. At that time, we had endured five hundred years of bloody civil war already, and didn't need any more trouble.

"The problem was, how to prove to him that he was mortal without killing him? There were some in the imperial court who thought of assassinating him for the good of the country, and some tried, but that is cowardly treason! How can one be disloyal to the emperor?

"After much thought, I came up with an idea: I dressed myself up as a demon, wearing white silk robes and a terrifying painted mask, stormed into his bedchamber late one night, and dragged him, screaming, out of bed. I told him that I was a visiting official from hell, and had heard that a god lived nearby. I asked if he was that god. He was shaking like a leaf, but he told me he thought he was, although he couldn't be sure. I screamed like a wild beast and said that if he was a god, he would surely know it.

"I picked up his jeweled sword and handed it to him, telling him that gods can break swords with their bare hands. He huffed and puffed, but of course he couldn't break the sword. Then I took it from him and busted it over my knee. I said that the punishment for pretending to be a god was to be eaten alive, and I started licking my lips! He started whimpering and begging for his life, so I told him that I would make a deal with him. If he would apologize to the gods right away and focus his mind on the affairs of state, I might be inclined to have mercy on him. He fell to his knees and promised he would do just that. Then I took his precious armor, saying that if he failed to keep his word, I wouldn't even wait for him to get dressed before dragging him down to hell to be tried and punished—I would have his wardrobe ready for him in my palace."

Hsun-ching decided to indulge his companion for a while. "But, Colonel Sun—wasn't Shih Huang Ti guarded around the clock by his most loyal soldiers? The history books say he was obsessed with treachery, and not even a mouse could get into his chambers without being cut down instantly."

Colonel Sun nodded proudly. "That is true. But mice can't fight very well against armed men, and I can. Shi Huang's bodyguards were quite special; they protected their emperor without any concern for their own lives. I had to kill three of them, and that was the first unfortunate result of my plan.

"The second was that Shih Huang Ti became so frightened of his eventual judgment in hell that he decided to create an army of spirit warriors to guard him in the afterlife. He had them fashioned out of clay at great expense to the nation, and arranged them in a giant underground palace. Then he slaughtered the builders and engineers so no one would know how to enter it, and buried alive all of his childless concubines to keep him company in the afterlife. Have you ever been to Hsien-yang?"

"No," Hsun-ching replied.

"There is a great mound there. Most people think it contains only the emperor's tomb, but under that mound, and under the ground for miles around, are thousands of terra-cotta warriors, horses, chariots, and weapons. Perhaps when we return from America, you can go there and see them, if you think I am lying."

Hsun-ching didn't know whether to laugh out loud or run away; the colonel spoke so earnestly that Hsun-ching began to wonder if he might not be a little crazy. "But, Colonel Sun," he said gently, "if you had taken that armor from the emperor, that would mean you are over two thousand years old. Right?"

"Yes."

Hsun-ching's mouth fell open in disbelief. "Are you saying you are two thousand years old?"

The colonel stopped walking and turned to face Hsun-ching. "Actually, I am not sure how old I am," he said slowly.

How could anyone believe such a story? It was impossible. But then Hsun-ching recalled how the colonel had ripped the tree out of the ground with a swipe of his staff. That was impossible too, wasn't it? A flicker of doubt crossed his mind, but it passed quickly. The colonel must have a reason for telling me these stories, he thought. I will have to be patient.

Hsun-ching chose not to ask any more questions that day, so they walked in silence until they reached the outskirts of Shao-yang. Hsun-ching went into town first and bought some ordinary clothes for Colonel Sun, then went to the bus station and bought two tickets for Kun-ming. When he returned to the forest, he saw his mysterious companion in a small clearing practicing maneuvers with his staff. He launched a savage, driving attack on an imaginary foe, then twirled the staff and threw it into the air. He caught it, drove one end into the ground, and used it to leap like a pole vaulter into a tree, all in the time it took to blink. When he saw how devastating the colonel could be with his crude weapon, Hsun-ching again felt afraid, but at the same time he told himself that anyone who could develop such remarkable physical skills couldn't possibly be insane.

When the man finished his exercises, he wiped the staff clean and joined Hsun-ching. "I'm getting old," he complained. "In my younger days, I could practice like that for hours without tiring. Now, after only a few minutes, my arms and legs start to lose their strength. If I had to fight more than twenty men, I would be in danger."

Wordlessly, Hsun-ching handed him the clothes, a bedroll, a duffel bag for his armor, and a pair of sunglasses to conceal his brilliant yellow eyes.

The bus for Kun-ming left early the next morning. At first Colonel Sun complained about being cooped up in a little metal box that traveled so fast through the jungle, but motion sickness quieted him down. He rode most of the way with his head out of the window, retching violently and cursing to himself. In Kun-ming they boarded the train for Heng-yang, and three days and two connecting trains later they stood on a hill in Shenchen, south of Canton, looking down at the border to Hong Kong.

"It's not just one fence," Hsun-ching said gloomily, "there are four or five of them. And look at all the guards! And up there on the hills—there are outposts with machine guns in them. We'll never get by them, and we don't have any money left to get to any of the other borders." He shook his head and sat down on the ground. But Colonel Sun did not seem discouraged at all; he rubbed his hands together and fixed his eyes on the point where the Hong Kong–Canton train tracks passed through the fence.

About half an hour later a passenger train came to the border. It stopped just short of a steel bridge over a small river that seemed to mark the actual border of Hong Kong, and twenty soldiers hopped on board to check the visas and passports of all the passengers. Outside the train, a team of soldiers checked under and around the train to make sure no one was trying to escape that way. After twenty minutes, the soldiers left the train and let it pass slowly across the bridge. Then the train picked up speed and rolled into the New Territories of Hong Kong.

"They checked that one pretty carefully," Colonel Sun said.

Two hours later a long, rusty train stopped at the checkpoint. The same two groups of soldiers came out of the guardhouse, checked the papers of the train crew, and looked quickly into most of the train cars.

"It's a livestock train—even from here you can smell it," Colonel Sun declared. "And those soldiers have to endure this every day! No wonder they rush through the search. Look how they open the wooden doors and pop their heads in and out—they aren't looking at all! That is how we'll get by!"

"But how will we get into one of the cars?" Hsun-ching asked. "There are soldiers standing all around it now."

Colonel Sun laughed and clicked his tongue. "We don't get in here—we double back until we find a curve in the tracks with a hill or tree alongside it. They'll have to slow down for the curve, and we'll hop onto the roof of one of the cars. Then I'll get us inside."

THEY FOLLOWED THE tracks north toward Canton for about three hours, and at last found a suitable spot. "It is lucky we're in southeastern China," the colonel said, "because if this were the northwestern desert, we'd have to walk six or seven days before finding a place like this." The spot he chose was a small graveyard carved out of the side of a steep hill about twenty feet above the tracks, protected from view on either side by thick bushes. They climbed up the side of the hill, and just as they reached the graveyard, an approaching train blew its whistle. Hsun-ching's heart pounded in his chest. "Is this the one?"

The colonel sat down against a gravestone, laying his staff across his knees, and shook his head. "A good soldier always brings whatever forces he can into play to help his strategy. Now it's daylight; if anything goes wrong and we're forced to try to escape, it'll be much easier for the guards to spot us. Also, at night they'll be more tired and impatient. We should wait until then."

As the train passed below, Hsun-ching looked at his companion doubtfully. "The train is still moving too fast," he moaned. "I'll never be able to hold on!"

"You won't have to," the colonel said. "You'll ride on my back, and I'll take care of the landing. A more important question for the moment is, what will we have for dinner?"

Hsun-ching pulled some more rice cakes out of his bag, but Colonel Sun made a face; he was tired of "monk food." He got up and told Hsun-ching to build a small fire, and promised to return with something more substantial to eat.

Half an hour later he came back with a goat. He threw the lifeless heap on the ground, and bared his teeth in a mischievous grin. "There's nothing like a good meal to give you strength before trying something dangerous!" he said. Hsun-ching nodded weakly, then watched queasily as the colonel skinned and cleaned the animal.

After it got dark, they packed their things and lashed them together. Colonel Sun tied this bundle to Hsun-ching's back, then sheathed his iron pole in a leather sling that he wore over his shoulder. They crouched at the edge of the graveyard and waited.

After what seemed an eternity, they heard the whistle of a train. "The last one was a passenger train," the colonel said, "so I think this is ours."

Before Hsun-ching could say anything else, the colonel told him to climb on his back and hold on tight. With Hsun-ching clinging onto him, Colonel Sun used the last bit of rope to bind them together in case Hsun-ching lost his grip in the fall. Then he stood up, his body tensed in preparation for the jump.

First the engine rounded the corner, and a blast of steam caught the two of them full in the face. Then a long series of oil cars followed. It began to seem that this might not be a livestock train after all, but at last some flat wooden roofs appeared around the corner, and the strong odor of manure filled their nostrils. "This is it!" the colonel cried, and as the train roared past, he made a tremendous leap and landed on all fours on top of one of the cars. They bounced once, and the car slid underneath them, but the colonel's strong fingers clamped down on the car's metal frame, and they stopped just short of tumbling to an unpleasant end.

"Aiyeeee!" the colonel yelled, exultant. He untied Hsun-ching, who fell from his back unconscious onto the roof of the car; the impact of their leap had smacked the iron staff against his forehead and knocked him cold. "Shit!" the colonel muttered. He tied Hsun-ching to the metal frame, then pried up a few boards so he could look down into the car. "Pigs," he scowled, "it would have to be pigs." He untied Hsun-ching and lowered him gently through the hole in the roof and dropped him into a soft pile of manure. "I hope he landed faceup," he said to himself, then he winced, ground his teeth, and jumped down beside his unconscious friend.

In a few minutes, Hsun-ching came to. He was in the middle of a dream in which he and Hamma were plotting to escape from the commune. They were making their plans in the one place where they knew they would not be overheard: the outhouse. Suddenly, they heard the sounds of a train bearing down on them, and as they ran out of the outhouse and saw a giant engine speeding toward them, he woke up.

"Where are we?" he asked.

"We're in a toilet for animals," the colonel grumbled. "How is your head? Can you stand?"

Hsun-ching rubbed the welt over his eye, and managed to get to his feet. "I'm okay, I guess."

"Good. Now listen carefully. We don't have much time. When the soldiers open the door, don't make a sound or even breathe! These pigs might get spooked, crowd over to one side of the car, and expose us."

"It's too bad they're not sleeping," said Hsun-ching. "We could lie behind them."

The colonel raised one eyebrow and nodded thoughtfully.

"Good idea," he said, then he picked up his iron rod. Hsun-ching watched in horror as he brought it down on the head of one of the pigs, crushing its skull and killing it instantly. When he had killed four of them, he dragged them to one corner of the car and arranged them as if they were sleeping. "You lie here," he said to Hsun-ching, pointing to a gap in the center of the inert pile, "and I'll lie right next to you."

When they were tucked snugly between the twitching corpses, the colonel said, "Now listen carefully. Only two men check each car, and I notice they keep their rifles slung over their backs. If anything goes wrong and one of them sees us, we'll have enough time to overpower them before they can get their rifles cocked and aimed. Something to keep in mind is that armies usually send their least talented men to guard borders, so even if they have their rifles ready, they probably won't hit us with their first shots. Have you ever killed a man before?"

Hsun-ching looked at him in horror. "K-killed a man? W-what are you talking about?! We're not going to kill anybody—we're just going to look for an old book! You must be j-j-joking!"

The colonel narrowed his eyes and shook his head. "Don't be a fool," he said quietly. "When you travel to strange places without an army, without the consent of your emperor, and without an invitation from abroad, you must be realistic. You must know beforehand that soldiers and criminals have one thing in common, and that is, they hurt people without thinking about what they are doing. The soldier does this because his superior tells him to; he feels complacent because he is doing his duty. The criminal hurts you because he has decided that whatever he wants is more important than your life. So you must be ready to strike first, without hesitation, when dealing with soldiers and criminals. Don't worry about them; they accept the risk of death when they choose their occupations."

Hsun-ching had begun to tremble. "If you're going to k-k-kill people, then we have to g-g-get out of here right now! What you're saying is r-r-ridiculous!"

The colonel's eyes opened wide with surprise. "This is a fine time to tell me you're a coward! I'm not saying we should kill innocent people! I'm telling you that, regardless of your intentions, you're about to start something that may get you in trouble. You must be prepared to defend yourself if you're threatened!"

"B-b-but w-w-w-w—"

"Didn't you see those men today? They are carrying guns! Their orders are probably to stop anyone who tries to get past the border, and shoot if he tries to escape. Does that make sense to you? You want to leave China to do an old man a favor, to make his life's dream come true, but those men are prepared to shoot you down if you try, and they think they have a right to do it! Well, I'm telling you they don't! They have no more right to do that than a criminal does to stab you for your money."

"B-b-but if they find us, they won't shoot us—they'll ask us to surrender first!" Hsun-ching argued. The colonel rolled his head in anger.

"I've been free all my life—do you really think I am going to turn myself in now, to a bunch of pimply-faced kids at a dirty little train station? I will never be captured alive!"

Just then they heard the train whistling its signal as it approached the border. Colonel Sun took hold of Hsun-ching's shoulder and said in an even, cold voice, "Are you prepared to do what you must to escape these men, or aren't you? If not, then we should get out of here right now, because the border is right outside the door."

Hsun-ching stared at the colonel, unable to speak. Then he looked at the dead pigs around him. He thought of the Red Guards, and of the soldiers who had sent him to the commune, and of poor dead Little Toad. He remembered that most of his young life had been wasted for him, without apology, as had been the lives of countless others. What the colonel said, mad as he was, was true; it did not seem right that he could not leave China freely.

"I c-c-couldn't possibly kill someone," Hsun-ching said at last, "and I won't h-help you hurt anyone, either. But I am going through that border. If you want to j-jump out now, you can."

The colonel growled with disgust and jumped up to the roof of the car. He climbed out through the hole, but dropped back in almost immediately.

"It's too late now," he said, crouching behind a bleeding sow. "There are big lights pointed at the car, and the soldiers are all lined up on either side. And this time, their rifles are in their hands. I guess they take extra care at night." Then he grinned at Hsun-ching. "You're stuck with me now, boy! If things fall apart and fighting starts, I recommend that you follow me out. If not, good luck." He made sure that his weapon was tied securely to his back, within easy reach, then dug himself low into the manure and waited for the door to open.

IX

THE TRAIN SCREECHED, GROANED, HISSED, THEN came to a stop with a loud clank. One of the soldiers called to the engineer, *"Hai pu hsing!* We aren't ready yet. You'll have to wait." A quarter of an hour passed, then another, and another. The animals became restless; they shoved against each other and kicked up filth, with a mighty chorus of mooing, crowing, and oinking. A huge pig stepped on Hsun-ching's shin, and he managed to keep from crying out, but when the pig began to urinate on his leg, he could not contain himself, and kicked it smartly in the rump. The pig screamed, frightening the others, and soon they were all screaming and flinging themselves against the walls of the car.

"Listen to the racket in this one," a guard yelled. "Better come over here."

"Let's see what the problem is here," said another. The door slid open and a guard reached in with a long pole, swatting at the pigs to keep them from jumping out. Two more soldiers scanned the car with their flashlights. Forty pigs huddled against the far wall.

"How come these pigs were making so much noise?" the guard asked one of the train crew.

"I don't know—maybe one of them is sick."

"Mm," the guard said. "All right, close this one up."

"Wait a minute," said the crewman, noticing the four pigs in the corner. "Those pigs aren't moving at all! Maybe they're all sick! I'd better check them." He started to climb up into the car, but the soldier grabbed him by the belt and pulled him back down.

"This is a border checkpoint, not an animal hospital! We don't have time for you to start taking care of pigs! You can do that when you reach Hong Kong. We still have more than twenty cars to check, so close this one up and let's go!"

The crewman shrugged, then closed the door and locked it.

HALF AN HOUR later the train blew its whistle and started moving again. It rode slowly across the iron bridge, then picked up speed as it crossed the border into the New Territories. Colonel Sun sat up in the darkness and poked Hsun-ching. "That wasn't so bad, was it? I told you it wouldn't be any problem." They climbed out on the roof as the train sped through the hills, and stared in wonder at all the brilliant lights in the high-rise buildings and along the highways.

Twenty minutes later, the train rounded a bend and slowed down as it approached Kowloon Tong, Hong Kong's largest train station. Hsun-ching was the first to notice the chain-link fences on either side of the tracks, but before he could say anything, the colonel pointed at the approaching station. "What are all those soldiers doing there?"

There were at least thirty soldiers standing on the tracks near the entrance to the building. They were dressed in smart black uniforms, carried pistols on their belts, and looked more relaxed and confident than the soldiers at the border.

"They must be Hong Kong soldiers," Hsun-ching guessed.

"What are they doing here? We already passed the border! What does that sign say?" Colonel Sun pointed to a big sign hanging over the entrance to the station.

"It says, 'Hong Kong Department of Immigration.' "

"Maybe Hong Kong doesn't want Chinese to come in any more than China wants them to get out," the colonel observed. "In any case, they look harder to fool than the soldiers at the border."

"What will we do?" Hsun-ching asked.

The colonel looked around quickly. "We can't jump off the train now. We're inside a fence. We can't hide in the pig car again, because now they'll be unloading it, and that crewman will want to find out why these pigs weren't moving."

"Well, whatever we're going to do, we have to hurry!" Hsun-ching yelled—they were only about one hundred yards from the station.

"There's only one direction to go, I guess," said the colonel, looking into the cavernous mouth of the station.

"Where?" asked Hsun-ching, his whole body shaking.

Colonel Sun pointed upward with his chin. He disappeared into the car and emerged a moment later with their two bags and his iron staff. He threw the bags over Hsun-ching's shoulder.

"No time to explain. Get on, and when I squeeze your arm, it means hold on tight. No time for rope now."

Hsun-ching put his arms around the colonel's neck and held on tight well before the colonel gave the signal. They crouched low, to avoid being seen by anyone as the train moved slowly into the cavernous station. The colonel squeezed Hsun-ching's arm hard, then made a tremendous leap upward. His fingers clamped down on a steel girder in the roof of the station, then he flung himself and Hsun-ching up into the shadowy ceiling with a mighty swing.

With Hsun-ching still on his back, the colonel perched on the six-inch beam and watched the train continue to move below them. One after another the cattle cars squeaked past, until the caboose came into view, then disappeared out the far end of the station building.

"The train didn't stop!" Colonel Sun hissed. "Why didn't it stop?"

A few moments later a second train pulled into the station, blew its whistle, and rumbled to a stop.

"A passenger train," the colonel moaned. "We could have

stayed on our livestock car and ridden it right out to the stock-
yards!" He shook his head and cursed, then told Hsun-ching he
might as well climb down from his back, since they would probably have to stay up in the rafters until late at night when the train
station closed.

"I can't," Hsun-ching said quietly.

"Why not?"

"Because I'm . . . I'm . . . I th-th-th-think I'm going to
f-f-faint. . . ."

It was the height. Ever since he could remember, Hsun-ching
managed to explain, he had been unable to climb even a ladder
without feeling dizzy. Colonel Sun told him to stay put and close
his eyes, because it would shorten their journey considerably if
he were to fall unconscious from the ceiling of Hong Kong's
Immigration Department. For nearly three hours the colonel
perched like a bird on the narrow steel beam, with Hsun-ching,
two bags, and his staff on his back. At last, the passenger train
backed out, the police locked the gates and doors, and the main
lights went out in the great station.

The colonel crept across the beam until it reached one of the
walls, then he managed to climb down and hop to the platform
without a sound. Hsun-ching let go of the colonel's neck and
tried to stand, but cramped muscles and vertigo had drained all
his strength, and he fell to his hands and knees. Colonel Sun
frowned at him and gestured for him to stand, but Hsun-ching
could only shake his head weakly and gasp for breath.

The colonel left him to rest and ran silently across the platform
to the train entrance. The huge iron gate was secured with a
heavy chain. Just outside, a few sleepy policemen in the guardhouse watched a news program on television. The colonel
paused, perplexed that a man would find it necessary to talk with
his head stuck inside a brightly lit glass box. Too late, he heard
something behind him, and turned to see Hsun-ching waving
desperately at him. A man in uniform was approaching from the
far end of the building, where the immigration offices were.
Hsun-ching managed to crawl behind a stairway, but the officer
had seen him. He pulled his pistol from its holster and crouched
a few yards from the stairway.

"*Mou tung!* Don't move!" he ordered sharply, and Hsun-ching froze with his hands in the air.

With the gun trained on Hsun-ching, the officer pulled a walkie-talkie from his belt with his free hand and called for assistance. Then he took out a pair of handcuffs and told Hsun-ching to lie on his stomach with his hands behind his back. Hsun-ching obeyed him, but instead of the cold steel clasp he expected, a crushing weight knocked the wind out of him.

"Get up," said the colonel, shoving the fallen officer to one side with his foot. Hsun-ching scrambled out from beneath him and rose unsteadily to his feet.

"What did you do to him?"

"He'll be fine," the colonel snapped. "Now let's get out of here!"

They ran toward the immigration building, but heard a commotion and the sound of many footsteps approaching. "These people sound wide awake from the way they are running," Colonel Sun said. "We're better off with the sleepy ones." He led Hsun-ching back toward the gate, then paused over the unconscious officer. He took the gun from the officer's limp hand and studied it for a moment.

"Do you know how this fire-spear works?" he asked, holding the gun out toward Hsun-ching.

"Yes, but—"

"Good." Before Hsun-ching could protest, the colonel handed him the gun.

"I'm going to bust this gate. We'll rush out, and you point this thing at those guards. I'll take their weapons away from them, and we'll see if we can get through the fence."

"But I told you, I won't—"

"You don't have to kill anyone!" Sun whispered violently. "You just have to do as I say! Now let's go!"

The colonel jumped in front of the gate, planted his feet wide apart, and severed the metal chain with a stroke of his staff. He kicked the gate open, and as soon as Hsun-ching was past, closed it from the outside and jammed it shut with a sideways blow of the staff. The police in the guardhouse jumped up and fumbled for their weapons, but Hsun-ching stormed through the door, pointed the gun, and yelled with all his might, "We are Chairman Mao's True Soldiers! Put your hands over your heads and surrender!"

The dazed policemen looked at each other, then slowly raised their hands. Colonel Sun jumped in through the window in a shower of glass, paused for an instant, then rushed toward the television. "You too! Shut up and come out of there!"

"It's just a television!" Hsun-ching shouted. "There's no one in there!" But when the colonel refused to move, Hsun-ching, seeing that precious time was being wasted, pointed the gun at the television and blew it to pieces with a single shot. "Get their guns!" Hsun-ching yelled desperately, and the colonel picked up the guns and followed him out the door.

The soldiers couldn't get the gate free, but they started to climb over it. Colonel Sun and Hsun-ching ran down the tracks until Hsun-ching gasped, "I can't run any further!" The colonel slowed down and looked around as Hsun-ching doubled over to breathe. There was moving traffic on the other side of the metal fence. The colonel dropped the guns and the bags, then planted one end of his staff under the fence and pried an opening large enough for a man to crawl through. He tossed the bags through the hole and pushed Hsun-ching after with a gentle nudge of his heel. Just as he was about to squeeze through himself, though, someone yelled, "Halt! Or I'll shoot!"

The policeman had his pistol drawn, and he was gaining fast.

"Run!" the colonel yelled to Hsun-ching, but Hsun-ching froze on the other side of the fence, unable to leave his companion.

"Put your hands over your head!" the policeman ordered. He was only about fifty feet away now. The colonel raised his arms up as he was told. The policeman walked toward him cautiously, keeping an eye on Hsun-ching. "Get down on the ground!" he ordered.

The colonel slowly lowered his arms.

"I said, get down on the ground!" the policeman shouted.

"You get on the ground!" Hsun-ching yelled at the policeman, pointing the gun at him, but then he felt a tingling pressure in his chest, the same sensation he had felt watching the colonel rip the tree out of the ground. He tried to say something, but found he was unable to breathe, and all the strength went out of his limbs.

Colonel Sun slowly raised his right hand and pointed at the policeman, who stopped in his tracks. He struggled to aim the gun at the colonel, clutching it with both hands. Then he took one of his hands off the gun and clutched at his chest. His knees buckled, and he made a last, desperate attempt to fire his gun, but it went off harmlessly toward the ground. The colonel walked toward him with a strange, gliding step—it looked to Hsun-ching as if he were walking on a sheet of ice—then he kicked the gun out of the policeman's hand and sent it clattering across the railroad ties. He held his iron staff up over the policeman, who lay on the ground gasping for breath, and seemed about to bring it down on the man's skull. One second went by, and then another, but still he did not bring the staff down. Other policemen were approaching now. The colonel backed away from the fallen officer, then, just in time, dragged himself through the fence and pulled it down again from the opposite side.

"I don't like these weapons," the colonel said angrily. He grabbed the pistol out of Hsun-ching's hand and threw it away as they ran toward the street. The soldiers fired warning shots into the air, but they did not dare fire in the direction of the street. Dodging cars and taxis, the colonel and Hsun-ching made it across the traffic and ducked into an alley. They followed the alley around a few corners, then jumped behind a garbage dumpster. Hsun-ching collapsed on the ground, gasping for breath.

"Do you realize what you have done?" the colonel demanded angrily. "You killed a man who was not even armed! He wasn't even in a uniform! After all your talk about not being willing to defend yourself against soldiers, you blow an innocent man's head off!"

Hsun-ching was near hysteria, and it took him a moment to realize what the colonel was talking about. "It w-wasn't a man!" he blurted out at last. "It was a T-T-TV! J-j-just a picture!"

The colonel frowned suspiciously, and asked how a painting could move.

Hsun-ching tried to explain, but Colonel Sun had never heard of electricity or cameras. Hsun-ching was able to assure him, though, that only the painting had been destroyed, not the real person. Then he asked, "B-b-but, Colonel Sun, what happened back there? What did you do to that man?"

"I didn't do anything to him! You saw me—I spared his life."

"No, I mean before that. You just looked at him, and he . . . fell down. And I felt something too, in my chest. . . . What did you do?"

The colonel waved the question aside. "There is nothing unusual about that skill. I have known men as physically weak as you who could do that."

"But what was it? You didn't even touch him, but he fell down as if he had been hit!"

"I cannot explain why it works, but it is a way of looking at a man," the colonel said. "If you fear nothing, not even death itself, then you grow strong. You can look at a man with an intent to cut through him, and he will feel crushed by your gaze."

"But how is that possible?" Hsun-ching asked.

The colonel shrugged. "A long time ago, before even your grandfather's grandfather was born, this was a fairly common skill. Many great warriors lived then who forged themselves through training and honorable combat. But the invention of fire-spears and cannons made that tradition obsolete. It takes decades to train a pure mind, but only a few minutes to learn how to use those cowardly weapons. That is part of the reason I am no longer a soldier."

Judging from his own experience as a "True Soldier," Hsun-ching did not see how any sort of fighting could be honorable, or give someone a pure mind. Still, he had just seen, and felt for himself, that Colonel Sun had exerted some kind of invisible power to disable the policeman. That, as far as Hsun-ching knew, was impossible.

"Colonel Sun," Hsun-ching asked gently, hoping to catch him off guard, "can you tell me what year you were born?"

The colonel gave him a withering glance, but he answered, "Yes I can. I was born in the fourth year after Duke Wen and his troops defeated the armies of Ch'u."

Hsun-ching, who knew very little about history, did not recognize these names. If this battle took place toward the end of the Ch'ing dynasty, however, that would make the colonel somewhere around sixty years old. Perhaps he was telling the truth now.

"But what year was that battle?" Hsun-ching asked.

The colonel scratched his chin thoughtfully, then said, "I believe it was the Year of the Rabbit. But I could be wrong."

Hsun-ching would have pursued the matter further, but now that the adrenaline was wearing off, he became aware of a new and more urgent problem. "Colonel Sun," he moaned, trying to avoid the stench of pig manure by breathing through his mouth, "I think we'd better find some new clothes."

The colonel pointed over their heads, where clotheslines heavy with laundry practically obliterated their view of the sky. "There are our clothes," the colonel said. "We could also use a bath. I think we should just go down to the shore for that. I could see it from the train, so we can't be far."

He shimmied up a drainpipe and chose a few items of clothing, then led Hsun-ching through a maze of alleys toward the ocean. Their path took them through downtown Kowloon, where even at two o'clock in the morning people milled in the streets, popular music blared out of the shops and restaurants, and flashing neon signs made it almost as bright as day. People sniffed, then turned to stare as the pair walked by even after the colonel put on his sunglasses in an attempt to make them less conspicuous.

"We really stink," Hsun-ching said.

"Haven't these people ever smelled pig shit before?" the colonel grumbled, baring his teeth at a pack of children who started to follow them.

AT LAST THEY came to a large pier, where hundreds of junks and small motorboats lay moored. They walked out to the end of the pier, stripped off their clothes, and jumped into the ocean. "This water doesn't smell much better than we do," the colonel observed, but they scrubbed themselves for a few minutes anyway, then climbed back onto the pier. Colonel Sun took out the clothes he had stolen, and let Hsun-ching have first choice. Hsun-ching took a plain white shirt, a pair of gray trousers, and some black socks. "Don't you want the fancy clothes?" the colonel asked him.

"No—you take them," Hsun-ching said.

Colonel Sun shrugged and put on the remaining clothes. His outfit consisted of a floral print yellow blouse and lime-green double-knit slacks. He replaced his sunglasses, and contemplated his reflection in a nearby porthole. "These clothes must be for an important official," he remarked proudly, puffing out his chest.

X

AFTER SPENDING THE NIGHT ON AN EMPTY JUNK, THE colonel and Hsun-ching began their search for a ship heading toward America. A fisherman preparing breakfast told Hsun-ching that oceangoing ships anchored at the international port on the other side of the peninsula. He seemed about to invite Hsun-ching to have breakfast with him, but when he saw the colonel standing nearby, he muttered, *"Sen-ging-beng!"* and disappeared into his boat.

"I think you might be wearing women's clothes," Hsun-ching remarked to the colonel.

Colonel Sun looked down at his outfit, and his face went white with rage. "Why didn't you tell me that before I put them on?"

"I didn't know," Hsun-ching said nervously. "I've never seen clothes like that before. And . . . you s-s-seemed to like them. . . ."

The colonel glared at his companion. "If you see me making a mistake, you tell me!" He squatted on his haunches and went as still as a statue, until Hsun-ching feared he would never speak or move again.

"Colonel Sun?" he asked.

"Yes?" The colonel looked up at him calmly; his anger had already passed.

"How are we going to eat?"

"Here." The colonel opened the duffel bag and pulled out his armor vest. It had several dozen pockets sewn onto the inside of it, and each of the pockets bulged as if filled with a heavy stone. The colonel tore open one of the pockets and pulled out an ancient, tarnished gold bar.

"I can't go into the city dressed like a woman. You take this to a merchant, have him weigh it, and get its worth in the local currency."

Hsun-ching took the bar and stared at it as it lay in his hand. "Is this real gold?" he asked.

"Of course it is."

"Where did you get it?"

The colonel shrugged and gestured for Hsun-ching to squat next to him. "When the Mongols rode south and brought an end to the Sung dynasty, one of the Mongol chieftains took his private army and stormed into the imperial treasury, murdered the grand secretary and his family, and stole a huge amount of gold from the Sung coffers. When his fellow chieftains arrived, he told them that the grand secretary had escaped with the gold, and search parties went out all over China. Of course, the secretary was never found; meanwhile, the chieftain distributed some of the gold among his army, then buried the largest portion of it just outside the city and waited for a good time to disappear with it.

"He waited more than five years, until nearly everyone had forgotten about the missing gold, then sent a memorial to the Yuan emperor requesting leave to return to the steppes of Mongolia to fetch his parents, wife, and children. The emperor granted this request happily, because this chieftain had been loyal to him for many years, and had been instrumental in the defeat of the Sung army. The chieftain put together a small caravan and left the city, camping near the buried gold on the first night.

In the middle of the night he and his most trusted soldier, who had seen him steal the gold years before, dug up the treasure and hid it in the packs his camels carried. When this task was completed, the chieftain betrayed his friend and stabbed him more than twenty times. Thinking the poor man was dead, the chieftain threw his body into a canal and went back to his camp.

"It happens that I was following that canal on my way to Ch'ang An. I usually prefer to travel at night, because I attract less attention that way. I heard someone choking, and came upon the soldier, who was drowning in his own blood. I asked him who had done this to him, and he told me what had happened, then died. Now, I'm not the sort of man to get involved in other people's business, but there are a few things that even I can't walk away from. One of them, as you know, is children being thrown off waterfalls. Another is betrayal of loyalty. I swore over the man's body that I would get revenge for him, then buried him so wild animals wouldn't eat his poor body.

"I managed to track the chieftain easily. It would have been a simple matter to walk into his tent and kill him, but I wanted something special for that man. Treachery, I believe, deserves more than an unexpected blow on the head with an axle. I decided to plan something unique for him.

"Time isn't a problem for me. Weeks and months on the road don't weigh on me the way they do on men whose lives are short, and who have things to live for. I followed the chieftain into Mongolia, and let him reach his family. He sent his servants back to China without any explanation, then told his family about the gold. They departed right away for deep Central Asia, where they could be fabulously rich, and safe from the wrath of the Yuan emperor. I let them travel a few days, then snuck into their camp one night and stole the gold. I loaded their sacks with rocks, so the chieftain would not suspect anything right away. Then I caught up with the returning servants, and told them that the chieftain and his family were actually heading west with the stolen Sung gold.

"When they returned to China, they told the emperor, who dispatched a small army to pursue the treacherous chieftain. I heard later that the army returned with the heads of the chieftain and his family decorating the ends of their spears. I laughed when I heard that, but not for long, because my informant told me that when the emperor asked the arresting officers where the gold was, they had replied honestly that the chieftain was only carrying rocks. The emperor suspected that he was being tricked again, so he had the officers beheaded. And that was the last anyone heard of the missing Sung gold, because, of course, I had it, and had nothing to spend it on."

Hsun-ching looked at the piece of gold in his hand, then asked quietly, "What did you do when you heard the officers had been killed?"

The colonel shrugged. "I felt bad about it, but not for too long, because the Mongols were all murderers anyway. Now—don't let anyone cheat you! That piece of gold should be worth enough to feed us for years, so make sure you get its full value. Merchants are the lowest sorts of men, and think nothing of letting men starve for the sake of profit. When you get the money, buy me some proper clothes and get us some food, then return quickly."

Hsun-ching put the gold bar in his pocket and left the dock, then wandered through the maze of crowded streets into downtown Kowloon. He didn't know what to think about the colonel's story. Am I going mad? he wondered. Am I starting to believe this man? It was utterly ridiculous—but if it wasn't true, where *did* he get all that gold? What kind of man could do the things Hsun-ching had seen the colonel do?

Hsun-ching forced these thoughts out of his mind and concentrated on the problem at hand. He had no idea where to go to sell a piece of gold, but when he saw a skyscraper with a sign that said BANK OF CHINA, he thought he might try there. He walked up to the large glass doors, then felt his heart race when he noticed two imposing Sikh guards on either side of the doorway, standing at attention with shotguns held across their chests. They wore heavy cotton turbans and had beards that hung halfway to their navels. Hsun-ching had never seen *waikuojen*—foreigners—before; the beards and the great beaklike noses, round eyes, and bushy eyebrows gave them the appearance of bears.

Hsun-ching took a deep breath and walked past them. The sounds of people talking and the ground beneath his feet had an unfamiliar, cushioned quality. He noticed that customers walked up to the long table and did business with the young women sitting behind it. It was like buying train tickets in China, he thought, except that you could see the person doing business with you instead of speaking through a little hole in the wall, and no one was pushing or shoving.

He looked around at the signs and pamphlets scattered around the lobby, hoping to find some clue as to how to initiate this transaction, but without success. Finally, he timidly approached one of the tellers. Wu Ch'eng-hui, read her nameplate, and below that, in English, Ruby Woo. Hsun-ching remembered that ruby was the name of a precious stone. Perhaps Miss Woo is in charge of buying and selling precious stones, he thought; in that case, she might be interested in gold.

"Can I help you?" she asked in Cantonese.

"Yes," Hsun-ching said. He put his hand into his pocket and pulled out the gold bar. "Will you buy this?"

Ruby blinked, then asked, "I'm sorry—could you say that again please?"

Hsun-ching felt his face go red. "This is gold. I want to sell it. Do you buy gold here?"

Ruby said no, but that they could put it in a safe-deposit box for him if he liked. Hsun-ching apologized and was making his way toward the door when a man standing in line put a hand on his shoulder.

"May I see that?" The man looked about Hsun-ching's age and spoke Cantonese with a heavy Fukien accent. He smiled warmly, so Hsun-ching handed him the bar.

The man looked at the piece of gold carefully, then asked, "You just came from China?" Hsun-ching became nervous, thinking that the man might be able to tell just by looking at him that he was an illegal immigrant. "Don't worry," the man said quietly. "I'm a friend."

Hsun-ching did not know what to say. He was by nature inclined to trust people, but in this strange environment, he thought everyone looked dangerous. He stared dumbly at the man, then said, "I want to sell this because I have no money."

"Where did you get it?" the man asked.

"I—I'm traveling with a friend. He has a few of these bars, but since we just arrived here, we don't have any local money."

The man smiled at Hsun-ching again and said, "Come on—I can help you. I know where you can sell this gold."

They left the bank, and the stranger led Hsun-ching into a noisy shopping district. The streets became more and more narrow and crowded. All of a sudden the man broke into a run and disappeared around a corner.

"Hey!" yelled Hsun-ching, and took off in pursuit, but the angry people the stranger had knocked out of his way wouldn't let him pass.

"Stop him!" Hsun-ching cried. "He stole all my money!"

When people up the alley heard that, they hurried out of the way of the stranger, not wanting to get hurt. That made it even easier for him to escape. But at the top of the alley, just as the stranger was about to duck around a corner, a middle-aged man wearing glasses jumped up from the table where he was having noodles and tripped the thief, then tried to wrestle him to the ground. The thief punched savagely at the man and managed to wriggle free, but the bar dropped out of his pocket. He darted around the corner, and disappeared in a crowd of shoppers.

Hsun-ching ran to the side of the brave man. "Are you all right?"

"I think so," the man said, brushing the dirt off his clothes and rubbing his bruised cheek. "I'm sorry he got away. Is that what he stole from you?"

Hsun-ching looked where the man pointed and saw his gold bar.

"Yes—yes, that's it! Thank you! Thank you very much!" Hsun-ching gasped. He stood there for a long time, staring at the bar and catching his breath. Then a fresh wave of despair rushed over him as he realized that he might not be able to find someone willing to buy the gold. And as if that weren't enough, he was completely lost in the streets of Hong Kong.

His rescuer noticed how miserable Hsun-ching looked, and asked him if anything was wrong.

"Well, I—" Hsun-ching stammered, "I'm lost."

"Do you want me to call the police?" the man asked.

Hsun-ching looked alarmed and shook his head, then made a

quick decision. "Sir, you were good enough to help me by stopping that thief. I've troubled you enough already. But—if you
could just give me some advice, I would be very grateful."

"I'll try. What's your problem?"

Hsun-ching told him that he and a friend had just arrived from
China, and had no money for clothes and food. "We have these
bars, but we don't know how to sell them. Can you help me?"

The man looked Hsun-ching over carefully, as if wondering
whether he might be a thief as well. At length he said, "Why
don't you calm down and sit with me for a moment, and tell me
more about this. My name is Yin Po-jan."

He led Hsun-ching over to his table and called for one of the
waitresses to bring a hot towel and another pot of tea.

At first Hsun-ching was too nervous to accept the man's hospitality, but the man insisted, and when Hsun-ching had wiped the
sweat off his face and had something to drink, Mr. Yin said:

"You said you just came from China—do you have any relatives here?"

Hsun-ching shook his head.

"How did you get here, then?" Mr. Yin asked.

Hsun-ching didn't know what to say. He knew if he tried to
make up a story it would sound preposterous. Mr. Yin broke the
silence. "I came here in 1958, as an illegal immigrant. My mother
was killed by the Japanese, and my father, who owned an um-
brella factory, was killed by the Communists. I snuck out on a
boat carrying our umbrellas from Shanghai."

Hsun-ching realized that if he was ever going to make it to
America, he was going to have to get used to relying on the
kindness of strangers. He confessed that he had also left China
illegally.

Mr. Yin nodded thoughtfully, then said, "It's harder to get
citizenship in Hong Kong now than in the fifties, but it isn't
impossible."

"But I don't want to live here," Hsun-ching explained. He told
Mr. Yin that he was on his way to America, then added, "I'm
traveling with a friend, as I told you before. He is the true owner
of this gold. He looks strange, but I assure you he is a good man."

Mr. Yin looked at Hsun-ching curiously. "Tell me," he said, "you were extremely lucky to make it to Hong Kong without being arrested. But without any papers whatsoever, how do you plan to get to America? Surely you realize that you can't count on being so lucky again?"

Hsun-ching hung his head and answered that they had no real plan at all, except that they hoped to find a boat willing to take them in return for hard work.

"I think you are going to rush yourself right into jail," Mr. Yin said. "Now that you're here, you should try to find work and in a few years apply for resident status. Then perhaps you could get a tourist visa to go to America. If you get there legally, it will be much easier for you to find ways to remain there."

Hsun-ching thanked the man for his suggestion, but replied that he could not follow it. He explained that he was an orphan, and that this trip was a favor to the old man who had raised him. "Master is very old, and I fear he will not live long much longer. There is something in America he has wanted all his life, and I must try to get it and bring it back to him now. It's the only way I can pay him back for all the kindness he showed me."

"You mean you will sneak back into China after going to America?" Mr. Yin asked incredulously.

"Yes."

"It's a strange mission you have chosen," said Mr. Yin, obviously intrigued by this story, "but I can understand how grateful you must feel toward the man who adopted you. In my own way, I have a similar debt to repay. Let me bring you to meet a friend of mine who might be able to help you. He is a retired seaman, and I think he's even been to America once or twice. And then maybe we can see about your gold bar. In the meantime, I will be happy to lend you enough money to buy some new clothes, and you and your friend are welcome to stay in my home until you decide what to do. We have an extra room for guests, and I'm sure my wife would not object. We've enjoyed helping other people just out of China before."

Hsun-ching felt embarrassed to accept so much hospitality from a stranger, but realized that he had little choice. He thanked

Mr. Yin again and again for his help, then followed him to Mong-kok, where, Mr. Yin explained, one could buy good clothes cheap.

While they shopped, Mr. Yin told Hsun-ching a little more about himself.

"I nearly starved when I first got off the boat here, and probably would have if it weren't for a very generous man. He met me in a public toilet! He went to use the bathroom out in the park, and found me sleeping on the floor there. He could have called the police, but instead he spoke to me, and when he heard that I was from Shanghai, his own hometown, he offered me a job in a warehouse he owned. I took the job and worked very hard, and in a few years became foreman of the warehouse.

"Meanwhile, he made arrangements to get me permanent-resident status. He and his wife treated me very well. They even helped introduce me to a young woman, who is now my wife. Eventually, I was able to save enough money to make my own investments, and start my own branch of the business. I am not a rich man, but I am no longer poor, either.

"My benefactor was a Christian, and he convinced me to be baptized. He told me that it was because of his adherence to the teachings of Jesus Christ that he helped me when I was in need, and he hoped that I would follow his example and do the same for someone else one day. You are a refugee from China like I was; if I can be of assistance to you, it will help me repay my debt."

When they had made their purchases, Hsun-ching and Mr. Yin went together to give Colonel Sun his new outfit. On their way to the docks, Hsun-ching asked Mr. Yin, "Do you know much about Chinese history?"

"A little bit. Why do you ask?"

"Well, do you happen to know when a Duke Wen fought a battle against the soldiers of Ch'u?"

This question struck Mr. Yin as a bit odd; he looked askance at Hsun-ching, then said, "I can't tell you the exact year, but I know that was during the Chou dynasty. That would be . . . oh, seven centuries before the birth of Christ. Why?"

Hsun-ching shook his head absentmindedly. "I was just curious," he answered.

When they reached the docks, Hsun-ching said, "I have to warn you again—Mr. Sun is very strange-looking; he's almost frightening when you first meet him. But he is a loyal friend. As a matter of fact, he saved my life when I was young." Mr. Yin promised not to be shocked by Mr. Sun's looks, and they hopped onto the docks.

As they approached the junk, they heard loud laughter. A gang of teenagers had surrounded the colonel and were pointing and laughing at his attire. The colonel was standing still as a statue with his arms folded across his chest, staring without expression at the biggest member of the gang.

Hsun-ching called out for them to go away, but he was too late; the large boy stepped forward to give the colonel a shove. With what appeared to be a single movement, the colonel swept the boy's feet from under him, lifted him over his head, and threw him over a boat and into the ocean. Then he turned on the rest of the boys, and within a few seconds all of them were bobbing and gurgling in the filthy water. The colonel looked up and saw Hsun-ching, straightened his blouse a bit, then said, "You were right about these being women's clothes. I've had a terrible morning."

XI

THE CAB STOPPED IN FRONT OF GAM GWOK DAAIH Haah, the "Golden Nation Building," and Mr. Yin climbed out to open the rear door for the colonel and Hsun-ching. Gam Gwok Daaih Haah was a fifteen-story apartment building in Wanchai, a neighborhood renowned for its nightclubs and prostitutes.

The driver looked nervous as Colonel Sun pulled his iron staff out of the car, and hurried away as soon as Mr. Yin paid him. The colonel noticed this, and asked Mr. Yin, "What was the matter with him?"

Mr. Yin smiled and said, "Nothing to worry about. Wanchai has a bad reputation, so he might have thought we wouldn't pay him. I think he was afraid your pole was some kind of weapon."

The colonel nodded and seemed satisfied. But Mr. Yin, who was now staring at the iron staff, scratched his chin and asked, "By the way, what is that for?"

Without hesitating, Colonel Sun answered, "It's a monk's staff—didn't the boy tell you? We're Buddhist monks. We're traveling to America to recover a sutra. Buddha be praised."

Mr. Yin looked surprised, but perhaps not

as surprised as Hsun-ching, whose cheeks flushed red. He didn't understand the need for this deception, and feared it would only bring trouble. Mr. Yin glanced back at the iron pole. "But didn't you say you were an army colonel?"

Without skipping a beat, Colonel Sun replied, "I was a military man once, it's true, but that was a long time ago. The title stuck with me because, even after I became a monk, I continued to practice martial arts—the kind you saw out at the pier. Anyway, the other monks seem to enjoy referring to me as 'the colonel,' and I have no objections."

Mr. Yin smiled and gave him a friendly pat on the shoulder. "I've always been a Chinese boxing fan! Do you practice Shaolin-style martial arts, or Wutang style?"

The colonel grinned, nearly letting his sharp teeth show, and said, "Neither. I practice my own style."

"It's obviously effective!" Mr. Yin said. "What do you call it?"

The colonel's eyes flashed behind his sunglasses as he answered, "I call it *Wu-k'ung ch'üan*—Aware-of-Emptiness Fist. To execute it properly, your mind must be completely empty; it must not stick to anything, for even an instant—not even on the opponent! That way, you can counter his attack before he even moves, because you are so clear you can sense his intentions. On the other hand, he cannot counter your moves, because you have no intentions—there is only action."

"I have always heard that martial artists had this ability," Mr. Yin said, "but I have never actually seen it. Is there any way you could demonstrate that on me without hurting me?"

The colonel seemed willing to oblige. He leaned his pole against the outside of the building, then said, "Try to hit me. As hard as you can, any way you like." Mr. Yin hesitated. Something about the colonel's confidence unnerved him.

"Don't worry. I promise I won't hurt you," the colonel said. Mr. Yin put up his hands into a Chinese boxing stance and knitted his brow. He stood there for almost thirty seconds without moving, waiting to catch his opponent off guard, but the colonel stood with his hands at his sides in a completely natural, relaxed stance. His face showed no tension or even interest in Mr. Yin; he looked as if he were completely unprepared for a duel.

At last Mr. Yin put his arms down. He was panting. "I—I give up! I had no chance!" He turned to Hsun-ching. "It was incredible! I felt as if, whenever I thought of throwing a punch, I could *feel* him hitting me first! I was defeated before I could even move!"

As they entered the building, Mr. Yin said, "Colonel Sun—I'm sorry that I didn't realize until now that you were Buddhist monks. Perhaps I should tell you, as I have told Hsun-ching, that my wife and I are Christians."

"But you are Chinese!" the colonel exclaimed, frowning. "That's a foreign religion!"

"Yes, but in God's eyes, we are all the same," Mr. Yin said gently.

"Mm. Does that mean you won't let us stay with you?" the colonel asked.

"Of course not!" Mr. Yin laughed, "You're welcome regardless of your faith! But I hope you won't be offended if we say grace at the table before dinner."

"It won't bother me," the colonel said, then he turned to Hsun-ching. "What about you?"

Hsun-ching shook his head. He was still flustered, wondering if anything he had already told Mr. Yin contradicted the Buddhist monk story. He also wondered if he would have to behave differently from now on to make the story believable.

"Fine, then," Mr. Yin said. "I spoke to my wife on the phone, and she is looking forward to meeting you." He looked thoughtful for a moment, then said almost apologetically, "I should tell you that my wife is very—well, enthusiastic about religion. She might want to tell you all about her faith in Christ. Please don't be offended, will you?"

"Not at all," the colonel said. "A soldier—a Buddhist, I should say—always keeps an open mind."

They got on the elevator, and Mr. Yin pressed the button for the fourteenth floor. The colonel became nervous when the door closed, and turned pale as soon as the elevator began to rise.

"What the hell is this?" he growled.

Mr. Yin laughed. "Haven't you ever ridden an elevator before?"

"No! What is it doing?"

"It's taking us up to the fourteenth floor! It's a lot easier than climbing the stairs."

When the door opened, the colonel rushed out and leaned against a wall. "Where are we now?" he asked urgently.

"We're on the fourteenth floor now!" Mr. Yin answered. "Did the ride make you queasy?"

"Yes," the colonel answered. "How does that box work?"

Mr. Yin explained how a cable, powered by a motor at the roof of the building, pulled the car up and down.

"And you trust that cable not to break?" the colonel asked angrily.

"Of course! They never break," Mr. Yin said. "You'll get used to it. You must really be from the countryside if you've never seen an elevator!" He led them down the hallway to the third door on the right. He rang the doorbell, and a plump woman with tightly curled hair opened the door.

"What took you so long?" she asked, "You called nearly an hour ago. Did you stop somewhere for dinner? I told you I'd cook something."

"No, no, we didn't eat anything," Mr. Yin answered patiently, "we just had to shop for some things first. Let me introduce you to Hsun-ching, the young man I told you about. And this is his companion, Colonel Sun. This is my wife, Yu-lan."

The colonel and Hsun-ching nodded politely. Mrs. Yin stared at the colonel, making no effort to conceal her shock at his appearance. "Are you a foreigner?" she asked.

A shadow passed over the colonel's face, but he answered evenly, "No, I am not."

"You don't look Chinese," she said, gesturing for them to come in. As they stepped into the apartment, Mr. Yin said to his wife, "Colonel Sun and Mr. Hsun are Buddhist monks."

"Buddhist monks? You didn't tell me that," she said.

"I didn't know myself until only a few minutes ago," he said. "I am curious to hear how religion is faring in the mainland these days."

"Hm," she said, staring openly at the colonel. "What is that pole for?" she asked him.

"It's a monk's staff," he answered. "We're pilgrims, so we

travel long distances on foot. This staff helps me; I have a bad leg."

"You don't limp," she observed. "And why do you wear sunglasses indoors? I never saw a monk who wears sunglasses before."

The colonel laughed mirthlessly and turned to Mr. Yin. "We've been on the road for several days without a chance to rest and clean up. Do you think we could retire for a few hours? Then we'll feel refreshed and able to talk all night, if you wish."

"Of course, of course!" Mr. Yin said. "Let me show you the bathroom, and the room where you will be staying. I hope you don't mind sleeping on cots—we don't have extra beds in this tiny apartment."

He showed them how to work the shower and the toilet. He had learned the hard way that people from the mainland often did not know how to use Western toilets. Then he led them to their room. It was small but neat, and looked out on another building. The colonel opened the window and peered downward. He winced, and closed the window gingerly. "What keeps these buildings from collapsing, or blowing over?" he asked.

Mr. Yin smiled and said, "This is nothing! Wait till you see some of the buildings downtown! There's no need to worry, though. All the tall buildings are reinforced with steel beams—they don't collapse easily."

"And what is that outside the window?" the colonel asked.

"That is the fire escape," Mr. Yin answered. "In case of a fire, you can climb down it all the way to the ground."

Colonel Sun seemed relieved to hear that. "Thank you very much. This is a fine room," he said.

"Let me know if you need anything," Mr. Yin said, backing out of the room. "I expect we'll have dinner ready in about an hour. Shall I call you then?"

"Yes, thank you," the colonel said, and Mr. Yin closed the door.

"Why are we saying we are Buddhist monks?" Hsun-ching asked.

Colonel Sun threw their duffel bags in a corner and leaned his staff against the wall under a large porcelain crucifix. He stared at the image of the bleeding Christ for a moment, then sat down on the edge of one of the cots. He took off his sunglasses and frowned at Hsun-ching. "Because that will make me easier to explain. What if this man, or his nosy wife, start wondering why I'm going with you?"

Hsun-ching looked down at the ground and didn't say anything.

"Look," the colonel said in a low voice, "what's more important? Making friends or getting that sutra? Sometimes telling the truth is important, but sometimes it isn't."

"It's just that I don't like lying," Hsun-ching said. "Once you start, what's to stop you from doing it all the time?"

The colonel clicked his tongue with impatience. "Common sense, unless you're an idiot."

Hsun-ching lay down on his cot and stared at the ceiling. The colonel went to his duffel bag and pulled out his armor. He took it over to Hsun-ching's cot and pointed to a rough slit in one of the leather plates.

"You see that?" he asked Hsun-ching.

"Yes."

"This is the closest I ever came to dying. Only a lie, and this armor, saved me. Let me tell you how it happened."

The colonel sat down on the corner of his cot and put the armor on his lap. "A long time ago, I crossed the Takla Makan Desert with a real Buddhist monk. We stopped for several weeks in a town called Turfan. Did you know that Takla Makan means 'Go in and You Won't Come Out'? That's how terrible the desert is. The prince of Turfan took a liking to us, and offered us an armed escort across the desert to the next oasis city. There were all sorts of bandits roaming around out there, and being a religious man, the prince wanted to do everything he could to help us complete the pilgrimage we were on.

"On the third night of our desert crossing, the bandits attacked. They waited in the hills until most of us had retired, then came charging into our camp riding Mongolian ponies. We had only eight men with us, and there were at least fifteen bandits. The prince's men fought bravely, and in spite of being surprised, managed to kill six of the bandits. I killed four myself, but then

I took an arrow in one shoulder, and another in my leg. Three of the little bastards jumped on me, and one of them must have hit me over the head with something, because I blacked out.

"Normally, I suppose, the bandits would have taken our booty then killed us all, letting the sandstorms cover all traces of the attack. But when they didn't find any booty in our sacks, only food, they must have thought they were being tricked. You see, no one crossed that desert unless it was to trade and make a fortune—you'd have to be mad to cross it for any other reason, because the Takla Makan eats up men and camels the way you and I step on ants. The bandits recognized the prince's soldiers and killed them right away, but they kept the monk and me alive.

"They asked us who the hell we were that the prince's soldiers would give us an armed escort. The monk told them the truth, that he was a Buddhist pilgrim doing a good deed. The bandits cursed their bad luck and decided to kill us instantly, of course. The leader took his spear and drove it into my chest, here, where the hole is.

"This is good armor; it was sewn for the emperor himself, after all. The bandit's spear didn't quite make it through on his first stab. As he pulled back to make a stronger thrust, I managed to say, 'I can't do it! I don't want to die, just to protect someone's else's money!' That got the bandits' attention.

"The leader said, 'Let's kill the monk and save the one who tells us about the money,' and he prepared to run him through. I should mention that I had been hired by that monk to take him to India, so I couldn't let him die if I ever wanted to be paid. 'No!' I shouted, 'Then it will be hopeless! I only know half the route to the silver, and he knows the other half! We have to keep him alive, and force him to confess his part of the secret.'

" 'All right,' the bandit leader said. 'So whose silver is this that you are on your way to find?'

"I told him we were servants of the T'ang court, and showed him the letters of introduction the T'ang emperor had given us. 'These letters say that we are Buddhist pilgrims,' I told the bandits, 'but that is our disguise. Actually, the imperial palace wants us to recover a huge shipment of silver that was buried four years ago, when the caravan lost its camels to a strange sleeping sickness. We are to confirm that it is still there, then the prince of Turfan will provide the men and animals needed to transport it back to China.' The leader seemed to believe this story, because he said, 'All right. If you tell your half of the route, and your friend tells his half, then I'll let you both go free.'

"Of course, you can't trust bandits to keep their word, so I said, 'Forget it—you'll slit our throats the moment we tell you the secret, and then what good will it have done us? We might as well die now, and know that at least you won't get the silver. No, we'll lead you to it. I'm willing to bet that once we show you the silver, you'll be too busy counting your fortunes to chase us when we run away. What do you say?' The bandits talked among themselves for a while, then asked, 'How many days' ride is it from here?'

'Two,' I said, hoping like hell I could come up with a good plan by then.

They tied the two of us up and made us jog alongside the ponies. I can't tell you how I cursed myself for not saying it was a two hours' ride, because the minute we started jogging, I knew what to do. But to make it believable, I had to wait until the end of the second day of running through that miserable desert before I announced that we had to go up into the mountains to the north.

"Once we got up there, I led them to a huge, twisted juniper tree growing right at the edge of a cliff. I told them they had to untie me and give me another rope, at least twenty feet long.

" 'What for?' said the leader, getting impatient, but I was ready for him. 'It's two hundred feet to the bottom of this cliff—do you think I can climb down using twenty feet of rope? My friend is tied up, and there's no one around for a hundred miles in any direction! What are you worried about? Just let me do what has to be done, and you'll get your silver!' The bandit laughed at this, but ordered his men to do as I asked.

"I tied one end of the rope around the tree. 'You see,' I said, tying the other end around my waist, 'the first thing I have to do is find the grotto over the edge here. Once I find it, then I'll pull the silver out and hand it up to you.'

"As I hoped, the five bandits walked over to the edge to have a look. I charged at them with all my strength, and all of us went

screaming over the edge, me screaming the loudest, I think, because I wasn't sure the rope would hold. It did, but it broke two
of my ribs when it went taut. Still, that didn't stop me from
laughing as the bandits fell away from me and then down onto
the rocks below, where their heads split open like ripe melons!
I climbed back up, untied the monk, and we rode on to the next
oasis, where we sent word to Turfan about the massacre of his
soldiers.

"Now tell me," the colonel asked Hsun-ching. "Do you think
it was wrong of me to lie to the bandits?"

An awkward silence followed, then Hsun-ching replied dis-
tractedly, "No—no, of course not." Then, after another pause, he
asked the colonel the name of the monk he had accompanied.

"His name was Hsüan-tsang."

Hsun-ching blinked a few times. "And you went with him to
India?"

The colonel nodded. He had found a loose stitch, and was tying
a little knot in it to keep it from unraveling further.

Now Hsun-ching knew who Wei-ching thought the colonel
was, and why Wei-ching had been so certain that the colonel
would accompany him on this pilgrimage.

Hsun-ching chewed his lip anxiously. "Colonel Sun," he
began, "when I was a boy, I read a book about a monk named
Hsüan-tsang who went to India in the T'ang dynasty. You don't
mean that Hsüan-tsang, do you?"

The colonel glanced up from his work at Hsun-ching, then
said, "Yes, unless there was another Hsüan-tsang."

Hsun-ching paused to consider his next question. "In the book
I read," he continued cautiously, "Hsuan-tsang had a companion
named Sun Wu-k'ung. Is that—was that you?"

"Wu-k'ung isn't my real given name. But some people called
me that because of the school of boxing I created."

A huge smile broke out on Hsun-ching's face. "You mean in
a past life!" he exclaimed, "You're talking about reincarnation,
aren't you! I've been so stupid!"

The colonel shook his head wearily. "No, I'm not. But by all
means, believe that if it makes you more comfortable."

Hsun-ching's face fell. "But, Colonel Sun—Sun Wu-k'ung wasn't a man, he was a monkey! A monkey with magical powers, who could fly and who fought with demons and monsters and—"

"Well, that's obviously a lot of crap, isn't it?" the colonel interrupted. "Do I look like a magical monkey? I can't fly any farther than I can jump, and the only monsters we encountered on the way to India were the bureaucrats we had to see to get our travel papers stamped."

Hsun-ching couldn't think of another word to say; he just stared at the colonel, his jaw gone slack. The colonel checked a few more stitches, then began cleaning the collar with a stiff brush he kept in an inner pocket. He seemed to be watching Hsun-ching out of the corner of his eye, though. At length he said, "You don't believe that I am the same man that traveled with Hsüan-tsang, do you?"

"Should I?" Hsun-ching asked, close to despair. "Can I? Would you believe me if I told you I was Confucius, or the Jade Emperor?"

The colonel nodded, holding the collar up to the light to check for small tears. "I've been in this situation before," he said. "And the fact is, there is nothing I can do or say that will prove that I am telling the truth." He put the armor down and looked hard at Hsun-ching. "But let me ask you this—does it really matter who I am? What difference would it make to you if you knew for a fact that I was only fifty years old? Would that change our travel plans?"

"No—but yes, it matters! You saved my life, and now you are risking yours to help me get to America! Of course I want to know who you are! I don't want to pretend to believe that you are a fairy-tale character!"

The colonel took off his soaked cotton shoes and lay down on his bed. "Who said I was a fairy-tale character? It's not my fault that you can't tell the difference between what is real and what you read as a child. Whether you believe me or not is your own affair. But whatever you decide"—he paused to stretch his arms out in front of him, making the bones in his powerful hands and shoulders crack loudly—"this is the last time I want to have this conversation. I do not enjoy trying to explain myself to people, and I have no need to prove myself to you or anyone. If you do not want my company on this trip, then just say so. If you do want my company, be courteous enough to stop telling me who I can or cannot be." The colonel lowered his eyes, took a few deep breaths, then became motionless as a stone.

XII

"O LORD, WHO ART IN HEAVEN, WE THANK THEE FOR this our daily bread. And we pray to Thee for the souls of our guests. Amen," Mrs. Yin said, then the four of them raised their heads.

"Is it over now?" asked Colonel Sun. He was very hungry, and hoped that there would be no more speeches before dinner.

"Grace is never over, Mr. Sun," she answered with a taut smile, "but you may eat now, if that is what you mean."

"Thank you," the colonel said, and he began piling food on his plate. Mr. Yin cleared his throat apologetically. "My wife and I are Christians, but we are Chinese, so of course we have a great respect for Buddhism. In fact, our reverend says that Buddha was a saint."

Mrs. Yin's lips tightened further, and she said in an even voice, "Yes, but the Lord told us, 'Thou shalt not worship false gods!' There is only one God, and Jesus is His Son."

None of this conversation seemed to bother the colonel at all, and he ate heartily. Hsun-ching, though, began to feel very uncomfortable. He shifted around in his seat, trying to think of something to say to relieve the tension. He forced a smile at Mrs. Yin.

"Your husband told me you are both from Shanghai—is that right?"

Mr. Yin nodded enthusiastically, grateful for the change of subject, but Mrs. Yin was staring at the colonel, who, she noticed, swallowed even the bones of the tea-smoked chicken she had prepared.

"You're still wearing sunglasses, I see," she said to him. "You haven't yet told me what was wrong with your eyes."

The colonel raised his head to look at her. "I wear these glasses so that people won't stare at me," he said, and with that he lowered the glasses and let her look directly into his brilliant yellow eyes. She gasped and put her hand to her mouth. "I became a monk because I couldn't stand being gawked at. Is it my fault I was born with yellow eyes? Or sharp teeth?" At that, he pulled back his lips to reveal his long canines. Even Mr. Yin gasped at the sight, and Mrs. Yin began to turn white.

"The other monks treat me like an ordinary man, because they know that all life is suffering, and in view of the fact that we'll all be born and reborn a million times, being ugly isn't a matter of importance," the colonel continued. "Does your religion have a similar view?" He pushed his sunglasses back over his eyes and stuffed a huge portion of shredded pork with carrots and peppers into his mouth.

Mr. Yin managed to nod. "Yes—yes, Jesus treated all men equally. It doesn't matter what you look like; the important thing is what you believe, and what you do in life. Isn't that right, Yu-lan?"

But Mrs. Yin wasn't listening to him. She stared at the colonel with barely concealed repugnance. "I hope you have enough to eat," she said in a strange tone of voice. "I see you are eating meat. I thought that Buddhist monks were vegetarians."

"Only in some sects," the colonel said cheerfully. "In our sect, we believe that the only way to break out of the cycle of karma is by reciting sutras. That is why we are going so far to find this one sutra; if you recite it properly, you will become enlightened no matter what you eat."

"I've never been to Shanghai," said Hsun-ching, trying desperately to alter the tone of their conversation. "I'm from Yunnan."

He began to explain how he had been raised by a monk, but Mrs. Yin interrupted him by pointing her chopsticks at a crucifix on the far wall and asking the colonel, "Do you know the meaning of the Cross, Mr. Sun?"

He looked at it briefly, then answered, "I knew some missionaries in Peking once. They told me that's where your god was nailed and left to die—isn't that right?"

Mrs. Yin nodded and said, "Yes, that's right. But then, after He was buried, He rose! He rose from the dead, and preached the Word of God! Do you believe that?"

The colonel wiped his mouth on his napkin and appeared to be thinking about something. "I wasn't there, so I can't say for sure. But—isn't it possible," he asked, "that he was just unconscious from loss of blood for those few days? Maybe he wasn't dead at all, but—"

"No," Mrs. Yin interrupted, "He was dead! But He is the Son of God, and He was granted Eternal Life, just as all those who are baptized and who believe in God will be! Don't you want Eternal Life, Mr. Sun? Immortality?"

The colonel glanced at Hsun-ching for a moment, who was by now green with misery. Then he rubbed his cheek with his palm. "Well, possibly. But are you sure immortality is such a good thing? Maybe it would be better to die, and be reincarnated as a tree or a beautiful bird or something. What do you think?"

Mrs. Yin shook her head. "No, I would not prefer to be a bird. I would prefer to be an angel in the Kingdom of Heaven. I shall pray for your soul when I get there, Mr. Sun."

"Thank you," said the colonel, helping himself to more rice. Mrs. Yin settled back in her chair and frowned at her plate. For the time being, she seemed exhausted in her effort to convert her monstrous houseguest.

"Yunnan is famous for its ham, I'm told," Mr. Yin said weakly to Hsun-ching.

"Yes, that's true," Hsun-ching responded, "the ham is very good."

LATER THAT EVENING Mr. Yin took the colonel and Hsun-ching to the home of his friend Mr. T'ang to discuss the possibility of traveling by sea to America. Mr. T'ang lived with his wife, two children, and three grandchildren in a two-room flat in the "Chinese City," a tiny part of Hong Kong that, because of a diplomatic loophole, still belongs to China. In fact, though, it is governed by no one at all. Built in the 1840's by Chinese wanting to protect themselves from British "barbarians," the Chinese City used to be surrounded by a huge wall, but that was torn down during World War II by the Japanese, who used the stones to build airport runways. Now, the Chinese City is something like a pirate island; drugs, prostitution, illegal medicine, and crime flourish, and the Hong Kong police are unable to do much about it, since the "city" is outside their jurisdiction.

Mr. Yin warned his guests about the danger on the streets and offered to visit Mr. T'ang by himself, but they insisted on going with him. The alleys were narrow and dark and full of suspicious-looking people, and the buildings were crumbling tenements. Mr. Yin had asked the colonel not to bring his iron pole, fearing it might be asking for trouble; as they walked deeper into the lawless district, though, the colonel began to regret its absence.

At last they reached the building where Mr. T'ang lived. They climbed a pitch-black staircase up to the third floor and knocked. Mr. T'ang called out from behind the door, "Who's there?" When Mr. Yin announced himself, Mr. T'ang unfastened a series of deadbolts and opened the door.

To the surprise of Hsun-ching and the colonel, the apartment was handsome inside. Elegant pieces of calligraphy hung on each of the painted cement walls. The furniture, though simple, was of classic Chinese design and carved of dark teak. Mr. T'ang's wife came out of the kitchen with a tray of sweets and a pot of tea. When she first saw the colonel, she gave a little start, but she regained her composure and poured tea for everyone.

They sat down at the one large table in the center of the room, and Hsun-ching could see the rest of the family sitting on flimsy beds in the other room, huddled around a TV set. The flickering blue light of the television was the only light in the apartment except for a single bulb above the large table, covered with the sort of lampshade one sees in Chinese restaurants, with red tassels hanging from it and miniature landscape paintings on its plastic sides.

Thankfully, Mr. T'ang and his wife made no mention of religion, although they were Christians like the Yins. They insisted on feeding their guests little snacks, refilling their teacups, and making polite small talk for some time without any mention of the journey.

At last the colonel became impatient. "How can we get to America?" he asked Mr. T'ang.

Mr. T'ang smiled and coughed politely. "Mr. Yin has already told me your situation. You just made it out of China, and you want to go to America, then back to China, all without passports or visas? You must be joking."

"No. We're not joking," the colonel said. He leaned back in his chair and scratched his chin, without taking his gaze off Mr. T'ang. "You've been abroad," he said confidently. "You know about these things. How can it be done?"

This time, Mr. T'ang's eyebrows rose in surprise, and his face broke into a smile. "How did you know that?" he asked, glancing at Mr. Yin. Mr. Yin shrugged.

"I can tell these things about people," the colonel answered. "Listen—we aren't smugglers or refugees. We are risking a lot to find an old Buddhist scripture, and we need help. Can you tell us how to get there and back, and how much it will cost?"

Mr. T'ang laughed quietly. "Well, I'll tell you what I know. As a matter of fact, I did go to America once. I used to work on boats that run back and forth to Indonesia. One time, before I retired, I went with a tanker that runs back and forth to Gam San—Gold Mountain. That's a city in America. We only had a weekend there. I didn't see much, but the foreign sailors are lots of fun, and love to drink."

"Excuse me, but what is the English name for Gold Mountain?" Hsun-ching asked.

"San Francisco."

Hsun-ching pulled out from his pocket the yellowed business card of the man who had taken the Laughing Sutra out of China. It listed his address as the Museum of Asian Antiquities, San Francisco, California. He showed it to Mr. T'ang, who nodded thoughtfully. "So you want to go to San Francisco illegally?" He shook his head and laughed. "You and about a million other Hong Kong Chinese. But then you want to go back to China! That's a twist! Unfortunately, the people at the borders don't know that."

"Do you think they might be able to borrow American passports?" Mr. Yin asked. Mr. T'ang laughed loudly at this idea.

"Everyone in Asia would have one if it were that easy!" His laughter turned into a fit of coughing that left his face nearly purple. "No, that won't do. And even if you could find out who deals in that sort of thing, and even if you could afford it, you wouldn't want to go through with it. If you're caught with fake passports, you're in a whole lot of trouble—much worse than if you're just sneaking across."

"So what should we do?" the colonel asked.

Mr. T'ang took a moment to catch his breath. "Mr. Yin tells me that you are a *moulum gousao*."

The colonel didn't understand the Cantonese expression; he glanced at Hsun-ching, but Hsun-ching only shrugged his shoulders.

"What does that mean?" the colonel asked.

"A high hand in the forest of heroes—it means you can fight. Mr. Yin said you tossed three punks into the ocean easily."

The colonel nodded. "That is true," he said, "but what does that have to do with getting to America?"

"Maybe a lot. I know someone who might be able to help you. But first, you have to be honest with me—do you know some sort of martial art?"

Without expression, the colonel replied, "I have never been defeated, in armed or unarmed combat. But I don't do people's dirty work for them."

"That's fine," Mr. T'ang said. "I didn't have anything like that in mind. But let me ask you this; if a man were to challenge you to a safe contest—wearing padded gloves, just for the sake of comparing skills—are you confident you could win?"

"Of course," the colonel sneered, "but why would I do something so foolish? Fighting is serious business, not a children's game. Why would any man demean himself by pretending to fight with little gloves on?"

Mr. T'ang nodded and said, "I have to agree with you there—I don't know what the point of boxing contests is. But I do have an idea for you." He refilled everyone's teacups, then settled back into his chair to tell them his plan.

"It must have been 1968 when I sailed to America—no, I think it was 1969. It was the summer before I retired, so that would be—well, I suppose it doesn't matter. The captain of the ship, whose name is Wong, has three loves in his life: one is gambling, another is whiskey, and the last is Chinese boxing. When I got the job on his ship, he and I hit it off pretty well, because I used to practice t'ai chi to keep in shape. Now it turns out that Captain Wong, although he loves Chinese martial arts, has almost no talent for it at all! So when he asked me to "push hands" with him, I beat him easily. He asked me to be his *sifu*, and in return he introduced me to whiskey."

Mr. T'ang's wife frowned when she heard that, but Mr. T'ang started laughing again and said, "My wife thinks it was a bad exchange, but I don't think whiskey is harmful, especially if you put a piece of ginseng root in the bottle and let it set for a few weeks. The ginseng counteracts all the poisons."

"Anyway," Mr. T'ang continued, "What a great voyage that was—it took thirty-one days to get there! Once we arrived San Francisco, Captain Wong insisted on taking me to his favorite place. It was a big gym near the docks with a bar attached to it! Every weekend the sailors and longshoremen would flock there, because there was a boxing ring in the gym where they could have their own matches, wearing big leather gloves, and those who didn't feel like fighting could bet on the matches. Everybody got drunk, including the fighters, and it was great entertainment.

"The night he took me there, Captain Wong got pretty drunk. There was a British sailor who was beating everybody up that night. After he'd really whipped a Filipino deckhand, he yelled out something about all Chinese people being weak. Shows you how much he knew—the guy he beat wasn't Chinese at all. Well, this got Wong all fired up, and he stood up and challenged the fellow!

"Now, even though I had had a few drinks myself, I still had enough sense to know that Captain Wong was going to get hurt. For one thing, he was nearly fifty years old, and he weighed only about a hundred and thirty pounds; the foreign devil was in his thirties and weighed far more. I reminded Wong of this, and he said, 'You don't need physical strength in Chinese boxing! Kung fu relies on internal strength!' Unfortunately, Captain Wong didn't have much of that, either. How could I sit there and watch him kill himself? Who would bring the ship back to Hong Kong? I pulled him down and said, 'I am your *sifu*, and I forbid you to fight!' This, it turned out, was exactly what he wanted. He shouted to the foreigner, 'Now you'll see real Chinese boxing! My teacher will kick your ass!'

"Before I could say anything, the crowd dragged me up to the ring. The whole place roared with laughter—after all, I'm hardly a big man. Someone put a pair of gloves on me, and the place went wild. Meanwhile, Captain Wong was betting everything he had on me. I didn't realize just how huge that foreign devil was, and how small I was, until I saw him standing a few feet away from me, literally steaming with sweat. The bell went off, and the giant just looked at me. I tried my best not to look afraid, but I think that made me all the more pathetic. And do you know what happened? He put down his arms, smiled, and announced, 'I call this a draw! And I'm buying this old man a drink!'

"He and his buddies took us from bar to bar until sunrise, and we had a great time—or at least, what I remember of it. They even got us tattooed—here, you see?" T'ang rolled up his sleeve to show them a small tattoo about halfway up his left forearm.

"That's the symbol for the British Navy. I never imagined that foreigners would know how to treat guests, but these navy men were all right. After he had recovered from his hangover, Captain Wong realized what a foolish and dangerous thing he had done, and he thanked me endlessly for risking my own neck to save his. But he told me that after losing face at the gym, he felt it was his obligation to China and all Chinese people to one day bring a real Chinese boxer to the West to prove that kung fu is real, and that

Chinese people are anything but weak. And, of course, he would make a fortune on the bets he would win.

"So this is my idea: Captain Wong still sails there—I know because I play mah-jongg with him every Chinese New Year's, and he's always telling stories about the latest fights at that bar. If you'd be willing to box one night there, I bet he'd take you both to America. If you could find that sutra fast enough, you could even ride back with him. The only catch is, you'd better make sure and win your matches, because if Wong loses his bets and his face again, the ride back could seem very long. What do you think?"

WHEN THEY RETURNED to Mr. Yin's apartment later that night, Mrs. Yin was still up. As soon as they walked in the door, she said to Hsun-ching, "May I speak to you for a moment here in the kitchen?"

Hsun-ching followed her into the kitchen, where she offered him a cup of tea. When he declined, she smiled and held out some pamphlets toward him. "May I give you some Christian literature?" she asked pleasantly.

"I—I guess so," said Hsun-ching, taking the materials.

"I'd like you to read them and tell me what you think," she said. "I think you'll find them very interesting."

"Thank you."

"By the way," she said in a conspiratorial tone, "that Mr. Sun—how long have you known him?"

Hsun-ching became nervous. "Well, not long, really. On and off, I guess—why do you ask?"

"I don't think he is who he says he is," she whispered.

Hsun-ching's heart pounded loudly in his chest. "Who do you think he is?" he asked her.

She looked around to make sure no one else could hear her. "I don't know, but he doesn't seem like a Buddhist monk to me. He seems very strange. How did he get that gold bar? I may be wrong, but I think there is something the matter with him. You should be careful if you are traveling with him."

"I'm very careful, Mrs. Yin," Hsun-ching said. "Thank you for the books. Good night." He squeezed past her and made his way to the guest room. When he told his friend about Mrs. Yin's suspicions, the colonel laughed bitterly. "You see? How long have we been traveling together? A week? Six days? And already it's begun. You asked me once why I hide in caves when I have what all men want—well, now you know. We'd better get out of here fast, before she rounds up a mob of fanatics waving those crossed sticks at us."

The colonel picked up Mrs. Yin's literature and glanced at it. "Look at this," he said, pointing to the cover of a leaflet that showed a family helping their father climb out of his grave. "What does the caption read?"

" 'The Truth about Eternal Life.' "

The colonel sneered. "How come he isn't rotted, after lying in a grave for years? *Pah!*"

They were both silent for a while, then Hsun-ching asked a question that had been on his mind all evening: "Colonel Sun—how did you know that Mr. T'ang had been to the West?"

The colonel smiled and stuck out his arm as if reaching for something, and pointed to his outstretched forearm. "When he poured the tea, his sleeve hiked up, and I saw that tattoo of his. It had foreign writing under the big ship. So I took a guess."

Hsun-ching nearly laughed out loud. If the colonel was trying to establish himself as some sort of shaman, he was not going about it in a very consistent way.

"For a while, I thought maybe you could read people's minds," Hsun-ching said.

"Wouldn't that be something!" the colonel said enthusiastically. "Imagine the kind of army you could have if your generals could look into the minds of their enemies! Or here is a thought for you—if you knew your enemy could read your mind, how would you adjust your strategy? How would you organize a battle?"

Hsun-ching noticed that the colonel became visibly excited by this idea. "Colonel Sun, do you like thinking about war?"

"Yes, I guess I do."

"But why? I think war is a terrible thing."

"So do I. I didn't say I like war—I hate it. But I like thinking about it, because if war becomes necessary, it is always better to be prepared for it. I have witnessed many, many battles, and they were all terrible. But I enjoy comparing each general's strategy, and wondering how it could have been improved upon. For most of my life I have been a soldier, so for me, the strategy of war is all I know. In many ways, a battlefield is the only place I can really be myself when I am surrounded by other men. War is a terrible fact of life, but if it is inescapable, then you must approach it as an art. Otherwise, defeat is certain."

Remembering the senseless carnage of the Cultural Revolution, Hsun-ching could not share the colonel's enthusiasm, so he turned the conversation back to their journey.

"If this Captain Wong agrees to take us," he said, thinking aloud, "we could be in San Francisco in a few weeks! Then we could return to China, and Master could have the text by the end of the summer."

"Maybe so," the colonel said. Then he asked, "Just out of curiosity—if we go with this Captain Wong, find the sutra, and then bring it back, what will you do then?"

"I don't know," Hsun-ching answered. "What do you think I should do?"

"How would I know?" the colonel asked. "I'm hardly an authority on carrying on a normal life. I guess I'm just wondering, if I knew I only had fifty or so years to live, and I could spend it like an ordinary man, what would I do?"

"Well," Hsun-ching said, "I don't really know what I want. Ever since I was born, it seems, everything has worked out wrong for me. But I think it would be nice to have a family, and some friends, and plenty of time to spend with them."

"Hmm. So why are you doing this?" the colonel asked. "Why didn't you just find a girl, get married, and start making a family?"

Hsun-ching started chewing his fingernails, a habit he had developed over the years in Hunan when he was perpetually hungry.

"I'm not really sure," he said unhappily. "I'm doing this for Master because it's the only way I can pay him back for taking care of me."

"You don't have to do anything, you know."

"Well, then—I guess I want to do it. But I want to get back soon."

A loud jet thundered over their building; the colonel didn't recognize the sound, so Hsun-ching explained it to him.

"This Hong Kong is a remarkable place," the colonel observed. "Only yesterday I wouldn't have believed that a man could ever fly. Now you tell me they do it all the time. And you say that America is even more advanced than Hong Kong?"

"That's what I've heard," Hsun-ching said.

The colonel fell deep into thought. He was quiet for a long time, then at last he said, "I wonder about this America—if men can fly there without any difficulty, maybe a man like me wouldn't seem special at all? Maybe I would seem like an ordinary man, or even less. I wonder if I will like it there."

XIII

OVER BREAKFAST THE NEXT MORNING, MR. YIN HAD some good news. "Mr. T'ang called earlier—he said that Wong's boat is docked in Hong Kong this week. If he gets a chance, he'll try to visit him this afternoon."

"Good," the colonel said. "Does he want us to meet him there?"

"No, he said he'd rather mention it to Wong casually at first. So I thought I might try to entertain you a bit today. Would you like to visit my factory, then have lunch and take a tram ride? It's the best way to see Hong Kong."

Hsun-ching agreed, but the colonel shook his head. "I think I'd like to wander around by myself today."

"Po-jan—you and Hsun-ching go on ahead," Mrs. Yin suggested. She nervously straightened the tablecloth. "I'll make a lunch for Mr. Sun that he can carry with him, so he doesn't have to worry about finding a place to eat."

"Oh—well, that's kind of you," Mr. Yin said, and he patted the colonel on the shoulder. "Yu-lan makes a good lunch, Mr. Sun! You shouldn't pass this up."

The colonel nodded and smiled in Mrs.

Yin's direction, but Hsun-ching could see that, behind the sun-glasses, he was not really looking at her. As Hsun-ching and Mr. Yin went out the door, the colonel said to Hsun-ching, "I might go sightseeing today. I was thinking it might be interesting to see that Chinese City by daylight."

Hsun-ching thought this a bit odd, and said, "But it's so ugly! Why would you want to see that again?"

The colonel stared at Hsun-ching and said in an even voice, "Curiosity, I guess. I'll be there, though, in case you want to meet me later."

As soon as Hsun-ching and Mr. Yin left, Mrs. Yin told the colonel to sit down while she prepared his lunch. She went into the kitchen and put a pot of leftovers on the burner for him, then came back out with a Bible. She sat across from him at the dinner table, setting the Bible facedown in front of her.

"Tell me, Mr. Sun," she asked, "where were you born?"

"A small village; you wouldn't have heard of it."

"I was born in Shanghai," she said. "That's where I grew up. Before the war, things were pretty good. But we had an awful time during the war. My sister was killed during one of the bombings."

"I'm sorry."

"Thank you. But we all lost family then, didn't we? Where were you during the war, Mr. Sun?"

"Which one?" the colonel asked.

That gave Mrs. Yin pause. She folded her hands in front of her. "Which war? Why, the war against the Japanese, of course! What other war could I mean?"

The colonel scratched behind one ear and nodded. "Of course. I was in Yunnan. That's where I live now."

Mrs. Yin unfolded her hands. "Were you in the army then?"

"No, no—I was already a monk by that time."

"There was a lot of heavy fighting in Yunnan. If it weren't for Chennault and the Flying Tigers, I think the Japanese would have taken the Burma Road. If that had happened, I think Chungking would have fallen, and we would have lost the war. Did you ever see them fly?"

"No—I was in the temple most of the time. Whenever we heard planes, we closed our eyes and started praying."

Mrs. Yin folded her hands again; she didn't seem to know what to do with them. Folded or unfolded, they sat there on the dark table like limp fish. They didn't seem connected to her body at all. She turned the Bible over in front of her. She smiled nervously at it, then turned it around to face the colonel.

"Have you ever read this?" she asked, trying to smile pleasantly.

"I'm sure I haven't."

"Would you like to?" she asked hopefully.

The colonel reached out and picked up the Bible. She paled at the sight of his powerful, gnarled hands, but continued to smile nervously.

"What book is this?" asked the colonel.

"It is the Holy Bible."

"Well, for one thing, I can't read." His lip curled into a sneer as he examined the book, noting that its leather cover was smooth and shiny from years of handling. "And even if I could read it, I'm sure I wouldn't understand it. Foreigners think differently than we do."

She shifted uneasily in her chair. "But this is the Word of God, not of man! The Lord doesn't distinguish between races and cultures; His Book speaks to all of us. Here—let me read you something." She opened the Bible and almost immediately found the passage she was looking for. "Luke, six, twenty-seven: 'But I tell you who hear me: Love your enemies, do good to those who hate you, bless those who curse you, pray for those who mistreat you. If someone strikes you on one cheek, turn to him the other also.' Jesus is telling us to love our enemies. That isn't hard to understand, is it?"

The colonel stifled a laugh. "It certainly is, coming from my profession—former profession, that is. If I had followed the Bible's advice on the battlefield, I would have had a very short career."

Mrs. Yin frowned and closed the book. "Mr. Sun—aren't you the least bit interested in the truth about Eternal Life?"

"No," the colonel answered. "I am interested in the truth about this life, right now. Wanting to live forever is just another way of saying you are afraid to die. I am not afraid to die, so I am not interested in Eternal Life."

"But what about truth?" she protested. "There is so much that Buddhism cannot explain! How do you explain the fact that Jesus rose from the dead and walked among us?"

The colonel sighed. "People will go along with any sort of myth, no matter how preposterous, to convince themselves that they will never die. Now it is my turn to ask you a question. How does your religion explain this?" He took off his sunglasses and looked straight at her. His eyes narrowed, and his gaze burned into her. She froze, her eyes wide with fright, and began to tremble. She felt as if he was squeezing the life out of her, yet he had not moved from his chair. He held her in his invisible grasp for a few seconds, then closed his eyes, releasing her. She gasped for breath and jumped up from her chair.

"I'll tell you a secret," said the colonel, grinning coldly. "Buddhism can't explain it, either."

Mrs. Yin grabbed the Bible, rushed into her bedroom, and slammed the door. The colonel began to regret giving in to the temptation to frighten her, but religious people were so insufferable, with their slavish yearnings for some cosmic emperor!

Outside, a police siren began to wail. The colonel waited impatiently for Mrs. Yin to come out and finish making his lunch. The siren became louder and louder, then stopped. The colonel went into the kitchen and took the pot off the burner himself. It was red-cooked chicken; he tasted a piece, and the anise-flavored morsel practically melted in his mouth.

"I'll just eat this here," he called toward the bedroom. "No need to pack it up for me."

Just then the hallway filled with loud footsteps. Someone pounded on the apartment door. "Open up! Police!"

From behind the bedroom door, Mrs. Yin screamed, "He's in here! Help me!"

The colonel leaped into the guest bedroom as two policemen forced their way into the apartment. Mrs. Yin propelled herself out of her bedroom, clutching the Bible against her chest with one hand and bearing a feather duster before her like a sword in the other. She pointed to the guest room with the feather duster, but before she could speak, there came the sound of shattering glass. The police kicked in the door to the guest bedroom, shaking the crucifix off the wall and to the floor, where it shattered into powder. The policemen gathered their wits and looked out the window.

"The fire escape!" one of them yelled.

"Aaaiiyaaa!" screamed Mrs. Yin, dropping the Bible and duster and pointing at the remains of the crucifix.

The policemen climbed out the window and looked down. What they saw left them speechless. A man was literally flying down the outside of the fire escape by letting himself fall from story to story, grabbing the metal frame only to slow his descent. Moreover, he was doing it one-handed; in the other hand he held two bags and an iron pole. The policemen couldn't shoot down into the busy street, and they knew they couldn't possibly catch up with him, so they watched him drop to safety, then radioed for more help.

"THIS IS ONE of our assembly lines," said Mr. Yin, pointing into a huge, dimly lit room. Hsun-ching stepped inside and saw hundreds of people, mostly young women, hunched in long rows, straining over their delicate work in the poor light. Two large electric fans stood on either side of the room, blowing the hot, stale air around a bit, and a small radio blared popular music. Some of the women sang along, but most of them worked in numb silence. Hsun-ching had never been inside a factory before; his first thought was that in the impoverished countryside you could at least work in the fresh air.

"What are they making?" Hsun-ching asked.

"It's a brand-new device, just invented in Japan. It's a tiny cassette player with earphones that you can carry in your pocket. You won't see it on the open market for another year or so. Would you like to hear what it sounds like?"

Mr. Yin took him out of the assembly room and into his office. It was a small room, with a single, sooty window overlooking an alley. He took a small metal contraption from a box, inserted a tape, and placed the earphones on Hsun-ching's head. "Press this button when you're ready," he said.

Hsun-ching pressed the button, and music flooded out from the center of his brain, as if the singers and musicians were sitting directly between his ears. The sound was unimaginably rich and beautiful. He stood there paralyzed, with his mouth wide open, until Mr. Yin reached out and pressed the "stop" button and the spell was broken. "I never . . . I never . . ." said Hsun-ching, and Mr. Yin laughed.

"You've probably never even heard a good phonograph before, have you? I wish I could be you just for a minute, to know what it must sound like! And this is nothing! You've only just arrived here in Hong Kong; wait until you see some of the other things you don't have in China! Just remember that if you decide not to go back, you have a job waiting for you."

They went to a small restaurant near the factory for dim sum. They had a plate of duck's feet wrapped in bacon, a fried noodle dish and some shrimp dumplings, and egg custard tarts and almond gelatin for dessert. Hsun-ching marveled at the variety of the menu and the energy of the waiters.

"In China people don't work like this," Mr. Yin said angrily. "That's the problem with their system—who's going to hustle if he can't get a raise? And who's going to care about doing a job right if he can't get fired for doing it wrong? That, among other things, is why I got out as soon as I could."

Hsun-ching, who was not used to such rich foods, felt overstuffed and dizzy. He leaned back in his chair and watched a large family celebrating a fiftieth wedding anniversary. The old couple sat across from each other at a large round table, surrounded by children, grandchildren, and great-grandchildren.

"Do you and your wife have any children?" he asked Mr. Yin.

Mr. Yin was silent for a moment, and a sad look passed over his face. "No, we don't. We wanted children, but . . . God works in mysterious ways. I'm sure He has a reason."

Then Mr. Yin smiled and asked Hsun-ching, "Pardon me if this is a stupid question, but can monks in your order get married?"

Hsun-ching flushed red with embarrassment.

"Is something wrong?" Mr. Yin asked.

"N-no," stuttered Hsun-ching, finding himself almost unable to think of an answer. "It's j-just that . . . in our sect, a monk can be married . . . if he is a lay monk."

"I see. So what about you? Do you think you will get married?"

"I hope so," answered Hsun-ching, relieved that he could answer something truthfully.

"That's nice! Marriage can be a wonderful thing. But be careful, because it can also be a burden. Make sure that you know a girl well before you marry her. My wife and I get along very well. We took our time before making any decisions. But lots of young people rush into marriage with the first person they meet; that can be a mistake, you know."

AFTER LUNCH THEY went back to the factory so that Mr. Yin could answer a few calls before taking Hsun-ching on a scenic tram ride up one of the emerald-green hills. "You'll love it," Mr. Yin was saying as they climbed the dusty stairs to his office. "From the top, you can see most of the islands of Hong Kong, and even part of the border between the New Territories and mainland China! That should send chills up your spine, I imagine!"

Just then a woman ran up the stairs after them. "The police!" she shouted in a heavy Shantung accent. "Something happened at your house! The police called, and they want you to call back immediately!"

Mr. Yin glanced nervously at Hsun-ching, then hurried into his office.

Hsun-ching closed his eyes and struggled to contain his anxiety. When Mr. Yin emerged from his office, his face was pale, and his eyes were glazed with confusion. He stared briefly at Hsun-ching, as if wondering whether to speak.

"The police say my wife called them about a dangerous man in the apartment. When they got there, things got confusing, and the man got away."

"Was your wife hurt?" Hsun-ching asked.

Mr. Yin shook his head slowly. "I don't think so. But she's very frightened." He blinked a few times. "The police said the man escaped by jumping down the fire escape. He was carrying a long pole and two bags." A desperate look came over his face. "I want to know what's going on here! What did that man do to her?"

Hsun-ching didn't have any idea what to say; he could only shake his head.

"You come with me," said Mr. Yin, grasping Hsun-ching firmly by the arm and hurrying out of the factory.

"HE WAS THE DEVIL I tell you! He tried to hypnotize me!" Mrs. Yin cried from the narrow sofa. She clutched the head of the shattered porcelain Christ in her trembling hands.

"Yu-lan, it's me—what happened?" asked Mr. Yin, taking her hand. A crowd of curious neighbors in the hallway jostled to see into the apartment.

"I was right!" she shouted.

"What were you right about, Yu-lan?" he asked.

"He was the devil! You were fooled, but I wasn't! I knew as soon as he walked in the door!"

"What happened, Yu-lan? Did he hurt you?"

"No, but look what he did to Jesus! Look!" She held out the ceramic face for him to see.

"Yu-lan—it's all right, do you understand? That's just a statue. You're safe now, and no one's going to hurt you. Now tell me—why did you call the police? What did Mr. Sun do?"

She closed her eyes and started to cry. "Because—he was the devil! I just showed him a Bible and tried to preach to him, and he said, 'See if your religion can explain this!,' and he pointed at me, and I couldn't breathe! He was hypnotizing me! So I ran into the bedroom and called the police! They went after him, but he got away!" She tried to stand up, but Mr. Yin eased her back down on the sofa.

"I wanted to save his soul, that's all! But look at what's happened!" She pointed around the disheveled room.

Mr. Yin stroked her forehead. "It's my fault, Yu-lan—I shouldn't have invited them here." He closed his eyes and sighed heavily. "But it's all right now. He's gone, and he won't come back. Listen to me now, will you? What the man did to you wasn't magic. There's nothing devilish about it—it's something martial-arts people can do. They can concentrate and send their ch'i out, and you can feel it. He did it to me, too, Yu-lan—it's nothing to be afraid of. Try to calm down."

Mr. Yin shook his head sadly, then turned to Hsun-ching. "I don't know what to think about this," he said quietly. "Maybe it's my fault for leaving him alone with her. I'm very sorry. But obviously I can't let you stay here any longer. Please forgive me."

IT TOOK HSUN-CHING several hours to find his way to the Chinese City. Once he got there, though, he had no idea where to begin looking for the colonel. Nor could he know whether the colonel had escaped capture by the police. He wished he could remember where Mr. T'ang lived, but the city was like a giant maze, and the alleys all looked the same. He wandered around until nightfall, but without finding any sign of T'ang's building or the colonel.

Hsun-ching had decided to accompany the colonel back to China as soon as possible. As much as Hsun-ching owed him, and as good as the colonel's intentions might be, he had a way of going about things that Hsun-ching could not abide. This time he had only frightened a woman badly, but what if he really hurt someone? Or what if he had been shot?

The darker it got, however, the more unsafe Hsun-ching felt, and the more he wished the colonel—crazy or not—were with him.

He noticed that a group of three men had started following him. They looked to be in their mid-thirties, and they stared at Hsun-ching malevolently while talking quietly to each other. Hsun-ching began to walk faster, calling the colonel's name, until one of the men yelled, *"Wai—ngo giu nei!"*

Hsun-ching wanted to run away, but he was afraid that might anger them; if they chased him, they could easily trap him in one of the alleys. He retraced his steps slowly. "What is it?"

"Who are you looking for?" said the man who had called to him. He had a scar that ran from just under his nose across both lips, making him look like a cat.

"My friend," Hsun-ching answered.

"What do you want him for?" said the man with the scar.

"I-I-I . . ." Hsun-ching stuttered, backing away instinctively as one of the men tried to circle behind him.

"Come here," said the man, then he nodded at the other two, and they lunged at Hsun-ching, grabbing him by the arms.

Hsun-ching cried out, but they paid no attention. They dragged him into a narrow alley. "Help!" he screamed, but the man with the scar pulled out a long knife. "Shut up! Or I'll rip you to pieces!"

Hsun-ching felt a loud buzzing in his ears, and the strength went out of his knees. The two thugs held him up, and the one with the knife growled, "Where's your wallet?"

"I-I-I d-d-don't have one," Hsun-ching spluttered. The man slashed with the knife, giving Hsun-ching a long cut across the stomach. Hsun-ching didn't feel anything, but when he looked down he saw blood seeping from under his shirt.

The man held the knife against Hsun-ching's throat and rasped, "If you don't have any money, why should I keep you alive?" Hsun-ching was about to faint when he thought he saw something moving toward them in the alley. One of the men holding Hsun-ching yelled, "Hey—you keep out of this!" but the shadow kept moving.

The man with the knife turned to look behind him. Hsun-ching heard a gasp of surprise and then a terrible crack before the man crumpled to the ground as if he were made of straw. Behind him the colonel crouched in readiness for his next attack, teeth bared and yellow eyes glittering. The other two thugs let go of Hsun-ching immediately and broke into a panicked run. The colonel moved to Hsun-ching's side.

"Are you all right?" he asked.

Hsun-ching dropped to his knees. He tried to speak, but could not control his breathing. The colonel tore open his shirt and examined the knife wound. "We have to fix this. Can you walk?"

Hsun-ching nodded, but when he tried to stand up, he felt dizzy, and he watched the colonel's face shrink into a little square of light, and then even that went out like a candle.

XIV

HSUN-CHING WOKE UP ALONE IN A SMALL GRAY
room with no windows. I'm in jail, he
thought. He tried to sit up in bed, but a sharp
pain in his abdomen stopped him. Then he
remembered that he had been stabbed; he
looked down under the sheet and saw that
someone had bandaged him. He looked
around the room. It was spotless, and contained only a desk, a sink, and a wastebasket.
One of the desk drawers was partly open,
and Hsun-ching could see a shiny pair of
long-handled medical scissors inside.

"I'm in a hospital," he said aloud to himself, relieved not to be in jail. He felt dizzy
and had no appetite at all. He wondered how
seriously he had been wounded. Then he
thought of the colonel. He fell into a troubled
sleep, and when he woke again, the colonel
was sitting at the desk.

"Colonel Sun!" Hsun-ching whispered.
The colonel turned to him and smiled.

"So you finally decided to wake up?" he
said. "You know, you look skinny, but carrying you around got to be a big nuisance. Especially with your guts sliding down the
back of my shirt." He roared with laughter,
then, seeing Hsun-ching's pale face, added

quickly, "But you'll be fine. The doctor stitched you up and says you'll be on your feet in two weeks. I watched him work. The healing arts have changed a lot since the last time I watched a doctor put someone together again. Did you know that they have a kind of acupuncture needle now that has a liquid in it that makes pain completely disappear for a few hours?"

Hsun-ching nodded, but he wasn't paying attention. "Listen . . . we've got to go back to China—as soon as possible, before anyone gets hurt. All of this is my fault."

"What are you talking about?" the colonel asked.

"Mrs. Yin was badly frightened! It wouldn't have happened if we hadn't stayed at their house. And you—did you get hurt? Are you all right?"

"I'm fine."

"What happened there? Why did she call the police?"

"Because she's a superstitious fool!" the colonel said angrily. "She lost her mind and called the police while I sat in the living room. They came, and I jumped out the window. But what does any of this have to do with us going back to China?"

Hsun-ching closed his eyes. "Don't you see? I wanted to make this trip to do Master a favor. It never occurred to me that I could get other people in trouble! I'm just like Li Shu-men! We're the same!"

"Who is Li Shu-men?" The colonel asked.

"The Red Guard! He burned Master's books, and took me away! Because of him, I spent ten years in the countryside, and poor Hamma—"

"How are you like him?" the colonel interrupted.

"We're both wrong!" Hsun-ching gasped. When he took a deep breath, his stitches pulled at his insides. "He wanted to go to Peking to make revolution! He thought he was helping people, but instead, he was killing them! I thought I was doing a good thing trying to go to America, but—"

"Enough!" said the colonel. "That woman was crazy long before she set eyes on us! Didn't you hear her, spewing out all that god-nonsense the night before? She was already lost."

"But—" Hsun-ching began, but the colonel would not let him speak.

"You know, you remind me of a soldier I once knew who fought with a division of Shih Huang Ti's army. It fell to him to bring word from the western front that the troops had been defeated at the river. On hearing this, the field commander realized that the battle was lost, and he went into his tent and cut his own throat in shame. When he saw the body of his commander, the soldier wailed like a dog and killed himself as well. He felt personally responsible for bringing the news that drove his commander to suicide!

"You can't live without suffering losses now and then, that's just a fact. But you can't lose spirit over it; it should strengthen your resolve! It would be different if, say, you or I had said to that woman, 'Shut up with all your foolish nonsense! It makes me sick!' and then stuffed a rag in her mouth and suffocated her. Then you might feel responsible, and want to repay Mr. Yin somehow. But you didn't do any such thing, and I didn't, either!

"If you look at all the trouble you are going through and all the risks you are taking, and all the sacrifices people like Mr. Yin will make to help you, then weigh it against the value of a single sutra filled with more worthless chatter in it, this trip looks foolish. But anything you do out of loyalty or friendship looks foolish when you add up the expenses! You decided to do this, and it was a good decision. Stick to it, and don't worry about what it costs.

"And remember, Mr. Yin took us into his house because he wanted to. Was it smart to let two refugees live in his house? Probably not, but he said he did it to repay a kindness someone showed him once, when he was a refugee. That's a kind of loyalty. What happened to his wife just happened, for reasons that don't concern us. And as for me, I am perfectly aware that I may be hurt or killed, and I accept that responsibility! There is no need for you to burden me with your worries."

They were both quiet for a few moments, then the colonel said, "I've said all I can say. I can't stand all this indecision! It's up to you now—you must decide if you are going to go through with this or not. If not, I'll carry you out of this room today and take you back to China. But if you decide to stick with it, I don't want to hear any more talk of turning back, do you understand? It is up to you."

Hsun-ching looked at the door for a long time. "You're right. I have to finish this."

The colonel nodded, then stood to leave. "Good."

"But I have to do it alone," Hsun-ching added. "I appreciate all your help, but I don't want you or anyone else to be hurt on my account. You could have been shot back there! I want you to promise me you will go back to China right away."

The colonel opened the door, revealing a spectacular slice of blue sky and water.

"Where—where are we?" Hsun-ching asked. Just then a man appeared in the doorway. He looked about sixty or seventy years old and was bald except for one long, dark hair that grew out of a mole on his cheek.

"He's awake?" the man asked.

"Yes," answered the colonel, standing up. "But he's weak."

The man nodded. "Well, I'm sure he'll be all right in a few days." He smiled and waved briefly at Hsun-ching, but seemed more interested in speaking with the colonel. "We start practicing on deck in about fifteen minutes. Will you be there?"

"Yes," the colonel answered. "I'll be right out."

"That was Captain Wong," the colonel said. "We are on his ship. We should be in America in about six weeks."

Hsun-ching shook his head in disbelief. "But how can that be? How long have I been asleep?"

"Not long—only last night and part of today."

"But how did we get here?"

"I told you, I carried you! This is why I mentioned the Chinese City to you yesterday morning. I was afraid something might go wrong when Yin left me there with his wife, and I wanted to make sure we had a plan in case we were separated.

"After the police chased me out of the apartment, I knew we had to get out of Hong Kong immediately. So I made my way to the docks and asked around until I found this ship. When I introduced myself to Captain Wong, I mentioned Mr. T'ang to him, and told him where we wanted to go. I told him I could win him some money at that wine house. He asked me to prove that I knew kung fu, and I threw one of his sailors overboard. He seemed impressed, and asked if I could also give him lessons while we were at sea.

"He looked like he was thinking about it, but then said he had to sail to a place called Bangkok first, then to Singapore, then to Indonesia, and then to America.

"From the way he looked, I thought he was going to say no. But just then, T'ang visited the boat to tell Wong about us. That made things go smoother. We had some foreign wine and shook hands on it. Then I went home with T'ang to the Chinese City.

"I hoped you might remember where he lived, so that I wouldn't have to wander around and pull you out of some alley, but that's where our luck ran out. So after a nice dinner with T'ang and his wife, I got worried and started searching. I heard you calling me, and I followed the sound, but it took me a bit too long to find you. Sorry about that."

"You saved my life—again," Hsun-ching said.

"It wasn't any trouble. I enjoyed it."

Hsun-ching frowned slightly, and said, "Just now, you said it was my decision whether or not to go on. But here we are on this boat. It wasn't my decision at all."

"It was your decision! I let you decide for yourself, and that was important, otherwise you could go on arguing with yourself about it endlessly."

"But what if I had said we should turn back? You said you would carry me out of this room and take me back to China today."

"Did I say that? Well, that was a lie."

"But, Colonel, I—I have to do this alone. When we get to America, I'll have to leave you. Please try to understand, I don't want anyone to be hurt—"

"If that is what you want, I'll do as you wish. I have nothing to gain or lose being with you. But we have six weeks at sea, and you may change your mind. Just rest for now." He started to leave, then hesitated. "One other thing," he said. "Since it bothered you so much when I told Mr. Yin that we were monks, I decided to tell the truth this time. So Wong knows all about you, and about me. He knows I am the Monkey King, and he'll keep quiet about it."

Hsun-ching's eyes opened wide. "What?" he whispered.

The colonel laughed. "You are so gullible! Do you know the story of General Tso? Once he was camped in a walled city with only a few of his men, waiting for reinforcements. During this vulnerable time, his enemies made a surprise attack. Tso and his men hadn't a chance, but Tso had an idea; he set up a table just inside the gate to the city, with the doors wide open, and sat there having tea so the barbarians could see him as they charged. They got suspicious when they saw him sitting there enjoying himself, and stopped not far from the gate. General Tso stood up from his table and invited them to enter and have tea with him. The gullible barbarians suspected a trap, and fled immediately—"

"Master Sun!" Captain Wong called out from the deck.

"Time to go," the colonel said. "Try not to be so gullible."

X V

ON THEIR FORTIETH DAY AT SEA, THE COLONEL AND Hsun-ching spent the afternoon sitting on the side of the boat with their feet dangling over the edge, watching a school of dolphins keep pace with the boat. The colonel had just been chronicling the first two thousand or so years of his life for Hsun-ching. In all that time, he reflected, the world hadn't changed much. But Hong Kong had taken him completely by surprise. Airplanes, skyscrapers, elevators, cabs—it was all like a dream.

They were interrupted by a commotion on the foredeck. Several of the crew were leaning out over the rail, pointing at the dolphins and shouting. One of them had a rifle; he wanted to practice his marksmanship by trying to hit one of the dolphins as it jumped out of the water.

Most of his attempts missed badly, but finally he succeeded in wounding one of the mammals. The crew cheered loudly and argued over who would have a chance to shoot next, but the wounded dolphin shrieked an alarm, sending the others under the surface just in time.

"Fools!" said the colonel angrily. "Even the stupidest hunter in the world knows it is bad to kill something if you don't plan to eat it. It disturbs the *feng-shui*! Now he will have bad hunting luck when he really needs to eat." He was silent for a moment. Then he said, "Let me tell you something about those big fish we just saw. A sailor a long time ago told me about them. They breathe air through a hole in the top of their heads, and will drown if they stay underwater too long. He said that one time his men tried to harpoon one, but only managed to wound it. The fish couldn't stay afloat and seemed about to drown, when all of a sudden three other fish swam under it and held it up so it could breathe. Do you suppose that the fish knew what they were doing? Or do you think it was just instinct, like the way people sneeze when something gets up their noses?"

"I don't know," said Hsun-ching, poking at the scars on his abdomen. "I think it's possible that animals have some thoughts. After all, we're just animals too."

The colonel slowly turned his head to look at Hsun-ching. His brilliant, unblinking eyes registered surprise.

"What do you mean, 'we're just animals too'?" the colonel asked.

"Scientists proved that we didn't just appear on earth looking like this," Hsun-ching said. "People were originally just monkeys, but over millions of years we stood up straight, our brains got bigger, and we changed to look like this."

As soon as he said this, Hsun-ching regretted it. He hadn't meant to imply that the colonel, with his vaguely simian appearance, might be some sort of evolutionary inferior. But the colonel only shook his head slowly, as if wondering how someone as reasonable as Hsun-ching could accept such a preposterous theory. At last he turned and looked back at their receding wake. "Anyway, I like that story about the fishes because I have always been fascinated by loyalty. It fascinates me because it doesn't make sense! For example, those fish continued to support their companion even when the men in the boat approached them. That allowed the men to harpoon all four of them.

"For humans—from what I have seen, anyway—success in life and war is not necessarily increased by keeping promises, and breaking promises doesn't necessarily lead to misfortune. But people still value loyalty. You would think that smart men

wouldn't indulge in tactics that don't bring consistent results—
and yet, many great statesmen and warriors insist on keeping
promises even when it destroys them."

"So?" Hsun-ching asked. "It's good to be loyal."

"Ah—that's just what I mean. That's the way most of us feel—
but why is it good to be loyal? Can you tell me?"

"Of course I can."

"I'm listening." The colonel had sewn a little canvas bag and
filled it with dried beans. He was tossing it back and forth from
one hand to the other, and squeezing it each time he caught it.
His grip was so powerful that Hsun-ching could hear the beans
being crushed. It seemed to be some sort of exercise for his already formidable grip.

"That's a silly question!" Hsun-ching blurted out. "If you
aren't loyal to your friends, what good are you? It's what sepa-
rates good people from bad people. If you aren't loyal, you can't
be trusted. If people didn't keep their promises . . . there would
just be chaos. There couldn't be any civilization. We'd be like
animals, thinking only about eating and sleeping. It's simple."

"I see," the colonel said. "But you know, that argument has lots
of holes in it. For one thing, some animals are more loyal than
many humans. Like those fish."

Hsun-ching began to get flustered. "So what are you saying?
That it's foolish to be loyal to other people?"

"I didn't say that. I just said that it is hard to explain why we
value loyalty so highly, because history has shown us that it
doesn't help us much."

"Not everything people do is just for themselves," Hsun-ching
said. "Loyalty is something we do for other people."

"Possibly. What do you think about the Peach Garden Oath?"

"The what?" Hsun-ching asked.

"You mean to tell me you've never heard of it?"

Hsun-ching shrugged.

The colonel shook his head in disbelief. "You—especially you,
who are making this big trip for that old man in Yunnan—and
you don't know about the most famous oath of all time! An oath
that cost hundreds of thousands of lives, and may have brought
about the fall of the Han dynasty!"

By now Hsun-ching was getting used to the colonel's dramatics. When he got worked up like this, it usually meant a good story would follow.

"Maybe you should tell me about the Peach Garden Oath," Hsun-ching said.

"Maybe I should," the colonel snorted. He put his beanbag down beside him, then began:

"After four hundred years, the ruling clan of the Han dynasty began to weaken. That's the way it is with the mandate of heaven; a new dynasty starts, full of strength and vitality, and its founders are men of character. But then, each emperor seems to get softer than the last; they spend more and more time painting little pictures and making love to their concubines, while the eunuchs and ministers get stronger and greedier. So it was with the Han, the longest and greatest of China's dynasties—its last emperors were miserable little fools. People were starving all over the country, while the court did nothing but build more gardens.

"A secret society known as the Yellow Scarves incited lots of poor farmers to overthrow the corrupt Han court. In desperation, the emperor appealed to his loyal subjects to join the army and fight the rebels.

"Liu Pei, a distant relative of the emperor, decided to join the army at once. On his way, he met Kuan Yu, a fugitive who had killed a corrupt official, and Chang Fei, a pig butcher. They were all patriots, fiercely loyal to the Han dynasty, and became friends at once. They went to a peach garden behind Chang Fei's farm and swore an oath of brotherhood, saying that they would combine their strength to overcome anyone threatening the Han rulers, and that if any one of them were to die in that struggle, the other two would avenge him immediately, even if it meant death for themselves. Then they drank themselves unconscious.

"They fought brilliantly to defeat the rebels, and when the Yellow Scarves were defeated, the emperor rewarded Liu Pei with an audience. During their interview, the emperor discovered that they were related, so Liu Pei, being the older of the two, came to be known as the Imperial Uncle.

"A man named Ts'ao Ts'ao was at that time the imperial chancellor. He was a ruthless, ambitious, and intelligent man. He was disgusted by the weakness and decadence of the Han imperial family, and wanted to take control from within the capital. Liu soon discovered Ts'ao's ambitions; after an unsuccessful attempt to poison Ts'ao, Liu fled the capital and settled in the West with Kuan Yu and Chang Fei, where they prepared an army to oppose Ts'ao and preserve the Han dynasty.

"Meanwhile, the southern part of China had become somewhat independent of the North, and its leader, Sun Ch'üan, had ambitions of his own. He figured that if Liu and Ts'ao fought, they would exhaust each other; Sun could just wait until the dust settled, then rush in and take over the whole country. So he was eager to provoke Ts'ao and Liu to battle. At the same time, both Ts'ao and Liu were trying to align themselves with Sun to prevent being outnumbered.

"Now I'll tell you who I think makes this story interesting. Not Ts'ao, or Liu, or Sun, or even the emperor—the one that fascinated me was Kuan Yu, the fugitive. He was a warrior of overwhelming physical talent; his favorite weapon was a saber attached to a long pole, which he called the Blue Dragon Sword. He was so adept with it that once he rode all by himself straight into the enemy's cavalry, hacked his way to the general, cut the general's head off, and managed to carry it back to his own lines. He is the only man I have ever known that I would not care to fight. But Lord Kuan was not a good strategist.

"Ts'ao Ts'ao managed to ambush Lord Kuan and take him prisoner. He also had Liu Pei's family under arrest. Rather than kill Kuan, though, he kept him alive and treated him exceedingly well. He hoped to convince Kuan to join him, but when he saw that was impossible, he decided to let Kuan and Liu's family go. He had two reasons for this. He knew that Lord Kuan was a man of honor before anything else. He reasoned that if things ever went badly in the war with Liu Pei, a sense of obligation on the part of Lord Kuan might prove useful. Secondly, by letting Liu's family go, he gave himself a reputation as a man who placed filial relationships above personal ambition. This would help him gain the trust and respect of the court scholars, whom he would eventually need to legitimize his rule.

"Sure enough, Ts'ao Ts'ao's armies were routed by Liu Pei

several years later. Liu had ordered Kuan to guard a pass that Ts'ao would have to flee through. When Lord Kuan and his fresh army ambushed Ts'ao's exhausted troops at the pass, he could have secured a victory right there and ended the war, and the Han dynasty might have continued even until today! But Ts'ao, brilliant man that he was, went bravely ahead of his soldiers, approached Kuan on his horse, and said, 'You have been well, I trust, since we last parted?' Lord Kuan was paralyzed by guilt; he couldn't bring himself to kill a man who had once shown him mercy. That sense of chivalry overrode his oath to fight in the defense of the emperor, so he let Ts'ao's army pass, reminding Ts'ao that if they ever met again, they would meet as sworn enemies.

"Ts'ao returned to the North, replenished his armies, and planned a new strategy for defeating Liu. One of his generals managed to capture Kuan again; knowing that Kuan would not be fooled a second time, Ts'ao had Kuan beheaded immediately. When Lord Kuan's head was presented to Ts'ao Ts'ao, he laughed and said, 'You have been well, I trust, since we last parted?'

"When Liu Pei and Chang Fei heard that Kuan had been killed, they invoked the Peach Garden Oath and attacked Ts'ao to avenge their brother's death. This doomed their overall strategy for defending the Han court, and they were both killed before they could even get near Ts'ao Ts'ao. All three of them—Kuan, Liu, and Chang—deemed their sense of loyalty to individuals more important than their loyalty to an entire nation. As a result, the nation fell, and they all lost their lives.

"So I ask you again," the colonel said, "what do you think about the Peach Garden Oath?"

Hsun-ching looked at the horizon; the sun was just about to dip into the ocean. "What do you mean, what do I think about it? What's to think? They did what they thought was right, and it ended up in tragedy. They couldn't have done any differently."

"No—that's not what I mean. My question is, why did they swear to die for each other in the first place? What purpose does loyalty to individuals serve, when it gets in the way of what is right for a large number of people, or even a whole nation? Hundreds of thousands of innocent people died in battles and famines that could have been prevented if Liu, Kuan, and Chang had defeated Ts'ao. But they failed largely because Lord Kuan insisted on placing chivalry above all else. Most people think of him as a tragic hero, and he will probably always be the one of the most beloved figures in Chinese history—but if you believe that a farmer's life is as precious as a general's, then he seems like a murderous fool. Don't you think?"

"I really don't know," Hsun-ching said finally. The sun dropped under the horizon, and the dinner bell rang below decks.

"I don't know either," said the colonel, standing. "That's why I keep asking people."

"How much longer until we reach America?" Hsun-ching asked. He was feeling more and more restless as the weeks dragged on, with nothing to do but watch the ocean pass by.

"Wong says we'll reach America very soon. Once we get there, we'll have to wait until the boat is properly docked and he takes care of all his business before he'll take us ashore. We're supposed to go to that *chiutien* where he wants me to box with some foreigners. While I'm doing that, you can go buy the sutra. Do you know where it is?"

Hsun-ching chewed on his lower lip. "The card Wei-ching gave me has the address of the museum the American collector used to work for. We just have to hope the sutra is in that museum."

"What's a museum?"

"It's a place where they keep old things. People can visit and see them there."

"That shouldn't be hard to find," the colonel said. He felt confident that Hsun-ching would have no trouble getting the sutra, with or without his help. If Hsun-ching didn't want him along, he would try to get Captain Wong to show him around America for a while.

But Hsun-ching had not moved. He just sat there biting his lower lip.

"You look worried about something," the colonel said.

"Well—it's just that I'm not sure you can buy things from museums. I know you can't in China."

"Yes, but China is commistun and America is capistal."

"What?"

"You told me that commistuns don't like money, and capistals do. American people are capistals, am I right?"

"*Capitalists.* It's *communist* and *capitalist.* I don't know—I'm just worried about it. Besides, I don't have any money."

"Don't worry. I'll give you money. What do I need it for? And if you can't buy it, you'll steal it—that's all. It was stolen from China anyway, so we'd be doing a good thing. Anyway, your job is to find out where the museum is while I'm breaking foreigners' noses at the tavern."

Hsun-ching looked even more worried. "Colonel Sun, you have to be careful! Don't hurt anyone there—in America, everyone has guns, and lots of people there are crazy! I read articles about it in newspapers in China. More than half the population is addicted to opium, and they don't care about human life or their families. The divorce rate is almost one hundred percent! And foreigners don't like Chinese people—they want to oppress them all the time. So you have to be very careful."

The colonel raised his eyebrows in surprise. "How can anyone stand living there if it's so awful?"

"I don't know, but we don't want to get stuck there. Just don't hurt anybody at that bar. Who knows what they would do if they got mad?"

The colonel frowned. "Wong didn't tell me about any guns. I think I'd better have a talk with him after dinner."

WHEN THE COLONEL knocked on his cabin door that night, Captain Wong was pouring his third tumbler of scotch, leaving just enough room in the glass for a single ice cube. "Who the hell is that?" he grumbled, but when he heard it was Colonel Sun, he rushed to the door.

"Master Sun—you should have just come in! No need to be formal about anything with me—you're my *sifu*, after all!"

The colonel saw that Wong was drunk. He accepted a glass of scotch, then sat down at the captain's table.

"Next week we arrive," Captain Wong said with a huge grin, "and then we show those black and white bastards real Chinese boxing!"

The colonel didn't smile. "Do people at that tavern carry guns?"

Wong looked surprised. "Of course not! Why?"

"Everyone knows that most people in America carry guns," the colonel declared confidently, "and that nearly all of them are crazy. I don't feel like getting shot because I beat some guy in a boxing match. You tell me straight—what will our situation be?"

Wong stared at him. Then a look of understanding came over his face. "Aaaaah . . . I know what this is all about! It's *hsüan-ch'uan*—propaganda! That's all bullshit! The party tells you that so you won't leave China! Ha ha ha!"

The colonel showed no signs of relief. "What's *hsüan-ch'uan?*" he asked sharply.

Now Wong really seemed perplexed. He tilted his head to one side, where it swayed for a moment, then said, "Propaganda! That's what the party tells you to make you think that life in China is better than anywhere else. What else did they tell you about America?"

"I heard that everyone smokes opium and that the dee-force rate is one hundred percent. And they don't care about their families."

"The dee-force rate? You mean 'divorce rate'?"

"Right. It's one hundred percent. That can't be good."

Wong shook his head and took a big swallow of scotch. "Listen—that's all bullshit. It's exaggerated, do you understand? Sure, there's guns and opium in America, but it's the same in Hong Kong. They tell you those things in China so that you won't complain when you find out how rich the rest of the world is. You forget all that stuff, understand? You go and look around and decide for yourself. But there's no guns at the bar. If you fight fair, you won't have any trouble. All right?"

The colonel's mind seemed elsewhere. "What do you mean, how rich the rest of the world is?" he asked slowly.

Wong laughed and raised his glass in a toast. "You'll see! And I'll bet you a hundred dollars you and your friend won't ride this boat back! To wealth!"

.   .   .

WHEN THE COLONEL returned to his room, Hsun-ching was practicing his English. With his extraordinary memory, Hsun-ching had
acquired a large vocabulary over the years, but he was not very
confident of his pronunciation. The sailors who spoke English
had been helping him, although the only literature they could
give him to practice with was pornography.

"Dear *Penthouse Forum*," Hsun-ching read aloud. "My girlfriend
likes to take bubble baths with me. The other day we were in the
tub and, well, I farted. I thought she'd be disgusted, but instead
she smiled and wanted to kiss the bubbles! Then she said—"

The colonel opened the porthole above their sink and looked
out at the stars. Hsun-ching asked him whether something was
the matter.

"What is the most powerful country in the world?" the colonel
asked.

"America. Or maybe Russia. One of those two."

The colonel sat down on his cot. "How powerful is China
today?"

"Not very. China is called a 'developing' country. That means
poor, basically. We have the biggest standing army in the world,
but our equipment is obsolete. America, Russia, the Western
European countries, Japan—they are 'developed' countries. They
are the powerful ones."

This news seemed to crush the old warrior. "China was always
the most powerful country in the world. All other countries were
just barbarian settlements! They paid tribute to China! How did
this happen?"

"I don't know," Hsun-ching said, "but foreigners are very
good at building things. They are very scientific. They make
better guns, better planes, better bombs, and better television
sets. During political-study meetings, we were told that it was
all because foreigners took advantage of China; they got everyone addicted to opium, then they came in and divided China up
and claimed to own parts of it. Then they declared wars of ag-
gression on China and killed the people. Then there were the
corrupt Nationalists who were supported by foreigners; they
starved the people. Finally, in 1949, the Communists took over

and kicked out all the foreigners. China has been trying to catch up since then."

"What have they been doing to catch up?"

"Well—mostly arguing about who is the best Communist. That way, we kill each other off without any help from foreigners."

The colonel sighed. "What sort of customs do the Americans have?"

"I'm not sure," said Hsun-ching, glancing at the *Penthouse.* "The newspapers in China say that American young people are kicked out of the house when they are sixteen, and have to pay rent if they want to visit their homes again. When parents get old, their children abandon them. They have music that makes them lose control of their minds; when they hear it, they dance like crazy people, shaking and writhing and committing obscene acts."

The colonel stared vacantly out through the porthole. "I wonder what that music sounds like."

Hsun-ching hung his head guiltily. "I know what you mean. The papers say we should be glad we don't have things like that in China, but I can't help being curious about it all the same."

"What else do these foreigners do?"

"Well, I already told you that most of them are opium addicts. And they are very materialistic. But their minds are empty. They don't have any feelings, or any human warmth. It's a very lonely society."

The colonel sneered. "You know," he said, "it seems to me I've heard all of this before! This is just what we said about the Mongols when they overran China—that they were cruel, heartless barbarians, and that they could never understand civilization. But it turned out to be a lot of crap—they were pretty much the same as us, except that they had better armies! I wonder how awful this America really is."

Hsun-ching grinned. "Well, you know . . . I met someone in the countryside who said he had relatives who lived in America. He said"—out of habit, Hsun-ching lowered his voice to a whisper—"that America was heaven!" He laughed nervously, then turned to the centerfold. He unfolded it and spread it out on the bed. The colonel leaned over and took a look at June's Pet of the Month. At first he looked stunned, but then a look of comprehension came over his face.

"This may be the reason right here," said the colonel, pointing at the woman's ample chest. "The foreigners grow to become powerful and ambitious because they are obviously well fed as infants."

XVI

HSUN-CHING WAS DREAMING. HE WAS RUNNING along the path to Wei-ching's hut to tell him he had returned from America. He saw the old monk weeding his garden and called out to him. Wei-ching turned around and at first he smiled, but then, to Hsun-ching's horror, his face began to change. He could hear bones cracking as Wei-ching's jaw protruded forward, his neck lengthened, and his forehead flattened out. His ligaments and tendons snapped, and his skin peeled off to reveal fur, and Hsun-ching realized that Wei-ching's face was becoming that of a cow. His mouth opened at last, but instead of speech, an eerie, long *moooo* came out of it.

Hsun-ching jerked awake in a cold sweat, but the mooing continued. Slowly, he realized that he was hearing the ship's foghorn. As each horn blast died away, another answered. "We're in America," Hsun-ching said aloud, sitting up in bed. He looked over at the colonel and saw that he was sitting up with his eyes half-open, laughing quietly.

"Why are you laughing?" Hsun-ching asked.

"I was just thinking," the colonel answered, "how pathetic it is that these huge boats have such ridiculous horns! If I built this ship, I'd want it to sound like an eagle or a tiger."

They got up and made their way to the bridge. Captain Wong stood at the ship's controls, and for the first time since the colonel and Hsun-ching met him, he seemed competent and in control. He barked commands to his crew and spoke crisply via radio to someone about approach speeds, channel currents, and docking order. Then he noticed his two friends. "You'll enjoy what you're about to see—if we don't hit it, that is."

They strained to look, but all they could see was fog. The ship continued to slice through the gunmetal-gray water, and several different horns could be heard now. Suddenly, out of the fog and only fifty yards from the bow of the ship, a great red object burst into view. It seemed to be the leg of a colossal sea monster whose body stood so high it was lost in the clouds. Then another leg appeared, and at last they could see the monster's body as it passed over them.

"That's the Golden Gate Bridge!" Captain Wong shouted. "The gate to Gam San!"

"Gam San?" the colonel asked with some interest.

"That's the Cantonese name for this city. The foreigners call it 'San Francisco.' We named it Gam San—Gold Mountain—because there used to be gold in the hills; that's why the first Chinese came to America."

"And over there to the north," Captain Wong continued, pointing to a dark smudge in the fog, "is Angel Island. That's where thousands of Chinese were held before they were allowed to come to America. Many of them spent years on that island, only to get sent back to China because the immigration quotas were already filled! I visited that island a few years ago. The walls of the compound are covered with sad poems. The Chinese carved them right into the wood and concrete."

"Why were they held on the island?" the colonel asked. "Were they criminals?"

"No—the white people didn't want Chinese to live in America! Foreigners are suspicious of anyone who looks different from them."

"In that respect, then," the colonel said bitterly, "they are just like Chinese people."

"What do you mean?" Wong asked. "We Chinese are very open-minded about foreigners! Look at Hong Kong—it's an international city!"

"Yes, but it's run by foreigners, isn't it?" the colonel muttered. "China is run by Chinese, and it's not very international."

"But look at you!" Wong argued. "You must be of foreign descent, and you grew up in China! You were even allowed to learn our Chinese kung fu, and now you are a master!"

"That's just what I'm talking about," the colonel said angrily. "What makes you think I'm a foreigner?"

Captain Wong didn't hear the question; he was busy again, shouting out more commands to his crew and radioing information to the approaching tugboats. "The harbor captain will be coming aboard any minute now to take us in," he said. "Excuse me while I get things prepared."

The colonel and Hsun-ching returned to the deck to get a better view of the city. The fog lifted enough for them to see all the way to Coit Tower; the pastel-colored buildings looked like jewels set into the hills. Hsun-ching felt a lump grow in his throat, and his sight blurred until the city resembled the colorful skirts young Tai women wear in Yunnan.

"I've never seen anything like this," the colonel said. "Every city has a special feeling to it. The Imperial City makes you think of power. The red walls look like they are smeared with blood, and the gold roof tiles look like the scales of coiled dragons. But this city . . . it looks like . . ."

"A young girl," Hsun-ching said, and the colonel had to agree.

SEVERAL HOURS LATER, as most of the crew busied themselves with unloading the ship, Captain Wong announced to the colonel and Hsun-ching that it was time to go ashore. "We'll go over to the bar and see what's what. Once I see who you'll be fighting, I can help you work out a strategy. I know how these foreigners fight. They tend to—"

"I don't need to know how they fight," the colonel interrupted.

"The important thing is getting my friend to the museum. While we're at the tavern, he should be getting that scroll. Can someone take him there?"

Captain Wong seemed slightly annoyed that the colonel did not appear to be taking the boxing matches seriously; he planned to bet quite a bit of money on him. "I can arrange a cab for him," he said impatiently. "That is the easy part. But you should prepare for this carefully, because—"

"I'm prepared. Shall we go?"

Wong frowned, but he only said, "Just remember—it is strictly illegal that I am bringing you ashore without papers." He looked at Hsun-ching. "Go to the museum, get what you have to get, then come right back. Don't get in any trouble! Because if you do—and this goes for you as well," he said, glancing at the colonel, "there'll be nothing I can do for you, and no one on this boat, including me, knows anything about you! Understand?"

Hsun-ching nodded. Wong reached into his pocket and took out his wallet. He handed Hsun-ching some green bills.

"This is American money. When we get ashore, I'll call a cab for you. Do you have the address of the museum?"

Hsun-ching showed him the yellowed card.

"Fine. When you're finished there, remember—we're at Pier Twenty-six, right under the Bay Bridge." Then he led them down the long iron gangplank to the dock.

It was the first time in six weeks they had stood on dry land, and at first Hsun-ching thought he was going to fall down. He had got so used to compensating for the gentle roll of the ship that now the ground felt as if it were tossing him around. Captain Wong went into an office building on the pier to call for a cab, leaving Hsun-ching and the colonel to marvel at the machinery used to unload the ships. One machine in particular, a huge crane, left them both in awe. "It's like the skeleton of a giant bronze elephant," the colonel mused.

When the cab arrived, Hsun-ching climbed into the backseat and gave the address to the driver.

"Good luck," said the colonel, pressing a gold bar into Hsun-ching's hand.

"Thank you. Please be careful, Colonel Sun. I don't want you to get hurt."

The colonel grinned. "I'll try not to bruise my hands."

The cab wound its way through the city, and Hsun-ching drank in the sight of the magnificent buildings, the lush trees, and the splendid potted flowers on the balconies and in the windows. The whole city shimmered as if it had just been washed, waxed, and polished. The brightly colored Victorians caught the late afternoon sunlight and glowed as if they had giant lamps inside. The cab took him into the exclusive Pacific Heights neighborhood and stopped in front of a dark, elegant brick building. A small brass plaque on the front door identified it as the Museum of Asian Antiquities. Hsun-ching paid for the ride, opened the heavy wooden door to the museum, and stepped into the cavernous lobby.

He had never been in such a large room before. The height of the ceiling and the echoing of voices and footsteps made him feel dizzy. He turned into a smaller room that contained ancient Chinese bronzes in spotless glass cases. He looked at a wine vessel, read the inscription inside it, and realized it was from the Chou dynasty; he was looking at a mug that Confucius might have used. He moved slowly past jade axes, bronze mirrors, and fired pottery into a room filled with paintings from the Sung, Yuan, Ming, and Ch'ing dynasties. For a while, he completely forgot about his mission and became lost in the paintings, wandering through his own country's cultural history. He knew that China had had periods of artistic brilliance, but he had only been able to imagine what that art looked like. He felt a wave of cultural pride swelling up inside him; at last China's claim to be the most civilized country in the world seemed justified. Then the thought that he'd had to wait twenty years and travel to a foreign museum to have such an experience depressed him.

A scroll of calligraphy reminded him of the sutra. Whom could he ask? he wondered. He saw a man in a uniform walking slowly through the room. He mustered the courage to speak, struggling to remember the phrases of greeting he had learned from the British primer Wei-ching had bought for him in Kun-ming. He strode up to the guard. "Lovely weather we're having, isn't it!"

"Pardon?" the guard asked.

Suddenly, it occurred to Hsun-ching that perhaps Americans, like Chinese, spoke regional dialects—what if this guard was from the countryside and couldn't understand Hsun-ching's English? He fumbled through his pockets and took out a pack of cigarettes one of the sailors had given him. He thought that perhaps in America, as in China, you had to soften petty bureaucrats with little gifts before they would help you. Hsun-ching extended a cigarette, but the man frowned impatiently and pointed at a sign on the wall. "There's no smoking in the museum."

Hsun-ching put the cigarettes back in his pocket. He decided to try pantomime. He extended his hands together before him, and moved his head back and forth as if he were reading. "I am looking for the famous Chinese book about laughing," he said, as clearly as he could.

The guard sighed. "Talk to the curator for the Chinese collection. He's probably down in his office. Go to the front desk and ask them to call him."

The guard pointed toward the front desk, but Hsun-ching hadn't understood him. He only nodded his head and smiled expectantly.

The guard rolled his eyes and led Hsun-ching to the front desk and called the curator's office himself. "Why don't you sit down over there," he said to Hsun-ching. "Someone will be up to see you in just a minute."

Hsun-ching nodded gratefully and sat down. He looked around the lobby and marveled at the full-sized potted trees reaching up nearly to the ceiling. What was the point? he wondered. Gardeners in China would spend decades to create a single miniature p'engching, known in Japan and the West as bonsai trees, whereas here they apparently made no attempt to limit the trees' size. Could it be that they had simply failed to train the trees, and were not ashamed to display the results? He had heard that foreigners had no sense of "losing face," so maybe that was it.

He heard a bell ring softly behind him, and turned in time to see the elevator door open. A young woman stepped out and came to the front desk. The guard pointed to Hsun-ching.

Hsun-ching stood to greet her, but he felt as if his knees might collapse. She had the most extraordinary skin he had ever seen. It wasn't so much white as translucent pink, and there was so much of it! By Western standards, she was not overweight at all, but to Hsun-ching, who had spent most of his life close to starvation, she looked like a luscious boiled shrimp. And her eyes! They were jade green, glowing as if they had tiny lights behind the irises, framed by a head of thick brown hair that fell around her face in unkempt curls. Slender rings of gold hung from her ears, and her fingernails glistened with red polish. When she stopped in front of him, Hsun-ching was nearly overcome by her perfume. He had heard that foreigners reeked of butter, but this woman smelled more like a tropical garden.

The woman introduced herself as the curator's assistant; the curator had already left for the day. She asked Hsun-ching how she could help him, but just then he was at a loss for words.

Everything about her is soft! Hsun-ching thought. Her skin, her hair, and even her voice. It sounded as though she had soy milk coating her throat. He wanted to touch her hair—would she mind?

"He says he's from China," the guard noted.

Hsun-ching struggled to concentrate on the task of speaking English. "Lovely weather we're having, isn't it! Please show me the Laughing Sutra as soon as possible, thank you. I have no time."

"I'm sorry—the laughing what?"

Hsun-ching quickly handed her the yellowed business card. "Thank you very much! But this man knows—take me to him as soon as possible. I have no time. Thank you."

The woman examined the card, then looked at Hsun-ching uncertainly. Hsun-ching wrung his hands. Didn't she recognize the name on the card? At last she spoke. John Volland had donated a large number of Chinese objects to the museum, she told him, but had also died at least a decade ago.

Hsun-ching's face went ashen, but he was determined not to

lose his composure. "Oh, I'm sorry," he said, searching for an appropriate phrase from his dictionary of English idioms. "R.I.P."

The woman stifled a laugh. She explained that in spoken English, one usually pronounced the words in full—"rest in peace"—but it was the thought that counted, and she was sure that Mr. Volland would have appreciated his concern. Hsun-ching noticed how she warmed to his use of an idiomatic phrase; he would have to think of more to help convince her to assist him. Would that be enough? he wondered. After all, she was a bureaucrat.

"Please listen to me! I risked everything to come here! You probably think I am a crazy, but I must find the Laughing Sutra! You are my only way! I will do anything for you if you help me! Your ask is my order!"

Now the woman laughed out loud. "We say, 'Your wish is my command.' Listen, I have no idea if I can help you or not, but why don't you come into the office and look through the catalog of the Volland Collection. If what you're looking for shows up there, the curator can show it to you tomorrow."

As she led him into the elevator, she smiled and said, "By the way, my name is Alison Weber."

"My name is Hsun-ching. I am . . . I worked on a farm."

"Oh really? But what about now? Are you a graduate student?"

"No—not really. I'm like you. An assistant."

"I see. So, you said you're from Taiwan?" She had a lovely smile, and the most perfect teeth he had ever seen.

"No, China. I came from China."

"Really?" she asked incredulously. "How?" At that time, China and America had not yet normalized relations, so only government-sponsored visitors from China were allowed in the United States.

"On a boat," Hsun-ching answered, smiling back. When he caught a glimpse of his reflection in the polished door of the elevator, though, he noticed that his own teeth were crooked and chipped, and he closed his mouth quickly. "By the way," he said cheerfully, "you are quite fat!"

Alison's face froze.

"In China, fat is very good!" Hsun-ching hastened to inform her. "You are very rich! Look at me! I am skinny because I am poor. Too bad, so sad. But you—congratulations! The more the merrier!"

The elevator door opened, and she led him into an office with file cabinets covering the walls. "Well," she said, pulling one of the cabinets open, "this is the catalog for the Volland Collection. Dr. Pertel, the curator, identified the pieces in English and in Chinese—you see, here in the upper right-hand corner? You just go through it and let me know if you find anything. I'll be here for another half hour or so."

She sat down at a desk nearby and started typing. Hsun-ching watched her out of the corner of his eye for a moment, then started leafing through the catalog.

There were categories for sculpture, porcelain, paintings, jade, earthenware, bronzes, and miscellaneous. Hsun-ching turned to miscellaneous and went through the entries one by one:

Shadow Puppet Figure, leather, Ch'ing dynasty. Honan province.

Carved Brush Holder, wood, Ch'ing dynasty. Shansi province. Snuff Bottle, glass, Ch'ing dynasty. Peking.

And so on. Hsun-ching went through page after page of entries, amazed that one man could own so much of the irreplaceable history of another country. There were inkstones, headrests, children's shoes, swords, seals, and hairpins. Some of the entries had a red stamp, a signature, and another date written next to them, but Hsun-ching couldn't figure out what they referred to. At last he came to a page headed:

Buddhist literature. Twenty-three scrolls. Not formally dated. Some in non-Chinese languages, including Sanskrit, Tibetan, and one unidentified. Known titles are:
1. The Diamond Sutra (Chinese)
2. The Diamond Sutra (Sanskrit) (water damage)
3. The Laughing (?) Sutra (Chinese, original translation from the Sanskrit)

"*Chaotaole!*" Hsun-ching yelled in Chinese. Alison looked up. "Did you find the book?" she asked.

"Yes—this one!"

She came and looked over his shoulder. Hsun-ching pointed to the entry. "So you weren't kidding—there really is a Laughing Sutra!"

"Yes, of course!" Hsun-ching exclaimed. "It tells you how to make your body never to dying—immortal!"

"Apparently, it didn't do the trick for Mr. Volland, though," Alison said.

"No—maybe he couldn't read Chinese! Ha ha! But there's no use crying over poured milk. Can you give the sutra to me now?"

"Uh-oh," she said, "there's a problem here." She pointed to a red stamp at the end of the list.

"What does that mean?" Hsun-ching asked.

Alison explained that before Mr. Volland died, he requested that the pieces of his collection that had any religious significance be given to an obscure Buddhist organization known as the Dharma Institute.

Hsun-ching felt his throat tighten. "Where is this other place?" he asked.

"Tell you the truth, I don't even know if it still exists," she said. "But let me check."

She looked in the telephone directory. The number was still listed. She offered to call and make inquiries for Hsun-ching, who nodded gratefully. As she dialed the push-button phone, Hsun-ching began to feel optimistic again; with equipment like that, surely finding the sutra would be a simple matter.

Alison explained to someone at the institute that a young man from mainland China wanted to see a scroll in their collection. She listened, then said, "Uh-huh," listened again, and again said, "Uh-huh." This went on for several minutes, then she hung up and looked apologetically at Hsun-ching. The good news, she said, was that the Dharma Institute did indeed still exist. The bad news was that it was a private organization and did not have the resources to display its collection of Buddhist antiquities to the public.

Hsun-ching felt his hands turn to ice. "But I don't want to just look at it," he said desperately, "I want to buy it!"

Alison was astonished. Was he buying it for a museum in China? she asked. No, he said, he just wanted to buy it. "You mean, just for yourself? To read?" she asked. Hsun-ching ran his fingers through his hair and explained that it was not for him, but for an old man in China.

Hsun-ching realized how outlandish his story must sound to the woman. He tried to imagine what he would have done if someone like Alison had suddenly shown up in Yunnan in search of, say, a cowboy hat taken out of America by a Chinese merchant—which she didn't want for herself, but for an old man in rural . . . Texas, was it?

Thinking quickly, Hsun-ching took out the red plastic work card he had been issued in Hunan. It had a small black-and-white photo of him, and identified which work unit he belonged to. He showed it to Alison as proof that he really was from China. Then he told her the story of how John Volland had taken the only copy of the Laughing Sutra out of China, and how his old master had wanted to recover it for nearly thirty years. He also confided in her that he had come to America for no other purpose than to find the sutra, and that when he found it, he planned to bring it back to China immediately.

"You would do all this for him?" she asked when he had finished.

"He cannot walk, and he is my father," Hsun-ching replied simply.

Still Alison looked doubtful. Hsun-ching leaned forward. "Call them again," he pleaded. "Tell them I will buy the sutra. And I will pay for it with gold." He showed her the gold bar the colonel had given her.

Alison really didn't know what to think of all this, but she decided there couldn't be any harm in making another call. And besides, this was easily the most interesting thing that had happened to her recently; her painting mentor had told her over and over that she lived far too sheltered a life to produce great artwork.

This time she explained over the phone that the gentleman from China wanted to buy the sutra, not just look at it.

"I'm awful sorry," she told Hsun-ching after hanging up, "but apparently they're not interested in selling their collection, either. But, listen—why don't you go to their office next week and tell them in person what you told me? They might change their minds, right?"

That would be too late, Hsun-ching thought; Wong's boat left at four o'clock Tuesday morning. If he missed it, how would he get back to Asia? Where would he live in the meantime? How would he eat? What if he was murdered by drug addicts or divorced people who didn't love their parents?

"I cannot wait!" Hsun-ching said desperately. "I must find it before Tuesday! That is when my boat leaves!"

But how, Alison asked, could he come all the way from China looking for a sutra without calling or even writing a letter to the museum beforehand, then show up unannounced on a Friday afternoon and expect to purchase it before Tuesday?

How could a foreigner understand? Americans could travel wherever and whenever they wanted, and they were so rich they could do or have anything. How could he explain that he was a fugitive, but not a criminal? The colonel could probably have thought of something to tell her, although it probably wouldn't have been true. So could Tom Sawyer, he thought, recalling the one book he read that was actually written by an American. And then, suddenly, it came to him.

"Do you know Tom Sawyer?" he asked her.

"What? Do you mean the book?"

"Yes—the boy in the book. Do you know him?"

Of course she knew about Tom Sawyer, she answered, but what did that have to do with anything?

"I am the Chinese Tom Sawyer!" he announced, touching her on the hand. "He went into the cave, but it was for a good thing! I am against the law to come here, to America, but it is for a good thing! I have no travel papers. I got out of China on a train full of pigs, and came here on a boat! All I want is this old book for an old man, because he is going to die soon. If you don't help me, I will fail. You are everything to me right now."

He stood up and showed her his hands, which were so callused from manual labor they looked like clumps of ginger root. "Look at these! I only know these things: dig hole, put little seed in, put dirt on top. Carry water in buckets, put it on dirt. But my master, his life has value. He knows lots of things. But he will die soon, so I want to give him something good, because he never got anything good. He wants this sutra, because he thinks it will make his body never to dying. Me, I think this sutra is nothing, just a piece of stupid paper. Maybe you think I am just a stupid boy. But I want to make my father happy—please help make my father happy."

His story moved Alison in a way he couldn't have expected. Hsun-ching, interpreting her silence as anger, apologized and tried to explain. "Maybe you don't understand, because in America you have so many things. But in China I have nothing except this old man. I want to give him this sutra because there is nothing else to give him! Please forgive me if I make you angry!"

Alison assured him that he had not made her angry. She was so moved by his speech, in fact, that she decided to take Hsun-ching to the Dharma Institute herself to make sure he got there before five o'clock. She led him out to her car, a beat-up old Rambler with only one headlight that she started with a screwdriver instead of a key.

The institute was in a wooded area right near the Presidio and the ocean, but they drove past it several times before they found it. Only a plain wooden post marked the unpaved driveway. They followed it through a grove of eucalyptus trees, then down a steep hill. Eucalyptus gave way to scrubby pine, then all of a sudden the road straightened out and they passed through an elaborate, carved wooden gate.

"This must be L. Ron Hubbard's house," Alison muttered to herself as she parked the car next to a long white limousine with darkened windows. They walked along a path of smooth white stones through a row of bamboo trees. There, the path opened up into a courtyard decorated with a Zen rock garden set in a bed of white sand. The sand had been meticulously raked in wavy patterns, like the ocean seen from far above. The building itself was a strange mixture of Asian and modern architecture, with bleached white stucco walls and a curved, gray-tiled roof. They passed through an elegant, spotless lobby filled with Asian sculptures and a working fountain into a huge reception room, where a young man wearing a white sweater and white pants greeted them. He glanced at a small clipboard and asked how he could help them.

Alison explained that she was the curator's assistant from the Museum of Asian Antiquities, and that she had a rather urgent question for whoever was in charge of the institute's collection. The young man looked again at his clipboard, then asked if she had an appointment. She apologized and said that no, she hadn't had time to make an appointment.

After a brisk discussion over the telephone, the young man at last pointed to a sofa and asked them to have a seat.

As they waited, Hsun-ching took a leaflet from a pile on the reception desk and read it. According to the leaflet, the Dharma Institute had been founded in 1965 by Mahavishnu Bob Corman, who attained supreme enlightenment in 1963. Mr. Corman, the leaflet stated, had up until that time been a disciple of a Yoga master from India, but in a sudden flash of insight gained a complete understanding of not only Yoga, but also Zen Buddhism, Taoism, and, indeed, all mystical religions. The institute's purpose was to promote the Mahavishnu's uniquely rich variety of pan-Asian philosophy as an antidote to ignorance, suffering, and conflict around the world. Hsun-ching tried to imagine how philosophy could have stopped the Red Guards, but his thoughts were interrupted by the receptionist.

"Miranda will see you now."

The receptionist led them down a hallway hung with Tibetan Buddhist murals, then pointed to a small office. A young red-haired woman wearing a flowing white robe stood up from behind her cluttered desk. She held her palms together in the Buddhist attitude of prayer and greeting.

"*Namaste,*" she said in a gentle voice.

"Hello," Alison replied, a little tautly.

Miranda offered them little round pillows to sit on, and offered them tea. Hsun-ching, who had not drunk tea in many weeks, happily accepted. But the strange, pale brew she poured him was so thick and sweet he almost choked.

Alison apologized for their sudden intrusion, then explained what she knew about Hsun-ching's situation and asked if there wasn't some way they could help him.

Miranda heard her out, nodding slowly. She never stopped smiling. Then she put her palms together again and said, "I'm sure Mahavishnu will be willing to help you out." When she mentioned the spiritual leader, a slightly beatific look came over her face.

"Well—can we speak to him?" Alison asked.

"Oh, Mahavishnu will be in Alaska all weekend leading a retreat. He'll be back Sunday night. Let me look at his schedule." She examined a thick leather-bound volume. "Why don't you come back on Monday morning? Is ten o'clock okay? He has a slot free then."

"Can't you use the telephone and ask him now?" Hsun-ching asked.

"Call him now?" she laughed. "No, I don't think that would be a good idea. We can't disturb them in the middle of retreat. You can understand that! But don't worry—he's a wonderful man! If you come back on Monday, I'm sure he'll be able to help you." The beatific look returned to her face as she showed them out.

ALISON BRISTLED WITH annoyance as they drove out. "I hate it when white people wear those robes! And those little guru pillows? They can afford chairs, for Christ's sake, can't they?"

Hsun-ching wondered why Alison was so worked up. The Dharma Institute seemed pretty harmless to him, except for the tea, which had made him slightly nauseated. Drinking it, he thought, was like being stuck headfirst in a giant honeycomb and having to chew your way out.

As they drove, Alison confessed to him that she had once been like the red-haired woman. She had moved to San Francisco after graduating from a Catholic women's college in Ohio. She had majored in art, against her father's wishes. She wanted to live in the Haight-Ashbury area and be a bohemian painter, but her first night in San Francisco she met a group of young people who invited her to a free vegetarian meal. After the meal, her hosts had pressured her to come out with them for a weekend to visit their "utopian community" outside the city and meet other artists and creative types. They had kept her for three weeks, practically starving her and pumping her so full of pseudoreligion and half-baked philosophy and feel-good mumbo jumbo that by the end she was convinced that being a part of their community was the best thing she could possibly do with her life. So she spent the next four months standing in airports and on street corners handing out organic snacks and inviting other lost souls to free vegetarian dinners. If it hadn't been for her painting teacher, she said, she might still be out there peddling carob cakes. But that, she said, was another story.

"So here I am, with the Chinese Tom Sawyer in my car! And today is your first day in America—the least I can do is take you out for dinner! No free vegetarian meals, I promise."

Hsun-ching was secretly delighted at the prospect of spending more time with her, but he declined out of politeness, saying that he had no way of returning the favor. Being Chinese, he explained, it would be very rude to accept a kindess that he could not repay. And she had already helped him enough as it was.

"Well," she asked, "what if you could help me with something? Then we'd be even. Would you let me take you to dinner then?" Of course, he answered, but what could he possibly do to help her?

Alison drove across town to the South of Market district, not far from the pier where Captain Wong's boat lay docked. She turned down a narrow street, passed by a long row of warehouses, and stopped across the street from a wholesale outlet for wedding dresses. Through the picture windows, Hsun-ching saw dozens and dozens of young girls in off-the-shoulder gowns, turning and preening before floor-length mirrors while fat, older women sat in chairs and watched. It occurred to him that he must be peeking into a foreign brothel, and he looked away quickly, hoping Alison had not noticed him staring, but she was busy unlocking the door of a warehouse opposite the dress store.

The warehouse turned out to be a studio owned by Alison's painting teacher, Sky Lucas. Overhead was a tangle of exposed beams, ventilation ducts, water pipes, and track lights hanging from the ceiling like a grotesque trellis that might tumble down at any moment. On the bare walls hung about two dozen canvases. They seemed to have been damaged beyond repair in some flood. Probably, they were being hung to dry out.

Alison looked around proudly. "Sky's having a show next week. The opening's on Sunday—maybe you'd like to come? There'll be a lot of interesting people here, and wine and cheese." After a moment's thought, she asked, "Do they have wine and cheese in China? Or did I read that people there don't eat cheese?"

"No cheese," Hsun-ching replied, "some wine." He was looking intently at one of the canvases. It was a jumble of spattered paint surrounding two sheets of paper, stapled one on top of the other and then directly onto the canvas. The visible sheet had letters typed all over it, but they did not appear to form words or sentences. The title of the work was "Thou Shalt Not."

Alison stepped up next to him and asked if he knew the story about monkeys and the Bible. She explained that a philosopher had once said that, if you had enough monkeys typing at random for eternity, sooner or later one would type out the entire Bible purely by chance. "So Sky spent a day at a maximum-security prison. He got a condemned murderer who is completely illiterate to just type away for a day. What Sky did is, he put one of the pages the murderer typed over an actual page from the Bible and stapled them together."

Hsun-ching was more baffled than ever.

"I should tell you," Alison went on, "that this whole show is part of a series Sky's been working on for about a year. It's called *Chaos Out of Order.* It's a study of how, even though it took hundreds of thousands of years for human beings to make order out of chaos—you know, civilization out of primitive conditions— it's only taking us one century to tear it all down. That probably sounds kind of weird just saying it like that, but look at the rest of the series and I think you'll get a sense for what Sky is saying."

One painting, titled "Florence Nightingale," was a portrait of a nurse with a pornographic magazine cover glued over her face. Another canvas featured a seascape, smudged with thick, greasy oil and studded with bits of polystyrene. "Polystyrene never disappears," Alison told him. She explained how marine animals eat bits of polystyrene floating in the ocean, thinking it food, only to die of starvation when the indigestible substance fills their gullets. "And when those animals die, their bodies decompose and the polystyrene floats out again, and gets eaten by other animals. It never ends, and almost no one knows or cares about it."

Suddenly, Hsun-ching brightened. "So this is propaganda?" Alison did not know that, in Chinese, the word for propaganda literally means to spread information, and does not carry any negative connotations. She replied testily that no, this was not propaganda, it was art. Real art, she added, not just pretty pictures.

"But art must be beautiful," Hsun-ching argued.

"What? Art doesn't have to be beautiful! It has to have feeling! Sometimes the feeling expressed is very ugly, but the important thing is that it is true."

Hsun-ching shook his head. In art, he knew, one first had to master technique. Only then could the work have feeling. Sky's work conveyed important information, but it showed no mastery of technique, and therefore could not be considered art. He pointed to a crude painting of a crucifixion scene, partially covered by Polaroid photographs of a television evangelist. "Even a child could do this," he pointed out.

Alison clicked her tongue with impatience, but did not argue any further. She had hoped that the value of Sky's work would be universal. But then, she thought, it would probably be impossible to appreciate conceptualist art without being familiar with impressionism, expressionism, and then post-expressionism.

Hsun-ching thought he had convinced her, and for the first time since arriving in America he felt a glimmer of self-confidence. "Is this what you wanted me to help you with?" he asked.

Alison laughed and said no, she didn't need instruction in art appreciation. What she needed was someone to help move her desk. She led him to a small, windowless cubicle on the far side of the studio, partitioned off by a plywood screen. She'd been wanting to move her desk for days so she could set up a large easel in her room, but hadn't been able to move it herself. "Sky has a bad back. He can't lift anything."

"Is Sky your husband?" Hsun-ching asked as they slid the huge metal desk across the paint-spattered floor. Her laugh was brittle. She explained that Sky was sort of a teacher, and he was helping her out by letting her rent this room for only a hundred dollars a month and giving her free painting lessons.

Hsun-ching noticed a group of unframed paintings leaning against the wall where the desk had been. When he asked about them, Alison sighed and said they were hers. As Hsun-ching leafed through them, she lit a cigarette and leaned against the desk. They were all portraits of very ordinary-looking people, but done in a bold, impressionistic style. One portrait of an old woman seated, painted in reds, browns, and oranges, seemed literally on fire. Hsun-ching gaped at it, then turned to Alison. "This is art! You should be teacher, not student."

Alison laughed until she started coughing. "You've got to be kidding," she groaned. "There's nothing original about my stuff! You see paintings like this in every art-school basement! Our bios would all read the same: 'favorite artist, Van Gogh; favorite subject matter, portraits of weathered faces. Hobbies, taking long walks in the rain and drinking black coffee.' I'm just good at imitating other painters, that's all. There's nothing new in what I paint."

But Hsun-ching wouldn't be swayed. Her paintings had impressed him as none of Sky's had, although he did feel sorry for the animals who swallowed the polystyrene. Alison told him he was just looking at appearances, and that underneath the colors and brushwork, her paintings were empty, whereas Sky's were exploding with anger and angst. But anyone can get angry, said Hsun-ching, while only a skilled artist could make something beautiful.

"That's just what I'm trying to get away from! I'm sick of beautiful art—it's so trite, so limiting! Why should art be only beautiful? Modern artists are pushing the boundaries back, they're redefining what art itself is! Doesn't that excite you at all?"

Hsun-ching let this notion sink in. He agreed that it was probably exciting that people were making new kinds of art. But he still liked her paintings more than the ugly ones.

Hsun-ching had never met an artist before, so he was awed by Alison and couldn't understand why she would be so hard on herself. He couldn't even imagine what it would be like to be so intellectual, to care so much about something so subtle and complicated, and to feel an urge, a need, to create. He felt so primitive compared to her! His main concerns were eating and sleeping and taking care of Wei-ching, and all he knew how to do was farm. If he were Alison, he thought, he would be so happy and proud of himself! Every day would seem like an adventure because in the daytime he would be at the museum, surrounded by beauty, and at night he would be creating more beauty! No worrying about droughts or floods or locusts spoiling crops, and no political-study meetings. What a life! He envied her more than any person he had ever met, anywhere. And now that he had helped her, he could accept her dinner invitation without feeling guilty, and learn more about her charmed existence.

Alison took him to her favorite café just around the corner. To start with, she ordered a plate of nachos and a pitcher of beer. Hsun-ching, who had never tasted beer before, nevertheless resolved to drink at least as much of it as Alison did. He was a man, after all, and it is a dismally universal truth that no man can bear the thought that a woman can eat, drink, smoke, or lift more than he can. His resolution turned out to be a foolish one, though, because Alison was fond of beer and had had lots of practice drinking it. They finished the pitcher before the nachos arrived, and Hsun-ching got so red in the face Alison thought he might have a stroke. She mercifully declined the waiter's offer to refill the pitcher, and instead ordered a round of ginger ale.

Unfortunately, Hsun-ching wasn't able to enjoy the nachos because of the melted cheese on top. He managed to find a few chips without the obscenely bright goo on them, but even those smelled spoiled to him.

Seeing that Hsun-ching was having trouble with the nachos, Alison asked him what he liked so she could order dinner for him. He didn't recognize anything on the menu, of course, so in the end Alison ordered spaghetti for him, remembering something about the Chinese inventing noodles and Marco Polo bringing them back to Italy. When the spaghetti came, Alison watched in amazement as Hsun-ching consumed his portion before she had even finished putting the condiments on her own. She asked him if he would like more to eat; in fact, he could easily have eaten another portion, but in China politeness dictates that the guest should always say no to offers of more food. The host, however, must always disregard this refusal and heap food on the guest's plate anyway. Hsun-ching waited expectantly, but in America, unfortunately for Hsun-ching, a no is a no, so Alison shrugged and ate her spaghetti as he watched her longingly, wondering what he had said or done to deserve this sudden cold treatment.

Anxious to get back in her good graces, and realizing that this might be his only chance to get to know a real American, Hsun-ching told her that up until today, all he knew about America was what he had read in Chinese newspapers. "What are the American people really like?" he asked.

"That's sort of a broad question," she laughed. "Why don't you tell me what you heard first, then I'll tell you if it's true or not."

Hsun-ching was hesitant to do this, but she insisted she would not take offense. "I read that Americans don't have *renqing wei,* which means 'human feeling taste.' For example, they don't love their parents, and their parents make them leave home when they are sixteen years of age. After that, if you want to visit your parents, you have to pay them to eat or sleep at home. Like a hotel."

"Well, that's not exactly true," Alison explained. "It's like this: Americans love their parents, but we argue with them a lot and *want* to leave home when we finish high school. Our parents don't kick us out, at least not usually. We like to be independent. After that, if you want to visit your parents, you don't have to pay rent, but you do have to be prepared to listen to them tell you how to run your life. That's the way it works for me, anyway."

"Did you leave home when you were sixteen?" he asked.

Before she could answer, the waiter interrupted them to ask if either of them would like dessert. Alison ordered a piece of blueberry pie, then asked Hsun-ching if he would like anything.

"Oh, no thank you," he answered cheerfully.

"Are you sure?" she asked him.

"Yes, I'm full," he said, this time less cheerfully. She can't be serious, he thought—of course she will order something for me.

"I guess nothing for him," she told the waiter, and Hsun-ching's heart sank.

"No, I was seventeen when I left home for college. I had a pretty easy childhood compared to most, I guess, but I argued with my folks a lot."

"Why?"

"Why?" she asked, laughing. "Why not? I didn't want to be like them. My father sells lamps, and my mother dusts—she lives to dust. And when they aren't doing that, they're both watching television. They just get older and fatter and grouchier, with nothing to look forward to except their annual trip to Florida, where they get sunburned."

"They have their own television?" Hsun-ching asked enviously. Alison suddenly felt ashamed; maybe to a Chinese person, her parents' lives would seem fulfilling. She explained that the way they lived worked fine for them, but she wanted something else. She wanted to live in a city and meet people from all over the world and have friends who had similar interests, but her parents had wanted her to stay in their hometown, marry a nice, dull man, and produce children. She left home to escape being told what to do.

Meanwhile Hsun-ching watched her eat the pie. The sight of all those dark, juicy berries nearly made him faint. When there was one bite left, Alison asked if he was sure he didn't want to try it. Still politeness did not allow him to accept, although his eyes pleaded with her. But she merely shrugged and left the piece on her plate. "I'm just too full to finish it," she said, and Hsun-ching nearly cried out when a busboy took the plate away.

"Excuse me, I will use the toilet," he said suddenly, and he rushed to follow the busboy toward the kitchen. When he was quite sure he was out of Alison's sight, he stopped the busboy, picked up the last piece of pie, and stuffed it into his mouth. It was far too sweet for him, though, and ended up making him feel dizzy again.

When he returned to the table, the Sex Pistols were blaring through the sound system, so loudly that the floor vibrated. "What do you think of this music?" Alison asked.

"Why is it so loud?" Hsun-ching shouted back.

"So you can hear it better."

Hsun-ching mulled that over. "I think it is very interesting," he shouted, "but it would be better if the angry man would stop talking."

"He's not talking, he's singing! This is real music—it's supposed to be strong!"

Hsun-ching nodded weakly, noting to himself that as advanced as they were in the fields of science and technology, foreigners had obviously neglected music in the course of their development.

After dinner Alison took him up to the roof of the warehouse, where they had a lovely view of the dark bay and of the lights on Twin Peaks. It looked as though someone had spilled a giant bucketful of stars all over the hills. Hsun-ching asked if all American cities looked like San Francisco.

"Nope. That's why I came here. I think it's the prettiest city we've got. What part of China do you come from?"

"Southwest part. Beautiful scenery, but China is very poor country. Life is very hard." He told her about the Cultural Revolution, and being sent down for ten years. She asked what he would do when he got back, and he confessed that he hadn't given it much thought.

"How can you not think about it? It's your life, isn't it? Isn't there anything you'd like to do?"

Hsun-ching thought hard, then shrugged again. "I only know two things: reading and farming. I don't like farming, and I can't get a job reading."

Alison rolled her eyes in astonishment. "You speak excellent English—how many people in China can do that? If we normalize relations with China, think of all the things you could do! You could apply to graduate school, or get a degree in business and then open up a store that sells—I don't know—Mao hats to Americans! You could do just about anything you want, it seems to me."

Hsun-ching smiled bitterly. "It is different in China than in your country. You don't choose your job, or apply to school. For me, it's impossible. The government chooses for you. I was punished for ten years for political crimes, and now I'm just a farmer. And I don't have a back door for things."

"What's a back door?" she asked.

"You don't know what is a back door? That is . . . if you want to get a job, and your uncle knows the work leader, you ask your uncle to help."

"Well, then, maybe you shouldn't go back," Alison thought aloud. "In a couple years, you could make enough money to hire a good immigration lawyer and become a citizen. Lots of people do, you know. My father did. He's from Germany."

Hsun-ching stared at her, completely dumbfounded. A thought like this had never crossed his mind, or if it had, he had chased it away so successfully he couldn't even remember it.

"I mean, you managed to sneak all the way here," she continued, "which is something a lot of people all over the world would love to do, if they could. Why go back if you've got nothing to look forward to? Once you get your citizenship, maybe by then Americans will be allowed to travel to China, and you could bring the sutra to your master then."

It was unthinkable. What if Wei-ching died before Hsun-ching could get back to China? "It's—it's impossible," he said, feeling guilty for even considering it.

Alison realized she had got herself all worked up on Hsun-ching's behalf, and she couldn't help laughing. "Listen to me, plotting out your life for you! I can't even get my own act together, and I'm telling you how to run yours! I sound like my father! Let me tell you how mixed up I am, so you don't feel bad: I got a degree in art when my father told me to learn business. I said I wanted to do something I enjoyed, and he said I'd end up as a secretary, and you know what? He was right! I'm licking envelopes in a museum just like a million other art majors, and only now figuring out that maybe I don't have that much talent as a painter after all. So don't take my advice on anything."

When Alison dropped him back at the piers, she wrote the address of the Dharma Institute on the back of a gum wrapper so that he could return there on Monday. She also put down the address of Sky's studio. "Like I said, his show opens tomorrow night. If you'd like to stop by, I think people would get a real kick out of meeting you. And you could ask them if they love their parents or not!"

Hsun-ching thanked her for all her help, and promised he would come to the party if he could. Instead of going directly to the boat, he decided to take a look at the bar to see if the colonel and Captain Wong had finished there. He thought it would be exciting to see the colonel box with the foreigners.

But as he drew near, he heard a tremendous shout as a man came flying through the front door, and he knew that something was terribly wrong.

XVII

THE BARNACLE STARTED OUT AS A WAREHOUSE, BUT in 1965 a group of retired longshoremen bought it and converted into a club for dock-workers and sailors. That gave everyone associated with the docks a convenient place to go to drink and unwind where they didn't have to compete for tables with bankers or college students. And with the gym, instead of getting in fights with locals or each other, they could box legitimately or bet on who-ever did want to box. That way, the club provided two of the most popular traditional forms of entertainment among sailors: drink-ing and brawling. Womanizing, another tra-dition popular among men of all professions, had to be done elsewhere; women were al-lowed in the club, but only if they were sail-ors or dockhands, meaning they were likely to respond to a pinch on the behind with an elbow to the jaw.

While Hsun-ching was on his way to the Museum of Asian Antiquities, Captain Wong had taken the colonel to the club. He told the doorman that a Chinese boxer had arrived. The doorman greeted Wong with a hearty slap on the back. He greeted the colonel and extended his hand to him, but the colonel did not respond, not understanding English.

"Shake his hand," Wong said. "It's the foreigner's custom."

The colonel extended his hand. The doorman, as was his habit, squeezed his hand tightly to show how strong his grip was.

"He's squeezing my hand, not shaking it," the colonel said to Wong.

Wong laughed; "Yeah, that shows he's a man! Squeeze it back and show him how strong you are!"

The colonel raised one eyebrow dubiously, then looked at the doorman. The doorman was grinning. The colonel grinned back and squeezed. The doorman's face went tense, started to twitch, and turned pale. "Damn!" he cried, wrenching his hand free.

Captain Wong slapped his thigh and guffawed, and said to the doorman, "You see? Chinese boxing! Ha ha ha!"

The doorman rubbed his hand and led them to the makeshift boxing ring. It was still afternoon, so the seats around the ring were empty, and only a few men were standing at the bar. A man was mopping the ring. Captain Wong strode over to greet him, then introduced him to the colonel.

"Master Sun, this is Bill McKeefrey. He runs the bar." The colonel nodded and extended his hand.

"Bill, this is Mr. Sun. He doesn't speak English, but you can shake his hand if you want!"

"Don't go near that guy's hand," the doorman said angrily.

Bill rested the mop against the ropes and chewed on his cigar for a moment. He looked at the colonel and frowned.

"Your telegram said this guy was big. He ain't no heavy-weight."

Wong grinned and said, "That's because you haven't seen him fight! He can handle himself."

Bill shook his head. "I can't let this guy in the ring. I don't need a Chinese guy with a broken neck on my hands."

Wong put his hands in his pockets slowly. With his eyes still on Bill, he said to the colonel, "He doesn't believe you're strong enough. You see that leather bag hanging from the ceiling over there? Hit it a few times and show him what Chinese boxing looks like."

The colonel hissed with annoyance. Some little man with a mop didn't think he was strong enough to fight! He considered hitting the man instead of the punching bag, but decided it was best to do as the captain suggested, since Wong knew the ways of these foreigners. He walked over to the leather bag and felt it. "How hard do you want me to hit it?" he asked.

"Hit it as hard as you can."

The colonel looked at the little man chewing on the soggy cigar, then back at the bag. A chain led up from it to an iron hook mounted in the ceiling. His upper lip twitched; he chose a spot on the bag and twisted suddenly from the waist, sending his fist into the bag with such force that the bag folded in on itself. The iron hook ripped out of the ceiling, bringing a shower of plaster and wood down on the floor. The bag landed on a wooden chair and shattered it.

The man with the cigar stopped chewing. The doorman stopped rubbing his hand and said, "God . . . damn!"

"He can take care of himself," Wong repeated, "and I brought him eight thousand miles for this fight. So don't tell me now that he's too small."

Bill chewed thoughtfully, then said, "All right, then. Bring him in on Tuesday. That's when the boxing starts up again."

Captain Wong's jaw dropped. "What do you mean, Tuesday? It's Friday night! This is the weekend! This is when the fights are!"

Bill spat out a mouthful of cigar and grinned. "Not anymore. We got somethin' on weekends now that brings better crowds. Boxing is Tuesdays."

Captain Wong's face turned purple. "But this is impossible! We leave on Tuesday morning! We've got to do it now!"

Bill shook his head and laughed. "Sorry, Cap'n. Nothin' we can do about that. But, listen—no harm done. Let your man compete tonight! If he wins, you'll make twice the money you could on boxing nights."

Wong's mouth opened and closed like a fish's. "Compete? Compete at what?" he spluttered.

"The hottest thing going now," Bill answered. "It's real big in
Australia, and in a few years you're gonna see it all over America:
dwarf tossing. You hire a dwarf wearing a special suit and a
helmet, then you get your people to see how far they can throw
him. You bet on who you think will throw him the farthest. It's
simple. And your man looks small; no one'll believe he can toss
more than three feet. His odds'll be huge. If he can heave a dwarf
half as good as he can hit heavy bags, you'll be a rich man by
tomorrow."

"I CAN'T BELIEVE THIS," Captain Wong said as he led the colonel
down Battery Street.

Colonel Sun shrugged. "What's the difference? Whether I
knock someone out or throw him across a room, I'm still going
to win."

Wong frowned at him. "What makes you so sure? You're a
great fighter, there's no doubt about that, and I'd be willing to bet
everything I have on it. But have you seen some of these foreigners? They're huge! It's a physical thing—they're bred that way.
And they eat raw meat all the time. How can you compete against
that? It's just muscle strength we're talking about—no skill involved. What makes you think you'll be stronger than any of
them?"

"You listen to me," the colonel hissed. "I'll win the contest, and
that's the last I want to hear about it. Now I'm hungry—you take
me to where we can get something to eat, and stop whining."

Captain Wong closed his eyes with resignation, sighed, and
said, "What kind of food do you want?"

"We're in America. I want American food."

"Are you sure?" Wong asked. "Most Chinese find it impossible
to digest."

"I'm not afraid of foreign food. What kinds are there?"

"There are two kinds," Captain Wong sighed. "One is steak—
that's the raw meat I was telling you about—and the other is 'fast
food.' We don't have much time, so we'll have some of that."

As they walked through the financial district, Wong tried to
introduce the colonel to American history as best he could. "This
is a nation of immigrants. Most people who come to America

were poor at home and hoped to make a fortune here. As a result, Americans are obsessed with making money. That's why, compared to us Chinese, they are shallow and uncivilized. In America if I go to your house and trip over a chair, I would bring you to court and sue you for allowing it to happen, just so I could get rich! In China, of course, I would apologize for bumping into your chair, and scold myself for not being more careful. After all, I have eyes, don't I?

"They'll do anything for money, in other words. And they want to do it fast—they don't like wasting time. They do everything fast; that's why they invented 'fast food.' It's already cooked, and all you have to do is order it, and they even hand it to you quickly! You'll see."

Wong took a short detour to take the colonel inside the lobby of a big hotel. It was like being inside a transparent pyramid. The lobby reached up almost twenty floors, and torrents of ivy spilled from the balconies of each floor. A reflecting pool, still as glass, lay in the center of the lobby surrounded by lush potted trees. An unbroken sheet of water spilled over the four sides of the pool, making a gentle hissing sound. The colonel winced, walked over to a potted tree, and started to undo his trousers.

"What are you doing?" Wong asked.

"I have to piss," said the colonel, fumbling with his sash.

"No, no—you can't do that here! Come with me!"

They hurried to the men's room, where the colonel relieved himself and sighed heavily. "Whenever I hear water running," he said, "I have to piss. It doesn't matter where I am, or what I'm doing. Everyone has a weakness."

Back in the lobby, a quartet of musicians dressed in tuxedos accompanied the quiet conversation of people sipping drinks on overstuffed sofas and dining in the hotel restaurant. An elevator with walls of glass rose and fell behind them without making a sound. To the colonel's eyes, the clean lines of the architecture, the overwhelming scale of the interior space, and the perfect balance of stone, water, and vegetation seemed otherworldly. He didn't know whether it was beautiful or horrifying, because he had nothing at all to compare it to.

"If this is what happens when people are uncivilized," he said at last, "then maybe we should think about becoming more primitive."

Wong laughed. For all their moral dissipation and crass behavior, he said, the Americans were capable of great things. "I remember the day they put a man on the moon. All the men on my ship went out on deck and cheered. It didn't matter if you were American or Chinese or whatever—the whole world felt proud that day."

"They put a man on the moon?"

Wong looked at the colonel with a blank expression. "You mean you don't even know that?"

Colonel Sun looked away. Putting a man on the moon did seem quite a feat, but since he had no idea how far away the moon was, or that there was no air in space, or how much power it took to send an object out of the gravitational pull of the earth, this news did not shock him much.

An Asian woman in a silver fox coat walked by; was she a Mongol? the colonel wondered. The Mongolians had ruled most of the Asian continent for hundreds of years, but then lost power and virtually disappeared. Perhaps they had migrated to America, the colonel thought. This woman could be a chieftain's wife.

"You see what I mean about the Communists?" Wong was saying. "They'll do anything to keep you in the dark! The Americans put a man on the moon almost ten years ago, and several more since then! Can you imagine that? A *huochien*—rocket—took them all the way to the moon. They even brought a little car with them so they could drive around up there!"

Huochien means "fire arrow"; the colonel tried to imagine a group of men clutching the shaft of a great arrow as it shot away from a colossal bow, and wondered how they could survive when it landed.

"What did they find there? Were there any people?" he asked, trying to sound politely interested.

"No. Just dirt and rocks. It's a very dusty place."

"Whatever happened to those men?" the colonel asked. He reasoned that without local people to help them or proper building materials, they could never build a bow large enough to shoot them back home. He thought of the poor explorers, sitting at the base of their great arrow in the middle of a field of rocks with nothing to do and no hope of seeing their families again.

"Who knows?" Wong answered. "America isn't sending men to the moon anymore."

They left the hotel and walked a few blocks to a McDonald's on the border of Chinatown. They took their place in line, and Wong pointed up to the menu above the counter. "It's printed in Chinese too," he said. "Order whatever you want."

The colonel squinted to look up at the characters on the menu. Then he shook his head and admitted to Wong that he couldn't read.

"Oh—well, I'll read them off for you. They have hamburgers, cheeseburgers, French fries, apple and cherry pie, milk shakes, Coke—what do you think you'll have?"

"I'll have whatever you usually have."

Captain Wong ordered a couple of cheeseburgers, some fries, and two large Cokes. On their way to a table, the colonel noticed a large plastic statue of Ronald McDonald.

"This statue here represents Mr. McDonald," Captain Wong explained. "He owns these restaurants."

"Is he an opera singer? Why is his face covered with paint?"

"No," Wong laughed. "He's a clown. Clowns in America look like this—they think it looks funny. You see? He's smiling."

The colonel shook his head. "His face is white. White is the color of death, a very bad color."

As they sat down, the colonel noticed another plastic statue. This one was a figure of Mayor McCheese, a cheeseburger with human characteristics. The colonel frowned and pointed at it.

"That man is deformed. How can they put these effigies like this in a restaurant? It's very bad luck, I think."

The colonel took a bite of his cheeseburger, chewed it for a moment, then spat it out on the tray. A look of deep suspicion came over his face. "I have never tasted anything like that before," he said slowly. "What kind of meat is that?"

"It's beef," Wong said. "America is most famous for its beef. They have huge cows out here. The meat is much more tender than the beef you get anywhere else in the world. What's the matter? Don't you like it?"

The colonel scowled and answered, "I was just remembering a story about a restaurant in China. You've heard of Wu Sung, haven't you?"

"The man who killed the tiger with his bare hands?"

"Yes. Not long before killing the tiger, he stopped at a restaurant to eat. They served meat patties. It turned out that the owner of the restaurant was insane, a murderer. He killed people and ground them up into patties, then sold them as food. Wu Sung discovered this and killed the man, of course." The colonel pointed at the statue of Ronald McDonald. "I wouldn't be surprised if this man were capable of such a thing! Look at his mad grin! He looks like he has blood on his mouth."

Captain Wong shook his head. "Listen. Just to make you feel better, I'll tell you why it would be impossible for McDonald's to be grinding up people for their hamburgers. This chain of restaurants is one of the biggest companies in the world—they have served millions and millions of hamburgers so far! If they were using human flesh, the entire population of the earth would have disappeared by now! So don't get all excited—relax and eat. You need all your strength for tonight."

TWO HOURS LATER, 329 large people and one dwarf jammed the Barnacle well beyond the fire marshal's limit. "We never had nothin' like this with the fisticuffs," Bill said to Captain Wong. "This dwarf business is gonna make me a rich man."

"What do I do?" the colonel asked.

"As far as I can tell," Wong answered, "you throw that man as far as you can." He pointed to the dwarf, who wore a red nylon outfit, a harness, and a white plastic helmet.

Bill led them to the bar, where a huge man with shoulder-length red hair, a handlebar mustache, deeply pocked skin, and a giant beer belly stood. He drank straight from the pitcher, his mustache flecked with foam and the front of his camouflage jacket soaked. He stood a full six foot seven, and his arms were as thick as the colonel's legs.

"This is Red," Bill said to Wong. "He's the grand champ when it comes to dwarf tossin'. Nobody yet come into this bar can toss half as far. And this here's my friend Captain Wong."

Red burped and smiled at Wong.

"And this is his friend Mr. Sun," Bill said to Red. "He come all the way from China to box, but we ain't got boxin' tonight, so he says he's gonna kick your ass dwarf heavin'!"

Red looked at the colonel's feet, then let his eyes travel slowly up to the colonel's face. He burst out laughing, spraying the colonel with beer suds.

Colonel Sun's eyes narrowed to slits. "What's he laughing at?" he asked Wong.

"Don't get worked up now," Wong said. "You can laugh back at him after the contest."

"I don't like him," the colonel said. Wong began to get nervous and asked Bill, "Listen, can we sit somewhere and have a drink before we get started?"

Bill led them to a table, then said, "I'll tell you somethin' funny about Red. He's got a real high voice, so he don't like to talk much. He sounds like one a' them fags over on Castro Street! Do you believe it? Har har har!" Bill laughed at his observation and slapped Wong on the back, but Captain Wong was not feeling happy. He wasn't confident that the colonel could win, and he was wondering how on earth to calculate odds on the contest.

"Could you do me a favor?" Wong asked Bill. "Since Mr. Sun and I have never seen dwarf tossing before, there's no way we can judge what kind of chance he has of winning. Do you think you could ask Red to heave the dwarf once, so we can see what we're up against?"

Bill took an imaginary puff from his unlit cigar and smiled. "Sure! Why don't you get your friend to ask him? Har har har!"

Wong shook his head and started tugging on his lucky mole hair. He was most enthusiastic about gambling when the game was fixed. He had to know if the colonel could really throw the dwarf farther than Red—then he could set things up right. If the colonel was the stronger of the two, then he wanted him to sit quiet and look feeble so the odds against him would be high. Then Wong would put everything on him and clean up. If the colonel couldn't throw the dwarf as far, all was not lost; Wong could provoke a fistfight between the two, and the colonel could show Red a little Chinese boxing. Then people might put their money on the colonel. In that case, Wong would put his money on Red and still come out ahead. If the colonel lost the fistfight, at least he wouldn't have lost any money.

"Listen, Master Sun," he said, "I know you could beat that man in a fight, but I'm not familiar with this contest. Since you've never done it before, how sure can you be that you'll win?"

The colonel turned his head slowly. He glared at Wong, unblinking, until the captain had to look down. "You just put your money on whoever you think will win," the colonel said. His voice sounded calm, but judging from the way he looked, Captain Wong decided that an honest bet might be the safest thing after all.

The colonel watched angrily as the bouncers placed a few foam cushions near the door of the bar. Meanwhile, the dwarf marched around the room swinging his arms, bending from the waist, and cracking his knuckles in preparation for being heaved. Red cut a swathe in the spectators as he lumbered from the bar to the heaving area. He put one hand on the dwarf's head and pumped the other fist skyward, and the crowd roared its approval. Bill happily chewed on his cigar, jumped on top of his table, and shouted, "It's shrimp-flingin' time!"

The crowd cheered again.

"Okay, sailor men," Bill announced, "you know the rules. Anybody wants to give it a shot come over here and say so, and we'll have the 'liminations. Each man gets three throws, and we put bets on who we think is gonna win. Then, the champ a' that round gets to go against Red, and a' course we'll be bettin' on that. An' if any man does happen to beat Red here, then he gets the 'Beat Red' pot, which as of last week is up to two hundred twenty-three bucks, so it's worth a hernia if you think you got it in ya."

Bill lifted a heavy glass jar full of cash into the air, and the crowd hooted and stomped their feet. Twelve men made their way over to the mats.

"You have to go over there with them," Wong told the colonel.

When he joined the contestants, the crowd burst into laughter. Next to Red and the other twelve men, who all stood over six feet tall, the colonel looked tiny, not to mention strange, with his ancient leather armor and his serious demeanor. That only made him seem funnier to the audience, who were by now mostly pointing at him, slapping their thighs, and choking on pretzels.

"Okay, settle in, men," Bill shouted. "He's from China, so he don't know you're supposed to have fun." The news that the angry little stranger was from China only provoked more noise from the audience. Finally, Bill managed to get them to quiet down enough for him to announce that betting would start and that everybody had ten minutes to get it all straight. A flurry of arguments and slips of paper went back and forth through the crowd, then at last Bill struck a garbage can lid with a crowbar and yelled out to the dwarf, "Helmet ready?"

The dwarf adjusted his helmet. "Helmet ready!" he yelled in a nasal voice.

"Then . . . let the games begin!" Bill screamed, and the crowd went wild. Captain Wong, who had placed a conservative hundred dollars on the colonel at four-to-one odds, downed a shot of bourbon, crossed his arms on his chest, and sighed.

The dwarf walked up to a competitor, gave him the thumbs-up sign, then faced the mats. The competitor, a beefy man with a bald head and a monstrous tattoo on his right arm, picked the dwarf up by the straps of his harness. The dwarf, poised like a torpedo with his head pointing toward the mats, folded his arms over his chest and tensed up. The competitor swung the dwarf once, twice, and on the third swing launched him onto the mats. "Eight foot three!" yelled Bill, who now stood at the far corner of the room with a tape measure in one hand and a mug of ale in the other. "Boooo!" howled the audience. Anything less than nine feet was chicken feed.

The man with the tattoo took three throws, each worse than the last. One by one, the dwarf went through the line of competitors, saving the colonel for last. When it was his turn, the dwarf said to him, "You sure you can get me to the mats, Grandpa? I don't want to get dropped short."

Even if the colonel had understood English, he wouldn't have been able to hear the question over all the catcalls and laughter. The best of the thirty-six throws so far had been eleven feet five inches, nowhere near Red's record of fifteen feet two. Red had gone back to the bar to refill his pitcher, since it was clear he wouldn't have to exert himself tonight.

The colonel picked the dwarf up by the seat of his pants and threw him without any preparatory swings. The odd thing about the throw, Captain Wong noticed, was that the colonel seemed to be throwing the dwarf down. The dwarf landed heavily and skidded several feet.

"Jesus Christ!" screamed the dwarf, "he's a maniac! He tried to break my neck!"

The crowd was uncharacteristically silent. Then Bill yelled out, "Twelve feet!" and all hell broke loose.

The colonel ignored all the cheering and backslapping and made his way to where Wong sat. He leaned down and said, "I'm tired of this game already. You come up here with me."

Wong felt it best to do as the colonel asked and followed him over to the heaving area.

"You tell this man," the colonel said pointing to Bill, "that I want this hurried up. Tell him to get the fat one with red hair over here."

Wong translated this as diplomatically as possible, and Bill shouted out, "Listen up, gents! The man from China is tired a' waitin' for Red! He says he wants Red to git up here quick so's he can kick his ass right now!"

The crowd went berserk, as they loved a good challenge— especially when it looked like the challenge would lead to a postcontest brawl. Red put down his pitcher and stalked over to the colonel. "You tell him," the colonel ordered Wong, "that this game is for weaklings."

Captain Wong swallowed hard and said to Red, "He doesn't think this game is hard enough."

The crowd cheered so hard it seemed some of them would pass out. This was the best entertainment any of them had seen in years.

The colonel pulled off the dwarf's helmet and threw it away, then said to Wong, "Tell this prisoner he is free! I'll see to it that he makes it out the door without being hurt."

"But, Teacher Sun," Captain Wong said, trembling, "he isn't a prisoner—he's—"

"I don't care if he's a prisoner or not!" the colonel yelled. "He's free now! Tell him!"

Wong said to the dwarf, "Mr. Sun says . . . he says you're free now. You can go."

"Fuck him, this is my job!" the dwarf squawked, and stalked across the room to find his helmet.

The crowd was out of control. Red, sensing that he was being made a fool of, began to look dangerous. His veins stood out as if they'd been squeezed out of a tube onto his forehead and neck. He was positively crimson.

"Now you tell the fat one," the colonel continued, "that we will finish the contest using a full-sized man."

"He wants to use a regular man for the contest," Wong said.

"Wait a minute—like who?" asked Bill, beginning to feel that maybe things were getting a little out of hand.

Wong translated for the colonel. The colonel pointed at Wong. "You."

"Me?" Wong yelped. "I'm not going to get thrown around—"

"You want to make money?" the colonel interrupted. "I'm showing you how! I tossed that little man into the ground for your sake! No one's going to believe I can throw you farther than that giant pink fool. You'll make plenty of money, and you'll be working for it yourself instead of making that poor little man with the hat and straps suffer!"

Captain Wong realized that he couldn't argue with the colonel. He had already made eight hundred dollars—if he bet six hundred of it and the colonel lost, he would still come up even for the night. How different this was working out from the way he imagined it! Chinese boxing—he was going to prove to them all that a good Chinese boxer could whup any foreigner, no matter how big he was. Instead, it looked like he was going to be heaved around like a sack of coal in a stupid contest that he might not make any money off of anyway. Most of all, he didn't like the idea of it. He was a ship's captain, and nearly sixty years old. Think of the humiliation if anyone in Hong Kong found out about it! And what if he got hurt?

"What's the deal?" Bill asked. "We're all gettin' edgy here."

Captain Wong took a deep breath, then stood up on Bill's table. "Listen to me!" he yelled. The crowd became quiet remarkably fast; no one wanted to delay the match and the fight afterward.

"I'm going to be thrown," Wong yelled, "but only if it's worth my while. I say my friend can win, and I'm willing to bet on it. If someone will take me up on it, then we'll find out for sure. If no one will give me a decent bet, then I'm going home!"

The crowd moved as a single organism, thrusting fistfuls of money up toward Wong to place bets. When the betting was finished—Bill penned the wagers on his arm—Wong had bet more than two thousand dollars on his teacher.

"All right, gentlemen," Bill laughed, "it's time to throw the captain!"

He pointed at the colonel. "You first, stranger."

The colonel held up three fingers and looked at Bill.

"That's right," Bill said, "three throws."

The colonel grabbed Wong by the shirt collar and the seat of his pants.

"Please be careful," Wong said.

He swung Wong once, twice, and on three let go. Wong landed with a thud.

"Eight feet even!" Bill announced.

Red sneered at the colonel. Then he grabbed Wong and casually threw him onto the mats.

"Eight feet ten!" Bill yelled. The crowd cheered, although not as loudly as before. The inevitable was taking place.

The colonel walked over to the spot on the mat where Wong had last landed. He picked Wong up again, swung him once, twice, then sent him flopping onto the mats like a cod.

A murmur went through the crowd, and Bill rushed over to the spot. He looked at it for a second, then jumped into the air. "Nine feet ten!" he shouted, and the crowd came to life again. How could this be happening? In spite of the fact that most everyone had bet against him, the colonel was beginning to acquire a certain underdog appeal.

Red sensed this and didn't like it at all. It was time to put the guy with the yellow eyes and the sideburns to bed. He grabbed

Wong roughly and dragged him to the heaving line. This time Red really used his warmup swings, and on three he let out a high-pitched yell and flung Wong with all his might.

"Ten feet!" Bill screamed, his voice going hoarse, and now Red had won the audience back. None of them had been able to throw the dwarf that far, much less the Chinese sea captain. Red pumped his fists up into the air, glared at the colonel, and squeaked, "Last throw, chump!"

A few men tittered at Red's tiny voice, but when he spun around, looking as if he might spit blood, the crowd fell silent. The colonel looked at the spot on the mat where Wong had fallen. Wong was rubbing a burn on his head where he had made contact with the mats. With his other hand, he was rubbing his right knee, which was painfully bruised and swelling fast.

The colonel stepped away from the heaving area, and the crowd started to boo. "Come on, you chickenshit!" Red squealed.

The colonel stopped at the bar and gestured to Captain Wong. Wong hobbled across the room to where he was standing.

"Now what?" he asked.

Without answering, the colonel grabbed Wong and held him in the ready position.

"Hey—what the hell is going on?" Wong howled.

The crowd couldn't believe their eyes—he couldn't be serious? He was fifteen feet away from the mats! But serious or not, they loved this moment more than any moment they could remember.

"You can't do this!" Wong pleaded. "You'll kill me!"

"You'll live," the colonel growled, "and think of all the nice money we'll make. Tell them to open the door."

"He says open the door!" Wong moaned.

The colonel planted his feet and his eyes. As he swung Wong, who was clawing piteously at the colonel's hands to try to escape, the crowd yelled, "One!"

On the second swing, Wong covered his head with his hands. "Two!" the crowd roared.

As the colonel pulled Wong back for the throw, he opened his eyes, shook all over, and let out an ear-piercing scream. Wong sailed through the air, over the mats, hit the ground beyond where Bill's tape measure reached, and tumbled out the door into the parking lot and practically landed on Hsun-ching, who was just returning from dinner with Alison.

The crowd didn't make a sound; they were all men who lived by the strength of their arms and backs, and had a pretty good idea what to expect in contests of strength. What they had just seen didn't have a place in that idea. The ugly little man from China had just thrown a 150-pound man at least twenty-five feet, maybe more, without even a decent heaving harness to grab onto.

The colonel decided it was time to settle his score with the hairy one. He stalked over to Red, reached up, patted the giant's cheeks, and smiled. Red saw the colonel's bared teeth for only a second; his face turned pale, and he opened his mouth to yell, but the colonel didn't give him a chance. He grabbed Red's mustache and yanked part of it out, then threw the howling giant over a table.

In an instant, awe turned turned to anger, and the crowd surged toward the colonel. If the fierce little man from China had thrown Wong twelve feet, or even thirteen feet, they would have held him over their shoulders and crowned him king of the gym, and would have laughed at the sight of Red picking up his mustache and eating humble pie. But twenty-five feet was too far—that made the colonel a freak from China, not a hero, and no good old boy from the docks was going to let a freak pull Red's whiskers out.

Nothing could have pleased the colonel more than the chance to blow off a little steam and crush a few barbarians. Still, he remembered the frightening power of the guns in Hong Kong, and Hsun-ching's warning that all Americans carried them, so he limited himself to knocking the wind out of his attackers or breaking their arms. Within moments, a heap of longshoremen lay strewn about the bar groaning like camels. The rest of the patrons of the Barnacle lost enthusiasm for the battle and slunk away, waiting to see what would happen next.

"You'd better get your money now," the colonel said to Captain Wong, who crawled in the door with Hsun-ching helping him.

"Never mind the money," Wong gasped, "you have to get out of here!"

"Why?" the colonel asked. "I've defeated everyone. There is no danger." Just then they heard a police siren start up about ten blocks away.

"That's why!" Wong said, "Listen to me—don't come near my boat, do you understand? Don't even go near it!"

The police were getting closer. The colonel's vision darkened. It was as if someone had placed a black felt cone over his face so that he could see only through a little tunnel in front of him. Something in his mind snapped, and pure anger burst behind his eyeballs and flooded into his brain. He wanted to stand his ground and crush everyone—the fools in the bar, the police with their guns, anyone who tried to hurt him—but then his head started to throb, and he knew he had to get out. He grabbed the "Beat Red" jar, rushed toward the door, and led the bewildered Hsun-ching down an alley toward the city.

XVIII

AT THE FOOT OF THE BAY BRIDGE, THE COLONEL AND Hsun-ching ducked under the concrete base of the ramp so that Hsun-ching could catch his breath.

The colonel described what had happened in the bar. "I should have won the contest and left quietly, but I failed. I lost my temper and acted badly. Now, because of my mistake, we will have to spend four nights on foreign soil. On the morning Captain Wong's boat leaves, we will go back to the docks, and I will get us on board." He winced and clutched his forehead, then slowly lowered himself to one knee.

"Forgive me," he said.

Hsun-ching helped the colonel up and begged him not to apologize. He noticed that his companion rose slowly, as if he were in pain.

"I would never have gotten this far if you hadn't come with me," Hsun-ching said. "And besides, its not your fault those people started a fight. But what's the matter with your head? Were you hurt?"

The colonel wobbled a bit, then shook his head. "It will soon pass." Then he fingered the empty leather sling over his back.

"I should not have left my pole in the boat," he muttered.

Hsun-ching was actually very glad that the colonel did not have his weapon with him. Look at the trouble he had got into with just his bare hands! Hsun-ching didn't want to imagine what sorts of terrible things might happen if he carried that pole with him through San Francisco for four days.

"The important thing now," Hsun-ching said, "is finding a place to sleep where the police won't know to look. I have located the sutra, and I should be able to get it on Monday."

"I know a place," the colonel said. "Follow me."

"AND DID YOU have a reservation?" asked the clerk at the big hotel.

"No," Hsun-ching answered. "We just arrived in San Francisco today. But your hotel is very famous, even in China. We have been looking forward to staying here for . . . for an eternity!" He hoped to flatter the man into letting them stay. In China, hotels always claim to be full because the workers do not want to have to clean the rooms. The only way to get a room is to have a "back door," or to bribe or flatter the clerks at the front desk.

The man eyed Hsun-ching suspiciously, then looked at the colonel, who sat in the lobby next to the reflecting pool, slumped on a couch with his head in his hands.

"And how will you be paying for this?" the man asked.

"How much does it cost?" Hsun-ching asked back.

When the man told him, Hsun-ching opened the "Beat Red" jar, dug around in it for exact change, and laid the money on the counter. "Is this correct?" The clerk looked at the money, then back at colonel. "Is he all right?" he asked.

"Yes, he's fine," answered Hsun-ching, thinking quickly. "He is a Peking Opera performer. He just gave his performance in Chinatown—that is why he is very tired. He hasn't even had a chance to change his clothes. Here—would you like a package of cigarettes?"

ONCE THEY WERE checked in, Hsun-ching led the colonel to the glass elevators. "No, no—" the colonel said, "I can't ride in one of these."

"But, Colonel Sun, we're on the ninth floor—you shouldn't walk up any stairs! Just close your eyes."

They got in the elevator, and the colonel gripped the railing nearest the door. As soon as the elevator started to rise, he opened his eyes, groaned, and pressed himself as hard as he could against the doors. The elevator stopped on the fourth floor, and as soon as the doors opened, the colonel spilled out and crashed into a group of Japanese businessmen.

Hsun-ching apologized for the colonel and helped the fallen men pick up their business cards, which were now scattered all over the hallway. A long sequence of bowing and counterbowing followed. It seemed the colonel had stumbled directly into a subordinate, who then crashed into his immediate superior, who then tripped and knocked the wind out the senior partner.

By the time the colonel and Hsun-ching got back into the elevator, the Japanese executives seemed paralyzed, each bent nearly double at the waist and each unwilling to be the first to straighten up.

At last the colonel and Hsun-ching reached the ninth floor and found their room. Hsun-ching helped him remove his heavy armor and brought him a glass of water from the bathroom. The colonel sat on the edge of the bed with his head in his hands, breathing rapidly. He took the glass of water, but as he moved it to his lips, a bolt of pain flashed through his head, and the glass shattered in his hand. Hsun-ching, remembering Hamma's encephalitic fever, soaked a towel in cold water and wrapped it around the colonel's head. This seemed to help, and after a few minutes the colonel was able to lie down.

When his breathing returned to normal and he was able to speak again, he announced that he was terribly hungry. Hsun-ching went down to the restaurant in the hotel lobby and ordered three bowls of beef soup. When Hsun-ching piled them up and started to carry them toward the elevators, the maître d' stiffly informed him that if he wanted to carry food to his room, he should call room service. A waiter took the bowls and carried them for Hsun-ching, who tipped him with a wrinkled cigarette. "Thank you so very much," the waiter snapped.

. . .

THE COLONEL WAS propped up in bed watching the in-house movie on television. It was a James Bond picture, and the colonel couldn't take his eyes off the screen.

"This man is very clever and powerful," the colonel whispered gravely. "Watch what he is doing."

Hsun-ching started to explain that it was just a movie, but at that moment Bond appeared on the screen, and the colonel hushed him. Bond had been pushed out of an airplane without a parachute. By adjusting the position of his arms and legs, though, he was able to swoop down like a bird onto a man who did have a parachute, wrestle it away from him, and tie it to his own back. Hsun-ching, who had never seen a movie using stunt-men or special effects, was as amazed as the colonel, and the two of them were unable to eat anything until the movie finished. When it was over, the colonel seemed deeply affected by it. Maybe he was wrong to think that there was no one else in the world with abilities like his own. If he were to meet the man in the picture box, he wondered, would they become friends or enemies?

"Who else can we see in the box?" the colonel asked. Hsun-ching found the guide and studied it carefully. "The next program is called *Superman*."

HSUN-CHING DIDN'T get to sleep until very late that night. The next morning he woke up with a hangover. When he sat up, the room did a somersault. He held on to the bed and waited for the walls and furniture to settle, but just as he felt ready to stand, he noticed that the colonel's bed was empty. He panicked for a moment, then noticed that the colonel was kneeling on the floor near the television. His eyes were half-closed, and he seemed to be in some sort of trance.

"Colonel Sun?" Hsun-ching asked gently. "Are you all right?"

"Yes," the colonel answered. His voice sounded much better than the night before.

"What are you thinking about?"

"Nothing."

Hsun-ching shuffled into the bathroom. He drank as much

water as he could, then took a hot bath. He couldn't believe how luxurious it was to be completely immersed in hot water in a spotless white tub, looking up at a spotless white ceiling. And so many fluffy towels! He was used to drying himself off with a rag the size of a handkerchief. He lay flat so that only his nose poked above the surface and slowly let all his muscles go loose. The water seemed to leach the toxins from his body, and soon he began thinking about Alison.

He wondered what she thought about him. Had she enjoyed being with him, or did she simply feel obliged to be helpful? After all, she was an artist with a college education and a car, while he was a fugitive orphan from a backward country.

To cheer himself up, he used all of the towels in the bathroom to dry himself off. He noticed that there was a telephone in the bathroom, right next to the toilet. *Aiya,* he thought, do foreigners talk on the phone even when they're doing that? Couldn't the person on the other end of the line tell? But then again, he recalled, foreigners are supposedly very quiet about certain things. For example, when they have soup, eat noodles, or drink tea, they never slurp. Maybe it was the same with matters of the toilet?

When he came out of the bathroom, the colonel was still in the same position, apparently in deep concentration. Hsun-ching did not want to disturb him, but he wasn't sure how long the colonel could sit like that, and it would be check-out time soon.

"Colonel Sun—I'm sorry to disturb you."

The colonel's eyes remained half-closed. "What is it?"

Hsun-ching explained that they didn't have enough cash left to stay in the fancy hotel for another night, so they would have to search for another place to sleep. The colonel nodded and stood up. His headache had cleared, but he seemed distant and worried about something.

"I'm sure that *Superman* movie wasn't real," Hsun-ching said, hoping to cheer the colonel up. "No one can fly without wings."

The colonel didn't seem to hear him at first. Finally, he turned to face Hsun-ching. "I cannot stay here long," he said. He stood up and looked in the large mirror over the desk. He had never seen such a clear image of himself. He moved his head from side to side, then opened his mouth so he could see his teeth. He closed his mouth slowly, turned away from the mirror, and sat down on the bed again.

"I'll tell you something," the colonel said quietly. "What happened to me last night, at the wine house and then with the headache, has happened before. It happened when I was in India. I don't understand it—maybe it is the *feng shui* in foreign countries, or the ghosts here. But when I am far from home and I must fight, I feel as if I'm going blind, and everything becomes like a dream. My body acts on its own, and . . . it's so easy for me to kill ordinary men. Afterward, the headache comes."

The colonel wiped his face with the palm of his hand. Hsun-ching noticed that he was flushed and sweating.

Colonel Sun stood up suddenly and looked at himself in the mirror again. "Isn't it enough that I have to look like this?" he said, his voice becoming desperate. "Why does this happen?"

Hsun-ching felt a chill go down his spine. He remembered that, in *Journey to the West,* the Buddha put a gold band around the Monkey King's head so that whenever he got violent, the monk Hsüan-tsang could recite a magic spell and the gold band would tighten and give Monkey an unbearable headache, crippling him so that he couldn't fight anymore. Maybe it was only a coincidence, but it unnerved him anyway.

The colonel sighed and looked away from the mirror. "I want to tell you something which may be of use to you someday. You asked me what I was thinking just then, and I said, 'Nothing.' I don't want you to think I was avoiding your question. I'll try to explain it for you.

"When the headache came, I felt as if my head was being split open with a blunt wooden saw. Last night, for the first time in many years, I thought I was dying, and I was afraid. Believe me, fear of death cripples a man more than anything else. Do you want to know the secret to my successes in battle? It was not my strength that saved me. It was that I had a clear mind, a mind without fear. And I don't just mean the sort of mind where, in your better days you say to yourself, 'I'm not afraid to die!' I mean a clear mind even when you are surrounded by your enemies, and death is certain! When your mind is really clear, it is like a polished mirror. Nothing disturbs it, and the enemy's movements become obvious even before they begin. That way you can cut through them like straw men."

He covered his eyes with his sunglasses. "Sitting like that is how I empty my mind of that fear," he said. "If you only remember one thing about me after we say good-bye, I hope it is this: All confusion, indecision, and suffering comes from fear of death. Rid yourself of it, and you will be free."

Fear of death was too big a subject for Hsun-ching to contemplate at that moment. Anyway, he believed that suffering came from having an unhappy life, not from the fear of death, and happiness depended primarily on circumstances beyond your control, such as when and where you were born, who your parents were, and whom you knew. There wasn't much you could do about being unhappy except avoid making it worse by doing things you would regret. For example, if a man sank up to his nose in quicksand made even the slightest false move, he would feel himself sink, experience a moment of unimaginable regret, then drown painfully.

He showed the colonel the gum wrapper Alison had given him with the address of the Dharma Institute on it. "I know where the sutra is," he reminded the colonel, "and we can get it on Monday. Then we go back to the boat before dawn on Tuesday. It's less than four days! Let's just try to relax and enjoy ourselves until then—if we don't get into any trouble, you won't have any more headaches. The woman I met at the museum invited us to a party at an artist's home tonight. We can go there and look at paintings! Please don't worry about anything anymore, Colonel Sun; we're almost finished here."

Down in the lobby, they happened to see two athletes checking in, wearing fancy sweat suits. "We should find clothes like that," the colonel said. "They look far more comfortable than those suits from Hong Kong." They found a sports store nearby, and with the last of their cash bought matching gray Adidas sweat suits, Nike sneakers, and gold football jackets that said SAN FRANCISCO FORTY-NINERS on the back. Then, using the position of the sun as a compass, they decided to explore the rest of the city before finding a place to sleep near the docks.

First they walked south into the Mission district. Hsun-ching, who had never heard Spanish before, wondered whether these were the oppressed Chinese-Americans he had heard about in China. He tried speaking Chinese to as many people as he could, but got only strange looks in response. The colonel laughed at Hsun-ching's efforts. "Can't you tell these aren't Chinese people? They're from India—anyone can see that!" To prove his theory, he tried greeting some of them with the one phrase of Hindi he remembered from his journey to the west, but again no one responded. "Indians are very suspicious of strangers," he explained. "I remember now that they often pretend not to understand you."

They turned onto Castro Street and followed it toward Market. Here, the streets were filled with pairs of men, some with their arms around each other's waists. In modern China, it is acceptable for male friends to hold hands or walk very close together in public, but not men and women, and Hsun-ching was glad to see that these foreigners could be such good friends. The colonel, on the other hand, assumed they had stumbled on a wealthy neighborhood; in ancient China, he remembered, homosexual love was quite common among intellectuals and the rich. The only thing they saw that seemed truly out of the ordinary was a man who came strutting out of a bar wearing only leather chaps that left his buttocks completely bare, and a pair of gold rings hanging from his pierced nipples.

"Look at that man," Hsun-ching whispered. "He has rings through his chest!"

"Yes, I saw," the colonel said. "Don't pay any attention to him. I've seen that before—he's a shaman. They go into trances and spirits go into their bodies, and then they put needles through their skin like that to prove that they feel no pain."

They continued west up a steep hill, then decided to start heading north again. They turned right on Ashbury Street and followed it down to Haight Street, where a completely different neighborhood began. Here, people looked a lot poorer; their clothes looked ragged and patched, and many of them wore shirts whose dyes had bled into chaotic splotches. Their hair was long and uncombed—even the men's—and some, who apparently couldn't afford proper shoes, wore only leather sandals. On the street corners, groups of them stood idly, talking or making music.

"This is where poor people live!" the colonel said disdainfully. "Here they are, in this dream nation where people can fly and drive their own fire-chariots, and they are too lazy to even comb their hair properly! Let's pass through quickly; areas like this can be infested with lice and ticks."

They hurried down Ashbury until they reached the Panhandle of Golden Gate Park. Hsun-ching thought that many of the cars parked along the Panhandle looked as if they had not moved for a long time. He was right; this was a favorite stopping place for homeless people who could afford only broken-down cars to live in. Because of its proximity to Golden Gate Park and the Haight, the Panhandle was a scenic and tolerant place to camp.

They passed a rusty, faded purple bus with a wooden chimney sticking up through the roof that looked as if it had grown out of the concrete like some sort of futuristic, industrial weed. A wisp of smoke curled from the chimney, carrying with it the smell of food. Hsun-ching and the colonel hadn't eaten since the night before, so they were famished. They had also spent the last of their money on their new clothes, so they would have to beg or forage for food if they wanted to eat. They approached the bus and knocked on one of the doors.

"Who's there?" an anxious voice demanded.

"Lovely weather we're having, isn't it?" Hsun-ching said cheerfully.

Someone peeked out from behind one of the shabby curtains. "What do you want?" the voice asked.

"We are from China!" Hsun-ching announced. "We have no money. Can you tell us where we can get some food?"

"Go to the soup kitchen," the voice advised.

The colonel thought it inexcusably rude that the man would not even open his door to speak to them. He stepped up to the bus, took hold of the sliding door on the passenger side, and gave a great tug. The door ripped right off its hinges, revealing a very surprised man with an enormous beard cooking over a small gas stove. The inside of the bus was strewn with clothing, paper, and boxes.

The bearded man went pale, and his eyes nearly popped out of his head. "I'm sorry," Hsun-ching said, pointing to the colonel, "he was only trying to open the door. He didn't mean to break it. We are from China, and we have no food. Can you help us?"

The bearded man grabbed a crowbar and held it in front of him. "Get away from my van," he shouted. The colonel, indignant that a man with unkempt hair and beard would threaten him with a weapon, charged into the bus and disarmed the terrified man. He pressed himself against the far side of the bus and yelled for help, but the colonel merely bent the crowbar in half for him to see and threw it to the ground. The man stared at the bent crowbar, then buried his face in his hands and started rocking back and forth. "It's just a bad trip," he moaned.

"Let's go," the colonel said to Hsun-ching. "I'm almost certain there are lice in here." On his way out, though, he noticed an omelet cooking on the little stove. "Eggs!" he exclaimed. "I love eggs!" He picked up the entire omelete with his fingers and consumed it in one bite. "Ask him if he can make more," he instructed Hsun-ching.

Hsun-ching thought it might be impossible to have any sort of normal relations with the bearded man at this point, but he did not want to anger the colonel. He entered the bus and found the bearded man trying to burrow under a pile of laundry.

"Please do not be afraid," Hsun-ching said gently. "Mr. Sun is sorry about the door. He is from China, so he was just angry that you would not open the door to talk to us. It's a terrible misunderstanding! Sorry! Could you just please make him some more eggs? Then he will be very happy, and we can be good friends."

"How did he bend that crowbar?" the man asked from under the laundry.

Yes, Hsun-ching acknowledged, Mr. Sun was very strong. Perhaps if there was any heavy work to be done around the van, Mr. Sun could do it in exchange for food?

The colonel was having difficulty seeing in the curtained bus, so he took off his sunglasses and looked around. The bearded man poked his head out to look, saw the colonel's brilliant yellow eyes, and nearly wet his pants when the colonel grinned and bared his sharp teeth.

"There are colors coming out of his eyes!" the man yelped.

"Oh yes," said Hsun-ching, "Mr. Sun looks very strange. He is a strange man, in fact. He even lives under a waterfall! But he is really very kind."

"Holy shit!" the bearded man half-howled, half-laughed. His terror seemed to be gradually turning into a kind of comic ecstasy.

"Could you please make him some more eggs?" Hsun-ching asked again.

"Eggs! He wants eggs?" the man gasped. He pointed at the plastic ice chest next to the stove and told them he had just used the last of the eggs—they could check for themselves. The colonel opened the cooler, which was now empty except for some nearly melted ice cubes.

"Look at this," he said to Hsun-ching. "He has a winter-box! Where do you suppose he gets the ice?"

Hsun-ching translated, and the bearded man explained that there was a market only three blocks away. This intrigued the colonel, so Hsun-ching asked the man if he would lead them there. He readily agreed; anything to get them out of his van.

The colonel was the first to step out of the bus, but in an instant he came hurtling back in. There were soldiers outside, he warned Hsun-ching. "They might be looking for us because of last night."

Hsun-ching pulled one of the curtains aside. Two policemen were walking along the sidewalk toward the bus.

"Please," he begged the bearded man, "the police are coming! They are looking for Mr. Sun, I think, but we haven't done anything wrong—please let us hide in here!"

Hsun-ching and the colonel rushed to the back of the bus and hid themselves the best they could. For a moment, the bearded man considered running out and asking for help, but then he remembered that he was not exactly on good terms with the police either. He was also high as a kite. Anyway, seeing the two strangers cowering from the police made him think that maybe these two weren't so bad after all.

When the police turned the corner, the bearded man told Hsun-ching and the colonel that the coast was clear. The colonel bowed gratefully.

"How come the police are looking for you?" the bearded man asked, making sure he was close to the door.

"Because last night, in a bar, Mr. Sun was attacked by some"— Hsun-ching couldn't remember the word for sailors—"soldiers from boats. He only defended himself, but he hurt some of them, so the police want to catch him."

The bearded man's suspicious expression gave way to open admiration. "He beat up some soldiers in a bar?" he asked breathlessly. Hsun-ching nodded, and suddenly the bearded man was all smiles. He gave the colonel a thumbs-up, then led them to the market to see the ice.

As they walked, Hsun-ching explained to the bearded man— whose name was Manny—that he and Mr. Sun were visiting from China for just a few days. They were going to find a Buddhist sutra, then go back right away. Manny didn't seem to be paying attention, though; he was staring intently at the sidewalk. When Hsun-ching asked Manny what his job was, Manny laughed and answered that his job was keeping on his feet, what with the earth's rotation and all. He explained that the earth was spinning on its axis at a very high speed, and sometimes you can actually feel the motion. When that happens, you have to concentrate pretty hard to keep from falling down.

The market, it turned out, was an enormous supermarket, the likes of which the colonel and Hsun-ching had never seen. The colonel was mesmerized by the giant freezer; how did they keep all that snow in that big open shelf from melting? Hsun-ching couldn't believe that so much fruit could be found in one place. He marveled that there were only ten or twelve customers in the store, casually wandering around as if the mountains of fresh produce were nothing special! In the outdoor markets in China, you were lucky to find more than a few piles of sour oranges and maybe some bruised, angry-looking little apples, and even then you had to compete for them with hundreds of people in the pouring rain.

Since it was his birthday, Manny decided to splurge. He

bought himself a cake and some tiny candles, and bought a pint of ice cream for the colonel and a bag of mixed fruits for Hsun-ching. Back in the bus, he explained the custom of the birthday cake to his guests, lit the little candles, and made a wish. He started to wish for an arms-free world and an end to starvation in the Third World, but since it was his birthday he changed his mind and wished to meet a nubile young woman whose ideal man was an aging draft-dodging activist who lived in a bus and ran a soup kitchen.

The ice cream was too cold for the colonel, so he had Hsun-ching ask Manny to cook it for him. Manny hesitated, then laughed and said, why not? He scooped some of it into his skillet and melted it into a steaming, milky soup. The colonel finished every drop. As for Hsun-ching, he relished the fruits as if they were the last food he would ever eat. When they had all had their fill, the colonel motioned to Hsun-ching. Although their host was poor and dirty, he had proved to be a generous man. "We should offer him something in return. Why don't you invite him to join us at the gathering tonight at the painter's house? Artists like it when one or two poor people come to their homes, because it makes them seem eccentric and unprejudiced. It gives them face with their artist friends. That way, we'll be doing both the artist and the poor man a favor."

Hsun-ching thought this was an excellent idea, and Manny was delighted to accept. They could take the bus, he suggested, and that way they'd have time to browse through the Arboretum, a gigantic greenhouse in Golden Gate Park. It was free, and they wouldn't believe the flowers.

Actually, the Arboretum did not impress Hsun-ching or the colonel nearly as much as the market. What could you do with flowers? How impractical! But they did enjoy seeing how much pleasure Manny wrung out of each flower. He gazed at every blossom, as if it were the first flower on earth, then moved on to the next with the same fresh enthusiasm. Hsun-ching didn't know what to make of this, but the colonel was impressed. He said to Hsun-ching, "I think there is more to this man than we first suspected. He does not seem to be a madman, since he can walk and talk without difficulty, but he is looking at things in a very concentrated way. I think if this man was a soldier, he would be very successful. Ask him if he was ever a soldier."

The question provoked a violent response. Hell no, said Manny—him a soldier? "How do you think I ended up sleeping in that bus? They wanted me to go to Vietnam, and I said no way! I burned my draft card and went to jail for five years. And here's the worst part—two months after I got out, they pardoned all the draft dodgers! I could've just gone to Canada and hung out all that time! Don't make me think about it."

Manny thought that, being Red Chinese, Hsun-ching and Mr. Sun would admire him for being unwilling to fight the North Vietnamese. But when Hsun-ching explained that Manny had gone to prison rather than go to war, the colonel looked thoroughly disgusted. "And to think I was beginning to respect this man!" he sniffed. "In China he would have been executed on the spot! Doesn't he have any sense of face? No one likes to fight! But how can he live with himself, knowing he is such a coward?"

"Maybe he isn't a coward," said Hsun-ching. "He refused to join the army, and he went to prison for it. That doesn't mean he is a coward."

"What else then?" the colonel boomed. "He disobeyed his superiors! Ask him why he wouldn't join the army! See what excuse he has!"

At that moment, Manny had his nose deep inside a tulip. He wasn't in the mood for politics, so he simply answered, "Because I'm a coward, that's why," and moved on to the orchids.

When Hsun-ching translated this, the colonel was shocked.

"You mean, he *admitted* it? He isn't ashamed to stand before us and say it out loud?"

"I guess not," Hsun-ching answered.

The colonel was dumbfounded. Then a bemused smile crept over his face. "Well, if it was up to me, I would have him beheaded for treason. But then I would hold a banquet and place his head at the table of honor! A man who speaks his mind should be celebrated in some way."

XIX

"I THINK THERE'S A PLASTICITY TO THIS SERIES THAT the *Damnation* series lacked," the man in the oversized wrinkled suit was saying.

"Yes, but that's not the point," countered the man with the diamond earring. "The whole thing isn't about the medium at all. It's about denying the medium—all of it—and I don't just mean art."

Alison refilled their glasses, then went to make sure there was enough pita bread to go with the humus. She was glad that the opening was such a success; more than fifty people had come, and it was still early. Sky worked so hard, but got so little pleasure out of anything. It tormented him that people didn't read anymore, that they didn't go to art museums, that they didn't care about the environment, and that the universe was expanding. All human ingenuity and inventiveness would be lost when the sun ran out of helium or nitrogen or whatever, and the earth would become nothing but a cold, dark rock hurtling through space, and yet people clung to pathetic, optimistic rituals like wrapping Christmas presents and saying "Have a nice day" to each other. She knew he was right about all those things, but she wished he would be a little easier on himself. But tonight he was happy. He stood apart from the others, sipping a glass of whiskey, staring at the floor, and pretending not to be listening to what anyone was saying. But she knew he was all ears.

She considered going over to speak to him, but then she thought better of it. He would just say that the reason he wasn't socializing was Alison, not the expanding universe or the polystyrene. It was always that way. If she was in a bad mood, he would pay attention to her and be nice as could be, but whenever she looked cheerful, he would accuse her of not loving him. She did, really, but not in the way he wanted her to. When she had first moved in with him, they had been lovers, but it was disastrous—for Alison, that is. It seemed he could only feel comfortable playing the role of her savior or mentor, and he never missed a chance to belittle her work, her Midwestern background, or her naiveté. He might have been a great guidance counselor, but he was a lousy lover. Still, she looked up to him and wanted his approval, and hoped that some of his genius would rub off on her. But she knew that she had to move out of the studio soon. He had a way of looking at her that was intended to make her feel guilty, but instead made her want to slap him. And he was looking at her like that more and more as time went on.

She didn't want to give him a chance to look that way tonight. She wanted to see him the way she liked to imagine him: the tortured artist, surrounded by, yet somehow aloof from, his admirers.

She was so caught up in her thoughts that the doorbell rang three times before she heard it. She made her way through a cluster of professional mimes discussing a painting entitled "Speechless."

"You came!" she said, delighted to see Hsun-ching.

"Yes! And I brought friends! This is Mr. Sun. He came with me from China to help me find the sutra. And this is Mr. Manny. He is our new friend! He lives in a car and gave us lunch."

Alison's smile froze when she saw the colonel, dressed in his Forty-Niners jacket and sunglasses, and Manny, in his filthy fringed leather coat, bell-bottom jeans, and cowboy boots, but she did her best to remain gracious. "Please come in!" she cried.

She prayed that Hsun-ching's scruffy companions wouldn't do anything to spoil Sky's opening.

Without even glancing at any of the paintings, Manny and the colonel marched directly to the food table and started to stuff themselves, but once they had had enough to eat, Hsun-ching led them through the show. He translated the titles of the paintings for the colonel and told Manny the story of how he met Alison. When Alison joined them again, she was relieved to see that the two strangers showed genuine interest in the paintings. Manny stared at each painting for a long time, pondering aloud on the title and its meaning in relation to the "chaos into order" theme. The canvases all seemed to be breathing, he marveled.

The colonel remained convinced that there was something vital and familiar about the way Manny behaved, and he watched his reactions closely to see if he could identify what it was. Occasionally, he would poke Manny's shoulder just to see how he turned, as easily as a child, to see who had touched him, then just as easily turned back to the painting. His consciousness was fluid, like a warrior's, the colonel observed. He wanted very much to invite Manny outside for a friendly duel, to see if he could maintain that fluid state of mind in light sparring, but he remembered his headache the night before and Hsun-ching's request that there be no more fighting.

"Is the artist here?" Hsun-ching asked Alison. "We would like to congratulate him."

Alison took them to Sky, who was on his fourth whiskey and getting unsteady on his feet. "Sky," she said, "this is the guy from China I told you about. And these are two of his friends."

Sky grunted and nodded at them. "They're not ready, though," he grumbled, gesturing at the paintings with his chin. "I should have waited."

"No way," Manny interrupted. "You're out of your mind, pal. I'm telling you, I spent five years in the joint after burning my draft card, and I had a hell of a lot of time to think about things, and I'm telling you, these paintings say what it is I was thinking."

"You did five years?" asked Sky, a glimmer of interest showing in his eyes.

"Five fucking years and ten days, man."

"What are you doing now?" Sky asked.

"Now? What can I do? I lost everything because of that fucking war! I'm living in a burned-out bus on the Panhandle! I run a soup kitchen for drug addicts and drunks and all the other people that got screwed by this country, that's what! You oughta send these paintings to the White House, man, or you oughta let the people I see every day come here and see 'em. This shit speaks to people like me, man, I'm not kidding you."

"Listen—do you want some scotch?" Sky asked.

"Does a pig like shit?" Manny answered.

Sky led Manny into the kitchen, and that was the last anyone saw of them for a good while. "You see," the colonel said to Hsun-ching, "it's like I told you. Artists like poor people. It's just one of those things."

Alison was overjoyed. She couldn't thank Hsun-ching enough for bringing Manny; she'd never seen Sky take to someone so fast.

"So you're from China too?" she asked the colonel. He didn't understand her, but bowed politely. Hsun-ching explained that he didn't speak English, but offered to translate if there was anything Alison wanted to ask him.

"Well, let's see," said Alison, rubbing her cheek thoughtfully, "Okay, I have one. I notice that all the Asian people I meet through the museum look a lot younger than they are. So ask him how old he is."

Hsun-ching stiffened, then nodded slowly. He turned to the colonel. "Colonel Sun—she would like to know . . . what the name of your home village is."

"I don't remember. It was a long time ago. But it was near a huge saltwater lake. And there were lots of Mongolians living there. So I guess it was in the western part of China."

"Mr. Sun says he isn't sure, but his guess is about sixty."

"Really! That's incredible! He looks like he's in his forties to me!"

"Yes, I think so too. Even I don't believe him when he says how old he is."

Alison excused herself to check on her guests. When she returned, she brought with her an elegant, well-dressed older woman with perfectly coiffed white hair and a string of rare black pearls around her neck.

"Hsun-ching, I'd like to introduce you to someone. This is Agnes Theriault. She works at the museum, and I told her a little about you. She's been to mainland China—you were invited by the Chinese government, weren't you, Agnes?"

"Yes," said Agnes, offering her hand to Hsun-ching. She let it droop a little from the wrist, the way a dog might extend a sore paw. Hsun-ching shook it gently, noticing how it seemed to have no substance at all, except for the rings on her fingers, which held jewels the size of Asian cockroaches. "But actually, it wasn't me that the Chinese wanted to see. It was my husband. He's an art historian. We were on a group tour for academics—can't you just picture it? All these absentminded professors losing their passports and forgetting their luggage all over the place, it was such a fiasco! Maybe that's why they let us wives and husbands tag along; somebody had to remember to buy things at the Friendship Store, right? So tell me—what do you think of America so far?"

Hsun-ching was not actually looking at Alison, but he was aware of her at the edge of his vision as he answered.

"Very attractive and big. For example, your city. The buildings are clean and painted beautiful colors, and the streets are very wide but with very few people on them. Also, the fruits. I have never seen such big fruits. And what did you think of China?" he asked, although he already knew the answer to that question; she must have hated it. A wealthy, cultured woman like her— what else could she have thought?

A smile came over Agnes's face, and she gazed up dreamily into the heating ducts. "It was positively *inspiring*," she said. "The people there are so unspoiled! There's a purity to them that just—I don't know how to describe it! Do you know what happened? When we got off the train at Beijing, we got about half-way down the platform when a conductor from the train—the *nicest* man you could imagine—came running after us, positively out of breath! One of the members of our group had left behind a cheap metal teacup, and the conductor came all the way out of the train to return it to us! Where else in the world would people do that? There's such a feeling of community there. I think it's just *wonderful.*"

Hsun-ching couldn't imagine why the woman was so impressed by the conductor's behavior. If his superiors learned that he had allowed a foreigner to lose something on a Chinese train, he would probably have been forced to clean toilets for a year. Of course he was out of breath; he was terrified!

"And I can't tell you how refreshing it was to see people from all walks of life treating each other as equals," Agnes continued. "At another train station, I saw an older man in an army officer's uniform squatting on the platform, eating those little sunflower seeds they all eat right next to a group of peasants, who were eating the same thing! It was so dear! Can you imagine that happening in this country? A five-star general squatting next to a bunch of disadvantaged people, eating little seeds? It would never happen here, I can tell you."

"But people are not equal in China!" Hsun-ching protested. "The army man sits on the ground because there are no chairs on train-station platforms! But once he gets in the train, he will have a seat even though the peasants have to stand. He will eat better food, and he will get tickets when he wants, and he will pay no attention to those peasants."

Agnes raised her eyebrows and shrugged. The whole two weeks she was in China, she insisted, she never saw anyone being discriminated against, or heard a single complaint against the government. All she heard, she told Hsun-ching, were rave reviews of New China, Chairman Mao, and his Great Proletarian Cultural Revolution, not only from the tour guides but from the academics to whom they were introduced. And all the issues of *China Reconstructs* magazine, which she subscribed to after the visit, were filled with optimistic news. "Although," she admitted, "my husband did think we were being fed propaganda some of the time."

"No, not propaganda! They were telling you lies!" Hsun-ching insisted, which left Agnes somewhat confused.

"What is the old woman talking about?" asked the colonel, noticing that the conversation had become animated. Hsun-ching did his best to summarize, and the colonel burst out laughing.

"How could she say anything so ridiculous? Is the farmer equal to the emperor? Is the son equal to the father, or the wife to the husband? There are natural laws that govern relationships between people, and if those laws are violated, why, the world would dissolve into disorder! Doesn't she know that? Ask her," he demanded.

"Mr. Sun would like to know what you think of the paintings," Hsun-ching inquired.

"Well," said Agnes, lowering her voice and putting her hand near the side of her mouth to speak confidentially, "I'm afraid it's a little over my head." She smiled at Hsun-ching and the colonel and winked mischievously. Hsun-ching told the colonel that she agreed with him completely, and that winking was the way foreigners acquiesced in an argument. The colonel nodded with admiration; this was the second time today a foreigner had shown humility and character by admitting to a fault without any argument or visible resentment.

"What do you mean, over your head?" Alison asked. "There's nothing obscure about what Sky does! How can you say that, when you can appreciate that esoteric Chinese calligraphy in the museum?"

"I guess I used the wrong expression," Agnes explained. "The meaning of each painting is clear, yes, but frankly . . . it just doesn't catch my eye. For me to enjoy a piece of art, it has to reach out and grab me just by the way it looks. Even though I can't read Chinese or Japanese, the calligraphy grabs me because it's so obviously beautiful. But Sky's paintings, for the most part, are a little too . . ."

"Too ugly!" Hsun-ching offered. Agnes gave him a playful frown, but her eyes said that yes, that was exactly the word she had in mind.

"I can show you beautiful paintings," Hsun-ching told her.

"Really? Are you an artist?" she asked.

"No. But she is," he said, pointing to Alison. "I saw her paintings. They're in the back room. I like them very much."

Agnes seemed genuinely surprised to learn that Alison was an artist. Obviously, Alison did a pretty good job of keeping her vocation to herself. She promised Agnes that she would bring some paintings to the museum for her to see, then excused herself to answer the door. Hsun-ching said to Agnes, "I like your idea. I also think a painting must be beautiful."

"Well, I'm afraid you and I are what we call old-fashioned," Agnes laughed. "Alison mentioned that you are here to find a Buddhist sutra, is that right? You know, I took some Zen classes through the museum last year. We had a real Japanese Zen master come to teach us and everything. We learned how to meditate— the roshi told us to count our breaths, very slowly, up to ten without losing our concentration. It was almost impossible! I kept thinking the silliest things. I ended up quitting the class because I couldn't sit like that, with my legs folded. My feet kept falling asleep, and then I had the hardest time driving home. But it was very interesting. Are you a Buddhist?"

Hsun-ching answered that he had been raised a Buddhist, but had since then lost interest in religion.

"Just as well," said Agnes. "I think it's all a bunch of hooey myself. I think we're all just biological accidents, a split gene here, a mutated chromosome there. The best we can hope for is to be reasonably healthy and try not to get too much in each other's way. What about Mr. Sun? Is he religious?"

The modern Chinese word for religion is *tsung chiao,* which literally means "ancestral teachings," and when Hsun-ching posed the question to the colonel, the colonel frowned. Of course, he said. Who would be so foolish as to ignore the knowledge of the past? "If I was ignorant of the strategies of Sun-tzu, for example, I would have died many times on the battlefield! And if I had not been fortunate enough to study the arts of war with great masters, how would I have learned how to release my mind and let it flow like water around my enemies? This woman is fairly old herself; surely she respects what has been passed down to us from antiquity?"

"But she means, do you believe in any gods?"

"Gods? *Aiya,* that's superstition. If there were any gods, they would be on earth making us do their laundry for them."

"But, Colonel Sun, you once told me you believed in ghosts, didn't you?"

"Of course! Something has to happen to your spirit when you die! That's just common sense."

Hsun-ching paused to consider all of this, then turned to Agnes. "Mr. Sun is very unusual. His mind is full of old Chinese ideas. He believes in lots of things, but I think most of all, he believes in duty."

"Duty? What do you mean?"

"I mean, if he says he will do something for you, he does it no matter what happens. He is very strong that way. Maybe something like your Knights of the Round Table."

"Well, that's romantic!" Agnes said. "Do you suppose the knight would like some more wine? His glass is empty, I see."

The three of them made their way to the refreshment table, which Alison had set up close to the door to her room. Unaware that in the West it is considered impolite to walk into someone's room without asking permission, Hsun-ching fetched the portrait he had admired so much, and brought it out to show Agnes.

"You see?" he said. "This is much better!"

Agnes didn't have time to say anything; Alison rushed over from the opposite end of the studio and hustled the painting back into her room. Red-faced as a cooked lobster, she was too flustered to say anything to Hsun-ching, but her jaw was set with annoyance. Hsun-ching was crushed; he had thought she would be pleased. Agnes excused herself. It was late, she said, and she had to be getting back. She said farewell to the colonel and then to Hsun-ching. "By the way, you're quite right," she whispered to him. She asked Alison to see her to her car.

When Alison returned, Hsun-ching approached her, his head hung low, and apologized profusely. She stopped him in mid-apology.

"I have to admit, I was very angry at you," she said. "I don't know about China, but here you never do something like that without asking first." She looked around the room to see if Sky was nearby, then added, "But it looks like Agnes's taste in art is as shallow as yours. She says she wants to buy it. So I guess I can't stay too mad at you."

To celebrate, she wanted to take Hsun-ching and the colonel

on an outing the next day, if they were free. When Hsun-ching asked where, she wouldn't tell him. She said it was a surprise, and since Hsun-ching was the Chinese Tom Sawyer and Mr. Sun was a modern-day knight, as Agnes had told her, they shouldn't be afraid of a little adventure.

XX

HSUN-CHING'S FIRST SENSATION WAS A PRICKLY heat on his face and chest. Gradually, he became aware that it was sunlight. He had no idea where he was, and in the dreamy half-state between sleeping and waking, he decided to see how long he could go without figuring it out. At last he opened his eyes. For a moment, his delicious confusion stayed with him, and even the blankets and laundry and sun shining through the curtains made no sense at all. But then, like scattered metal filings jumping toward a magnet, the images around him leapt into order, and he remembered with a pang of anxiety that he was in the messy van with Manny and the colonel.

What am I doing here? he wondered. What will happen to me? What if the police find me and the colonel here and throw us into prison, or what if I get the sutra and return with Captain Wong only to be arrested in Hong Kong? All of a sudden the absurdity of his journey struck him like a clumsy slap in the face. All this for a worthless book? Why couldn't Wei-ching have realized long ago that religious books are all a waste of time? After all, he'd read thousands of them in his life, maybe tens of thousands, and what good had it done him? How could one more make any difference at all? If he could forget about the sutra right now and do whatever he wanted, what would he do? he wondered. Would he stay, as Alison had suggested? What did he want? These thoughts ran over and over in his mind until he was sick with worry. At last he sat upright, and slowly his head began to clear. He remembered that today Alison was going to take them on an adventure, and that cheered him up.

When Alison arrived, she found Hsun-ching and the colonel squatting on the sidewalk next to the bus. Hsun-ching apologized for Manny. Between the whiskey and some other substance Hsun-ching couldn't pronounce, Manny wasn't feeling well and had decided to stay in for the day. The colonel found it curious that Manny seemed to have lost his extraordinary concentration so suddenly. It had been his experience that soldiers who had cultivated a similar concentration never lost it, even when drunk or in pain. He had even heard of a swordsman in Japan who, on the day he died from stomach cancer, composed the following poem:

> Tightening my abdomen
> against the pain—
> The caw of a morning crow.

What a magnificent death, the colonel thought.

Alison noticed that Hsun-ching and the colonel were wearing their matching Forty-Niners jackets again.

"Are you guys into football?" she asked as they climbed into the car. Hsun-ching admitted that he didn't have any idea what the emblem on their jackets meant. "Mr. Sun insisted on having them," he explained, "because they are gold and red, the colors of the Forbidden City."

The colonel, who sat in the backseat, leaned forward to ask about the plastic Godzilla on the dashboard. "Why does she have a dead lizard placed there?" he asked.

Hsun-ching translated this question for Alison, who described the famous movie for them but then had a difficult time explaining the meaning of "retro" and "kitsch."

"I think she is saying," Hsun-ching said in Chinese as the car pulled away from the bus, "that since Americans can have beautiful, modern things whenever they want, they enjoy buying old, ugly things because it makes them laugh and feel happy."

The colonel nodded, but thought to himself that this concept must have lost something in the translation, because no one in his right mind would prefer an ugly thing to a beautiful thing.

"What does Mr. Sun do in China?" Alison asked.

"Oh . . . he was a soldier. But now he is retired."

Alison glanced at Colonel Sun in the rearview mirror. She remembered that he was supposed to be around sixty years old, but she still found it hard to believe. "Tell him to take off his sunglasses for a second," she said.

Hsun-ching passed this request on to the colonel, who hesitated, then slid the glasses off and looked at Alison in the mirror.

His eyes reminded her of the bright yellow marbles she used to play with as a child. Their color was so intense they seemed to glow as if lit from inside. She had to remind herself to watch the road to pry herself loose from his gaze.

The colonel wanted to know where they were going.

"Well," Alison said, "I told you I wanted to show you something I didn't think you could see in China. Have you ever been to an aquarium?"

Hsun-ching said that he didn't know what an aquarium was. Alison explained it briefly, then said, "But I don't want to tell you anything more about it, because I want it to be a surprise."

Hsun-ching turned to face the colonel. "It sounds like we're going to some kind of fish market."

Colonel Sun nodded without much enthusiasm; he hated fish.

WHEN HE SAW the line of people waiting to buy tickets at the entrance to the Peninsula Marine Park, Hsun-ching smiled. "There is a rumor about America that people tell in China, and now I see it isn't true."

"What rumor is that?" she asked.

"In China people say that in America there is so much food you never have to line up to buy things. There is a story that Communism, Capitalism, and Socialism decided to have lunch together one day. Communism and Capitalism were on time, but Social-ism arrived late. He said, 'I'm sorry I am late, but I had to queue up to buy a sausage. Communism said, 'What's a sausage?,' and Capitalism said, 'What's a queue?' ''

Alison laughed. "But this line isn't for food, it's for tickets."

"Oh."

"What are you talking about?" the colonel asked.

"Apparently, you have to buy tickets just to get *into* the mar-ket."

"They must have expensive fish in there," the colonel said.

Alison led them into the main building. At first they couldn't see anything; the room was pitch-black, and hushed by a sound-proofed ceiling. As their eyes adapted to the darkness, though, dim flashes of color appeared around them. Gradually, they could see that they were standing in a corridor, with rows of windows on either side. Through the windows they could see tropical fish, giant lobsters, sea horses, moray eels, and octopuses, all under water and lit by tiny spotlights.

"Come look at this!" said Alison, pointing into one of the tanks. It contained a fish that had an almost perfectly rectangular shape. "What I want to know," she asked, "is why a fish like this exists? It can't swim very well, it's ugly as sin, and it's not even poisonous. Why do you think it's shaped like this?"

Hsun-ching thought for a moment. "Maybe it's broken."

Further down the hall, a special exhibit had caught the colo-nel's attention. The tiny fish behind the glass were dull-colored and almost invisible, but when you pressed a button next to the window, the light in the tank went off and the fish glowed with their own strange, chemical light.

They have tiny flames inside! the colonel thought. While he pondered the convenience of having fish that cooked themselves, Alison and Hsun-ching moved on to the next room, where a group of plump seals flung themselves around their tank. Every once in a while one of them would surface near the balcony outdoors, where a crowd of children leaned over to watch, then slap the water hard with one of its flippers to drench the squeal-ing children.

It came as something of a revelation to Hsun-ching that ani-

mals—sea creatures, no less—did things for fun. The only animals he'd had contact with in China were raised for work or food,
and they had all seemed pretty wretched.

The other interesting thing about these animals was that many
of them reminded Hsun-ching of people. One large seal, sleeping
in the sun, looked particularly human. Hsun-ching could imagine
it wearing a Mao cap and sitting in an office, sleeping next to a
cup of tea and a stack of newspapers like the cadres he saw in
Hunan, and he started laughing out loud.

"That one is a party member!" he said.

Just then a tiny otter slid into the water and started chasing one
of the seals. It looked like a little boy trying to play with an older
brother, and it reminded Hsun-ching of Hamma.

The colonel caught up with them, and Alison led them outside.
"We're just in time to catch the noon performance," she said.

"What kind of performance?" Hsun-ching wanted to know.

"That's the big surprise."

They filed into a large outdoor stadium with a giant pool in the
center, and sat down in the front row of bleachers.

"I hope you and your friend don't mind getting wet," Alison
said.

An athletic young man with bleached-blond hair and a wire-
less microphone stepped out onto a diving board at one end of
the pool and welcomed the audience to the Peninsula Marine
Park. He wasn't sure if the star of the performance was going to
show that day, he announced. "She's been hiding somewhere
under the bleachers, and we can't get her to come out. But that's
all right, because she isn't much to look at anyway. . . ."

At that moment, a sixteen-foot, three-thousand-pound killer
whale shot straight up out of the water, righted itself at the peak
of its leap, and stuck its pink tongue out at the announcer. It fell
with its body stretched out parallel to the water in what had to
be nature's greatest belly flop, sending a massive sheet of water
out over the announcer and a good part of the audience.

Hsun-ching screamed with delight and the shock of the chilly
water, as did Alison. But the colonel did not make a sound or even
move; he just sat there with water droplets all over his eyebrows
and whiskers and his jaw slack with disbelief. In over two thou-

sand years of an eventful life, nothing he had seen or even heard of could compare with the sight of this colossal sea monster. He felt terribly vulnerable without his iron pole, but since women and children were sitting all around him bravely enjoying the show, he forced himself to stay put.

Next, the announcer threw a beach ball into the pool, which the whale balanced on its nose and threw back. Then, unbelievably, the young man put down the microphone and jumped into the pool with the beast. He disappeared underwater, and for a few seconds, the colonel thought he must have been eaten. But then the blond daredevil popped out of the water, balanced on the whale's back. He rode the whale for a whole circuit around the pool, waving at the crowd and smiling as if it were a perfectly ordinary thing to do.

Hsun-ching had never been so entertained in his life. He shouted and cheered with abandon, and clapped his hands like a child. For the finale, man and whale disappeared underwater. Twenty seconds passed, then thirty. The colonel held his breath. He imagined that the sea monster was holding the brave man under water in its terrible jaws, ripping him to pieces like a roasted squab. All of a sudden, the whale roared straight out of the water like a rocket. This time the tanned hero was crouched on the whale's snout, and at the peak of the monster's leap he sprang up, arched, and followed the whale into the water in a perfect swan dive. The colonel was overcome. Clenching his right fist and placing it in the open palm of his left hand, he rushed to the edge of the pool, knelt down, and gave the man a warrior's salute.

"*Ch'iao ye!*" he shouted in Chinese. "Unsurpassed!"

He turned to Hsun-ching, his face glowing with excitement. "Have you ever seen anything like it? A marvelous fish! An excellent fish!" he exclaimed, bowing in the direction of the whale.

FOR LUNCH THEY had hot dogs.

"Hm," the colonel said after his first bite, "this doesn't taste like dog meat to me. It tastes more like pork." He was feeling perplexed. He had insisted on meeting the whale trainer, expect-

ing him to exude an inner strength the likes of which the colonel
had not felt in many centuries, and even thought that perhaps he
would find a kindred spirit in the blue-eyed man. Ever since he'd
left China and seen how drastically the world had changed in the
last century—especially after seeing the James Bond movie—he'd
been troubled by this question: Would the men and women he
found in this new world be so extraordinary as to make him seem
merely ordinary? If so, could he find a place for himself in that
world and, for the first time, true companionship?

He had fixed his eyes on the trainer and directed his spirit
toward him, reaching out with his will to communicate in the
manner of warriors. But instead of replying to the colonel's
strength, the young man clutched his throat, turned blue in the
face, and fell coughing to the ground. The colonel felt the boy
collapse like a termite-ridden house; his mind had no foundation!
How he dominated the giant sea monster remained a mystery to
the colonel, who released the boy from his gaze and walked away
shaking his head.

When they had finished their hot dogs, Alison took them to the
water slide, an enormous steel and fiberglass structure that
twisted, turned, and roller-coastered before climaxing in a near-
vertical drop. It ended in a shallow pool, from which a group of
exhilarated children was just then wobbling back to land.

Alison insisted that they try the ride, although neither the
colonel nor Hsun-ching was enthusiastic.

"It would be a great loss of face if I were to die falling off a giant
foreign toy," the colonel said.

"It looks too dangerous," said Hsun-ching.

"It's not dangerous at all," she assured them, "and since you're
already soaking wet, you've got nothing to lose! Come on—I'll go
first and show you."

She peeled off her sweatshirt and jeans; underneath she wore
a lavender bathing suit. The sight of her so affected Hsun-ching
that he changed his mind about going on the ride. If he didn't join
her, he reasoned, she might put her clothes back on. He pulled
off his jacket and shirt and rolled up his sweatpants. Resigned,
the colonel stripped down as well.

They had to take a lift to get to the top. There, a young attendant handed each of them a square of plastic to sit on, and they took their place in line behind a group of noisy children.

Some of the children went down feetfirst, some headfirst, and some side by side to race to the bottom. When they had all pushed off, Alison said, "The best way is to sit down on the plastic with your feet pointing downward and then lie flat. That way you can slow yourself down by stretching out your arms and legs." She gave them a little salute, then pushed off. In an instant, she disappeared around a sharp curve. Hsun-ching and the colonel looked at each other.

"I'll go first," Colonel Sun said bravely. He sat down on the little plastic square and pushed off.

It was a descent into madness. He clawed at the blue trough, trying to control his speed, but it was futile. All his strength and prowess were rendered useless by the silly plastic square and the running water. Instinctively, he curled himself into a ball, which only made him pick up speed. He tumbled helplessly through a seemingly endless series of twists and turns. When he felt himself slow at last, he opened his eyes—just in time to see the edge of the final drop. His self-control burst, and he let loose a bloodcurdling scream until the slide gradually straightened out, and as gently as you could imagine, spat him into the wading pool right next to Alison. He tried to stand, but his legs were so weak he stumbled. He looked around to orient himself and saw Alison doubled over in hysterics. The noisy children who had been ahead of them were laughing and pointing at him.

Shaky with adrenaline, the colonel slowly realized that the whole point of the slide was to make you scared. His first reaction was to feel angry. But when a little boy came flying down the waterfall right behind him squealing with delight, he felt ashamed of himself for his lack of control.

At the top of the slide, Hsun-ching was letting people pass in front of him. Now that he was up so high looking down at all that rushing water, he felt as if his legs and chest were filled with lead. The ride reminded him of the waterfall in Yunnan. He closed his eyes and tried to think of something pleasant to loosen himself up a little, but it didn't work. He knew he couldn't go down the slide.

An attendant asked him if he was all right, and Hsun-ching asked if there was any other way of getting back down to the ground. The attendant led him to a stairway that looked like a fire escape. Hsun-ching descended with both hands clutching the rail, like a mountain climber rappeling down a sheer cliff. When he reached the bottom, Alison was waiting for him.

"I'm sorry," said Hsun-ching, feeling embarrassed. "I—I'm afraid of water."

Alison told him not to worry and apologized for urging him to try it. Hsun-ching looked around, but didn't see the colonel anywhere.

"Where is Mr. Sun?"

Alison grinned. "He's on the lift. I think he wanted to try it again." She and Hsun-ching took a seat on a bench facing the waterfall and waited for the colonel to come down. She leaned back and tilted her face up toward the hot sun. Tiny golden flecks in her makeup glistened on her wet face, making her look like a marble statue come to life.

"How old are you?" Hsun-ching finally asked her.

"Twenty-four. And you?"

"Almost twenty-one. But you seem older than twenty-four."

"How is that?" she asked, smiling.

"Because you are so . . . *independent*," he said. He remembered that word from the Gettysburg Address, which he'd memorized from one of the English books Wei-ching had bought him in Kun-ming.

"What makes you think I'm so independent?" she asked, a little wary. Her experience had been that "independent" meant "good" when men applied it to Third World countries, film companies, and polling agencies, but something like "stubborn" when they applied it to women.

"Because you choose your own job, make your own money, choose your own city to live in, and even choose your own car."

His answer was sobering to Alison. Independence was an attitude she didn't think she possessed. She still worried about what people thought of her, her artwork, her appearance. Sometimes she wasn't sure if she was doing things to please herself or to please other people so they would like her. But for this young man from China, independence seemed to mean being able to buy a used car when you wanted to.

"Well, I'd say you're pretty independent yourself," she remarked. "After all, not many people would travel all the way around the world without a passport."

"But this wasn't really my decision," Hsun-ching said.

"What do you mean? No one made you do it, did they?"

"No, but I did this because I should do it. It is the only thing I can do for my father, so . . . I feel that I must. You are independent because you can decide things for yourself."

"I must be missing something," she said. "Here you are in America! You could start your life from scratch here if you wanted to!"

"But," Hsun-ching admitted, "I don't know what I want."

A loud shriek from the waterfall interrupted them. They looked up just in time to see the colonel hurtle down into the wading pool, this time with his arms up over his head and his legs spread wide. He hit the deep water with a great splash, then came bounding out of the pool glowing with pride.

"Wu hu ai tsai!" he shouted in Chinese. "I have nearly mastered it!"

As he scrambled back toward the lift, Alison turned back to Hsun-ching. "The truth is, I don't know what I want either. For the longest time, I thought I just wanted to please my parents. But it didn't work out. As soon as I got old enough to pick my own clothes out, I knew I couldn't possibly wear what my parents wanted me to wear, and so on and so on."

She brought her knees to her chest and folded her arms around her shins. A narrow bracelet glittered on her right ankle, and her toenails gleamed with crimson polish. Even her pinky nails, which were each about the size of a grain of rice, looked as if a drop of fresh blood had been dropped on them. Hsun-ching imagined how small the brush must have been, and how carefully she must have painted to cover those tiny nails, and his heart filled with longing for her.

"I don't want to end up with a crappy life," she said abruptly. "Plastic furniture covers, family portraits in soft focus, Cup-a-Soup for lunch just in time to see *As the World Turns*! None of this means anything to you, but I am describing a life of sheer, un-mitigated boredom. With all the libraries and museums and zoos in Ohio, my parents would rather stay home and watch television game shows where other people win prizes! It's a waste of a lifetime is what it is, and I'll do anything to make sure it doesn't happen to me."

Hsun-ching was amazed that anyone could feel so passionately about what he perceived to be subtle differences in lifestyle. To go to the library or watch television, to be bored or excited. He didn't think it mattered much as long as you had a choice—that was the luxury he dreamed about. Still, he respected her for it. He knew that many people in China would think Alison was spoiled and ungrateful, but he didn't. If she was sitting in her parents' home and moping, he would think she was spoiled, but she was working hard, all by herself, to make her dreams come true. How many young people in China did that? Most of them lived off their parents until they were thirty, and then did what-ever their work unit told them to do, lived where they were assigned to live. If they suffered, they suffered in silence. He thought Alison was brave, and he wanted to be more like her.

"What about you?" she asked. "Are you happy with the way your life is going?"

Now it was Hsun-ching's turn to laugh. Of course he wasn't happy with the way his life was going, how could he be? His life had been terrible up to now, and would probably stay that way. But he did have his daydreams.

"What are they like?" she asked.

"It's very simple: In my dream, I have a family and some friends, and they can stay in one place together. Nothing bad happens from outside people. We can enjoy our lives day after day and not feel lonely, and have enough to eat. Then I would be happy."

"So what are you going to do about it?" Alison asked.

"What am I going to do?"

"Yes, what will you do to make it happen?"

Hsun-ching smiled to himself; in China to have such a wish come true would depend mostly on things beyond his own con-trol. But he didn't tell Alison that. He wanted her to know that he could have deep feelings too. So he imagined for the moment that he lived in his own house in America and had a job that he had chosen, like being a gardener for a rich man.

"I am going to search all over, maybe over the world, until I find who will be my wife. Then we will have a family, and I will work hard so they have lots to eat, and they will live close to me and be happy and keep me company, even when I am old."

WHEN ALISON DROPPED them off in front of the purple bus that evening, she wished them a safe journey back to China. She wrote her address once again on the back of a gum wrapper, this time along with the zip code, and handed it to Hsun-ching. "When you get back, will you send me a letter? It'd be nice to know you arrived safely, and then I'd have a Red Chinese stamp for my collection."

He promised he would. She started to drive off, but Hsun-ching ran after the car and yelled for her to stop. He waited for her to roll down her window. "I almost forgot."

"What?" she asked.

"I wanted to tell you. Out of everything I saw here, you were my favorite American thing."

Alison laughed and shut off the engine. She stepped out of the car and gave Hsun-ching a hug. He had never held a woman in his arms; his happiness was indescribable, and although he barely touched her, as if her body were just a puff of smoke, he wondered if she knew he was clinging to her for dear life. Then she kissed him good-bye, so lightly he thought he might have dreamed it.

Long after her car had disappeared, Hsun-ching stood in the same spot, trying to hold on to the sensation of her lovely arms around his back, and her lips when they touched his. He was in love with Alison, but he knew he would probably never see her again. It was as if his wish had come true—for a few moments— but as always, it had slipped from his grasp.

MANNY WAS ASLEEP when Hsun-ching and the colonel knocked on the door of the bus. He got up to let them in, looked at his watch, and then flopped back down on the mattress. "I'm late for work again," he groaned. "Fuck it. I'm not going," he decided, and covered his head with a handful of laundry. But the colonel dashed his hopes of going back to sleep. "What a magnificent park!" he effused. "Is there no limit to what Americans can do? Imagine, taming a sea monster like that! Unthinkable! And then to build a giant waterfall, not just to look at but to sit in! All purely for the sake of enjoyment!" He clicked his tongue thoughtfully. "Even though they are foreigners, I think China could learn from these people."

He nudged Hsun-ching, who hadn't heard a word he'd said. The colonel wanted to know if Manny could explain the mystery of how a weak-willed boy could control such a gigantic beast.

When Hsun-ching described to Manny what they had seen at the park and how impressed the colonel had been, Manny looked disgusted. "He liked that, did he? I'll bet he'd love Disneyland too, huh? Listen—you tell him bullshit like that is just what's wrong with this country! We have people starving all over the world while we're building nuclear weapons big enough to wipe out a whole state, we have cancer, we have people killing each other, and what do we do? Build a million-dollar slide for adults! Great! That way, everybody can forget how we're screwing the whole planet, what the hell. I can't believe you guys—you're from China, for chrissake, how can you fall for stupid stuff like that? Pretty soon the whole country will be one big Disneyland! Fake trees, fake mountains, fake plastic birds with hinged beaks that sing through little speakers in their heads, and the real animals will be gone, ground up and dried to make alligator purses, or swimming around in pools with blond guys on their backs! I thought this was just the sort of thing you people were trying to get rid of in China, man."

Hsun-ching said to the colonel, "Manny hates this park very much. He thinks it is a waste of time. He thinks Americans should spend their time and money on stopping wars, helping poor people, and things like that."

The colonel took off his sunglasses and stared at Manny. "How can he say that the fish-tamer is wasting time? The fish-tamer has accomplished a great thing, whereas this man lies around in his own garbage all day long and does nothing! How typical of a degraded man. He brings himself to poverty through his own laziness, then resents it when hardworking people seek entertainment. We should leave this place at once. I'm sure I was bitten by lice last night."

"What's he saying?" asked Manny, groping around on the floor of the bus for his aspirin bottle. He found it and popped three aspirin into his mouth and tried to swallow them without water. His mouth was so dry he couldn't get them down, though, so he opened a warm can of beer and washed them down with that.

"Mr. Sun liked the park," Hsun-ching summarized.

"Oh yeah?" Manny laughed sarcastically. "I tell you what. I'd like to invite you to dinner."

"Dinner?" Manny made the invitation sound like a challenge, so Hsun-ching wasn't sure how to respond.

"Yeah, dinner—at the soup kitchen. My treat. It'll be an education."

Hsun-ching thanked him for the dinner offer, but declined. He was too distracted to eat.

"What about Sun?" asked Manny, pulling his jeans on while still lying down. "He doesn't need to understand English to get the picture."

MANNY'S JOB WAS helping to prepare the meals at the Downtown Soup Kitchen, which was located in a huge, unfinished church basement. Manny gave the colonel a paper plate and a cup and took him through the food line, then led him over to a long folding table and sat him next to an elderly Asian man. "Enjoy your dinner." To the colonel, it looked like an opium den: old people who shuffled along, staring vacantly at nothing in particular, a tired-looking woman with three ragged little children, young men with bloodshot eyes, ravaged skin, and matted hair hunched over polystyrene coffee cups who nodded to each other and hardly spoke.

The colonel turned to the old man sitting next to him. He brought each spoonful of vegetable soup to his mouth deliberately, as if it took all of his concentration to keep his trembling hand on course.

"Aren't you Chinese?" the colonel asked.

"Mm," the old man grunted.

"What are you doing in this place?" the colonel sneered. "You're Chinese! Don't you have any sense of shame?"

The old man seemed to pause for a second, but didn't look up from his bowl. The colonel grabbed him roughly by the collar of his filthy sweater. "Opium nearly destroyed our country! Everyone knows that! You shame China with your weakness!"

The old man turned slowly and glared at the colonel with eyes fogged over with cataracts. "What the hell are you talking about? There's no opium in here," he growled in a heavy Toisan dialect. His voice was gravelly with cigarettes, but his speech was perfectly coherent. Opium addicts didn't talk like that, the colonel realized. He let go of the man's collar. "What are you doing here, then, with all these foreign drunks?" he asked.

"The same thing you're doing here, getting something to eat! Why don't you mind your own damn business!"

"I was invited here," the colonel said haughtily.

"Yeah, by who? A social worker? *Hou sau*," the old man snapped, then returned to his soup. Confused, the colonel watched a girl of not more than fifteen join the tired-looking mother at a nearby table. The girl was alert and animated as she told some sort of joke to the children. The colonel didn't know what to make of it; only some of the people looked like drunks, actually, and none of them seemed to be drinking anything but water or that dark, bitter-smelling tea, so this couldn't be a wine house. The only thing they all seemed to have in common was their appetites and their shabby clothes.

"What is this place?" he asked his companion. "Some kind of shelter for criminals?"

The old man dropped his spoon with a clang. He turned to the colonel angrily and rasped, "What are you, stupid or something? This is a place where people who got no money can get some hot food! Even a kid could figure that out. Now shut up and eat."

The colonel wasn't used to being talked to that way, but he didn't get angry. He was intrigued by the old man; usually people reduced to charity shrank and groveled in the presence of self-sufficient men, but this old gentleman seemed not only unashamed but indignant.

"All right," the colonel said amiably. "I apologize for my rudeness. I arrived in this country only two days ago, so everything is still unfamiliar to me."

"Where'd you come from?" the old man asked curtly.

"China."

The old man shook his head in disgust. "No wonder you don't know shit about anything, then," he grumbled, then he picked up his bowl and started to leave. The colonel pulled him back. "What is that supposed to mean?" he asked.

"Communism killed our country," said the old man, jabbing a shaking finger at the colonel. "Look at you, proud as can be, making fun of an old man! You're all the same! You come crawling out of China, begging for us overseas Chinese to help you out, and when you get here, what do you do? Nothing, that's what! You're all too lazy to work! You don't know what work means! All you can do is complain! And you soak up the worst of your new country in no time at all—look at you! Look at those stupid sunglasses—thugs wear those! And your jacket! You look like a foreign gangster!"

The colonel stood up slowly and took off the sunglasses. He took off the jacket, too, revealing his suit of ancient armor. The old man squinted. When he looked into the stranger's yellow eyes, he felt a tingling sensation in his chest, and his heart began to beat wildly.

"You disgrace your country with talk like that," the colonel said quietly. He put his hands on the table and leaned toward the old man, who seemed to shrink under his gaze. "Now you tell me, old man: You accuse me of not knowing how to work, but here you are in a beggar's tavern eating other people's food! Who are you to accuse anyone of laziness?"

The old man was terrified, but he was no weakling. He drew himself up and returned the colonel's gaze. "I worked all my life, harder than you can imagine, and now I have nothing. I have no choice but to come here for food."

The colonel was impressed. Even the brave young monster-tamer had withered under his gaze, but this frail old man found the will to stand up to him. Now here was a man of character.

"Why aren't you eating at home? What's happened to you?"

"I have no home!" the old man hurled back. "It was torn down! And now that I'm going blind, I cannot work."

"What about your family? Why aren't they taking care of you?"

"Family? What family? I don't have one. It wasn't allowed."

Slowly, he told the colonel his story. His name was Wong Shek-kin, and he was born in 1896 in Toisan village, Kwangtung Province. He was married in 1920. Shortly after, a rare opportunity presented itself. A distant relative who lived in America returned to the village with the sad news that his young nephew, who had been born in America and was an American citizen, had died of influenza. He offered to take Shek-kin back with him, posing as the nephew. Gruesome as it seemed, that was one of the few ways a Chinese person could get to America at the time. Shek-kin decided it was a golden chance to make a fortune in "Gold Mountain," and escape from China's famine and civil war. Once he was established, he promised himself, he would send for his wife.

His plans failed, however. The only work he could find was as a cook in Chinatown, which paid almost nothing. Still, he sent every penny of his savings back to his wife so that she could purchase a ticket on a steamer as soon as he had cleared the way for her passage. In 1921, however, Congress passed an Immigration Act to keep "undesirable elements" from becoming citizens. That included alien-born women, even if their husbands were already American citizens. But Shek-kin kept his hopes alive, and after three years had saved up enough to hire a lawyer to examine his case. After taking all of Shek-kin's money, the lawyer regretfully announced that Congress had just passed yet another Immigration Act, which made it impossible for any "aliens ineligible for citizenship"—meaning primarily Asians—even to visit the United States. After that, all hope was lost. But Shek-kin continued to send most of his savings to his wife and fellow villagers in China for the duration of his working life.

Shek-kin was not alone. In the twenties, Chinese-American men outnumbered Chinese-American women twenty-five to one. Thousands upon thousands of lonely men like him toiled their lives away in kitchens and sweatshops in Chinatown, unable to marry or to send for their wives. It would have been suicide to return to China during the war with Japan, and when the Communists took over, Shek-kin heard that many of his fellow villagers were killed or imprisoned because they had relatives abroad. His wife pleaded with him to stay in America, where he would be safe. She died in 1974, about the same time Shek-kin had to stop working because of his failing eyesight.

He had almost no savings, since he had sent most of his money home, and no pension. He was able to earn a few dollars a day tending a newsstand in Chinatown, enough for a cheap room in the International Hotel, where many elderly Asians like himself lived out their last years. In August 1977, in the middle of the night, hired strongmen threw all the inhabitants of the hotel out on the streets so that it could be torn down to make way for a commercial building. The owners of the property couldn't decide what sort of building, though, so it stayed an empty lot while many of the hotel's former tenants were forced to sleep in the streets.

After Wong Shek-kin had told the colonel his story, he picked up his soup bowl and returned it to the counter, then shuffled up the stairs and out of the church basement. Later that night, when he curled up to sleep in the heated doorway he had found in a downtown building, he would discover a hard lump in his pocket. At first he would think it was a stone, but on closer examination he would see that it was a tarnished bar of gold stamped with the imperial seal of the Sung treasury.

WHEN MANNY AND the colonel returned to the bus, Hsun-ching was still awake. Manny was eager to know what the colonel thought after seeing all those poor people who had been tossed away by society like garbage. The colonel did not want to talk about that, however. He wanted to know how much Manny was paid to feed the poor people.

"Paid?" Manny asked, "I don't get paid for that! I just get the food, that's all."

So how did he survive? the colonel wanted to know. By selling marijuana, Manny replied. He lit a joint and offered it to Hsun-ching and the colonel. The colonel recognized the smell from the time he had spent in India. "That's a kind of opium he's smoking," he told Hsun-ching. "Don't go near it. It makes you dizzy and confused."

So Manny smoked alone. "Listen, buddy," he said to Hsun-ching, "I want you to tell your friend something. I threw my life in the toilet when I burned my draft card. I went to jail, and now I can't get a job, and I hate living in this stupid bus. But I don't regret it one bit, because at least I didn't kill anybody. Your friend may think I'm a dope-smoking bum, but he didn't have to throw everything away just to do the right thing. I don't care what he thinks. Tell him that."

Hsun-ching related the gist of Manny's speech, and the colonel grinned. "He is drunk now. Let's not make him upset. Tell him I admire him for helping those unfortunate people."

Manny seemed pleased, and smoked in peace until he fell asleep. The colonel said to Hsun-ching, "I have gained knowledge by coming with you on this journey. This man," he said, pointing to the snoring Manny, whose beard was bent upward by the edge of his sleeping bag so it covered his face, "is not a coward like he said yesterday. I was mistaken. He is loyal to poor people like himself, and I am now inclined to think that he was brave to defy the army the way he did, even though he committed treason. As he said, he sacrificed himself to do what he thought was right. Unfortunately, he has paid the price. Look at him now—isn't it sad? He will probably never recover. Opium and wine and self-pity will sap his courage, and then he will be just like the people he is trying to help. How sad."

The colonel contemplated Manny for a while in silence, then said, "I have seen enough of this country. We must find the sutra first thing tomorrow morning, then make our way toward the docks before nightfall. I want to be near that dock all night, so there is no chance we will miss that boat in the morning. There are wonderful things to see here, but terrible things as well. I could not live here. I met a man tonight who had a will of iron and a pure heart; a true man of character. But he was defeated! Ground into nothing by stupid ideas enforced by stupid people! In any civilized country, his devotion to his wife and home village would have been recognized and rewarded, but here he was tortured for a lifetime. He was pulled from his home in the night so that the landlord could tear it down—can you imagine such treachery? These people may be able to send their people through the sky on giant flaming arrows, tame the beasts from the four oceans, and defy their own armies to defend their own individual beliefs, but they fail to recognize the most important human quality of all, the one that means the most to us when we face our inevitable deaths. Dignity."

"But, Colonel Sun, people don't reward that quality in China, either. At least not nowadays."

The colonel sighed and squatted down next to the warm stove. "Maybe you're right," he said. "But at least I don't get headaches there."

XXI

"THIS DRINK IS TOO SWEET," THE COLONEL COM-
plained after trying Miranda's herb tea. "It is
suitable for hummingbirds, not for men."

Hsun-ching silently nodded his agreement, and waited anxiously for Miranda to
get to the Laughing Sutra. Everything had
gone well so far; there was only one embar-
rassing hitch, when Miranda led them
through the lobby and the colonel passed by
the fountain. He nearly didn't make it to the
bathroom in time.

Miranda sat down on her little cushion,
tilted her head to one side, and blinked her
eyes compassionately. "I am *really* sorry," she
said, "I was just *totally* off base when I told
you Mahavishnu would have more time
today. I completely forgot he had a visitor
coming today."

"But I can still see the sutra?" Hsun-ching
asked hopefully.

Miranda winced faintly, then smiled.
"Well, I asked him, but, see, it's hard because
it's in the basement with all sorts of other
stuff, and only Mahavishnu really knows
what's what down there. It would take him
days to find it, it sounds like. And he just
doesn't have the time."

Hsun-ching's face went pale. The colonel noticed and asked what was going on. When Hsun-ching replied that it seemed the head monk of the temple had refused their request for the sutra, the colonel set his jaw. "We must take this woman prisoner and demand the sutra as ransom," he proclaimed.

Hsun-ching suppressed an urge to panic. He didn't want any part of the colonel's feudal military operations, and besides, he reminded the colonel, someone would summon the police, and then they would surely miss the boat home. The colonel maintained that if he could get past Shih-huang Ti's private army and walk away with the emperor's armor, it couldn't be hard to steal a dusty scroll from a bunch of pale-skinned weaklings. He was anxious to get the sutra business over with as soon as possible; his headache was getting worse.

Hsun-ching pleaded with Miranda. "We came all the way from China! Can't your leader can just talk to us? You promised! Tell him we can pay for it in gold!"

Miranda was sorry, but once Mahavishnu made up his mind over something, there really wasn't any room for discussion. Just then the limousine Hsun-ching had seen at the institute three days before pulled up outside. Miranda looked distracted.

"Excuse me," she said. "I'll just be a minute." Hsun-ching and the colonel watched from the doorway as two ascetically slender men glided past them down the hallway to greet the arriving guest. The shorter of the two had taut, shiny skin and thin black hair combed straight back. He had no eyebrows or eyelashes, apparently the result of a burn, giving his dark eyes an unnerving vacant expression. He walked without any movement in his shoulders, as if he didn't want to aggravate a stiff neck.

The other man was elegant, white-haired, and tanned, and looked completely at ease. He was dressed exquisitely, in soft leather shoes without socks, white cotton pants, a tan crew-neck shirt, and a silk sports jacket the color of the ocean. When the door of the limousine opened, the white-haired fellow pressed his palms together and bowed his head. *"Namaste."*

The visitor emerged from the limousine and returned the gesture. Hsun-ching was surprised to see that he was short, had unkempt hair, and wore blue jeans and a rumpled gray sweatshirt. Only his easy manner suggested that he was an important man.

Hsun-ching decided to take a chance. "Mr. Corman?" he called.

The white-haired man turned slowly, still smiling. The black-haired man stiffened and moved cautiously to the side and a little bit in front of the white-haired man, as if to shield him if necessary.

"I came from China to see you!" Hsun-ching shouted. "Please, I must speak with you!"

Corman exchanged a quick glance with the black-haired man. "Why did you want to see me?" he asked calmly.

"You have a Buddhist sutra—it used to be in the museum—I came from China to see it! Please—then I will go back to China! That is my only wish!"

Corman was very sorry, but the Dharma Institute was an organization for spiritual research, not an antique gallery. He thought he had made that clear to Miranda, he said. The visitor interrupted. "Hey, if the guy came all the way from China to see a sutra, I think he ought to be able to see it, don't you? That's the longest pilgrimage I ever heard of."

Mahavishnu Bob Corman smiled thinly. "We'll certainly arrange for him to see the sutra. But we'll need time," he said to Hsun-ching. "We're not prepared for a visit today."

Hsun-ching stepped forward, trying to explain why he was in such a rush. Quickly, the black-haired man stepped between him and Corman, indicating that Hsun-ching should come no closer. Just as quickly, the colonel stepped between Hsun-ching and the black-haired man.

"Excuse me," the visitor said, looking closely at the colonel. "Are you Tibetan?" The sect of Buddhism to which he currently swore allegiance had its spiritual base in Tibet, and he had been trying for several months to locate an authentic Tibetan holy man whom he could lure to the West. Although he had never seen a real Tibetan monk, he had heard that they looked somewhat wild and untainted by "civilization." Colonel Sun, with his hairy face, long fingernails, and strange armor, fit that description pretty well.

Before Hsun-ching could answer on the colonel's behalf, the visitor said, *"Ku-sho-ku-su de-pa yo-pe?"*

Colonel Sun looked surprised. *"La au-tse yo. Ku-sho ku-su de-pa yo-pe?"* he responded.

"Sorry—that's the only sentence I know!" the visitor blurted out. "Hey, Mahavishnu—this is a Tibetan!" He pressed his palms together and bowed his head toward the colonel, who looked confused.

"How come that foreigner speaks Tibetan?" the colonel asked Hsun-ching.

"I don't know—how come you speak Tibetan?"

"I don't," the colonel answered, "I just know that one sentence. Tibetans say that to each other when they meet."

"Why didn't you say you were from Tibet?" said the Mahavishnu. "I am a great admirer of the Dalai Lama. I met him in India, as a matter of fact. He is a very holy man."

Hsun-ching didn't know what to make of all this, but he came to the conclusion that he had a much better chance of getting to the sutra as a Tibetan than as a Chinese.

"Why don't you have some tea with us in my office?" Corman asked, gesturing toward the stairway. "Let me introduce you. This is Jeremy Thorp," he said, pointing to the visitor. "He is an American film star, and he is also my student. He has been practicing Tibetan Buddhism for several months now."

Thorp bowed again, and this time Hsun-ching returned the greeting. The Mahavishnu pointed to the black-haired man. "This is Vajrapani. He is also my student, and my chief assistant here at the institute." Vajrapani nodded slightly, but he did not look at ease. "And now, why don't you tell us who you are?" Corman asked Hsun-ching.

"I am Hsun-ching, and this is Mr. Sun," he answered.

Corman smiled, but his eyes narrowed slightly. "But those sound like Chinese names, not Tibetan names," he observed.

"Ch-Ch-China controls Tibet," Hsun-ching said, beginning to stutter, "so we must learn Chinese in school. We have to have Chinese n-names."

"That's got to stop," Thorp said, disgusted. "Tibet should be an independent state! It's ridiculous that the Dalai Lama is in exile. He belongs in Lhasa."

"This is a spiritual sanctuary," Corman gently reminded them. "We leave political and material concerns outside the gate." He led them into his stark, cavernous office and motioned to the rows of little black pillows facing his desk. "Please be seated."

"I founded this institute in 1966," Corman began to explain to Hsun-ching. He paused and gestured to Miranda, who gave a start as if waking from a daydream and hurried out the door to fetch more tea. "That was a terrible year for America," Corman continued. "The whole country was shaken by violence and confusion. Perhaps it was something like China's Cultural Revolution."

Hsun-ching shuddered at the mention of that phrase; the English words seemed to give the awful event new life. This was the first he had heard of the United States suffering a similar period of calamity.

"It was inevitable, though," Corman continued. "Western civilization had reached a crisis point. We followed the path of materialism, and it led us to a dead end." He paused and daintily removed a peach-colored rose from the black vase on his black desk. He looked at it gratefully, sniffed at it, then returned it to the vase as if he were setting it free. "Did you know that if you sniff a rose for more than five minutes, you will no longer smell its fragrance?" he asked. "That is where Western civilization led us. We grasped at the material world, at our mechanistic theories of life, at our vain hope that physical comfort, wealth, and life insurance would bring us peace of mind—and do you know what happened?"

He smiled gently at Hsun-ching, but his eyes were afire with evangelical zeal.

"What happened?" Hsun-ching asked.

"We couldn't feel life anymore! We became numb to it! So we became desperate, trying to squeeze meaning and pleasure out of life. We needed bigger houses, more sex, longer vacations, and more powerful drugs to feel alive! And the more desperately we grasped at life, the more it slipped through our fingers."

"We were on a collision course with ourselves," Jeremy Thorp added solemnly.

"In the 1960s," Corman continued, "the younger generation sensed this dilemma, and abandoned the values of Western civilization. But they did not know what to replace those values with! They sensed a need for a spiritual life, but they did not have the discipline or knowledge to distinguish between what is spiritual and what is merely sensual. As a result, young people are rushing back toward materialism with a vengeance. I predict that by the 1980s, a whole generation of gluttons and cynics will have emerged."

Miranda returned with a bowl of fruit and a tray. She handed each of them a cup and a teabag. Hsun-ching looked at the little pouch uncertainly.

"It's tea!" Corman said. "You just put it in the cup, and I'll pour you some water."

Hsun-ching sniffed the bag, then apologized for his stupidity. He ripped it open and poured the leaves into his cup.

While Corman poured for the others, the colonel whispered to Hsun-ching, "This man is the abbot of his temple, and yet he pours for a couple of strangers. There is a saying: 'If a general massages the sore feet of his lowly scouts, he is either brilliant or foolish, but in either case dangerous.' Something seems strange about this man; he doesn't seem like a regular priest. And his assistant, the one with no eyebrows—something seems wrong about him too. I have a bad feeling about this place."

Corman resumed his brief history of the Dharma Institute:

"I have devoted most of my life to the task of—how shall I put it?—bridging the gap between the material and spiritual world. But in the 1960s, I realized that this could no longer remain a personal quest. So I founded the Dharma Institute, a place where spiritually advanced men and women could meet and work together. We are building a new spiritual foundation for Western civilization, taking what we can from Asian philosophy and applying it to Western life."

"Tibet's the key, though," Jeremy Thorp said, nodding conspiratorially toward Hsun-ching.

Corman smiled stiffly. "Jeremy is convinced that Tibetan Bud-

plain. "The information in the sutra belongs to everyone." He stood up and brushed the front of his immaculate blue jacket. "Why don't we move over to the next room, where we have our library, and have a look at something first?"

He led them across the giant room and into a smaller but equally beautiful room. Like Corman's office, the library had sliding-glass doors leading out to a balcony, black cushions on the floor, and a single teak desk in the middle of the room. Its walls, however, were covered from floor to ceiling with Korean wooden cabinets and dark ebony bookshelves. Corman leafed through a catalog on one of the shelves, put on a pair of silk gloves, then opened one of the cabinets. He took out a long, narrow box and carried it over to the desk, then sat down with his back to the ocean.

"Why don't you have a seat?" Corman suggested. Hsun-ching and Jeremy Thorp sat opposite him at the desk, but Vajrapani and the colonel remained standing. The Mahavishnu opened the box and took out a long cloth bag. He untied the bag and carefully pulled out a silk scroll, brown with age and crumbling at the edges. He laid down on the desk facing Hsun-ching and slowly unrolled about two feet of it. To Hsun-ching's dismay, it was not the Laughing Sutra; whatever it was, it wasn't written in Sanskrit or Chinese.

"What is this?" Hsun-ching asked nervously.

"I was going to ask you," answered Corman, glancing at Vajrapani. "It's Tibetan. I was hoping maybe you could translate it for me."

Hsun-ching realized he was in trouble. He asked the colonel if he had any idea what the writing said, but the colonel shook his head. "I already told you. I never learned to read, much less a language used by savages. Fake it—after all, how will the foreigners know the difference?"

Hsun-ching chewed on his lip and tried to look as if he was concentrating on the text. "This is a book about Buddha," he began, running his finger over the characters as if he were reading them. "It starts with his life as a prince."

Without a word, Corman rolled the scroll up and put it in its box. "Wrong," he said. "This is the *Tibetan Book of the Dead*. Any Tibetan would recognize it. And I'll tell you why I had a feeling

dhism is the most advanced of all spiritual traditions. He is very anxious to invite a Tibetan lama to the institute. Perhaps you can help us."

Behind Corman a pair of spotless sliding glass doors allowed a breathtaking view of the Pacific, glazed with sunlight and slanting dramatically up toward the horizon. Only a single, gnarled pine tree interrupted the view of sky and water. The scene had a profound calming effect on Hsun-ching. His quest was nearly over, he realized; soon he could go home. Then some movement in his field of vision jarred him out of his reverie.

He looked around him. Miranda and Corman were sitting on the cushions with their legs crossed and backs perfectly straight, in what the Buddhists call a full-lotus position. Only years of practice made that posture a natural one, and how easily one sat that way was a fairly reliable gauge of one's efforts at meditation.

The colonel had planted himself in his usual half-kneeling position, sitting on his left calf and crossing his arms over his raised right knee. That way, he had once explained to Hsun-ching, one could be relaxed but also prepared to leap forward if necessary. He had become accustomed to sitting that way when, as a young soldier, he frequently accompanied important generals to banquets. Such men were especially vulnerable to assassination attempts during festive occasions.

Vajrapani had been in a lotus position, but now he was kneeling like the colonel. He gazed down at the floor, but it was obvious that his attention was strongly focused on Colonel Sun.

Meanwhile, Mahavishnu Bob Corman had concluded his speech. "We're very lucky to have generous benefactors like Jeremy; surroundings like this make our work much easier."

Thorp looked at Hsun-ching. "You can't reach *satori* in an apartment downtown. You Tibetans know that better than anyone—that's why you're living in the highest mountains in the world, right?"

"*Satori?*" Hsun-ching asked.

"You don't know what *satori* is?"

"*Satori* is the Japanese pronunciation of a Chinese character," Corman said. "I'm not sure how you pronounce it in Chinese, but it's written like this."

He raised his finger into the air and drew an invisible character. Hsun-ching recognized it right away. "Oh—we say *wu.* It means . . . I don't know the English word, but something like 'to wake up.'"

"Precisely," Corman said. "The English word is 'enlightenment.' The sudden awakening of the spirit, the moment when rational thought gives way to intuitive understanding, the release from the endless karmic cycle of birth and death! In other words," he said, brushing his hand slowly over the polished surface of his desk, "immortality."

Hsun-ching knew that word; it was one of the first English words Wei-ching had taught him. Wei-ching, after all, had spent most of his life trying to figure out what immortality really meant. He had also spent most of his life believing that the Laughing Sutra, which Corman had tucked away somewhere in this building, contained the answer.

"Do you believe in immortality?" Hsun-ching asked Corman. The Mahavishnu continued to brush his open palm across the desk, as if it were a giant rosary bead.

"Yes, I do. That is what my . . . our work is all about."

Suddenly, Corman lifted his hand from the desk. It was a tiny gesture, but Hsun-ching felt it in his stomach as if an electric current had been broken. "But what about you?" Corman asked. "Tell us more! You say you came all the way from Tibet to look at one sutra in our collection. Do you mind if I ask why?"

Hsun-ching thought for a moment. "Since you know Chinese characters, I will show you something." He traced two invisible characters in the air. Corman frowned in concentration, then imitated the strokes.

"To look for a scripture," he said.

"Yes," Hsun-ching said. "In Chinese, those characters are pronounced 'hsun' and 'ching.' Those are the characters of my name. Now I will show you two more."

He drew two more invisible characters in the air. Corman concentrated again, then shook his head. "The second character is scripture again, but I don't recognize the first."

"The first is pronounced 'wei,'" Hsun-ching said. "It means to protect. That is the name of my . . . father. 'Protector of Scrip-

tures.' He believes he must protect Buddhist sutras, because they are being lost. He has collected and made copies of almost all of them. But there is one sutra that he cannot find. That is why he named me Hsun-ching; he wanted me to look for it."

"And which sutra is that?" Corman asked.

"It is called the Laughing Sutra. The T'ang dynasty monk Hsüan-tsang carried it, with many other sutras, from India to China more than one thousand years ago. He stored them in a cave in Kansu Province."

"Oh?"

"Yes. When Wei-ching traveled there to see them, the people who live there said that foreigners had stolen most of them. They said that one of them was called the Laughing Sutra, and it was about immortality. That one disappeared after John Volland visited the caves."

Corman shifted on his cushion. "Yes, I remember John talking about the Tun-huang caves. But he didn't *steal* any sutras from there," he announced, putting his teacup down and leaning forward. "He bought them. Frankly, I'm getting tired of hearing the Chinese government complain that their art treasures were 'stolen' by Westerners. If Volland hadn't bought a lot of that art and put it in good museums all over the world, most of it would have been destroyed during the Cultural Revolution. Isn't that true?"

"That isn't important to me," Hsun-ching answered quickly. He didn't want to get Corman angry, not when he was so close to accomplishing his goal. "All I want is to buy this sutra from you and bring it back to my father. I will pay you more than it is worth."

This offer caught Corman by surprise; he looked at Hsun-ching suspiciously for a few seconds. "How much were you thinking of?"

"You tell me a price. If I have enough money, I will give it to you."

Jeremy Thorp, whose back was aching fiercely now, squirmed on his cushion and said, "Don't let me interrupt or anything, but is it customary to bargain over sacred books?"

The Mahavishnu evidently did not want to upset Jeremy Thorp. "Oh no, don't misunderstand me," he hastened to ex-

you wouldn't recognize it," he said, explaining for Jeremy Thorp's sake. "No real Tibetan would offer money for a sutra. No way."

Hsun-ching opened his mouth to explain why he had lied, but no sound came out. The words were jammed up tight in his throat; it looked as if he were choking.

Vajrapani had put one hand inside his corduroy jacket threateningly; with the other he grasped Hsun-ching by the collar and pushed him toward the colonel.

"What exactly is our situation?" the colonel asked Hsun-ching. His voice sounded relaxed, almost sleepy, but his body was tensed like a coiled spring. Hsun-ching couldn't answer, but gestured with his hands that the colonel should do nothing. The colonel stayed put, but took off his sunglasses and fixed his blazing yellow eyes on Vajrapani. His upper lip twitched, then pulled back in a sneer that revealed his wolflike teeth.

"Whoa!" Jeremy Thorp gasped. The Mahavishnu's face turned pale, and Vajrapani seemed to be on the verge of panic. Miranda gasped and slumped off her cushion in a dead faint.

There was a long, tense silence. At last Corman pointed ominously at Hsun-ching. "You and your friend are going to leave now, and you are not going to come back! I am a forgiving man, but I don't like liars, and I won't be so lenient next time! Now, Vajrapani—would you mind seeing them to the door?"

"IF I HADN'T l-l-lied about us being Tibetan, this wouldn't have happened," Hsun-ching cursed. He and the colonel had made their way down a steep path to the ocean. The colonel was combing the beach for smooth, round stones. When he found one about the size of a large egg, he put it carefully into one of the many pockets in his armor.

"The lie got us into the priest's office," the colonel argued. "That was all it needed to do. But by hesitating just then, and not allowing me to take action when the opportunity presented itself, you may well have spoiled your chances of returning to China with the sutra."

"What could we have d-d-done?" Hsun-ching gasped.

"It would have been simple. Our only danger was the guard with no eyebrows. If I had removed that danger, the priest would have been frightened and given us the sutra. Then we could have escaped."

"B-but I told you! I don't want to hurt anyone! It's not worth it, for some old book!"

The colonel sighed. "As you wish. But now you will see how wrong you are, because now the priest and his guard will be more alert. They will be ready for us. To get back in there will be very dangerous, and it is likely that not only the guard will be hurt."

"No one's going to get hurt," Hsun-ching said darkly.

"Oh, but I think it is inevitable! The only way we can get the sutra now is by breaking into the temple. I think we can climb up the side of it and get in through the roof. There was a window up there. Then, since the guard will undoubtedly detect us, I will have to use one of these stones on him, otherwise he will have time to remove that gun from his jacket, and then we would be finished. With all that going on, the priest may have time to call the police, so we may have to cope with them as well. It will be much more difficult this way. If you had paid attention to the things I have told you these last weeks, you would not have weakened just then. But you didn't listen, and now you will see for yourself how terrible the consequences of indecision can be!"

The colonel collected another couple of stones. "I am ready," he announced. But Hsun-ching was looking out across the water, and didn't seem to hear him.

"What's the matter with you?" the colonel shouted. He grasped Hsun-ching by the shoulders and shook him, as if waking him up. "This is the critical moment of your journey! Don't falter now! Get control of yourself and prepare for your struggle! Otherwise you will kill us both."

Hsun-ching closed his eyes for a moment. "Colonel Sun. Please forgive me. I'm not going to get the sutra."

"What?"

"I don't want to get killed. I don't want you to get killed, either."

The colonel looked stunned. "You mean, after all this, after coming all this way, you would dare go back empty-handed?"

Hsun-ching shook his head slowly. "No. I'm not going back. I'm staying here."

XXII

"ARENT GOING BACK?" THE COLONEL ASKED. "Aren't going back where?"

"To China. I'm not going back there. I want to stay here," Hsun-ching answered. He couldn't bring himself to look at the colonel.

For the first time Hsun-ching could remember, the colonel blinked. "How can you not go back?"

Hsun-ching pulled his fingers through his hair roughly, and avoided the colonel's gaze. "Why should I go back?" he blurted out. "I've never been able to enjoy anything without having it taken away from me! My whole life has been miserable in that country, the same as Wei-ching! Why should I return to it? Now I have a chance to start a new life— my own life, for a change! I'm twenty years old, don't I deserve that?"

"Your own life?" the colonel asked. "How has your life not been your own? Who possessed it up until now?"

"Ai, that's not what I mean . . . no one possessed my life, but other people controlled it. Someone made me an orphan, then someone else dragged me into an insane 'revolution,' then someone else sent me to the countryside for ten years, and now I'm supposed to go all the way back to that nightmare just to tell poor Wei-ching that I couldn't get his book for him? Is that—"

"You can get it!" the colonel interrupted. "I have collected all the tools we will need."

Hsun-ching turned away, wringing his hands in frustration. "Even if I could get the sutra, I still wouldn't go back! The book is worthless—Wei-ching is dying and I can't cure him, and neither can any mystical formula. You know that as well as I do."

"You knew that before you left China," the colonel argued. "The value of the book never had anything to do with it."

Hsun-ching turned around, and this time looked the colonel right in the eye. "I love him like a father—you know I do! He's the only father I've ever known! But don't you think he would want me to stay?"

Colonel Sun didn't reply. He just stared evenly at Hsun-ching.

"Well, don't you?" Hsun-ching pleaded. "I have a chance to be happy here—don't you think Wei-ching would want me to stay here?"

"If you asked him, he would probably tell you to stay, yes."

"Then why are you staring at me that way—as if I'm doing something terrible?"

"Because you promised you would get the sutra and bring it back for him."

"All right, I did—but maybe it was a foolish promise!"

The colonel shook his head. "That isn't important. When you make a promise, you carry it out, regardless of how foolish it may seem."

"But that's so stupid!" Hsun-ching suddenly shouted. "That's a stubborn, old-fashioned, dumb thing to say! Why should you do something if you realize it isn't the best thing to do?"

"Because that is what a loyal man does," the colonel answered patiently.

"A *loyal* man? What happened when those three loyal men you told me about made a promise in a peach garden? A dynasty fell, and hundreds of thousands of people died in the wars that followed! It was a disaster! How can you tell me now that loyalty is so precious?"

The colonel fell silent for a long moment. It appeared that he could not, or would not, answer the question. Then he stood up a little straighter, looked at Hsun-ching, and said quietly, "Maybe it is because loyalty is the only sort of beauty a man like me can hope to possess."

When Hsun-ching made no response, the colonel nodded, then faced the ocean. "Your mind is made up, then?"

"Yes."

"Then there's no point in my staying here longer. I must get back to the dock as soon as possible." He saluted Hsun-ching in the ancient manner. "I wish you better luck on this side of the world than you had on the other." He turned and started walking north, toward the bay.

"Colonel Sun," Hsun-ching said, "please don't be angry with me."

The colonel looked back at Hsun-ching. "I'm not angry with you," he said. "But the only reason I am here and not closer to the boat is that I assumed you wanted to get the sutra, at all costs. And I promised to help you. Since you have changed your plans, it is time for us to say farewell."

"But, Colonel Sun, why don't you stay here with me? Things could be different for you here; there are a million things you could do here, instead of sitting by yourself—"

"I would rather sit by myself," the colonel interrupted, "than be surrounded by ugliness. From what I have seen, this country has no soul. It has only appearance."

Hsun-ching began to follow him up the path toward the city. Without stopping or turning, the colonel laughed and said, "We're old friends now, you don't have to be polite with me. You've walked me far enough."

Hsun-ching hung his head. "Thank you for all you did for me."

"No need to thank me. Good-bye, Hsun-ching."

As the colonel walked out of sight, Hsun-ching realized that that was the only time he had ever called him by name. He went back down to the ocean, lay down on the beach, and began to think.

He imagined returning to China to find Wei-ching lying on his poor cot, struggling for breath, and then telling him, "I found the sutra, but could not take possession of it." He could see the disbelief spread over the old man's face, then turn to bitter disappointment and despair. He tried to imagine being married to someone in China, living in a village growing cabbage, raising children as poor as himself, and growing old without anyone understanding what he had seen and done on his journey to the West.

Then he imagined himself caught trying to get back into China without even reaching Wei-ching. He guessed that he would have to spend another ten years in a work camp, this time perhaps in the deserts of Ch'ing Hai Province or the ice forests of Manchuria.

He turned these images over and over in his mind, hour after hour, until he felt he could have convinced anyone in the world that he was justified in staying. Then he had one last daydream: He imagined Wei-ching lying in his damp hut for the duration of the Cultural Revolution, wondering the whole time if the boy he had raised was alive or dead. He had had to wait ten years already; how in the world could Hsun-ching make him wait the rest if his life?

Hsun-ching didn't get up right away. He closed his eyes and listened to the ocean for a while. It reminded him of a chapter of the *Tao te ching,* a Taoist classic Wei-ching had made him read, which explains how water—although it is soft—can wear away even stone. Hsun-ching always had trouble with that chapter. The Taoists claim that it is because a yielding nature is actually stronger than a resisting nature. But Hsun-ching had argued that anything dashed against rock for millions of years will wear it away. If you threw hard things against the rock, it would wear away even faster. To Hsun-ching, the real point of that chapter should have been that infinite patience, not a yielding nature, will allow even a weakling to enjoy success. And the ocean was patient, that was for sure. Think how many waves must have pounded against this shore since the earth was formed?

Hsun-ching sat up all of a sudden. Sometimes ideas came in the strangest ways; here he was, thinking about the ocean, and all of a sudden he knew how to get the sutra without hurting anyone, and in time to catch Wong's ship back to Hong Kong.

He waited down by the beach until late afternoon, then followed the path back up toward the institute. Walking quickly to lessen his chances of being seen, he passed through the wooden gate at the entrance and in through the front door. This time, instead of following the hallway down to the reception room, he turned right at the fountain and darted into the men's room. He went into one of the stalls and locked the door, then stood on the toilet so no one would see his feet. And then he waited, determined to be as patient as the ocean.

As it turned out, the Mahavishnu was leading a seminar in Kundalini Awakening that night, so people were trickling in and out of the bathroom until almost ten o'clock. Each time someone would use one of the stalls on either side of Hsun-ching, he would hold his breath and hope that no one could hear the pounding of his heart. Once, when the other stalls were occupied, a man noticed that there were no feet under the middle stall door and knocked to see if anyone was using it. When no answer came, he tried the door. Finding that it was locked, he stood up on his toes and reached his arm over the door, hoping to unlock it from the inside. His fingers stretched downward to within an inch of the lock, but then someone flushed the toilet in the adjacent stall and the arm slid back over the door.

At around eleven o'clock, Hsun-ching heard the front door close as it had many times that night. This time, though, a series of clanking sounds indicated that it was being locked. Hsun-ching waited another ten minutes just to make sure, then slowly lowered himself from the toilet and crept out of the bathroom. He tiptoed down the hall and had just reached the reception room when he heard a loud thump upstairs, followed by the sounds of footsteps coming down the front stairs, near where the bathrooms were. Hsun-ching clapped his hand over his mouth to stifle a gasp and darted around for a place to hide. He felt like a drop of water skittering on a hot plate. Just as the footsteps rounded the corner and started down the hall, he managed to squeeze himself under the receptionist's desk.

The footsteps moved slowly down the hallway, past the reception room, then down another stairway. A few minutes later Hsun-ching heard shuffling sounds from the room below him. It sounded like someone was reorganizing shelves. Someone working late, Hsun-ching thought blackly. Now what will I do?

He waited for nearly half an hour and listened closely as whoever was downstairs seemingly went from reorganizing shelves to reorganizing the furniture and then to tossing it around for good measure. Finally, though, the sounds ceased. Had whoever was down there decided to spend the night, or was there a basement exit? Hsun-ching realized that he had no more time left. Even if he found the sutra right now, he thought, he might not make it to Wong's boat in time. He could wait no longer.

He crept to the top of the stairs, then paused, cupping his hands to his ears to hear better, but the basement was silent. He felt his long earlobes cradled against his thumbs, and remembered how Wei-ching had told him that they were omens of good fortune. He tugged at them and silently urged them to give him good luck just this once, especially since they had failed him so many times before. Then he took off his shoes and started down the stairs.

There was a light on in the basement. When Hsun-ching reached the bottom of the stairs, he realized he was in a giant storage room. Boxes and wooden crates were lying all around in complete disarray, and a jumble of statues, paintings, incense burners, and scrolls was strewn about on the floor. Hsun-ching was wondering how on earth anyone could find what he was looking for in this mess when a large object streaked within an inch of his head. It moved with such speed that the air in its wake struck him with the force of a slap. The missile hit a sandstone Buddhist statue like a cannonball, and the statue disappeared in an explosion of sand and powder.

Unable to move or even breathe, Hsun-ching could only look in the direction where the projectile came from and wait for the next, fatal shot. Then he saw a glint of yellow, and the colonel's head emerged from behind a crate.

"Hsun-ching!" the colonel cried.

Hsun-ching's knees went weak, but he managed to stay standing. The colonel hopped out from behind the crate and rushed over to the pulverized statue. He shook his head and smacked his lips thoughtfully.

"I never was a very consistent shot," he murmured, then he smiled at Hsun-ching. "But it's a good thing, isn't it? If I had hit you just then, I would have regretted it deeply. I'm glad you are alive."

"Wh-what are y-you doing here?" Hsun-ching stammered.

The colonel almost looked embarrassed. He frowned, then muttered, "I was going back to China anyway, how much trouble could it be to get one little roll of paper for an old man?"

"So you found it?" Hsun-ching asked anxiously.

The colonel looked down at the ground and said nothing. Hsun-ching looked around him and noticed that all of the crates, and all of the scrolls for that matter, were identified in Chinese characters. The colonel couldn't read! He had risked his life to come back to this building without any possible way of knowing which was the correct sutra, yet still he had tried.

Shame spurred Hsun-ching to finish what the colonel had started. He tore through the crates like a madman until he found one marked "Volland."

With the colonel's help, he ripped the crate apart, and a hundred or more scrolls rolled to the floor. Hsun-ching felt as if a switch had been turned on inside his skull, flooding his brain with light. He scanned the inscriptions on the outside of the scrolls, which were written in a very obscure script. The Gracious Will Sutra, the Homage to Bhutatathata Sutra, the Mahprajnaparamita Sutra, the Western Heaven Sutra, the Precious Authority Sutra, and the Correct Commandment Sutra. At last he found it: the Laughing Sutra. He stuffed it inside his jacket, and, without a word, the two moved as one person up the stairway and out of the basement.

Hsun-ching thought they would escape through the roof, the way the colonel had apparently come in, but the colonel shook his head no. He pointed to the front door and smiled. It was the strangest thing; the sensation of light in his brain also gave Hsun-ching the uncanny feeling that the colonel could communicate with him without words. He understood instantly that for a man like the colonel, it would only make sense to leave through the front door. How undignified, how unchivalrous, to do otherwise!

When the Mahavishnu returned the next morning, he would at least have the small consolation of knowing that he had been robbed by brave men, not thieving cowards.

Unfortunately, medieval Chinese chivalry developed its glorious traditions some time before the invention of the burglar alarm. When the colonel and Hsun-ching opened the door together, arm in arm, a piercing wail shattered their euphoria. The colonel, not understanding electronics, rushed back into the building in search of the hidden sentry, and spent a few precious moments ripping the reception hall apart and challenging the coward to come out and defend his temple instead of hiding and screaming like a cat in heat.

At last Hsun-ching grabbed the colonel by his armor and dragged him outside, and they sprinted through the gate, hoping to reach the city before the police came. But they were too late; the institute's alarm system was connected to a security service, which dispatched a car immediately, and now it came barreling down the gravel driveway.

Hsun-ching and the colonel turned and sprinted toward the path leading down the cliff. Hsun-ching disappeared over the edge of the cliff before the car came through the wooden gate, but the colonel deliberately hesitated until the car's headlights hit him for a full second before he flew down the path after Hsun-ching. He wanted the guards to think that only one man had robbed the institute. That way, if it was necessary, he could draw the guards into a chase while Hsun-ching escaped.

Hsun-ching and the colonel were grateful for the moonlight, for without it they would surely have stumbled and fallen onto the rocks below. When they reached the beach, they turned south and ran toward where the cliff flattened out; they could slip back into the city easier there than up north, where the cliffs got even steeper. Unfortunately, the beach to the south also had street access, which a police car now made good use of as it roared out over the sand, pointing its lights up the coast. Hsun-ching and the colonel managed to jump behind a shallow dune just before the lights hit them. Behind them, they could hear the security guard yelling down to the police from the top of the cliff.

"We're trapped," Hsun-ching whispered.

The colonel shushed him and surveyed their position. They were lying in a shallow dune about twenty yards from the water, and maybe sixty yards from the foot of the cliff. The police car had stopped about two hundred yards south of them. The security guard at the top of the cliff was staying where he was; apparently he was going to let the police do the hard part of catching the criminal.

"Listen carefully," the colonel whispered. "I will walk down the beach toward the soldiers. They will point their torches at me. When they do, you crawl on your stomach toward the cliff. Then, hug the cliff and run north! You can hide in the boulders until they leave."

"But what about you? What will you do?"

"I will escape another way! I managed to slip through Shih Huang Ti's guards, remember? This will be easy for me. And they will not bother with you, because they don't know there are two of us. The guard only saw one of us go over the cliff."

"You don't have your pole!" Hsun-ching remembered. But the colonel dismissed all such concerns with a wave of his hand and stood up. The police saw his profile against the water and shined their spotlight on him. The colonel started walking slowly toward them, angling gradually toward the water.

Hsun-ching was sure the plan would end in disaster, but he obeyed the colonel's instructions and started crawling, military style, with his arms locked in front of him, toward the cliff. It seemed that an eternity passed before he pressed himself into a little depression in the cliff, where the guard above couldn't possibly see him. There, he hesitated; he had to see if the colonel was going to be all right. He poked his head out and looked down the beach. Bathed in the stream of light from the policemen's searchlight, the colonel now stood with his feet in the water, with his back to the ocean, facing the two policemen. The police were ordering him to put his hands over his head, but of course he didn't understand them—and if he had, Hsun-ching knew, he wouldn't have obeyed them anyway. He stood there like a consummate actor, forcing all who watched him to pay close attention now, because the performance of his life was about to begin. Then he put his hand inside his armor and took out the last of the stones. He stepped forward with his left leg and pointed with his left hand. He looked like an archer, poised at the highest tension, waiting patiently for the perfect moment to release the stone. Then his right arm swung forward, and the rock hit the spotlight with a deafening crash.

The colonel went dark, but in the moonlight Hsun-ching saw him charge forward and heard a bloodcurdling battle cry. Then there was a loud pop, and a flash of light, and for a moment Hsun-ching was blinded. When his eyes adjusted to the darkness again, he saw the colonel lying on his back, struggling to get up. For the first time in his life, Hsun-ching's stutter was a blessing. His mouth opened and his chest heaved, but no sound came out. Meanwhile, the shadowy forms of the police began cautiously approaching the fallen man. The colonel, sensing the decisiveness of the moment, brought himself to his feet with his last strength. With a final, desperate shout, he turned and cast himself with all his might into the ocean. He churned through the water until it was up to his waist, then plunged in and flailed at the water to drag himself as far out to sea as he could. The police stood at the shore in apparent disbelief. Minute after minute, Hsun-ching waited for the colonel's strength to give out and the waves to deliver his body to the police. But he kept going, swimming farther and farther in the moonlight, until he hit a current that started pulling him out toward the open ocean. Then, his arms started to slow down, and then stopped moving altogether. For a few minutes, Hsun-ching could see the colonel's head bobbing up and down in the waves as he drifted out to sea; then, without a sound, he disappeared utterly.

Hsun-ching had known despair before. He knew what it was like to be consumed by fathomless terror; it had nearly made him mute for life. He waited for the approach of the madness and gave himself up to it. But suddenly, he felt once again the irresistible sensation of light pouring through his mind and bathing the world around him in a weird, throbbing glow. It occurred to Hsun-ching that he might really be losing his mind, but the feeling persisted.

He decided that rather than trying to cross the city, he would run along the coast all the way around the peninsula to the docks.

He ran his heart out, until he thought his ribs would crack and his lungs would burst like overinflated balloons. But his mind was clear, like a bright mirror, and no thoughts disturbed him. He was only his pain, his legs, the sand, the rocks, then the piers, the ships, and soon the Bay Bridge.

Tasting blood in his throat, he followed the wire gate surrounding the piers until he reached Pier 26. The gate was locked. Hsun-ching could see Wong's boat; two tugs were attached to it, and all its lights were on—it was already moving!

Hsun-ching felt no panic. He started to climb the gate, but the cyclone fence at the top tore deep gashes in both his hands. The pain did not disturb him at all, but he realized that he simply could not make it over. If he struggled any harder, he would become hopelessly tangled in the barbed wire.

He pounded on the gate, calling for someone to come open it. But the longshoremen had already untied the thick docking ropes and gone back inside the building, where they could not hear him over the din of the tugboats. Hsun-ching watched as the huge ship pulled away from the dock, and the light began to fade.

But then another light flashed on behind him. He turned around to face it, and saw that there was one beam, moving toward him. It must be the police, he thought. They knew I would come here. When they were only a few yards away from him, the door of the car opened and a single person got out. She was carrying a painting.

"God, I thought I was too late!" Alison said. "I remember you said the boat left at four, so I got here at three-thirty. But there was no one here, and I couldn't get through this gate, so I've been driving up and down here looking for you just in case. Here," she said, handing Hsun-ching the portrait of the woman in red. "I can sell Agnes another one. I wanted you to have it."

Then she saw the blood on his hands and forearms, and the wild look in his eyes.

"I missed the boat," was all Hsun-ching could say. "I got the sutra, but I missed the boat." He opened his jacket and looked down at the crumbling scroll. His chest was still heaving.

"Come on!" Alison shouted, pulling Hsun-ching toward her car. "Get in quick!"

He hesitated in confusion. Alison's appearance was a miracle, but what could she do now? She grabbed his jacket and pulled, and when he turned to look at her, something wonderful happened. Again, suddenly, he understood, as if she had spoken and explained it to him. He jumped into the passenger seat, and Alison threw the car into reverse and screeched backward. Then she stopped the car, took a deep breath, and gunned the engine.

"You are the female Tom Sawyer," he yelled as she popped the clutch.

The chain lock didn't break when Alison's car hit, but the doors of the gate bent enough to let someone crawl through. She had hoped to drive Hsun-ching right down to the end of the dock, but they had to abandon the car and run to the end of the pier. There was no time even to yell good-bye. Hsun-ching ran on a last shot of adrenaline. He sailed out over the edge of the dock and hit one of the giant airplane tires lashed to the side of one of the tugboats. He clawed at it and held on for dear life, but his hands were slippery with blood and his legs were dragging in the water and he felt himself slipping. He didn't think for a moment of what would happen to him if he lost his grip on the tire; he thought only of the sutra. He couldn't allow it to get wet! A ferocious tenacity welled up inside him, and he sank his teeth into the tire and bit down so hard a molar cracked. That was all he could do. Then he felt a hand as strong as a vise on one of his wrists. But only when another powerful hand slapped him on the crown of the head and told him to open his damn mouth did he loosen his jaw.

He ignored the bewildered crewman and turned to look at the dock. Alison was standing there, surrounded by a group of shouting men. She wasn't paying attention to them, though; she was just standing there with her painting in a dim circle of light, watching the tugs and Captain Wong's boat slip out into the bay. Hsun-ching and Alison, paying no attention to the men screaming at them, waved to each other silently, and Hsun-ching wished more than anything in the world that he could have taken the painting with him.

XXIII

HSUN-CHING APPROACHED THE BULLETPROOF-GLASS window and spoke through a tiny metal grate to a severe-looking woman sitting behind a desk reading a Hong Kong newspaper. "I am a refugee from China," he said wearily. "I fled from there earlier this year, but now I am surrendering myself. I wish to be sent back to China. I will accept whatever punishment the party chooses for me. My only wish is that this scroll, which I stole from an old man's library in China, be returned to him."

The visa officer didn't even bother to look up from her newspaper. She just pointed to the sign in the window: LUNCH HOUR. CLOSED UNTIL ONE-THIRTY.

Hsun-ching laughed mirthlessly. He rapped on the glass and yelled, "I'm not a tourist—I'm an illegal alien from China! I snuck out here, but now I'm surrendering voluntarily! Can't you hear me?"

The woman flashed him an angry look from behind her thick black plastic-rimmed glasses. "Can't you read?" she squawked. "It's lunchtime! I'm off-duty! Come back later!" Then she went back to her paper, and Hsun-ching had no choice but to reflect on

how much he hated the sound of the Cantonese dialect, and sit
in a little wooden chair and wait.

At one-thirty Hsun-ching went back to the window, where the
woman was still reading. "It's one-thirty," Hsun-ching said quietly. The woman paid no attention to him.

Hsun-ching punched the glass as hard as he could. "Are you
deaf, you stupid party hack? I said I'm surrendering! I'm probably
the only man in the world trying to defect *back* to China, and
you're too busy reading your goddamn newspaper to come out
and arrest me!" The woman looked startled, then disappeared
into a back room. Hsun-ching kept banging on the glass until
three grim-looking men in gray Mao suits took him by the arms
and led him through a heavily bolted door into the offices of the
embassy.

IN HIS WRITTEN confession, drafted for him by several of the con-
sulate officials after hearing his oral statement, Hsun-ching admitted to: "Betraying the trust of the party, the party leaders, and
the broad masses by abandoning the socialist motherland. Em-
bracing poisonous bourgeois-liberal ideology. Harboring capitalist fantasies at the expense of the workers, peasants, and soldiers
of New China. Breaking the laws of the party by crossing provin-
cial and national borders without the necessary paperwork or
permission. Riding the train to Hong Kong without a ticket," and,
in a clause insisted upon by the woman with the thick glasses,
"trying to force an official of the Chinese Communist party to
work during off-duty hours, and when she politely refused to do
so, threatening her with terrible curses and physical harm." To
protect Mr. Yin, Mr. T'ang, and Captain Wong, Hsun-ching
claimed that he had escaped from China six months ago and had
been living in the streets since then.

After he had signed the document, the officials confiscated the
sutra, and Hsun-ching was handcuffed to a party official and
taken by train to Canton. There, he spent twelve weeks in a
detention center where no one would tell him what would
become of him, or what had happened to the Laughing Sutra. The
time passed neither slowly nor quickly for Hsun-ching. The
death of the colonel had sunk in once he had boarded Wong's

boat, and he had been so tormented with guilt and remorse that by the time he reached Hong Kong he was too worn out to care what happened to him anymore. If they had said they planned to stand him up against a wall and shoot him as a socialist deserter, he would have accepted his fate passively. He still wanted to finish his task and get the sutra to Wei-ching, but it was a mechanical wish, driven more by momentum than any clear sense of purpose.

One day, without any warning or explanation, he found himself sitting in the Guangzhou Public Security Bureau, staring across a table at five men in a room lit by a bare light bulb.

They interrogated him exhaustively. When did you leave China? Why did you leave China? Who helped you? Who influenced you to leave China? They asked these same questions over and over again for more than three days. At last they asked him, "Why did you turn yourself in?"

"Because I realized I had to come back to China," he answered.

"Why did you have to come back to China?" they shot back.

"Because I realized that if I didn't come back, I couldn't have lived with myself. I would have felt too guilty."

"Guilty for what? What would you have felt guilty about?"

"About not coming back."

They went through this dialogue at least fifty times before the interrogating officials called a halt to the proceedings and moved to an adjacent office to discuss the case. They left Hsun-ching alone in the dark room, without food or water, for another six hours. At last one of them returned.

He sat down heavily, lit a cigarette, and sighed. "I am Comrade Shuang. It is my responsibility to decide how the state shall deal with you," he said, making no effort to conceal his lack of enthusiasm for the task. "The usual punishment for attempting to flee China is a prison term, but why should the party feed you and let you sleep all day when instead we could put you to work?"

"I am familiar with that policy," Hsun-ching muttered. "I worked for the party in the countryside for ten years."

The official exhaled a thick cloud of smoke, then watched it curl up lazily toward the light bulb. "Yes, I know all about that," he said. "It's all in your file. Orphan, Red Guard, rehabilitated, released. Just between you and me," he said, leaning forward across the table and speaking in a low, contemptuous voice, "I'm surprised a troublemaker like you would come back." Then he sat back in his chair and continued, "But here you are, and here I am, having to do something about you. Tell me. What do you think I should do?"

"It isn't for me to say. All I ask is that you return the scroll I took from Wei-ching—"

"The man who raised you, I understand," Comrade Shuang interjected.

Hsun-ching was shocked that they knew this much. "Yes," he said pensively, "the man who raised me."

"And why did you steal this sutra?" the official asked.

"Because I thought it would bring me good luck."

"I see," the official said. "Are you a Buddhist?"

After a pause, Hsun-ching said that he was.

"Really?" the official asked. "Are you sure? The villagers in the Hunan commune you lived in say otherwise. They say that after the death of a certain young friend, you renounced religion completely."

Hsun-ching's eyes glazed over. How did this man know so much?

"And your friend Wei-ching tells me that you didn't steal this sutra from him at all—that you in fact went to America to recover it from an American who stole it from China thirty years ago. That you made this journey for Wei-ching's benefit, not your own, and that you planned to come back all along."

Hsun-ching began to tremble with anger. He wondered what they had done to Wei-ching to get this information. Comrade Shuang blew some more smoke up toward the light bulb, then asked, "Are you surprised that I know all this?"

"Yes."

"Well, it's not that surprising. As you so colorfully pointed out to the consular secretary, it is not often that someone defects to China. Last year there was a Taiwanese air-force pilot, now it is you. Understandably, we give such cases our full attention. It was my duty to find out everything I could about you."

"Where is Wei-ching?"

"He is in a Kun-ming hospital. He was not very healthy when I went to visit him, but we transported him to a good hospital and assigned the very best doctors to treat him."

"Why are you doing this?" Hsun-ching asked.

The official inhaled deeply from his cigarette, then smiled thinly.

"Because you could be very useful to the state if you decided to cooperate."

"How could I be useful?"

"Well, as a traitor and foreign lackey, you will only occupy prison space. But as a reformed Chinese patriot and filial adopted son, you could set a great example for our disaffected youth."

"I don't understand," Hsun-ching said.

"Let me tell your story from another point of view. Let's say that after the ravages of the Cultural Revolution, you felt that China had taken away ten years of your life and left you with no future. You heard exaggerated stories about how comfortable life in the West was, so you decided to sneak out of China and head toward the 'Promised Land.' But when you got there, you realized that it was not at all as you imagined. That the society was chaotic, selfish, and lonely, and in a short time you felt disgusted by the self-indulgence and hypocritical attitudes of Americans. You realized that, at heart, you were Chinese, and that you had an obligation to care for your adoptive father in his old age. It was an irrepressible morality in you, a uniquely Chinese morality, that made you surrender and come back, regardless of the consequences. And once you got back, the state recognized your sincerity and, instead of punishing you, allowed you to return home and care for the old man. What would you think of that?"

"But what would I have to do?" Hsun-ching asked.

"It's very simple. You agree to tell your story, exactly as I have told it to you, to whoever asks. There would be a certain amount of publicity—you would be expected to make speeches, grant interviews, and make occasional appearances."

"Can I give Wei-ching the sutra?"

Comrade Shuang suddenly turned very serious. "We will let him read it; there is no harm in that. But then it will be given to a museum in China, where it belongs. You will make absolutely no mention of it to anyone whatsoever, and this office does not want to know where you got it or how. Your trip to the West had nothing to do with any sutra, and as far as you know, sutras are a kind of Indian food. One thing China does not need," he said, shaking a tobacco-stained finger at Hsun-ching, "is to be accused of supporting international thieves."

The official leaned back in his chair and relaxed once again. "It so happens that since this sutra was stolen from China in the first place, there are some of us who are inclined to think that you have done China a small service. But that must not become public knowledge." He put out his cigarette and folded his hands in front of him on the desk. "What is your answer?"

"As long as Wei-ching gets to read the sutra, I'll do whatever you say."

The official nodded and opened a bag next to his chair, pulled out the sutra, and handed it to Hsun-ching. "I have nothing else to add except that, if you should choose not to heed our agreement, then you will face, in addition to your present waived charges, the charges of obstruction of justice, lying to the state, and, most serious of all, taking part in counterrevolutionary activities. I take it you are familiar with the gravity of those charges."

"Yes, I am."

Comrade Shuang smiled. "In that case," he said, extending his chunky hand for Hsun-ching to shake, "welcome back to the motherland."

THAT NIGHT, IN his room in the detention center, Hsun-ching opened the scroll. It began with an introductory colophon, written in Hsüan-tsang's own hand:

> The Sutra of Divine Laughter, in twenty-three chapters, in which the means are divulged by which a man or woman may attain immortality. I, Hsüan-tsang, a humble servant of the Imperial T'ang Court, submit with shame this uneducated translation of the original Sanskrit text, acquired in India in the fourth year of the

glorious reign of the Sustained Brightness Emperor. May the August Presence allow His keen eyes to glance over these poorly written characters, and forgive His servant for his ignorance and lack of skill.

Then the actual sutra began. Hsun-ching slowly unrolled the scroll from right to left and read through the chapters, but it was written in such highly specialized language that Hsun-ching couldn't understand most of it. He skimmed through the whole text, then noticed that Hsüan-tsang had added another colophon at the very end. It read:

This unworthy monk presents this scroll to the fearsome Dragon Throne as an example of the sort of corrupted texts which are now becoming popular both in China and in India. While the sutra begins properly, noting that all ignorance, and therefore all suffering, springs from our attachments to the illusory realm of the senses, it then diverges from the Path. It suggests that spiritual disciplines are just as deluded and illusory as material attachments. It claims that the Buddha revealed this to his most fervent disciple, who meditated constantly for over seven years without result. When he heard that, the disciple (who was very attached to his spiritual life) flung himself wholeheartedly into all sorts of depravity. By doing so, he supposedly lost his appetite for it, like a guest at a banquet who overeats until he vomits and then no longer wishes to eat any more. Having thus momentarily freed himself from desire, the disciple suddenly realized that his own desire for enlightenment was, in reality, no different from a greedy man's desire for wealth and fame. When he understood the unity of all desire, he became enlightened and laughed very hard.

While this anecdote sounds attractive, it cannot be true. It is well known from experience that the more depraved a man is, the more depraved he wishes to become; moreover, the depraved man often erroneously believes that he is experiencing great pleasure while indulging in lustful excesses. This is, of course, false pleasure and not useful to us in our search for Truth. We must avoid false pleasure at all costs, and must condemn literature of this type as worthless.

Written on the fourth day of the second month of the seventh

year of the Sustained Brightness reign, under the glorious patron-
age of the August Emperor, in whose Presence this servile monk
trembles with awe and gratitude.

Hsun-ching read and reread the colophon in sheer disbelief. He
must be reading it wrong. Hsun-ching knew that the scroll was
worthless, but he didn't expect it to proclaim itself so. What
would Wei-ching do when he discovered that the precious
Laughing Sutra was as silly and misguided as those Christian
comic books of Mrs. Yin's? Would it cast him into despair for the
remaining days of his life? Would it have been better if Hsun-
ching had never found it, so that Wei-ching could at least die
hoping to read it in his next life, and the colonel might have
lived?

THE FLURRY OF attention, interviews, questions, and speeches did
not seem real at all to Hsun-ching. He felt as if he were watching
a movie of himself as he said the correct things, gave the correct
answers, and played the correct role of the Prodigal Socialist.
After a very busy week, during which he became a familiar face
to over a billion people, the propaganda organs of the party
decided the time was ripe for Hsun-ching to return to Kun-ming
for the much-awaited reunion with his ailing "father." He flew
west from Canton with an entourage of reporters, photographers,
publicists, and, of course, Comrade Shuang.

At the entrance to the hospital, Comrade Shuang turned to
Hsun-ching. "You will have a practice reunion first. Wei-chung
has been advised what to say when he sees you, and I am sure
you are by now familiar with what you should say. Then we will
reenter the hospital for the official reunion, which will be re-
corded on camera and tape. After that is finished, we will allow
you some time alone with Mr. Wei, during which you may show
him the sutra."

When Hsun-ching saw how frail Wei-ching looked, he nearly
cried. Wei-ching had tubes up his nose and down his throat and
attached to both wrists. Hsun-ching sat down gently on the bed
next to his old friend and put his hand on Wei-ching's arm.

Wei-ching opened his eyes and smiled faintly. "Are you all right?"

"I should be asking you that," Hsun-ching said.

Wei-ching laughed weakly. "At my age, it's better not to."

Comrade Shuang reminded them that in five minutes they would have to reenact their joyful greeting for the reporters. "It would be best if, Wei-ching, you begin by saying, 'I knew you would come back to China,' and Hsun-ching, you respond with, 'I couldn't leave China or you behind.'"

The required phrases were uttered, albeit stiffly, and Comrade Shuang deemed it a success. After all the reporters had left, Shuang asked the attending nurses to leave the room and stood guard outside the door himself to make sure no one interrupted them.

Hsun-ching laid the sutra tenderly on Wei-ching's chest, and the old man's eyes glistened with tears.

"You found it!" he gasped. "Buddha be praised! I must read it!"

As weak as he was, Wei-ching managed to lift the sutra with his own hands and unroll it, section by section, holding it so close to his face that it grazed his nose as his cloudy eyes struggled to make out the millennium-old writing. Hsun-ching, meanwhile, sat by the bed and smiled to himself. He was smiling because he knew Wei-ching would not have to endure the agony of reading the damning colophon; he had cut it off with a pocketknife and thrown it into a panda-shaped trash bin.

It took Wei-ching nearly an hour to finish. When he came to the end, he let the sutra fall back on his chest. A look of sadness passed over his face, then he closed his eyes. Hsun-ching thought the old man was about to cry, but then he thrust his toothless jaw forward and, with great effort, sat up in bed. He rolled the sutra up and handed it back to Hsun-ching. "I am ashamed and very sorry to tell you this. This sutra has no value whatsoever. It contains nothing but superstitious nonsense. And I am deeply shocked that Hsüan-tsang did not realize this when he translated it for the emperor. Perhaps he was a better traveler than scholar."

Hsun-ching could not look at Wei-ching. What a mess.

But then, Wei-ching began to laugh.

"Excuse me for laughing," Wei-ching said. "But it is called the Laughing Sutra, after all. At least it was appropriately titled."

"I'm very sorry," said Hsun-ching.

"Don't be!" Wei-ching answered cheerfully. "I spent most of my life waiting for this book, and now I learn that it is useless! That is a terrible thing. But imagine how much worse it would have been if I hadn't found that out? Even if I live for only a day now, it is a day of freedom from yet another sort of ignorance!"

Wei-ching's eyes shone with inexpressible gratitude.

"Don't you see?" he cried. "You have released me! The boy I tried to teach Buddhism has taught me the greatest lesson of all! Buddha be praised for sending you to me! It is as Buddha said all along: Enlightenment cannot be found in books. It must be experienced directly! Foolish as I was, I did not take him at his word. But now I do! I am free!"

He was so exhilarated he nearly fell out of bed. "And now it is my turn to give you something," he said. "Is that Communist clodhopper out of the room?" Hsun-ching checked to make sure Comrade Shuang was not peeking through the window. "Remember when you came back from meeting Sun Wu-k'ung at the waterfall, and he refused to go with you to America? At that time, I was confused, because I thought it simply had to be Buddha's will that he go with you. I was wrong about that, but Buddha's will is fathomless, and cannot be understood by men. Even though Sun Wu-k'ung did not go with you to America, he has helped you nonetheless!"

"What do you mean?"

Wei-ching grinned mischievously and said, "He visited me at the old temple just before the Communists took me to this hospital! That would be two weeks ago. He knew you were coming back! And he said that Buddha wanted you to be rewarded."

"That's impossible!" Hsun-ching cried. "He's dead! I saw him die myself!"

"Did you?" Wei-ching asked. "Then it must have been his ghost that gave me this gift. He wanted you to have it."

Wei-ching's wrinkled hand dug around under his blanket for a moment, then came back out and stopped right under Hsun-ching's nose. In his palm lay a tarnished gold bar, with a misshapen chunk of lead buried deep in its center. Hsun-ching felt a weak but familiar tingling in his chest and immediately rushed to the window. He looked down at the street, where hundreds of people were riding their bicycles and milling on the sidewalk. One man stood out from all the others; he was not moving at all, and seemed to be staring up at the hospital. He wore dark glasses and leaned against a shiny metal pole. Hsun-ching was speechless; he held up up the gold bar with the bullet lodged in it so the man down below could see it. The colonel lowered his sunglasses, nodded, and gave the thumbs-up, an American custom he had come to like.

Wei-ching enjoyed nearly two weeks of liberation from ignorance, then died in his sleep. Hsun-ching declined the local Propaganda Bureau's offer of a state-organized memorial service, choosing instead to take Wei-ching's ashes to the Pure Land Temple on the outskirts of Kun-ming, where they had heard the nuns chanting so many years before. The two nuns who had survived the Cultural Revolution chanted the funeral service.

Then Hsun-ching and the colonel took Wei-ching's ashes back to the site of his old temple and tossed them on the river. As his friend's ashes floated downstream, Hsun-ching recited a passage of the poem Wei-ching had taught him when their old white cat died:

> I make offerings of rice and fish,
> bury you in the river,
> and chant from the sutras—I
> wouldn't slight you.

"Now we must say farewell properly," the colonel said. "I am feeling tired."

"We can spend the night here at the temple," Hsun-ching suggested. "Why do we have to say farewell? Where are you going?"

The colonel laughed quietly. He did look tired, Hsun-ching noticed. "I'm going somewhere where I can really rest. This hut won't do. Haven't you wondered why I never sleep?"

Hsun-ching had always assumed that when he slept, the colo-

nel slept as well. But now Hsun-ching remembered that whenever he had gone to bed, the colonel had always been sitting up
or lying with his eyes open. And whenever Hsun-ching woke up,
the colonel was in the same position, with his eyes still open.

"Your days are like moments to me," the colonel explained.
"You woke me up when you knocked my pole down in the cave.
I tried to get back to sleep, but couldn't, so I decided to join you
on your trip. Now we've come to the end of my day."

"Will you go back to the waterfall?"

The colonel laughed again. "What if you decide to go on another trip? I don't want you stumbling around my bedroom again
looking for company."

Hsun-ching hung his head. The colonel smiled and touched his
arm. "You have been a good friend—maybe the best I have ever
had. You didn't want anything from me, and you didn't turn
against me. And you are a loyal man. It is difficult to be loyal in
times of war, when the world is burning around you, but it is
perhaps even more difficult to be loyal in times of peace. You
were loyal to that old man, and I admire you for that. But when
it is time to sleep, you have to sleep. Who knows? Maybe you
will live longer than you think. When I wake up, I'll look for you.
Perhaps we'll meet again. If not, though, remember what I said
about fear. When you are facing your last moment on earth, be
strong. Don't squirm. Then you will realize in an instant that
there is no such thing as time. In that instant, it will seem as if
we had never left each other. I look forward to it." The colonel
kneeled and bowed his head. Hsun-ching returned the gesture,
then accompanied him part of the way down the path before
watching him disappear into the forest.

WHEN HSUN-CHING returned to Kun-ming, Comrade Shuang informed him that because of his English-language ability and his
experiences abroad, the state would generously provide him with
a job as a writer of travel brochures for the Yunnan branch of the
China International Travel Service. A few months later, the government announced that diplomatic relations had been restored
with the United States of America. The first thing Hsun-ching did
that morning was to write to Alison. He told her everything that

had happened since he had left her on the dock. He sent it off, skeptical that the Chinese postal system would actually deliver a letter to America, but three weeks later he got a telegram. It read:

DEAR HSUN-CHING, VERY VERY DELIGHTED TO RECEIVE YOUR LETTER. ALWAYS WANTED TO SEE KUN-MING. HAVE APPLIED FOR TOURIST VISA, THE MUSEUM IS HELPING, MAY TAKE TIME BUT YOU'RE NOT GOING ANYWHERE, ARE YOU? WILL BRING PAINTING, YOU OWE ME DINNER. BEST, ALISON.

ABOUT THE AUTHOR

MARK SALZMAN began studying Chinese martial arts, calligraphy, and ink painting when he was thirteen. He graduated from Yale in 1982 with a degree in Chinese language and literature. From 1982 to 1984 he lived in China, where he taught English at Hunan Medical College. In 1987 he began work on a feature film based on his book *Iron & Silk,* which was shot on location in China, and in which he acted. Filming was completed on June 3, 1989, the night of the Tiananmen massacre in Beijing. Now he and his wife live in Los Angeles, where they dream about moving back to San Francisco. They have two cats, Fog and Smog.